"I p...
your guardian angel."

"Yeah, right. More like a fallen angel."

"Some of the best guardian angels fell at one time," Trond said. "Besides, I'm disliking you less since the near-sex episode."

"I want to apologize for practically attacking you." This was the least she could do.

He grinned at her. "I've been meaning to talk to you about that near-sex event."

"I'd rather forget about it, if you don't mind."

"Oh, let's not." He continued to grin. "I was thinking about giving you another chance to try again."

"Try again?" she gurgled.

"To turn me."

He reached a long hand over and patted her bottom . . .

SANDRA HILL

KISS OF SURRENDER

A DEADLY ANGELS BOOK

AVON

An Imprint of HarperCollinsPublishers

AVON BOOKS
An Imprint of HarperCollins*Publishers*
10 East 53rd Street
New York, New York 10022-5299

Copyright © 2012 by Sandra Hill
Excerpt from *Kiss of Temptation* copyright © 2013 by Sandra Hill
ISBN 978-0-06-206462-2
www.avonromance.com

First Avon Books mass market printing: December 2012

Avon Trademark Reg. U.S. Pat. Off. and in Other Countries, Marca Registrada, Hecho en U.S.A.
HarperCollins® is a registered trademark of HarperCollins Publishers.

Printed in the U.S.A.

10 9 8 7 6 5 4 3 2 1

This book is dedicated to the twenty-two brave SEALs who died in August 2011 when their Chinook was shot down by Taliban insurgents outside Kabul. They and all SEALs . . . in fact, all our special forces . . . are the silent warriors putting their lives on the line every day so the rest of us can be free.

God bless America but especially those soldiers of all the military branches, along with their families, who sacrifice so much.

KISS of SURRENDER

Prologue

In the beginning...

In the year 850, in the cold darkness of the Norselands, Trond Sigurdsson snuffled and snored and burrowed deeper into his bed furs. He was a man who held a deep appreciation—some might say an unnatural appreciation—for his creature comforts, and that included rest. Lots of rest.

In truth, he would not mind sleeping the winter away like a graybeard, which he was not at only twenty and nine, but a shiver passed over his body as he noticed that even the hair on his head felt frozen. Despite his druthers, he started to twitch and awaken. Which was a shame because, as jarl of these estates, there was naught he *had* to do.

So why bother rising? This time of year, the gods graced them with only an hour or more of sunlight, and he was not about to go out to the barns or stables and engage in menial labor. For all he knew, or cared, the teats had already frozen into icicles on his milch cows. Who needed milk anyhow?

Of course, there had been those pleas from the

villagers yestereve—and the day before, truth to tell—begging him to come rescue them from an impending Saxon assault. Or was it the Huns? How ridiculous! Surely, even Saxons were not so demented as to engage in slaughter on a cold, dark winter's day. And Huns were more like to attack the keep itself. Still, he should go check, or send a *hird* of his soldiers to check. Trond might be lazy in many regards, but he was a far-famed warrior when the mood favored him, and he did have responsibilities as jarl of this region.

With a sigh, he contemplated his choices. He would have to rise, clothe himself, rouse his soldiers who were no doubt suffering the alehead, break his fast on cold fare, have horses readied, and ride through the blistering wind through withers-high snow for a half hour and more. All for foolish, no doubt unfounded fears.

Mayhap later.

Trond stretched out one bare toe to the left, and found naught but cold linens. And to the right. More cold linens. He understood now why he was freezing; 'twas the lack of body heat. Frida and Signy must have slipped out to their own bed closets off the great hall during the night. No swiving to while away the waking hours, he concluded with a jaw-cracking yawn. Then immediately recoiled at his own stale mead-breath. No wonder his concubines had left his presence. No doubt he had let loose ale farts in his sleep as well, as was his habit, or so some maids had dared to complain. Should he get up and rinse his mouth with the mint water he favored? And wash the night sweat from his odorsome body? Nay. Best he stay abed and rest.

And so he drifted off to sleep once again.

When he awakened next, the room was alight with the brightest sunshine. How could that be? At this time of the year? Sitting up, he let the furs fall down his naked body and blinked against the blinding light. Only then did he notice the stranger standing in the corner.

He jumped off the mattress and stood on the far side of the bedstead, broadsword in hand. A tall man stood there, arms folded over his chest in a pose of impatience. He wore a long white gown, tightened at the waist with a rope belt, like a woman's gunna or a robe worn by Arabs he'd met in his travels. Despite the loose garment, Trond could see that he had a warrior's body. And he was a beautiful man, Trond observed, though he was not wont to notice such things about other men, being uncommonly handsome himself. In this case, it was hard not to admire the perfect features and long black hair hanging down to his shoulders. Or the strange light shimmering about his form.

"Ah, at last the slugabed rises," the man observed.

Trond had felled men for such disrespect, but that would require more energy than he was ready to exert. "How did you get in here? Where are my guards? Who are you?" Trond demanded.

"It is not a question of how I got here, Viking, but why." He said *Viking* as if it were a foul word. "Do not concern yourself with who I am but what I will be . . . the thorn in your backside. Forevermore."

"What? You speak in riddles. Are you a god?"

"Hardly," the man scoffed.

"Did Odin send you? Or Thor?"

"Do not blaspheme, Viking. There is only one God."

Trond nodded his understanding. Actually, he

practiced both the Norse and Christian religions, an expediency many Norsemen followed.

"I am St. Michael the Archangel," the man informed him.

And I am King David. "Is that so?" Trond replied skeptically. "An angel, huh? Where are your wings?"

To Trond's amazement, a set of massive wings unfurled out of the man's back, so large that the snowy white tips touched the walls on two opposing sides of his bedchamber, and feathers fluttered to the rush-covered floor. "Convinced, Viking?"

Trond just gaped. Was he in the midst of some *drukkinn* madness? A dream, perchance?

"You have offended God mightily with your sloth," the angel pronounced. "You and your brothers have committed the Seven Deadly Sins in a most heinous manner." He shook his head as if with disbelief. "Seven brothers . . . seven different sins . . . what did you do, divvy them up? Or did you draw straws?"

Trond assumed that was some attempt at warped angel humor. He did not laugh. Instead, he glanced at the doorway and asked, "My brothers? They are here?" Last he'd heard, his six brothers were scattered throughout the Norselands on their own estates, hunkered down until springtime when they could go a-Viking once again. When the angel declined to respond, Trond went on, "What's so wrong with a little sloth, anyhow?"

The angel's upper lip curled with disgust at his question, but then he pointed a finger into the air betwixt them where a hazy picture appeared. 'Twas like looking into a cloud or a puff of swirling smoke, and what Trond saw caused him to gasp with dismay.

"Because you were too lazy to get up off your sorry arse, this is what happened today," the angel told him.

It was the nearby village being besieged by marauding soldiers. Saxon or Hun, 'twas hard to tell. They were covered with furs and leather helmets. More important, his people were being slain right and left, heads lopped off, limbs hacked away, blood turning the snowy ground red. Women and children were not being spared, either. It was a massacre. One soldier even impaled a still wriggling infant onto a pike and raised it high above his shoulders.

Gagging, Trond turned aside and upheaved the contents of his stomach into a slop bucket.

"And that is not all," the angel said. "Look what pain your indifference has caused, over and over in your pitiful life."

Now the cloud showed Trond as a youthling watching indifferently as other Viking males beat Skarp the Goatman almost to death. Skarp had been a fine archer at one time, but later became the object of ridicule due to a head blow in battle that had rendered him halfwitted.

Then there was a view of himself not much older, fifteen at best, though already a soldier, observing his comrades-in-arms raping a novice nun in a Frankland convent following a short bout of pillaging, short because it had been a poor convent with little of value to pillage. Although he had not engaged in the sexual assault, he'd done naught to intervene, despite the blood that covered the girl's widespread thighs. Odd how he could recall so vividly the red splotches on her white skin! And the screams. Now that he thought on it, there had been much female screaming. And male laughter.

"Was that the beginning, when you first began to hide behind your shield of apathy? For surely, you followed a path of indolence thereafter. Like a slug you are, slow to move, except for your own wants and needs."

One image after another flickered through the mist. Him ignoring a fourteen-year-old dairymaid who claimed to be carrying his child. Later, he'd heard that her father had turned her out, and she'd died of some fever or other.

Then there was his mother seeking a boon from him, which had been inconvenient at the time. The expression of hurt on her face showed clearly, as did the coldness in his. Had that favor been so important to his mother? Why had he not bothered to find out? She'd died soon after of a wasting disease whilst he'd been off a-Viking.

Trond felt sickened when he saw himself and all his sins. What was wrong with him? Why didn't he care? About anything or anyone? It was selfishness, of course, but more than that. To his surprise, he felt tears wet his bearded face.

"I suppose you have come to take me to your Christian hell in payment for my sins," Trond said with resignation.

"Not exactly," the angel replied. "God has other plans for you."

Trond arched his brows in question.

"Satan has put together an evil band of demon vampires to roam the earth harvesting human souls before their destined time. Lucipires, they are called. Our Father has charged me with formation of a different type of band to fight those evil legions. Vikings, to my eternal regret."

Trond's brow furrowed with confusion. "*You* are

going to lead Viking warriors in battle against some demon vampires?"

"Not exactly."

Trond didn't like the sound of that. "What exactly?"

"Viking vampire angels," St. Michael explained. "Vangels."

Trond started to laugh. "You are going to turn Vikings into angels? You would have better luck turning rocks into gold."

The archangel was not amused by his laughter. "Viking *vampire* angels," he emphasized. "For seven hundred years, you and your brothers will lead the fight against the Lucipires."

"With your magical powers," Trond said, waving a hand at the cloud picture and at the shimmery light that surrounded the angel, "why don't you just annihilate the demon vampires yourself?"

"That is not the way God works."

Trond mulled over everything that the angel had told him. "Seven hundred years is a long time."

"It is. Or you can spend eternity in Satan's fire."

Death by fire was ne'er a pleasant prospect. He'd seen Olaf the Bitter consumed by fire from a pitch-lit arrow. Yeech! And *eternal* fire? "Not much of a choice there."

St. Michael shrugged. "Do you agree?"

Trond was no fool. He could tell that the archangel would just as well see him on a quick slide to Hell. "I agree." But then he asked, "What exactly is a vampire?"

The archangel smiled at him, and it was not a nice smile. Before he had a chance to ponder that fact, Trond's body was thrown onto the rushes. Pain wracked every bone and muscle in his flailing body, especially his bleeding mouth and shoulder blades, where it felt as if an axe was hacking away at the bones.

"It is done," the archangel said after what seemed like hours, but was only minutes, and disappeared in a fading light.

Done? What is done? Trond felt himself rise above the floor, viewing his dead body, which lay on its one side, curled in a fetal position. Fangs stuck out of his mouth, like a wolf, and there were strange bumps on his shoulder blades.

But then in a whoosh of movement Trond was back in his body, and he was flying through the air, out of the keep, into the skies. Where he would land, he had no idea. He was fairly certain Heaven was not his destination. Nor Valhalla.

One

You could say he was a beach bunny . . . uh,
beach duck . . .

"If it looks like a duck, and walks, like a duck . . .
hey, Easy, can you give us a quack? Ha, ha, ha!"
Trond Sigurdsson, best known here in Navy
SEAL land as Easy, gritted his teeth and attempted
to ignore the taunts military passersby hurled his
way, especially when he noticed that the bane of his
current life, Lieutenant Nicole Tasso, was standing
there, along with Lieutenant Justin LeBlanc, or Cage,
who'd been the one teasing him this time. Cage was
LeBlanc's SEAL nickname, appropriate considering
his Cajun roots. Cajuns were folks who lived in the
southern United States—Louisiana to be precise—
and were known to eat lots of spicy foods, drink
beer, play loud rowdy music, and be generally wild.
A little bit like Vikings, if you asked Trond, which
no one did.

He didn't mind the teasing all that much, but no
red-blooded male—and, yes, his blood was still red,

and, yes, he was still a man—wanted a good-looking woman—even one Trond absolutely positively did not desire or even like—witnessing him down on his haunches, walking around like a friggin' duck, making an absolute ass of himself. A duck's ass!

"You're working Gig Squad? Again!" Nicole just had to remark.

As if it is any of her business! But then Nicole was a nosy, bossy, suspicious woman who'd made it her goal in life to uncover Trond's secrets, or improve him, or both. *As if!*

Gig Squad was a SEAL punishment that took place every evening in front of the Coronado, California, officers' quarters where Navy personnel leaving the chow hall could witness the humiliation of the punished trainees. Squats. Push-ups. And, yes, duck walks.

His infraction? Jeesh! All he'd done was hitch a ride on a dune buggy when told to jog this morning in heavy boondocker boots for five lackwitted miles along the sandy shore. What was wrong with the ingenuity of taking the easy way to a goal? "Work smarter, not harder," that was his motto. The SEAL commander, Ian MacLean, apparently did not appreciate ingenuity. Not this time, and not when he'd slept through an indoctrination session, or yawned widely when a visiting admiral came to observe their exercises, or complained constantly about the futility of climbing up and over the sky-high, swaying cargo net when it was easier to just walk around the blasted thing.

Truth to tell, he was not nearly as slothful as he'd once been now that he was a vangel . . . a Viking vampire angel. Nigh a saint, he was now. Leastways, no great sinner. But Mike—as he and his fellows

vangels rudely referred to St. Michael, their heavenly mentor—kept hammering away at him that
sloth embodied many sins, not just laziness or indifference. Supposedly, Trond was emotionally dead,
as well. Insensitive. Ofttimes apathetic and melan-
choly. "You have no fire in you," Mike had accused
him on more than one occasion, as if that were a
trait to be desired. "Your foolery and lightheated-
ness mask a darkness of spirit. You are sleepwalk-
ing through life, Viking. A dreamer, that is what you
are."

So here he was, more than a thousand years later,
still a fixed twenty-nine years old, still trying to get
it right. Before vangels were locked into modern
times, a recent happenstance, their assignments had
bounced them here and there, from antiquity to the
twenty-first century and in between, back and forth.
He'd been a gladiator, a cowboy, a Regency gentle-
man, a farmer, a pilot, a ditch digger, a garbageman,
even a sheik. A sheik without a harem, which was a
shame, if you asked him, which no one did.

And now a Navy SEAL, even as he continued to
be a VIK, the name given to him and his six brothers as head of the vangels. He understood the VIK
mission and how it applied here, as it did with all
assignments . . . killing demon vampires and saving
almost-lost human souls. Still, many of the SEAL
training exercises were foolish in the extreme, if you
asked Trond, which no one did. Walking around like
a duck . . . Was that any way for a thousand-plus-
year-old vampire angel to behave? And a Viking at
that!

It was demeaning, that's what it was. And PITAs
like the always bubbly, always on-the-go, always
mistrustful "Sassy Tassy" didn't help matters at all.

By PITA, he didn't mean a pet lover, either. More like a Pain in the Ass. He tried ignoring her presence now, but it was hard when Cage added to his embarrassment and Nicole's amusement by further taunting in that lazy Southern drawl he was noted for, "Why dontcha fluff yer feathers fer us, Easy?" He was referring to the exercise where a detainee not only waddled around like a duck but flapped his elbows at the same time. Twice the pain and twice the humiliation. To Nicole, Cage added with a shake of his head, "That Easy, bless his heart, is the laziest duck I ever saw."

The final insult was Nicole's smirk at Cage's remark. Oooh, he did not like it when women, especially Nicole, smirked at him. Then she added further insult by telling Cage, loud enough for Trond to hear, "Maybe he should just ring out and save us all a lot of trouble."

SEAL trainees could "volunteer out" at any time by ringing the bell on the grinder, the asphalt training ground at the compound. Actually, huge numbers of those who started out in SEAL training dropped out. Quitting was not an option for Trond.

Once Trond managed to control his temper and the huffing of his breath—it was hard work, waddling was—he duckwalked toward the woman whose back was to him as she continued talking, in a lower voice now, to Cage, who idly waved a hand behind his back for dismissal of the Gig exercise. At the same time she was standing in conversation, she bounced impatiently on the balls of her boots, as if raring to get off to something more important. The blasted woman had the energy of a *drukkinn* rabbit.

Meanwhile, the SEAL charmer was smiling down at Nicole, and she was smiling back, even while she bounced. Nicole had never smiled at him, but then he'd never tried to charm her, either.

Trond noticed that Cage's eyes were making a concerted effort not to home in on her breasts, prominent in a snug white razorback running bra with the WEALS insignia dead center between Paradise East and Paradise West. Leastways, they looked like Paradise to a man who hadn't had hot-slamdown-thrust-like-crazy-gottahaveyougottahaveyou sex in a really long time. Or any other *real* sex, for that matter. Near-sex, now that was a different matter. He was the king of near-sex. *Not that I'm planning any trips to Paradise, near or otherwise. Nosiree, I'm an angel. Celibacy-Is-Us. Pfff!* In any case, WEALS—Women on Earth, Air, Land, and Sea—was the name given to the female equivalent of SEALs, which stood for Sea, Air, and Land. A female warrior, of all things!

He shook his head like a shaggy dog . . . or a wet duck . . . to rid himself of all these irrelevant thoughts.

"Are you sure about that, darlin'?" Cage was saying to Nicole.

Trond had no idea what they were talking about, but one thing was for damn . . . uh, darn . . . sure, if he'd ever called Nicole *darlin'*, she would have smacked him up one side of his fool head and down the other.

Trond was still down in his duck position while the other poor saps had risen, their punishment over for now. Without thinking (Trond's usual MO, unfortunately) he leaned over and took a nip at Nicole's right, bouncing buttock, which was covered nicely by red nylon shorts. Luckily, he'd been a vampire angel long enough that he could control his fangs; otherwise, he would have torn the fabric.

With a yelp of shock, Nicole slapped a hand on her backside and swiveled on her boot-clad heels. SEALs and WEALS were required to wear the heavy boots to build up leg muscles. Hers were built up very nicely, he noted with more irrelevance, although the shape of a woman's body was never irrelevant to a virile man. And Vikings were virile, that was for sure.

All this exercise must be turning me into a brain-rambling dimwit. Or is it the celibacy?

"What? How dare you?" she screeched.

I dare because I can, my dear screechling. Rising painfully on screaming knees, he stood, reaching for a towel and wiping sweat with purposeful slowness off his face and neck. His drab green T-shirt with the Navy SEAL logo clung wetly to his chest and back. "Oops!" he said, finally.

"Oops? That all you have to say for yourself?"

You don't want to know what else I have to say. "Sorry. I thought it was a big ripe apple, and you know how ducks like apples." He grinned.

Usually women melted when he grinned at them. He had nineteen different grins in his repertoire, at last count. This was his how-can-you-be-mad-at-a-sexy-guy-like-me grin.

She was not melting. Not a bit. "Did you see that, Cage? Did you see what he freakin' did to me?"

Cage was laughing too hard to answer Nicole's question, as were the other idiots who'd been released from Gig duty. To say SEALs were often politically incorrect would be an understatement. Like Vikings, Trond thought once again.

"Did you say *big*?" At least she wasn't bouncing anymore. "Did you actually say that I have a *big* butt?"

Huh? Uh-oh. He recalled then how modern women were fixated on the size of their posteriors. Little did they know how much men adored them. The consternation on Nicole's face would have daunted a lesser man. Or a smarter man. "Did I say your buns"—that was a contemporary word for *buttocks*—"were like *big* apples? I meant to say *juicy* apples. Or melons." He batted his eyelashes at the bothersome witch.

"Melons! You . . . you . . . you . . ." she sputtered, casting a glare at him and then at all the other laughing hyenas around them. With a snort of disgust, she stomped away.

"Uh, *cher*, I'm thinkin' you need to do a little damage control," Cage advised him. "You doan wanna make Sassy Tassy your enemy. Uh-uh! Talk about! Pissing off a female officer? Can you spell sexual harassment?"

Her-ass, for sure. But Cage was right. He was supposed to be blending in here. Taunting the irksome woman who was already suspicious of him was not a good idea.

With a sigh, Trond tossed aside the damp towel and hurried after her. "Sassy," he called out, trying his best not to notice the up-down bounce of her butt cheeks in the brief shorts, cheeks that were not too big at all.

Should he point that out to her?

Probably not.

"Nicole?" he tried then, figuring she might be more inclined to answer to her real name.

Still nothing.

"Hey, slow down," he yelled.

She stopped in her tracks and turned, frowning at him from under a brimmed cap. Her curly, light brown hair was gathered into a tail that emerged from a hole in back of the cap. Her heavily-fringed, honey-colored eyes sparked gold fire at him. Being of Greek descent, she did in fact resemble Helen of Troy, whom he'd seen from afar on one occasion, right down to the light olive cast to her skin and the slight Mediterranean bump on her arrogant nose.

"What?" she demanded, catching him in the midst of ogling her.

Talk about cold! With that attitude she couldn't launch a longboat, let alone a thousand ships. "I might have crossed the line back there," he offered.

"Might have? You are such a dickhead. Is that supposed to be an apology?"

Well, yes. "It is what I said, is it not? We dickheads are thickheaded betimes."

"Betimes!" she snorted. "That's the most lame apology I've ever heard."

He counted to ten silently in Old Norse, then said as sweetly as he could, "I am sorry if I offended you."

She arched one brow skeptically.

His tongue, which seemed to have a mind of its own these days, unfurled like a banner on the wind. "Your buttocks aren't too big. Not at all. In fact, when you wiggle—"

"Whoa! You need to stop when you're ahead." Shaking her head at his hopelessness, she resumed walking.

He walked beside her. " 'Tis your fault."

"This should be good. How is it my fault?"

"For one thing, you are always hurling those lackwit motivational proverbs at me, mostly dealing with my attitude, which is just fine, if you ask me." Which no one did.

"That's because you need a major attitude adjustment."

He'd like to adjust something on her, and he'd like to do it with his fangs. "For another thing, you are always pulling rank on me, even though my captain standing in the Jaegers is probably comparable to yours as lieutenant in the U.S. Navy." Trond and one of his fellow vangels, Karl Mortensen, had joined BUD/S, Basic Underwater Demolition SEAL, the SEALs training program, under the pretext that they were Jaegers, the secretive Norwegian special forces, equivalent to the SEALs. Not that he'd been back in the Norselands for the past one thousand, one hundred, and sixty-three years. But Mike had set up this cover story to get them into the training compound.

There were people in the U.S. government who would swear that the security surrounding their special forces was ironclad, that no one could enter their ranks undetected. Little did they know the power and craftiness of an archangel!

"Maybe I do that because I don't believe your story. Maybe I suspect you're here for some ulterior purpose. Maybe my detective instincts tell me you're hiding a secret. Maybe I'm repulsed by your laziness. Maybe I think you need a few motivational courses."

A fount of information, most of it unsolicited, on motivational courses, Nicole apparently had dozens of books on the subject of inspiration, ones that could be downloaded onto an mp3 player and listened via ear buds. Inspiration to overcome fears, inspiration to increase focus, inspiration to lose weight, inspiration to gain weight, inspiration to achieve success, inspiration to reach potential, inspiration to be inspired. In his case, she'd offered to lend him one called *The Power of Pure Energy*. And she made the offer repeatedly, sometimes alternating with *Attitude Is Everything*. Each time he declined with a cool politeness, she was surprised that he wasn't jumping with joy to soak up her wisdom.

Nicole had been a police detective before joining the female SEALs. Another job better suited to men. Not that he would say that aloud in the presence of a woman who might just clout him upside the head, as one had done at a NOW rally back in 1972.

That's what he thought, but what he said was, "That is a lot of maybes. What do you care about my background as long as I get the job done? You cannot deny that I hold my own in SEAL training."

"Yeah, by wheelbarrow management. You're one of those people who only work when pushed."

Oooh, she was really getting on his nerves now. "I am a Viking. We have our own way of doing things." Which was a load of boar droppings. Even he knew he was not typical of Viking men. Certainly not like his brothers, who had managed to find a place in this new world: Vikar, who was successfully managing the VIK headquarters in a rundown castle in Transylvania, Pennsylvania; Sigurd, a physician at Johns Hopkins Hospital; Cnut, an international security expert; Harek, a computer whiz who was setting up an angel blog on the Internet; Ivak, who was presently managing his lustful inclinations in a prison; or Mordr, a soldier-for-hire, who should have been the one sent here, not him.

Nicole shrugged. "It's the way you do things that rankles. And what's with all this Viking crap you're always spouting?"

Viking *crap*? Oooh, how he would like to tie her tongue in a knot! "I *am* a Viking, and I have no idea what Viking *crap* you refer to."

"You're always saying things like 'Back in the Norselands, our weapon of choice was the broadsword.' Or 'We Vikings are known for our battle skills and our extreme good looks.' Or 'I am Viking, hear me belch.' "

He stiffened with affront. "I did not say that last thing." Trond prided himself on having refined his cruder habits over the centuries. He only belched on rare occasions now, and then in private. Mostly.

"Earth to clueless swabbie. There are no Vikings today. They died out about a thousand years ago."

That's what you think. "Some of us are still around."

"Pure-blooded Viking, huh?" she jeered.

"That's right." *I wonder how many years of additional penance I would get for tying her tongue in a knot.*

"Like a shitzu?" She grinned.

A big knot. "More like a pit bull," he said and made a growling noise at her.

"You're a ghost, you know."

"Huh?" He was dead, but he wouldn't call himself a ghost.

"I ran a search on you in my old police database. You don't exist. Nor does your friend Karl."

Nosy, nosy, nosy! "Must be the Jaegers have buried our identities." *Or good ol' Mike.*

"Do you know Max from SEAL Team Five . . . Torolf Magnusson? He and that whole Magnusson clan claim to be Vikings." The way she tossed a question at him suddenly, without warning, was no doubt some detective skill intended to trip him up. "Even Commander MacLean is married to a Viking, Max's sister. And there's a whole herd of that Magnusson family up in Sonoma."

By the runes! This woman could talk a cat out of a tree, or a lustsome man out of a cockstand. Not that he had one. Not over her. Not that he couldn't muster one up, given a chance. Not that he was taking that chance.

I swear, my brain is melting. Must be the heat. After the extreme cold of the Norselands, you'd think I would cherish this warmth, but a Viking is not meant for these climes.

"I asked you a question," she prodded. The whole time she interrogated him, she shifted from foot to foot, as if impatient to be off to her next important mission. Did she never stand still? Was it a physical condition? Or something she did just to annoy him?

He crossed his eyes, and this time he counted to twenty in Old Norse. "No, I have not made the acquaintance of Max yet. He has been away on field operations while I've been here, and when he returned, I was at jump school at Fort Benning. I look forward to meeting him, though." In fact, he'd heard so many odd things about the Magnusson family that he was curious.

"I got a new catalog from Audible Books today," she said. Another out-of-the-blue remark meant to disconcert him, no doubt. "There's a book there you might like. *Outwitting the Devil.* Interested?"

How appropriate! He couldn't help himself. He burst out laughing.

She scowled at him.

They'd reached the parking lot, not the female officers' quarters where he'd thought she was headed. He recalled then that Nicole lived off-base in Coronado in a small house she shared with two other WEALS. Trainees like him were not given that option.

"Well, do you accept my apology?" he asked.

Tilting her head up at him—she was a mere

five-five or so to his six-foot-four, not that their size disparity daunted the pixie at all—she eyed him suspiciously. Like a show dog on point she was with him. "What you really mean is, will I be reporting you?"

He shrugged. "That, too." Where were all the biddable women in the world, that's what he wanted to know. Had they become extinct, like Vikings?

"No, I won't be reporting you, but I will be watching you," she warned. "I'm on to you, buddy."

He doubted that sincerely.

"You're hiding something." She stared at him, as if waiting for him to reveal all.

Not in this lifetime, or a hundred others! "Aren't we all?"

An expression of pain crossed her face for a brief moment, stunning him into silence. *She has secrets, too?* Was it possible . . . Oh please, do not let it be so. Was Nicole Tasso the person he was sent to save?

His only clue as to the mission he and Karl were to accomplish here was to take out terrorists working for Jasper, king of the demon vampires, and to save one, or several, SEALs in danger of falling to the "other side."

"You look like you smell a rotten egg," Nicole said, opening the door to her little red Mustang convertible.

Which would have been appropriate since Lucipires, on being annihilated, melted into a pool of slime that smelled like sulfur, or rotten eggs. Not that she was in any way a Lucie; he would have known that right off the bat. But she could have been fanged by one and be in need of a vangel transfusion.

Maybe if I thrust my fangs into . . .

No, no, no! No thrusting.

Oh Lord! Let it not be so! he prayed. And it was definitely a prayer, not an expletive. Vangels never, or almost never, used God's name in vain.

He leaned in closer and sniffed.

"Are you smelling me?" The outrage on her face was almost comical. "First you imply I have a big bottom, and now you imply I have body odor. What a charmer!"

He just smiled. There was no scent of lemons, the usual clue that a person had been infected with the sin taint. No fang marks on the neck, either. *Whew! Thank you, Lord!*

I wouldn't be thanking anyone yet, a voice said in his head. He'd recognize that voice anywhere. Mike. And the voice was laughing.

Two

Why are women always attracted to losers? ...

Nicole sat in her car, stunned, with the motor idling. Trembling with emotions she'd thought long dead, she stared at Captain Trond Sigurdsson as he strolled away from her. The biggest loser to walk the face of the earth! And also the sexiest.

No rushing for him. Nope, he just swaggered in a loose-hipped, lazy sort of way. He had the gait of a confident man. Too confident, in her opinion.

And talk about buns! His were choice.

Height was not a requirement for Navy SEALs, just upper body strength. As a result, many SEALs were of average height, or even short. Not this knuckle-dragging baboon. He was six-foot-four, and all of it lean muscle.

She flicked the air conditioning on to full blast to cool her overheated body. And not just because of the outside temperature.

What was wrong with her? What was this strange inner excitement that flooded her? Big men did not attract her. With good reason. Her ex-husband, Billy, a Chicago policeman—a sergeant now, despite his sins—had been over six feet tall, a weekend body builder and amateur pugilist who packed a mean punch, as she knew all too well.

She shivered in memory and reminded herself how far she'd come. People meeting her today would never believe she'd once been so weak and insecure that she'd let a man use her for a punching bag, *and* blamed herself. In fact, when she thought back ten years, she barely recognized the eighteen-year-old girl who'd fallen in love with a rookie cop noted for his twinkling green Irish eyes and lop-sided grin. Not so noted as a wife abuser. She'd been an energetic, full-of-life, hopeless optimist before that. After three years, Billy had turned her into a whimpering doormat. That's why it rankled when people like Trond the Troll berated her for being too peppy or pushy; all she could say was, "So, sue me!"

It had surprised the hell out of everyone back in Chicago, including her family, when she'd left Billy, who gave the outward appearance of a nice guy who'd never in a million years strike a woman. Hah! It had also surprised everyone when she'd gone to the police academy in another state and worked her way up to detective. Sort of an in-your-face flicking-the-bird at her ex. Or at her father, if you could call him that. Daddy Dearest had preferred his code of silence to his fellow men in blue over his own daughter. Said she always was a flake, needed a bit of discipline. And her mother, the original Church Lady, had advised her to "offer up" her suffering for the souls in Purgatory. An act of grace, she'd called it. Hah! What grace was there in being a human punching bag? Her only sibling, Teresa, had been only eight at the time and clueless.

Soon after that, Nicole had been recruited for WEALS, not so much for her detective skills but because she'd become an award-winning marathon runner, as well. The SEALs and WEALS did like their buff bodies.

Which brought her to the present and the puzzle of why she was drooling over another big man with twinkling eyes, albeit blue this time, and a killer grin. One who sure as sin was hiding something, if her detective radar was any indication. Was she a masochist?

"Hey, Tasso, who's that sweet thang you're oglin'?" asked her housemate Marie Delacroix as she dumped her duffel bag into the backseat and opened the front door to slide into the passenger seat. An ex-Marine from Louisiana, like Cage, Marie had been in the charter class of WEALS back in 2007, while Nicole had graduated this past year. Marie had joined the SEALs after losing her father in the Twin Towers attack.

"I'm not ogling the jerk. I was glaring."

"Uh-huh." Marie appeared unconvinced as she peered into the distance—Trond was about a half block away now—and pretended to fan herself. "Holy crawfish! That is one fine ass!"

"I hadn't noticed," Nicole lied.

Marie glanced her way and they both erupted with laughter.

"I thought you had to stay for 'drownproofing,'" Nicole said as she engaged the car and backed out of the lot.

"Got canceled. Thank God! I just got highlights last weekend, and that chlorine is a killer for the hair."

With all the attention the news media gave to Navy SEALs lately, they usually fixated on how strenuous BUD/S, the training program, was. What the public didn't realize was that SEALs, and WEALS for that matter, had to continue that brutal physical program even after graduation into the teams. And that included "drownproofing," where the person had hands and feet bound together and was then tossed into the water to "bob for life." Great fun! And, yes, it was a killer on the hair, even with a rubber cap. Not that the SEALs with their high-and-tights minded, but the women did. They all recalled the time Candy William's bottle-blonde hair turned green after a drownproofing session.

"Not my favorite rotation!" Nicole agreed.

"I'm starved. Wanna go out for a pizza?"

"I can't. I'm teaching a motivational class at the teen center at seven, and then I'm taking a Zumba class at the aerobics studio at nine."

"I swear, girl, do you ever just relax and do nothing? It's Friday night, for heaven's sake!"

"I like to keep busy."

"There's busy, and then there's *busy*. You've got more energy than a school of Asian carp."

"Carp?"

"Yeah, remember that *National Geographic* special we watched where the carp were so big and so over-populating lakes that they were jumping out of the water like popcorn? Do you mainline Red Bull?"

Nicole laughed. "Natural metabolism." Well, that was only part of the picture. In truth, she was always aware of those three wasted years where she'd done practically nothing, except what Billy had allowed her to do. No going outside, especially not shopping or doing lunch with the few friends she'd retained, not even to go jogging; she'd loved running, even then. No books or magazines, unless they were ones he approved. TV forbidden during the hours when he was on shift because he believed she was being influenced by shows like *Oprah* or *The View*.

Now that she could do whatever she wanted, she wanted to do it all. Seven years since she'd left, and she was still letting the brute affect her life!

She and Marie talked about everyday things then. Base gossip. What they'd done that day. What was coming up the next week. As they talked, Nicole drove and enjoyed the passing scenery in her peripheral vision. The idyllic resort community of Coronado, where she lived, was nestled between the massive North Island Naval Air Station and the much smaller Naval Amphibious Base on the Silver Strand, with the Special Warfare Center located on the ocean side of Highway 75 bisecting the base. The small touristy town boasted white sand beaches on the Pacific side and a marvelous view of the San Diego skyline on the other.

As she pulled into the driveway of their cottage on the palm tree–lined street, she could hear music blaring through the open windows. Blues queen Etta James was wailing out that classic "Stormy Weather." Their other housemate, Donita Leone, must be back from her mission to Fallujah.

She and Marie exchanged worried glances. When Donita played the blues, it spelled trouble. Mostly she preferred upbeat songs by Lady Gaga, or even Marie's rowdy zydeco CDs.

Entering the small living room, she and Marie followed the music to the tiny kitchen where Donita stood in all her five-ten, ebony-skinned glory, stirring a pot of what smelled like Crab Alfredo. On the counter was a freshly baked chocolate cheesecake. Of course, Donita didn't have to worry about gaining weight. As a former Olympic swimmer, she had a body to die for.

But the cooking, along with the blues?

"I smell trouble." Marie was sniffing the air, and it wasn't the food she was referring to as trouble.

"Donita?" Nicole said, walking up and placing a hand on her arm. She saw then how red-rimmed her friend's eyes were.

"I hate the bastard."

"Uh-oh!" Marie said behind her.

They both knew who the bastard in question was. Sylvester "Sly" Sims had been a well-known black underwear model before joining the SEALs after 9/11. Like Marie, Sly had lost a family member in the 9/11 attack on the Twin Towers; in his case, a brother. Sly and Donita had been involved in an on-again, off-again, love-hate relationship for the past five years. He must have been on this mission with Donita.

"What'd he do this time?"

"He's engaged."

"*What?*" she and Marie both exclaimed. As many times as Donita and Sly had broken up and made up over the years, there had never been any question that they belonged together.

"Are you sure?" Nicole asked Donita, who was dumping pasta into a pot of boiling water. A pigload of pasta! Was she expecting company, or was she expecting them to eat all this stuff?

"Oh, I'm sure, all right." Donita swiped the back of her arm over her teary eyes. "Kendra Black is sporting a diamond the size of a golf ball."

"No way!" Nicole's jaw dropped. "Did you talk to Sly?"

Donita shook her head. "He tried to talk to me, but I told him to go fuck himself. He had the nerve to say, 'You snooze, you lose, babe. I got tired of waiting, and Kendra gives good—' That's as far as I let him go. The two-timing rat bastard! Honestly, he's been different lately, ever since he came back from survival camp on San Clemente Island. He even wanted me to . . . well, never mind."

If a black woman could blush, Donita was doing it now.

"What did he want you to do?" she and Marie both asked.

"A threesome." The look of disgust on Donita's face was nothing compared to theirs.

"Eeew!" Nicole said.

Marie's curiosity got the better of her, though. "With whom? I sure hope he meant another guy joining the sheets, not another woman. Never mind, the whole idea sucks big-time. I can just hear it now," she said in an imitation of a deep, male-husky voice, "I love you, baby, but I gotta share you with my friends." Reverting back to her own voice, she concluded, "Yeah, right, that's love."

"I really thought Sly loved me," Donita said, more tears slipping down her face.

"Honey, he probably does, but men are as loyal as their options," Nicole told Donita, handing her a tissue.

Donita blew her nose loudly and tossed the tissue in the trash. "I'm a good-looking woman. I take care of myself. Why is it that the grass is always greener in some other woman's yard?"

"I still believe there are good men out there who don't feel compelled to mow every pretty lawn in sight," Nicole contended.

Marie gave Nicole a disbelieving look and glanced pointedly at a pile of her motivational books-on-tape that sat on the counter. Her roommates thought she was a Pollyanna for always looking for positive sides of everything. Well, not everything, or everyone, Nicole thought. She certainly had negative thoughts about Trond Sigurdsson.

Donita and Nicole jumped when Marie suddenly slapped a hand down on the countertop with anger. "Here's a news flash, ladies: Men! Fucking assholes! They go apeshit over any woman who twitches her ass at them. And Kendra has been twitching her ass at Sly for a looong time. Talk about!" Normally Marie was supportive of Donita's relationship with Sly, probably because of their shared grief over 9/11, but friendship trumped unfaithfulness.

That was true about Kendra, but probably unfair. Kendra was a fellow WEALS whom they all knew well. Women everywhere twitched more than their asses around Navy SEALs these days, especially after the Bin Laden killing. Not just Kendra. In fact, there was an expression called "yo-yo panties" that referred to the climate on any military base the day before deployment. These days, the expression applied to SEALs just about all the time. It was sickening, really.

On the other hand, Nicole had heard that due to all the physical endurance exercises in SEAL training these elite forces were known to exhibit some remarkable, let's say, endurance in making love, too. No wham-bam-thank-you-ma'am for them. Not that she knew that from experience.

For some reason, an image of Trond Sigurdsson came to mind. *Bet my latest motivational book series he knows a lot about endurance.* She shook her head to clear it. No way was she going *there*! Besides, he was so lazy, he probably wouldn't make the effort to prolong sex. Too much work!

"I know what you need . . . what we all need," Marie said.

Oh good Lord! Is she reading my mind?

"Screw your classes for tonight, Nicole. We're taking Donita to the Wet and Wild for a girls' night out."

Oh, that. Whew!

The Wet and Wild was a bar frequented by Navy personnel, men and women alike, but especially SEALs and SEAL trainees. The hangout featured a wet T-shirt spraying machine at the doorway, like a mini car wash with side sprayers. The doorman waived cover charges for any women willing to walk through it. Lots of them did. Political correctness was not a priority around military men, especially full-of-themselves SEALs, and some women just wanted to let loose and have a good time.

"Sly and Kendra might be there," Nicole pointed out.

"All the better. Show him you don't care," Marie advised Donita.

Donita turned off all the burners on the stove and said, "I'll go, but only if we all wear our Slut Sisters outfits."

Oh my God! Donita was referring to the skinny black jeans, sparkly tube tops, and red cowboy boots the three of them had bought for Mardi Gras a few years back. Cowgirl hats and Band-Aids over the nipples optional. "I can skip my Zumba class, but I have to show up at the teen center for the motivational class. There's no one to substitute for me on such late notice and no way to notify the kids of a cancellation."

"Honey, we can go to the Wet and Wild *after* your class. Besides, if you show up in your cowgirl slut outfit, that'll be more motivation than those teens ever got." This from Donita, who was already piling dirty dishes into the sink. She looked up pleadingly. "So, are we agreed?"

Hesitantly, Nicole joined her two friends in a three-handed high five.

"All for one and one for all," they shouted.

Was she the only one who recalled the last time they'd worn those outfits? They'd gotten arrested for inciting a riot.

But then Marie expounded that famous Louisiana philosophy, "*Laissez les bons temps rouler.*"

Let the good times roll.

Something was going to roll, all right, but Nicole was afraid it was going to be their sorry behinds.

There's more than one way to go a-Viking...

Trond was splatted out, facedown, on his cot in the two-man room of the SEAL bachelor quarters that he shared with Karl. Because he and Karl fell into that ambiguous category of visiting special forces, they hadn't been forced to bunk with the other trainees, which was a blessing considering the secrecy the two of them had to employ for some things.

Trond wore only boxer briefs in light of the poorly functioning air conditioner and the ninety-degree heat outside. This being Friday night, he wouldn't mind sleeping until Monday. But he couldn't do that. There was a half day of PT for trainees in the morning.

After a shower, a six-pack of reconstituted Fake-O blood that he and Karl had shared surreptitiously, on top of ten hours of SEALs training, not to mention Gig Squad, he was flat-out beat, mentally and physically. Besides that, a quick check of e-mail had shown messages from each of his brothers and one alarming IM from Mike:

Why have you not yet saved the sinners, Viking?

Well, gee, Mike, it would help if I knew who those sinners are.

Why are the Lucipire terrorists still thriving, Viking?

Earth to Archangel: You expect me to save the entire world all by myself?

IMO, if you have time to jest, I have not given you enough work to do, Viking. LOL.

Trond was going to LOL someone, probably his brother Harek, who'd taught Mike how to use a computer.

So, did Mike mean sinners, as in plural, or was that a keyboard error? Talk about pressure! Ever since Mike had discovered the Internet, the archangel sent him messages via the computer, rather than in his head. Way too many of them! Never cheery ones, either, like "Good job, Trond! How are you? Anything I can do for you?"

Karl came in, making enough noise to wake a hibernating grizzly with his new pair of rubber-soled shoes that squeaked with every step he took. Squeak! Squeak! Squeak! Each squeak was like scraping fingernails on a weary concrete brain.

Trond cracked open one eye and saw his partner was fully dressed in T-shirt, open button-down shirt with silver angel epaulettes on the shoulders, jeans, and the irksome athletic shoes with the tortuous squeak. As Karl sat down on the opposite bunk to tie said athletic shoes, Trond asked, "Where you going?"

"Down to the exchange to buy a few things."

"Condoms?" Trond inquired teasingly, knowing full well that Karl wouldn't be having sex with any woman, and not just because he was a vangel. Karl had been twenty-two when he died in 1972 during the Vietnam War. He was still a perpetual twenty-two since he'd joined the vampire angel network. Unfortunately, or fortunately, Karl's wife was still alive. Despite her being sixty-three years old now, and despite Karl not being permitted to show himself to her, he still remained faithful to his marriage vows.

"Hah!" Karl snorted. "More like deodorant and cigarettes."

Karl smoked every chance he got, which wasn't often here on base where "No Smoking" signs were posted everywhere. He couldn't blame the man, though. There weren't many sins a vangel was permitted. And while smoking might be a stinking habit, chances of the vangel smoker dying of cancer were nil since he was already—ha, ha, ha—dead. Besides, Karl claimed the "coffin nails" relaxed him and helped him play his role, blending in with humans.

"Of course, I could buy some condoms for you," Karl said. "Maybe you'll get lucky sometime soon."

"Yeah, right. The only kind of sex I have doesn't require protection." And he hadn't even had that kind—his famous "near-sex"—in ages. Literally.

"Listen, buddy," Karl began, "the Fake-O just isn't doing it for me anymore. Being out in the sun so much is a killer. I can feel my skin color fading, despite the SPF 1000, and my energy level is zapped with the least exercise. I'm finding it harder and harder to keep my fangs retracted. You've had centuries more experience with it than I have. We need to feed from a saved sinner sometime soon, or kill a few Lucipires."

Blood, pure blood, taken through the fangs was essential to the Viking vampire angels. Contrary to popular opinion, vampires . . . or vampire angels, leastways . . . could go out in sunlight, providing they'd blood-fed properly to avoid their skin getting whiter and whiter, eventually translucent.

In an emergency, they used blood ceorls in their community or the unsatisfactory Fake-O. Or, as his brother Vikar had discovered recently, he could flourish off the occasional feeding on his life mate, or eternity mate in their society. But the best way remained drinking blood of a person they had saved from Satan's vampires, once purified by repentance or failure to act on sin.

Fake-O was a product that had been invented by their very own ceorl chemist. Not as good as real blood, but it sufficed as a stopgap. Back in the old days, like the Roman empire, there had been no sunscreens or tanning salons, obviously; so, the vampires had to hide out in caves until nighttime, thus giving rise to all the idiotic notions about vampires needing to sleep all day, usually in coffins. Yeech!

Satan's demon vampires, on the other hand, needed the blood of their victims in order to contaminate them. They preyed on humans who were on the brink of some grievous sin, giving them that little extra boost toward damnation. First, they bit the neck of their victims, bringing them to stasis, after which they blew their unholy breath into the person through any bodily orifice, preferably the mouth or ear. This made the victim weak and open to temptation. Once they took the "bait," acting on temptation, and committed the sin, the demons drained them dry and took them to the underworld. All this in a matter of seconds. Their human bodies just disappeared.

Trond sat up with alarm. Karl wasn't a complainer. If he was worried about lack of pure blood, there was a problem. Except for not having tanned-to-the-point-of-leather skin, he looked just like any other SEAL. Short, almost bald hair, muscle-toned body, a rigid military demeanor in the way he carried himself.

"You can always feed on me," Trond offered.

Karl shook his head vigorously. "No. That is an absolute last resort. It would weaken you in an environment where we have no backup. I'll return to Transylvania, or have a blood ceorl sent here for a few days, before I take your blood. Thanks for the offer, though, my friend." Karl hated using the female ceorls because of his marriage vows. Even though feeding from a blood ceorl wasn't normally a sexual act, Karl considered it a betrayal of sorts.

Trond homed in on something else Karl had said. He was glad to hear Karl refer to him as friend and not master, as he'd been wont to do for a long time, being lower down the vangel totem pole. Trond and his six brothers, the VIK, were considered the jarls, or upper class, in the vangels. It would have been way too hard to explain "master" to this bunch of freedom fighters.

"We have to figure out which of these SEALs is ready to turn bad, or has already made the transition," Trond said.

"Any clues?"

"Not yet. In addition, we need to get ourselves assigned to a mission where we can battle some Lucipires. I heard some rumblings today of an active op brewing. This might be it."

Karl stood and shook out the legs of his jeans. "Okay, I'm out of here. Do you need anything?"

"No, but, Karl, you'll tell me if things get too bad, won't you?"

"I will."

Trond sat on the edge of his cot after that, elbows on his knees, face in his palms. Being a Viking vampire angel was the pits sometimes.

"Whoa! No sad sacks allowed!" said Cage, whose room was across the hall, or leastways it was his room when he decided to stay on base. He had an apartment over in San Diego. That's what he and Karl should do—get a place off-base—once they finished this training program, assuming they would be staying here that long.

"What the hell's a sad pack?"

"Not a sad pack. A sad *sack*. A depressed person. As my mawmaw allus sez, 'You have a face so long you could eat oats from the bottom of a barrel.'"

Trond glanced up with disbelief. First, motivational sayings from Nicole, now hokey Cajun sayings from Cage. "I'm just tired."

Cage was wearing tight denim braies, or pants, an

equally tight black T-shirt with the logo "It's Only Kinky the First Time," cowboy boots, and a cowboy hat tipped rakishly on his long hair. Full-fledged SEALs did not have to adhere to strict military appearance, the rationale being that they could infiltrate foreign countries better if they didn't resemble white-walled jarheads. Trond, for one, intended to let his own hair grow from now on.

"We're all tired, *cher.*"

"Where are you off to tonight?" He gave the Cajun's attire another full-body scan, shaking his head with amusement. "The rodeo?"

Cage grinned. "I wouldn't turn down a rodeo or two, if you get my meaning. But, no, we're off to the Wet and Wild. Me, JAM, Geek, and F.U. Cold beer and hot women ring any of your bells?"

Oh yeah. Clang, clang, clang. Those two—alcohol and sex—would quench two of his always throbbing bodily appetites, thirst and hunger. But the temptations in such a wild spot might be too much for even a thousand-plus-year-old vangel to withstand. After all, his original "penance," or assignment, had been for seven hundred years. He and his brothers should have been done by 1550. Not surprisingly, they, being Vikings, had erred on occasion, little sins here and there—okay, a few big ones, truth to tell—which kept piling on the years.

"Nah. I think I'll stick around here. Order a pizza. Watch a few *Band of Brothers* DVDs that I've missed. Thanks for asking, though."

Just then, JAM stuck his head in the door. That would be Jacob Alvarez Mendozo, a former almost Jesuit priest, of all things. The fine hairs rose all over Trond's body as he stood and stepped closer. Yep, the scent of lemons, a clear sign of a sin taint.

But wait, maybe JAM was wearing some citrusy cologne. Menfolk in modern times tried everything in their power to hide honest male sweat. Some men even shaved their chest hairs. What was wrong with men being men? That's when he noticed the two small marks on JAM's neck.

He and Karl, who had returned, exchanged glances.

Trond did a mental fist pump in the air. Finally, *finally*, he had found his mission. Or at least part of his mission. This must be the SEAL they'd been sent to save. All along he'd been thinking it was someone like the obnoxious Frank Uxley, aptly named F.U. Never had it occurred to him that their target was a seemingly religious man like JAM. What exactly had he done or was he contemplating doing?

"Uh, maybe I'll go with you guys, after all."

Three

Satan's bedfellows . . .

Jasper, king of the Lucipires, was about to hold court with his commanders, who made up the Lucipire Council, in the great hall of Despair, his palace in the remote icy mountains of northern Scandinavia, sometimes known as the Land of the Polar Night. A U-shaped conference table had been set up with comfortable armed chairs, everything made ready for the arrival of Jasper's guests.

Most humans couldn't withstand the extreme cold or long periods of total darkness beyond Svalband, Norway, the northernmost inhabited region of Europe, but those were the very conditions that appealed to vampire demons. A person had only to spend an hour in Hell, let alone hundreds of years, to appreciate the cold and snow of this Arctic wilderness. Plus, lack of neighbors was an asset for the type of activities Lucipires engaged in, not the least of which was torture. Welcome Wagon would have to be pulled by a dogsled here.

Of course, the long period of polar nights also

led to what was commonly known as Land of the Midnight Sun, days and days of nothing but sunshine. The Lucipires relocated during those times or stayed in the windowless dungeons.

Jasper's band of Lucipires had been almost totally annihilated by those damnable Viking vampire angels following the Sin Cruise, one of his most creative projects, if he did say so himself, even though it had failed. If that hadn't been bad enough, their cave headquarters had been destroyed by St. Michael the Archangel himself, Jasper's most hated enemy.

The Lucipires had learned from their mistakes, though. Lucifer, their master, had made sure of that before sending reinforcements to replenish their depleted ranks, which were a thousand strong now, and growing.

Jasper was now forced to work side by side with Heinrich Mann, a former Nazi general who was . . . well, a Nazi about organization. Who ever heard of demons getting orgasmic over spreadsheets and P&L statements, the profits and losses referring to victims? If it were up to Heinrich, their victims would be forced into regiments that goose-stepped, German army–style, to and from their killing jars in the torture chambers.

Jasper had been a Seraphim angel at one time, one of the fallen princes exiled from Heaven along with Lucifer; therefore, he was superior in authority to Heinrich, who was a mere mung demon. However, the casual observer would never know it by the constant interference of the arrogant bastard. Mungs were a species of great size, often seven feet or more, oozing a poisonous mung or slime from every pore.

In addition to the Seraphim demons and the mungs, there were also the prestigious haakai demons, such as the five who were walking into the hall now with great pomp, their magnificent capes trailing behind them. Lucipires were humanoids; they could transform their bodies into any outward appearance they wanted, but their basic form was scaly skin, red eyes, fangs, and sometimes tails. Kneeling next to each of the five chairs were five young, newly turned human girls, naked, with their hair pulled back to expose their necks. Just in case his guests wanted a "beverage." He knew from personal testing that these five were especially tasty . . . damn sweet.

His haakai commanders bowed first in deference to him as their king before taking assigned seats at the conference table, where brass nameplates spelled out their names and territories.

Finally, accompanying these lords of the Dark Side, came the imps and hordlings, Satan's foot soldiers. Each commander had a hundred or more serving him . . . mungs, imps, and hordlings. The goal was to increase that number tenfold in the upcoming years. Talk about pressure! It was enough to give a demon ulcers. As it was, he'd taken to popping antacids like PEZs.

"Hector," Jasper greeted the first of the haakai to come forth. Hector wore the attire of a Roman soldier under his cape, his occupation when he'd been alive. "How are things in Terror?" Terror was the name of the hidden catacombs under the Vatican that Hector used for his Italian headquarters. A classic case of hiding in plain sight.

Hector shrugged. "The catacombs are actually quite comfortable, and many sinners come to Rome, as you know. We can fang them before they have a chance to repent. But all that hymn singing above us is . . . well, annoying. Holy this! Holy that! Praise God ad infinitum!" He rolled his seeping red eyes at Jasper.

Jasper understood completely. Hadn't he lived for years in a cave in America? Try sleeping to the sound of bat wings fluttering. Lots of bat wings! That's why he'd chosen to build a castle for himself this time, albeit in the land of glaciers. No bats here. Too cold!

Next up was Haroun al Rashid, the Silk Road merchant who had been responsible for hundreds of slave deaths in his greedy human life. Haroun did the touching of heart, mouth, and above the head form of obeisance to him before saying, "Greetings to you from the Arab lands." Haroun lived in Torment, a tent city in some remote Afghan region that he'd furnished lavishly to fit his tastes.

"No need to ask you how things are going," Jasper chuckled. The battlefield was a great harvesting ground for demons.

After that came Yakov, the Russian Cossack who had established a command center in Siberia aptly named Desolation, and Zebulan, the Hebrew warrior, who lived in a honeycombed volcanic ruin on a Greek island called Gloom. Then, there was the only woman in their command group, Dominique Fontaine, a six-foot-tall, black-haired voodoo woman, whose New Orleans mansion, Anguish, had a popular eating establishment and a torture chamber that defied description. To say that Dominique was a repulsive demon was an understatement, even for Jasper. One of Dominique's passions was snakes. At the moment, she had one of the diamond-headed monsters draped around her neck like a feather boa. Both of them presented impressive fangs. Dominique bowed to him, and he bowed back. Words were unnecessary. He did not like the woman, and she did not like him.

Jasper rapped his gavel on the table as a call to order. It was the femur bone of his very first vampire angel kill eons ago. At the same time his femur gavel hit the wood, his assistant, Beltane, a French hordling, came up to whisper in his ear, "He is here."

No need to spell out who *he* was. Heinrich liked to arrive late and make a grand entrance. He was dressed in his old Nazi uniform, loaded with medals, his back ramrod stiff. No tail today. Nor was he oozing slime as most mungs did. In fact, he was looking rather dapper with his blond hair parted on one side and slicked smoothly off his face. *"Heil!"* he said, stretching his arm outward toward Jasper, as if he were a frickin' Hitler, when everyone knew Der Führer was roasting in Satan's own version of Auschwitz.

News flash, Heinrich. You lost the war. Jasper nodded to the seat beside him and rapped on the table once again.

"Sorry I was late, everyone, but I was in conference with Luce," Heinrich told them with an exaggerated grimace of apology. Luce being Lucifer, of course.

What a name-dropper! Jasper seriously considered sticking his gavel up the asshole's asshole, knobby end first.

"Proceed!" Heinrich waved a hand airily, as if he were in charge of this meeting, and not Jasper. Most mungs were mute; unfortunately, Heinrich was not. *How much trouble would I be in if I amputated his tongue? Hmm.*

Jasper bared his teeth at the idiot and hissed. His fangs were so long they almost touched his jaw.

Heinrich glanced over at him and said, "Oops! Did I step on someone's tail?" Then he pulled a laptop out of his leather shoulder bag and proceeded to tap away at the keys.

What the fuck is he doing now? E-mailing Satan? Holy Hades! Is there wireless in Hell? Jasper couldn't allow the mung's insolence to go unchecked, especially when all the haakai were watching for his re-action to his authority being undermined. "The next time you arrive late, *Heiny*, the doors will be locked to you. I would suggest that you check your attitude before addressing me in future. You will not like the consequences. I'm thinking you would look good with a humpback."

Jasper turned away then, but not before noticing Heinrich's appearance begin to revert. His pretty Aryan skin was turning red and scaly. Apparently he had no fondness for humpbacks.

Good!

Zebulan, at the other end of the table, grinned with satisfaction. Heinrich hated Zebulan with an unholy passion since he was of Jewish descent. Zeb-ulan suffered no love for the Nazi, either. More than once, the two had tried to fang each other.

"Now, let us hear reports from each of the com-manders," Jasper said, "starting with Dominique." Let Heinrich try to interrupt *her* and see what hap-pened!

Dominique spoke of all the victims she'd lured to her dungeons by way of her four-star restaurant and she told them with relish about some of the new tor-ture methods she was experimenting with to turn her victims more quickly. Most of them involved snakes.

"So, do you serve snake on your restaurant menu?" Zebulan inquired with a grin.

Dominique licked her fire-red lips with a tongue that would do Gene Simmons proud while giving Zebulan a lascivious once-over. "No, *mon ami*. Just Hebrews."

They all laughed, even Zebulan.

After that, Jasper turned to Haroun.

"We took a dozen Al-Qaeda members just last week, Lucifer be praised," Haroun informed him. "And many soldiers of all countries who were at their tipping points for sin. Most important, I am well pleased with the progress we are making in turning Najid bin Osama, who, as you know, is from my territory. It helps that he is the long lost son of Osama bin Laden, one of dozens of his sons, lost or otherwise."

"And a wonderful job you are doing with him, Haroun."

"By the by," Heinrich interrupted, "Satan is having a grand time 'playing' with Osama bin Laden down there in his deluxe suite." Heinrich grinned, which, with his fangs exposed, gave him a most ludicrous expression, like a clown.

Ignoring Heinrich, Jasper addressed Haroun once again. "The havoc Najid is creating worldwide is leading to something special, I presume."

"Most definitely." Haroun passed folders to everyone at the table. "September 11 of this year, the anniversary of that most infamous event, we have planned multiple events around the world."

Everyone skimmed the documents, and various members of the council praised Haroun's efforts.

"Well done, Haroun! Well done!!" Jasper said, clapping his hands. The others joined in.

After each of the other commanders discussed

issues of importance in their territories, with special emphasis on newly killed humans and newly created Lucipires, there was another round of applause. Five hundred and sixteen kills in the past three months! Not bad!

"Master?" Heinrich said then, raising his hand for attention.

Jasper wasn't fooled by the sudden deference, but he tilted his head in recognition.

"Lucifer has a particular interest in the Special Forces Project that was started recently. Can we hear more about this?"

"Haroun is heading that project, as well." Jasper sat down and gave the floor to Haroun.

The Arab stood. "As we all know, for many centuries our emphasis has been on increasing our kills and expanding our ranks, part of that through reorganization around the world." He nodded to others around the table for emphasis. "But then, several months ago, a suggestion was made that we could increase our stature if we were able to add some of the military special forces to our side. Although we don't have any firm 'recruits' yet, there have been ten initial fangings that we intend to follow through on. Two of them are Navy SEALS, two Delta Force, two Mossad, two British SAS, and two Russian Spetsnaz."

"I thought our goal was to get some vangels in our nets, especially one of the seven VIK. I would love to nab one of those seven brothers." Yakov, the Russian Cossack, licked his lips at the prospect of such pleasure.

"Wouldn't we all?" Dominique remarked. "The things I could do with one of The Seven! Pleasure-pain is my specialty, you know."

Yes, they all knew!

"Aren't we overextending ourselves a bit?" Zebulan asked.

Jasper could feel Heinrich stiffen beside him. Any opinion the Hebrew extended would be rejected by Heinrich out of hand.

"Wouldn't we be better off directing our energies where they would be most effective . . . the general population?" Zebulan continued. "Those special forces guys are a breed apart. I mean, they might be wild on occasion, but bravery and fidelity and discipline and all those graces are hard to dilute with a sin taint."

"We just have to work harder on those fellows," Heinrich interjected.

Any more interjecting, and Jasper was going to interject something in him. And wasn't it ironic how Heinrich always said *we* but never managed to exert himself into any significant doing.

"And, by the way, there are female SEALs now, too," Heinrich interjected, then ducked his head when he realized he'd spoken out of turn again.

"Did you see all the press on those Navy SEALs when they took down Bin Laden? Superheroes turned into demons? I don't see it happening," Zebulan argued.

"Zebulan makes a point," Hector agreed. "We are working hard enough to rebuild our ranks. Why lose momentum now?"

"Because one of those SEALs would count for a dozen, two dozen others," Heinrich replied. "Imagine what we could turn them into? Super demons."

There Heinrich went with the *we* business again.

Jasper hated to agree with Heinrich, but he had to in this case, even though he did consider himself super. "We are always on the lookout for the vangels.

No matter what other goals we may have, capture or killing of a vangel supersedes everything. But the special forces kills would be almost as good."

"In a way, the Special Forces Project would be the icing on our devil's food cake," Zebulan remarked with droll humor.

Everyone groaned at his joke.

"As I mentioned earlier, our most revered leader, Lucifer, is so impressed with this project that he wants it to be expanded," Heinrich relayed, more serious now.

This was news to Jasper. Not that Lucifer liked the project, but that he wanted it expanded. Jasper was going to have his own chat with the boss.

"I was going to wait until later to mention this, but I need to give up control of the project. I have too much on my hands as it is with the war in my country," Haroun said.

"In what way does Satan want us to expand?" Jasper asked Heinrich.

Heinrich spread his arms. "Everywhere. Somalia. Cuba. Libya. Scandinavia. Spain. Canada. Germany. Everywhere. Most countries have special forces of some type or other. Wouldn't it be impressive if we had Lucipires in all these units?"

Zebulan made a snorting sound of disbelief.

Jasper liked Zebulan. He'd been around almost as long as Jasper, but he was getting a little surly of late. Perhaps he needed a reminder that he followed orders like the rest of them. "I nominate Zebulan to be the one to take over the Special Forces Project."

"What?" Zebulan stood, knocking the young blood offering to her naked ass.

"No, Zebulan, do not object. Hear me out." He could tell that Heinrich objected to his choice—

surprise, surprise!—and was tapping away on his laptop as fast as his scaly fingers could move. That just reinforced Jasper's decision. "Consider it a challenge, Zebulan. I would assign you extra hordlings, but I think you need to be covert on this operation as much as possible." He thought for a moment and offered something he rarely did. "I'll help you, personally, wherever I can. And Haroun can of course advise you on what's been done so far."

Finally Zebulan agreed with an angry exhale of exasperation, probably because he could see the smoke of indignation coming out of Heinrich's nostrils. "I'll do it, but my way. Start with the SEALs, then move to the other services. One at a time."

"That will take forever," Heinrich whined.

Jasper agreed, but he wasn't going to side with the whiny-assed Nazi. "With a small troop on call, Zebulan should be able to accomplish all our goals more efficiently than if we spread ourselves too thin. Now, if we've covered all business on our agenda, I have some treats to show you."

"Some new torture implement?" Dominique asked excitedly as Beltane rolled a long dolly into the room on which sat two life-size killing jars in which newly dead human souls fought wildly to escape the glass sides. To no avail, of course. The jars were soundproof, but by the wide-open mouths of the victims he assumed they were screaming.

Jasper likened his victims to butterflies; they even flailed their arms like wings when first put into the jars until they finally reached a state of stasis. After that, he pinned them to his display boards with three-foot pins through their no-longer-beating hearts, taking them out on occasion for playthings. Pets, really.

A hordling wheeled in his new torture device. It resembled a two-man or -woman rowing machine with enormous phalluses projecting in either direction from the center.

There was a communal sigh of appreciation at his creativity.

He smiled. "I call it the Impaler."

As Beltane began to unscrew the lids, screams emerged that could probably be heard all the way to the Arctic Circle. Not that anyone was about to heed those screams. And, truly, screams were music to a Lucipire's ears.

Seven sets of fangs elongated in lust.

Four

Yeah, Toby, we love this bar . . .

Trond was glad he'd come out tonight. He hadn't had a chance to talk in private with JAM yet, but the beer here at the Wet and Wild was cold and strong, the company of fellow soldiers was welcoming, and the music, though loud, was pleasantly rowdy. As a Viking, Trond knew rowdy well; it was in his blood.

And, really, every once in a while, a man just had to let loose and howl. Not that he was planning any howling tonight. That came too close to wolf behavior, and to his mind, that meant fangs. The one thing he could not do was expose his fangs, lest he scare the crap out of his comrades, get himself shot on sight, or land himself in some Frankenstein science lab like a bigfoot monster, or an alien. No, he would just stick to watching other men howl. Vicarious pleasure. Rather like near-sex. Nowhere near the real thing, but pleasurable just the same.

Why am I thinking about sex all the time lately? he asked himself.

Lately? he scoffed. *Let's face it, those who can, do. Those who can't, think about it. A lot.*

On the other hand, even when I could, I thought about swiving all the time. Must be sex is in my blood. Like rowdiness.

Many of the customers were singing along—rowdily, of course—with the three-person band—one woman and two men—to a song called "It's Five O'Clock Somewhere."

"I don't understand the words," Trond finally admitted.

"Easy, what planet you been livin' on? The lyrics mean that men can drink beer whenever they want since it's quitting time in some part of the world," Cage explained.

"What? You American men are such halfwits! If there is one thing we Viking men know better than any other, it is that beer needs no excuse for drinking. Ah. It probably has something to do with you modern men . . . I mean, American men . . . being too much under the thumb of your women."

The band had just finished the song, and in the brief pause everyone at the table had been listening to his words of wisdom. In fact, some of their jaws were dropped with amazement. Vikings tended to have that effect betimes.

"You dumb fuck! Are you sayin' we're pussy-whipped?" F.U. snarled. The short SEAL with his shaved head resembled a pugnacious bulldog with its lower lip thrust out.

"Cool your jets, man," Cage advised Trond under his breath.

In the old days, Trond would have knocked out a few of the aggressor's teeth, just because he annoyed him. Like a bothersome gnat, F.U. was. Being a sort-of angel was a drag, with "sort-of" being the key because his brother Vikar was the only one of the seven brothers who'd earned his wings, and even his were come and go. All these shoulds and should-nots! Trond settled for a mere shrug.

Which of course infuriated the gnat, who snarled some more. "I'm sick of you so-called Vikings infiltrating our SEAL ranks. All the Magnussons. Ragnor and Max. Pretty Boy's Norse wife, Britta, who was a frickin' WEALS for a while. Even the commander's shrewish wife, Madrene. You're all full of shit, if you ask me."

Trond started to rise from his seat, but a voice in his head warned, *Viking! Remember. Turn the other cheek.* He knew that fighting without just cause—and F.U.'s insults were mere bug bites on the slate of life—was not the angel way. So, curbing his anger and his fangs, which tended to come out in times of high emotion, he said as calmly as he could manage, "You are right, F.U. I have not met the other Norse folk you mentioned, but 'tis true, Vikings are full of shit on occasion."

"Fuck you!" F.U. replied.

Okaaay! That went well. I have no more cheek to offer, unless I drop my pants. I should have just knocked out a tooth, or two. "Thanks, but that's an invitation I'll have to decline."

Others around the table were laughing . . . at his uncharacteristic meekness and F.U.'s snarly disposition.

But then, he couldn't help himself. He positioned himself so that only F.U. could see his face. With a hiss, he flashed his fangs at the man. It all happened so fast that F.U. just blinked at him, then howled at everyone else. "Did you see that? Did you see that? He's got bloody fangs? Holy shit! Easy is a vampire!"

"What?" Trond said with brows raised in innocence. Then he winked at everyone at the table, as if to say, *That F.U.!*

Now F.U. was alternately shaking his head to clear it and frowning at Trond as if he'd just pulled some prank on him, which he had.

Trond turned to his other side toward the baby-faced SEAL known as Geek. Darryl "Geek" Good was about thirty years old, but he had the face of a youthling. Being of superior intelligence, a computer genius whose skills were highly valued by the military, he milked his innocent façade for all its worth; women apparently loved "babying" him. Meanwhile, when he was not being a SEAL, he was making vast amounts of money on some of his Internet projects.

"I understand you own an interesting company associated with the website www.penileglove.com," Trond remarked politely. But what he thought was, *Why would any man in his right mind put a glove on his cock? Oh, maybe it is a type of condom.* "What exactly do you sell?"

Geek grinned at him. "Sleeves of wax to be warmed in hot water or a microwave. When a man dips his dick in the warm wax and then removes it from the sleeve, the wax hardens like a tight glove. Pulling it off creates an orgasmic sensation that can only be described as magic down yonder, if you get my meaning. I have samples in my car if you're interested." He waggled his eyebrows at Trond.

Not for the first time, Trond concluded that modern men were a bit demented, even as he wondered if sex with a bag was a sin. "What is wrong with using a woman's sheath and her warm 'wax' to put a shine on a man's lance?"

"There is that, but my penile glove beats jacking off. And some guys claim their ladies like to dip Mr. Happy for them."

Mr. Happy? Hah! His Mr. Happy hadn't been happy for a long time, and a bit of wax in a bag wasn't going to put a smiley face *down yonder*. A twitch of a grin, maybe. A full-blown smile, no. But what he said was, "Uh, I think I'll pass for now."

The female band member tapped the microphone for attention, and said, "I know we have a few SEALs here tonight . . ."

Trond's tablemates sank down in their seats, not wanting to call attention to themselves here at the back of the drinking hall. He'd noticed that wherever they went, the SEALs seemed to isolate themselves from others and tried to appear inconspicuous, not always successfully.

". . . and I know some folks . . . not me, of course"— the woman rolled her eyes with mock innocence— "think they're a little bit arrogant . . ." She put a forefinger and thumb about an inch apart to illustrate.

More than a few people snickered at that observation.

SEALs *were* notoriously arrogant, and some of their conceit did come off as standoffishness, but that isolationism was mainly due to shared experiences, some of them horrific and bloody. They stuck to themselves because, well, how could they speak with others of what they had seen and done?

Like vangels.

". . . but, man oh man, when those SEALs with balls of steel took Bin Laden down," the woman continued, "I'll bet a few of them had this to say, and who can blame them?" The band then blasted into Toby Keith's "How Do You Like Me Now?"

Laughter and applause resounded around the room.

JAM, who sat directly across from him, was the only one not laughing. In fact, if Trond didn't know better, he would have thought the Hispanic man was on drugs. He fidgeted. He flexed and unflexed his fingers. His eyes darted hither and yon. Could the Lucie fanging have this type of side effect? He'd never seen it before, but one never knew what Jasper would come up with next.

The music was too loud to carry on a conversation across a table. So, taking his bottle of beer in hand, Trond stood and walked around to the other side, sitting down next to the obviously disturbed man. The things he wanted to say to JAM should not be overheard.

"What's up, JAM? You're strung tighter than an archer's bow," he said right off.

JAM stiffened at what had to appear as an inappropriate question from a near stranger. "Just pumped to deploy again. Rumor is, there's something big in the works. An important new SEAL mission. Almost as big as Geronimo." Geronimo had been the code name for Bin Laden.

"Terrorists?"

JAM nodded and blew out a breath of exasperation. "There are too damn many tangos out there, and they're multiplying like cockroaches in a candy factory."

Tangos was the SEAL name for bad guys, or terrorists. Trond understood the cockroach comparison. Lucipires could be crushed in one spot, but they always popped up somewhere else, in greater numbers, too.

"Sometimes I think we should just drop a bomb

on those raghead countries and wipe 'em out once and for all."

Whoa! *Raghead* was a politically incorrect word to blanket an entire Arab race. Not that SEALs were known for their PC-ness. Nor were Vikings. But *raghead* was much like the N word for black folks, or *wetback* for Mexicans, as JAM should well know, being of Hispanic descent. And what was that about bombs?

In truth, Trond had observed that some SEALs, after years under their military belts, got too good at killing. Some even came to enjoy it. A dangerous line divided justifiable killing and murder.

"Do you really mean that about bombing them all?"

"Damn straight I do. I'm friggin' sick of taking down a few here and a few there. They all need to die."

"Even if there's collateral damage? What about all the innocent men, or women and children, who would die, too?" Trond couldn't believe he was asking that question. He who had let an entire village perish without a second thought. Could it be that he was learning from past mistakes? Finally?

"Hey, some of these women and kids are as evil as the men."

"Were you always this cynical?"

"What? Don't you dare try to psychoanalyze me. I'm not F.U. I like the Magnusson family, weird as they are, but you're crossing the line, buddy, just like they always do. Mind your own stinkin' business."

Trond took a long draw on his beer, realizing that he had moved too fast with JAM. "Sorry, man. I was out of line."

"Why are you looking at me so funny? Why are your eyes getting sort of silvery. Oh, crap! Another weirdo! You really are just like the Magnussons, aren't you? Another fuckin' time traveler."

"What? No. Huh? Time traveler? No, I am not one of those. Ha, ha, ha!" *The Magnussons are time travelers? Now that is interesting.*

JAM quirked a brow with suspicion.

"I am something else."

JAM's second brow joined the first. Doubly dubious now.

With a sigh of surrender, he revealed, "Suffice it to say, I have been sent to help you." Then immediately bit his tongue at his hasty words.

Instead of being pleased, JAM was indignant. "By whom?"

He couldn't stop now. "Mike."

"Who in bloody hell is Mike?"

Not hell. That other place. "Perhaps we could meet privately tomorrow. This is not really the time or place—"

"Who in bloody hell is Mike?" JAM repeated through gritted teeth.

"St. Michael the Archangel."

JAM was startled for a moment. Then he burst out laughing. "Jesus H. Christ! Can my life get any more screwed up than this?"

"Actually, yes, your life can get more screwed up than this." *If the Lucies pull you into their camp, you will be screwed tighter than any mortal coil.* "By the by, please do not blaspheme."

"Huh? Are you some kind of religious nut? No, that can't be. I've heard you toss the F-bomb around a time or two."

"F-bombs and other vulgarities are all right. Well, not all right, but not majorly sinful. Taking the Lord's name in vain is a major no-no."

"I need another beer, or five," JAM said, shaking his head with disbelief. He probably thought he was drunk and had misheard him or that Trond was drunk and had misspoken.

Another Navy SEAL approached then, with a woman tucked under his arm, close to his side.

"Here comes Sly," Cage announced to the table, as if they all didn't recognize the big, black dude from Harlem. "He's got Kendra with him. Whatever you do, don't ask about Donita."

Military men were like women when it came to gossip. Probably stemmed from so much time together in close quarters. Trond had already learned over the past few days that Sly, who'd once posed for magazine pictures in his tighty-whities, had been involved for years with Donita Leone, one of the female SEALs, but he'd broken up with her suddenly and was now betrothed to another of the female SEALs, Kendra Black. Apparently it was an awkward situation because the SEALs and WEALS were all acquainted with each other.

Of course, the first thing out of F.U.'s mouth when Sly and Kendra sat down at their table was "Where's Donita?"

"Why should I care where the bitch is?" Sly said. "I've got a new bitch, don't I, honey?"

Everyone, except F.U., flinched at Sly's coarse comment, especially the blushing woman who started to turn away, but Sly forced her face back toward him and kissed her, hard, in a way intended to be publicly demeaning.

"Have you flipped your lid or somethin'?" Cage asked Sly when he raised his head. "You've turned into a world-class asshole."

"Listen, redneck, you got something against black

men asserting themselves? You thinking I should be down on your bayou plantation saying, 'Yes, massa, whatever you say, massa'?"

Cage started to rise, but Geek shoved him back in his seat. "Knock it off, Sly. You know Cage is no bigot."

"Yeah, well, keep your Ragin' Cajun nose out of my personal life," the black man grumbled.

That was when Trond noticed the smell. Lemons. Like waves, the lemon scent was wafting out of Sly's pores. Peering closer, he saw a Band-Aid on his neck. Did it cover a fang mark?

The implications hit him like a sledgehammer to the forehead. The sin taint! It wasn't just JAM who had been infected, but Sly as well. He'd heard different SEALs say over the past few days that Sly was behaving strangely ever since he'd come back from some SEAL survival training exercise on San Clemente Island. That must be the reason. Had JAM been on that same mission?

But Trond had no time to ponder all this because just then, Cage exclaimed, "Holy friggin' crawfish! Wouldya look at that!"

All heads turned toward the entrance where three women were laughing as they walked—nay, strutted—boldly through a spraying machine. Three WEALS, that was, wearing low-riding black jeans that could have been painted on their luscious bodies, red high-heeled boots, and almost-nothing sparkly tops in red, white, and blue that left their arms and shoulders and necks bare, as well as an enticing stretch of skin between their abdomen and navels.

The one wearing the red upper garment was none other than the bane of his life, Nicole Tasso, and Trond couldn't stop staring at her. It wasn't only his eyes that were appreciating her, either. Another part of his body was on full hot-damn-gotta-have-*that* alert.

And then he noticed the most amazing, alarming things of all: the expanse of bare skin from her midriff to her navel where a small gold ring winked at him. Leastways, it felt as if the wink was directed at him personally.

"I think I've died and gone to Heaven," Geek said with a mischievous chuckle.

Or somewhere else in my case.

Sly looked as if he'd swallowed bad meat, watching intently as other men ogled Donita in a stretchy white top through which brown nipples stuck out like pretty sentinels.

F.U. was sitting a little straighter in his seat in an attempt to add height to his short stature. If he only knew, it wasn't his size that repulsed women.

Cage laughed. "The last time they wore that gear, we had to bail them out of the city lockup." Then, to Trond's horror, Cage waved at the women to join them. In fact, he was already pulling another table over to connect with theirs.

The band began to play, "R. E. S. P. E. C. T.," that song that was like a woman's anthem in this country. But in Trond's head, another word entirely was being spelled out, T. R. O. U. B. L. E.

Clueless men are ageless . . .

"Oh, this is bad. Really bad," Nicole muttered as they made their way across the tavern.

And Nicole wasn't referring to the wolf whistles

and lecherous looks they got in a pathway that opened as a gauntlet for the three women. Sly and Kendra were sitting at the table where they were headed. That was bad. But what was really bad was sitting dead center . . . the T in what was bound to be trouble for her tonight. Trond Sigurdsson.

She should just tuck tail, turn around, and go home.

But wait. Maybe this would be her opportunity to get a little closer to him, to discover what secret he was hiding, to find out if there was something in his background that could endanger the special forces teams here at Coronado. She'd already gone to Commander MacLean weeks ago with her suspicions, and he'd told her that Trond's paperwork from the Jaegers was ironclad. Unless she had concrete evidence against the man, he advised her to stop her private investigating.

That had never stopped her in the past, and it wouldn't stop her now. If she'd asked more questions before marrying Billy, maybe . . . well, just maybe things would have been different.

So, with a bravado fueled by good intentions, she sat down next to him and tried her best not to notice how good he looked and—*mercy!*—even how he smelled. His dark hair was military short, shaved on the sides and only about a half inch on top. He'd shaved this evening and showered; she recognized the Axe deodorant soap, but even that couldn't mask his own unique skin scent. He wore a short-sleeved denim shirt with epaulettes on the shoulders that resembled silver wings. In a crowd of unisex T-shirts, his shirt seemed odd. Not unattractive, just odd. It was probably some designer fashion in Norway or maybe something associated with his Jaegers. The shirt was tucked into straight-leg jeans. Nicole's old detective skills helped her to make these kinds of quick observations. Of course, not usually with so much appreciation.

She decided to follow up on her idea to lure him into revealing his secrets with a little politeness since outright suspicious questioning hadn't worked in the past. "Hi!" she greeted him with a bright smile.

He jerked away from her, as if stunned that she could be pleasant. Or maybe it had been her peppy "Hi!" She knew from past experience how much he disliked her "peppiness." Then he said, "I can see your nipples."

So much for pleasant! She glanced downward and could have died. *Oh God! I forgot the Band-Aids.* "I swear, Easy, if there were a jerk parade, you'd be the drum major."

"What? Sassy, Sassy, Sassy, you earn your SEAL nickname when you wear a garment like that. And then you are offended when men notice." His eyes were glued to her chest, and their usual pale blue shade seemed to be morphing to silver. It must be the lighting.

"Most men wouldn't be so crude as to comment."

"Why not? I like big nipples."

She felt herself blush, from her forehead to her toes. "So, now I have big nipples as well as a big butt?"

"Easy bit her butt during Gig Squad today," Cage informed the rest of the table, every one of whom turned to stare at Trond with incredulity.

"I never said she has a big ass," Trond insisted.

Be nice, Nicole. Think positive. Look for the good in people and events. Part of Nicole's healing after she'd left her husband seven years ago had involved a concerted effort to avoid negativity. Even when she felt like she was drowning in depression, she put on a smile, and, yes, she'd developed a peppy attitude. She'd found that eventually outward optimism worked its way inward. If that made her seem like a Pollyanna, so be it. Women found their survival skills wherever they could. This guy, though, would be a challenge to Norman Vincent Peale himself.

She started to turn away from him, but the idiot was on a roll. "In my ti— I mean, where I come from, big nipples are an attribute to be desired. The better to suckle a man's babies." Under his breath, he added, "And the man, as well, of course."

JAM choked on the beer he'd just drunk. Cage had his face down on the table, shaking with laughter. Geek was grinning from ear to ear, no doubt waiting with anticipation to see what the goofball would say next. Sly and Kendra were doing their best to pretend Donita wasn't there, and Donita was doing her best to get JAM's attention to make Sly jealous. Marie had gone to the ladies' room, to check her nipples, no doubt.

"If I were you, I would shut up about now," Nicole warned Trond.

But did he listen? Nah!

"And, personally, I wouldn't mind at all if you remarked on the bigness of some of my body parts." Then he smirked.

The smirk was what did it.

Standing, she picked up a pitcher of beer and dumped it over the jerk's head. "Oops!" she said, then stomped off toward the ladies' room. She passed Marie coming back on the way and told her not to worry, that she just needed a breather.

Almost immediately, she felt like an utter fool.

What was wrong with her that she'd overreact to a little teasing? SEALs were masters at the art of the tease, much of it politically incorrect. It was harmless, really. And she'd just given them ammunition for more teasing. She could practically hear their communal thought waves following her: *PMS!*

About fifteen minutes later, Donita and Marie came into the rest room and pulled her out of the stall where she'd been sitting, fearing that she might be crying. She never cried, she never allowed herself to cry. Not anymore. And she sure as soap didn't let anyone see her break down. With a self-deprecating laugh, she assured her friends that she was all right. Probably that time of the month, she remarked.

She gave each of her friends a hug. *Good Lord! How pathetic am I being when Donita is the one in need of sympathy tonight.* "Are you okay?" she asked.

Donita nodded. "I'm planning on getting blitzed *and* laid tonight, preferably in that order."

Nicole laughed, which was just what she needed. A little humor to relieve the stress. "Any prospects?"

"JAM is number one on my list at the moment, but, hey, anything can happen. The only thing I can say unequivocally is, not F.U."

They all smiled at that. Poor F.U. had learned sensitivity from the Howard Stern School of Charm. He was an extreme sports enthusiast . . . skiing, hiking, and all that, which should have made him interesting, and there must be SEAL groupies out there who welcomed his advances just because he was in the elite force, but she didn't know any WEALS who'd let him within breathing distance. The nail in his yuck coffin came the day someone overheard him say, "Never trust anything that bleeds for five days and doesn't die."

"Anyhow, hurry and fix your makeup, honey. You're missing the big show," Marie told her. "JAM went out to get Trond a spare T-shirt he always carries in his vehicle, but Trond didn't want to put it on over all that sticky beer. So, as we speak, he is washing the beer off his head and bare chest . . ." She paused in a ta-da fashion. " . . . in the spraying machine."

"Better than porn." Donita waved a hand in front of her face.

"Every woman in the joint is getting a hot flash," Marie added, also fanning her face.

Nicole could only imagine. Unfortunately.

Within moments, they were all back in the bar, halfway across the dance floor, staring like all the other fascinated females and amused men as Trond stepped out of the spraying machine and used a bar towel to begin drying off his head and chest, seemingly oblivious to the stir he was causing, or perhaps he was just used to that type of attention.

Suddenly, as if he sensed her presence, he glanced up and over at her. Their gazes held for a long moment before he winked. At her!

She had fully expected anger, or mocking. But a wink?

No, no, no!

That wink said in body language as old as time, *I have you in my cross-hairs, babe. Beware!*

A laughing JAM handed the idiot a metallic gray T-shirt that Trond proceeded to pull over his head and tuck into his jeans. Even the tucking was an erotic exercise.

"Ho-ly mo-ly!" she whimpered.

He couldn't possibly have heard her this far away, and yet his head shot up, and he raised his eyebrows in question. He knew! The overconfident man knew precisely what effect he had on her.

Now that the "floor show" was over, people were returning to the bar or their tables to drink, or to the dance floor where the band was now playing that ultra sexy "Need You Now." She needed to get out of here before she made a fool of herself, or an even bigger fool than she'd already been. There was a back exit, she recalled, and spun on her heels, heading that way.

She'd gone only a few steps across the dance floor when she was yanked to a halt by a hand on her upper arm.

It was Trond, of course.

"What do you want?" She glared at him over her shoulder.

"You."

She turned, inch by inch, incredulous at such an outrageous lie. He'd shown her fifty ways to Sunday since she'd met him how much he disliked her. And now he wanted her to believe he wanted her? Another ploy to move his secret agenda? How dumb did he think she was?

And he dared to look at her with such unwavering innocence. Men! They were clueless to the bone.

She did the only thing she could then. She burst out laughing.

Five

Some chains are of our own making . . .

N icole, you misunderstood."
She stopped laughing for a moment.
"I misspoke."
"Oh?"
"When I said I want you, I didn't mean *want* want."

She started to laugh again.

Laughter was not the reaction any man wanted to his lustful inclinations, even if those lustful inclinations were all in her head. Okay, they were in his head, too, and some other places, but only because she'd brought up the subject.

"So, you don't want me in *that way*?"

That way and a dozen others. Maybe two dozen. "Are you on offer?" *What? Did I really ask that? If I had any hair on my fool head, now would be the time to start pulling it.* "When you asked what I wanted, I said you, but I never finished the sentence. I want you to stand still long enough so that I can apologize."

"Apologize?" she scoffed.

A pair of dancers—Cage and Marie, doing an energetic Cajun two-step—slammed into Nicole's back, shoving her against his chest, and he put his hands on her hips to steady her. With the high-heeled boots she wore, she fit nicely against his much taller frame, hip to hip, and other equally tongue-and-groove parts. Especially when she linked her hands behind his neck, preparatory to dancing. How he had moved from his apologizing to dancing was a leap he found hard to fathom. "I hate to dance," he told her.

"I love to dance," she replied.

Which meant that they continued to sway from side to side in a close embrace.

Holy clouds! Modern men have it good! Dancing as foresport? Whoever would have predicted that? Lot less energy required to get a woman in the mood!

But, no, he had to get his mind off that sex pathway to nowhere and on to the matter at hand. He inhaled and exhaled before saying, "I am really sorry."

"For what?"

"For hurting your feelings."

"You overestimate your powers."

"There is no excuse for a vang . . . a man to use words as weapons with a woman," he barreled on, as if she hadn't spoken. "Yes, you provoke me. Sorely, betimes. And, yes, the mere sight of you ignites this spark within me, and I must needs either kill you or kiss you. And, yes, you are forbidden fruit to this hungry soul. And, yes, I have had two bottles of beer, but I am not *drukkinn* by any means, lest it be drunk with lust, which men have been known to release in anger when unrequited, but still . . ." He released a long breath after that ridiculously long blather. "Please accept my apology."

"That is the most half-assed apology I have ever heard." With her hands still on his shoulders, she leaned back to see his face better.

The arching of her body caused her nether parts to rub against his crotch, and he could swear he saw stars behind his eyelids. Or maybe it was just the disco-style lights blinking off her belly button ring or off her breasts that were nigh naked under the little sparkly stretch top. *One flick of my finger and it would be gone. Do I dare? Maybe if I . . .*

"Somehow I don't see you as the humble type. Did Cage tell you to apologize?"

Shaking his head to clear it, he looked down at her and smiled. "Cage called me a dumb shit and likened me to an armadillo crossing a superhighway every time I am around you."

"Smart guy, that Cage!"

He squeezed her hips in reprimand.

"So you're bird-dogging me now because Cage told you to."

"That is not what I said." *Bird-dogging?* He knew what that meant, and it was not an attractive picture. Nor did he like the image of himself as an armadillo. Hah! She ought to beware of him lest his fangs emerged full-throttle. She would know then that he more resembled a wolf . . . a fierce, proud, beauteous beast of the wild.

Nicole must have noticed the indignant expression on his face because she tilted her head in question.

"A dog? A smelly, ball-licking, hairy hound? That is how you see me?"

Her eyes widened before she laughed. "Get over yourself."

Bird-dogging? Trond could still not get over that

assessment. He had never chased a woman in all his sorry life, and he was not about to start now with the most irksome female to walk the planet. He gritted his teeth and told her, "Must you missay me at every turn? That is not why I followed you. I saw the hurt in your eyes, and I was ashamed of myself." *There! That is all the humility I am going to engage in. Take it or leave it.*

"Oh good Lord! That wasn't hurt, you sorry excuse for a sweet talker, you. It was anger. And even if you had the power to hurt my feelings, which you don't, the last thing I need from the likes of you is a pity party."

I knew this would happen. I knew it, I knew it, I knew it. That's what happens when a man apologizes to a woman. Sets himself up like a target for the arrows of a shrew's verbal darts.

"Frankly, I'm the one who needs to apologize for dousing you with beer."

Huh? Oh. Well, that is better. Maybe she is not such a shrew, after all.

"I don't usually behave in such an impulsive way. Even when I'm provoked."

Nay, she is a shrew, all right. "Apology accepted," he said quickly before her blathering tongue could launch more insult bombs at him, but then he thought of something else. *Do I sense an opportunity here?* "Shall we kiss and make up?"

"Only if you want a karate chop to your family jewels!"

They were still only swaying from side to side. No twirls or fancy steps. But just then Trond noticed that the band had changed songs. "Oh no! Not now!" he said on a groan. Coming to an abrupt halt, he pressed his forehead against Nicole's.

"What now?"

Why does she say that as if I'm always in trouble?

Maybe because I often am. "It's that song," he explained and groaned again.

"Aretha Franklin's 'Chain of Fools'? What about it? I know you're a fool, but what else is new?"

Sarcasm ill suits her, but I will not tell her so. See, I can be wise. Is anyone listening up there? "Did you ever see the movie *Michael* starring John Travolta?"

"Yeah," she replied, frowning with confusion.

"My brothers and I have watched it dozens of times," he revealed. If she only knew, a bunch of vangels didn't have much else to do on long winter nights when holed up together. That and Michael Jackson videos to appease the youngest vangel in their ranks, who fashioned himself a born-again moonwalk dancer, like the King of Pop. He only hoped the band didn't decide to play "Thriller." He might just have to slit his wrists and drink his own blood dry.

"And the chains song?" she prodded.

"Makes me want to dance," he admitted, reluctantly.

"I thought you didn't like to dance."

"I don't."

It was probably some subliminal impulse implanted by Mike into the vangels, or at least the VIK. Sort of an archangel joke. Stepping back from her, he closed his eyes in concentration, then began with his arms raised, palm spread as if feeling for something in the air. *I must look like every village idiot ever born.*

"Are you crazy? Stop it! People are staring," he heard Nicole say in a mortified whisper as she tried, to no avail, to tug him off the dance floor.

The beat of the music was in his bones now. He
opened his eyes and did the forefinger pointing
move with four rhythmic steps to the right, then
four rhythmic steps to the left. Then he repeated
the pattern, grinning at Nicole the whole time. You
couldn't help but grin when you did the *Michael*
dance.

He heard Cage yell out, "Hey, guys, come here.
You've gotta see this. Trond has turned into John
frickin' Travolta." Cage was considered a really
good dancer. If he was impressed, then Trond must
be doing something right. Or wrong.

A gleeful F.U. yelled, "Shake yer booty, Easy."

He was going to shake something on F.U. sometime soon, and it wasn't going to be his ass.

"Show us your moves, stud!" Nicole's housemate
Marie urged.

He had moves, but they weren't ones to be dis-
played in public.

People were starting to clap and the crowd began
to sing along whenever the band got to the "Chains,
chains, chains" refrain. Now that he was in the
groove, he glanced around. Son of a troll! He was
the only one dancing.

He continued to dance, sometimes bending his
knees and thrusting his hips, other times using his
fists in a punching motion as he danced forward.
The whole time he kept beckoning Nicole with the
fingertips of both hands to come closer. She kept
shaking her head no, and laughing, even though
some women, and a few men, began to join him in
a line dance.

She wasn't the only one laughing. So were Cage,
Sly, JAM, Geek, and F.U., who stood behind her. As
well as Donita, Marie, and Kendra.

Just great! That's me. A Viking court jester! Lord of the Fjord Dance! "C'mon, Nicole. Be a sport," he urged. *Said the dancing spider to the fly.*

"No way!"

Trond put his hands over both eyes as if wounded by her rejection, but her refusal was a challenge he couldn't ignore, and he danced over to cull her out from the herd, so to speak. Hey, he could be a cow person, too. Now that he was behind her, he put one arm around her waist and tugged her close to his body. Real close! When his hips swayed, hers did, too. Against her ear, he whispered, "Gotcha!"

"That better be your belt buckle pressing against my rear."

He just laughed, and polished his "buckle" against her curves. Oh, he wasn't quite doing that dirty dance move called daggering, but it was close.

Dozens of couples began to crowd the dance floor and play "follow the leader" with all his moves. They bumped. They ground. They spun on their boot heels. They did the *Michael* line dance moves. In the end, when the band finally ended its extended version of the song, he twirled Nicole three times under his arm, then into a close embrace where he kissed her quickly before she had a chance to smack him silly. Or worse, *kiss* him silly. Just that brief touch of lip on lip was enough to show Trond that there was an important zing going on here. And it had nothing to do with her constant snarking at him. He had no time for zing in his life. He was not allowed to have zing in his life. But, oh, the zing felt so good.

When the song ended, everyone clapped as he looped an arm over her shoulder and started walking back to the table. That's when he sensed a sinister presence in the tavern. It was over by the door. He stiffened, and told Nicole in an undertone, "Go back to the table. Quickly."

"What? What's wrong?" Of course, the stubborn woman would argue with him now.

He gave her a soft shove and turned away, scanning the room. Over there. The man in the baseball cap stared at him, then turned and sauntered toward the exit. Faster than any human could travel, Trond was on his heels.

They were just outside the door in the parking lot when the Lucipire turned. Despite the extended brim of the Blue Devils baseball cap that hid his upper face and despite the long, exposed fangs, Trond recognized a familiar foe. It was Zebulan.

Zebulan recognized him, as well. Not a good thing! "Well, well, well! Aren't you a welcome surprise? A VIK in Navy SEAL land. Be still my heart. Oops, I forgot. My heart no longer beats. I thought you were back in ancient Rome gladiating."

The two of them were circling each other, moving away from the lighted entrance and across the lot toward a wooded area. Trond's fangs were out now, too, and he suspected the wispy blue wings were emerging, as well, as they did when he was about to do battle. He didn't want to be caught in that condition by humans in the area.

"Gladiating? Zeb, Zeb, Zeb, you have a warped sense of humor."

"In our line of work, a sense of humor is a survival skill betimes, don't you think?"

Trond shrugged. The two of them had come into contact many times in the past, sometimes violently. "What are you doing here, Zeb?" Suddenly, Trond knew. Two Navy SEALs sin-tainted. A high-ranking

Lucipire in the area. The connection was obvious. And he would bet his real wings, if he ever got them, not these ethereal foggy images at his back, that more sin taints on the elite special forces were planned. What a coup that would be for Jasper and all the Lucipires! "Wouldn't it be more efficient for you Lucies to work in the general population?"

Now it was Zeb's turn to shrug. "A challenge is welcome in our ofttimes mundane lives. Yours and mine both."

Trond didn't like being likened to demons in any way. "First *gladiating*, now *mundane*? Holy horseradish! You been reading the dictionary for kicks?"

"We get our kicks any way we can, as you well know. I saw you dancing with the slut. Is she someone special to you? Are you vangels allowed to fuck now? Wanna share?"

Trond knew that Zeb was just yanking his chain. If he protested the derogatory term for Nicole or the sexual implications, the Lucipire would know to make her a target to trap him.

There was a reason that the Navy discouraged marriage or committed relationships (lot of good that did them!). The enemy could get to the soldier by way of his loved ones.

It took all Trond's willpower to restrain himself from reacting.

"That was unkind of me," Zeb said, surprising the hell . . . or something . . . out of Trond.

Trond shook his head to clear it. "Are you going to report my presence here to Jasper?" Silly question! Of course he would.

"Probably."

Probably. Why not absolutely? Something is strange here. Trond leaned down and pulled a blade from his boot—a special blade quenched in the symbolic blood of Christ. If he killed Zeb with this blade, Zeb would not just dissolve into a pool of sulfurous slime, but would be gone forevermore, never to materialize again as a demon vampire. Just a permanent resident of the deepest bowels of Hell, where he would pay horrendously for having failed. But then, Zeb took a metal object from his pocket, like the hilt of a weapon, which soon proved true. When he pressed a button, the object turned into a retractable short sword. *A switchblade sword? Cool! I'll have to order one or five when I next talk to Mordr.* Trond was not fooled by the size and flexibility of that blade, though; it was no doubt tainted and could not just kill Trond, but render him into a stasis where he could be taken back into the demon vampire's lair, possibly turned to the Dark Side forevermore if he was unable to withstand the torture.

"I might let you go . . . for now . . . if you give me the two SEALs that we've already tainted," Zeb offered, crouching into an attack position. "I'll wait and finish them off on a mission away from here, and no one will know what happened when their bodies disappear. Blame it on Al-Qaeda."

Trond was in an attack position now, too. "You know I can't do that." An idea occurred to him then. "I like you, Zeb. Despite your evil ways, there is something about you that speaks to me." He put a hand over his heart for emphasis. "You would make a good vangel."

Zeb stepped backward and gasped as if he'd stabbed him through the heart, good and true. "That is impossible. The things I have done . . ."

"The things we all have done!" *And wasn't that the truth? Sinners one and all.*

"It is cruel of you to offer such a suggestion to me, Trond. Oh, I know I have no right to expect consideration. Still . . ."

"Is there even a speck of goodness left in you, Zeb? Have you never wished to escape your fate?"

"Only every minute of every day for the last two thousand and some years. But this is a futile conversation. It has never been done before."

And probably never will be. "I am not the person to be discussing this with you. But I can put you in touch with someone who can."

Zeb arched his brows.

"Michael."

Zeb made a snorting sound of disbelief that St. Michael the Archangel would ever speak with him. Then he lunged with his sword.

Trond just barely managed to swerve at the last second, and the sword tore off a portion of the sleeve on Trond's T-shirt, rather JAM's T-shirt. That was close, too close for comfort. They went at each other in earnest then. Thrusting and parrying, slicing and stabbing.

"Trond? What's going on?" a female voice asked.

Oh crap! It was Nicole.

"What are you doing out here?" The voice was getting closer.

Zeb smiled.

"Don't you dare," Trond warned.

Zeb licked his lips.

"Don't you dare," Trond repeated.

"She's safe . . . you are, too . . . for now. But I'll be back." Zeb was backing up into the woods. "And when I return, I'll be taking you with me."

"Threats now? You could try."

Just before Zeb disappeared into a poof of noth-

ing, he said, "Not threats. Promises. And I will succeed in the end. Evil always wins."

"Who are you talking to?" he heard a female
voice ask.

*Nicole! Who else would it be but the persistent barna-
cle on my butt.* "Go away," he ordered, quickly willing his fangs and wings to disappear.

Of course she stomped over the loose gravel of
the lot to stand beside him, peering into the woods
where he was still staring. He surreptitiously hid
the knife in his boot once more. "Who was that?"

"No one. I just came out here to piss." *Is that the
best I can do? Jeesh!*

"And the other guy just had to pee at the same
time, so you decided to have a pissing contest?" she
jeered. "By the way, what was that blue smoky stuff
at your back? Were you smoking weed?"

Go away! "No, I was not smoking anything, but,
yeah, sure, on the pissing contest. Why not?" *Now,
go away.* He was still scanning the area, making sure
there were no other Lucies about.

"Why not use the men's room inside?"

He crossed his eyes with frustration. "Maybe
I have a phobia about public rest rooms." *Which is
ludicrous, considering some of the primitive privies and
garderobes I've had the misfortune to visit over the years.
For example . . . well, never mind.*

"Are you playing me?"

*I'd like to play with you. Dirty play. No, no, no. I don't
mean that. Go away!* "Would I do that?" he asked
with a sigh of resignation as he drew her away from
the woods and back toward the building, glancing
over his shoulder to make sure they weren't being
followed. For some reason, he trusted Zeb's word
that he wouldn't attack *this time*. Still . . . what was

that old proverb? Trust in God, but sharpen your sword.

She shrugged his hand off her arm. "I was right about you. Oh, you are good at deflecting attention away from your secret activities, but I know you're up to something."

This was bad. She was going to cause trouble for him with the commander. He just knew she was. He tried to think of some secret a man might have that he would want to hide, other than the fact that he was a Viking vampire angel and a thousand or so years old.

Oh no! Not that.

But it was the only thing he could think of on such short notice.

"Wait!" he yelled to her retreating back. "I'll tell you what my secret is."

She stopped and turned to look at him, skeptical.

He took a deep breath and said, "I'm gay."

Six

Honey, I'm home ...

Trond got back to the BQ shortly after midnight. Alone. The other guys had made connections with women. Love connections, that's what they called them in this time. More like lust connections.

That was one big difference between Viking men and modern men. Vikings told it like it was. "Do you want to swive?" "Can I tup you?" "Let's shake the bed furs." None of that flowery "make love" business. No sugarcoating.

Speaking of sugar, he reached into his back pocket.

Karl, propped against several pillows on his cot, looked up from the book he was reading, one of his favorite science fiction thrillers, something about overendowed dragons and dominatrix mermaids. Karl just barely caught the several shrink-wrapped packages Trond tossed his way. Raising rimless glasses that had been perched midway down his nose, he read aloud, "Penile Glove? What the fuck?"

"Honey up, soldier," Trond told him with a grin at his own jest. "They're a gift from Geek. Read the directions and make sure you don't get it too hot or you'll melt your . . ." He waved a hand downward.

Karl winced but then he actually read the instructions with interest, after which he remarked, "Cool!"

Cool? What alternate universe have I landed in?

"I take it by that scowl that you didn't get lucky tonight."

"Pfff!" was Trond's only response as he sat on the opposite bunk and began to unlace his shoes. "I'm gay."

"What?" Karl sat up straighter. "Are you sure? I had a sneaky suspicion that you were hiding something in your closet."

Trond threw one of his shoes at the teasing idiot.

Karl caught it with a laugh and tossed it back at him.

As Trond continued undressing, he threw his garments on the floor. His beer-sodden shirt, his briefs and denims, and the T-shirt JAM had lent him. Then, with a sigh of disgust, he rose and picked up each of the items, folding them carefully and putting them in his foot locker, except for the shirt, which he put in the laundry bag. A guy wasn't allowed even a little sloth in the Navy.

"So, what's the deal, gay dude?"

Trond explained what had happened. By the time he got to Nicole dousing him in beer, Karl was laughing. By the time he got to him doing the *Michael* dance, Karl was both laughing and wide-eyed with incredulity. By the time he got to the parking lot scene with his hasty confession to being gay, Karl was bent over holding his sides. "This is the most fun I've had since I ate roaches in 'Nam," Karl choked out.

How pathetic was that? And sad? Both the roaches and the lack of fun. "You won't think that's so funny when people suspect you're my girlfriend."

That stopped Karl mid-chuckle. "How come I'm the girl? I'm more macho than you."

"Dream on, buddy."

"Suddenly this mission is sounding a bit more interesting. Don't look so gloomy. Being gay is just a speed bump in your looong life."

"I am not gay. Don't even use those words. And, frankly, my looong life has been nothing but speed bumps."

Karl just grinned. "I can't wait to see what you pull next."

Me too. "I have to admit, this whole situation would be funny if it weren't happening to me." A thought came to him of a sudden. "Don't you dare tell my brothers."

Karl just continued to grin.

Trond went on then to explain what he'd discovered so far about both JAM and Sly being sin-tainted. They made plans to get closer to both men, which might be a bit difficult if word got around that they were gay. In addition, he told Karl about rumors of an impending mission of huge importance. They'd have to keep their ears to the ground and make sure they were included. Somehow.

Going over to his desk, Trond logged onto his laptop and in a specially encrypted e-mail account, notified all six of his brothers that Zebulan, one of Jasper's commanders, was in the area. While they'd been aware that at least one of the SEALs had been targeted, that could have resulted from a fanging by any Lucie, even a lower-level mung, but Zeb's presence here in Coronado could only mean that Jasper had bigger plans.

Vikar was the only one online at the moment, and he responded immediately to his IM message.

Should we come?

Not yet.

Any news on the mission?

Just rumors.

I have a bad feeling.

Me too.

Don't hesitate to ask for help. No sense being a hero.

Me? LOL!

This could be the biggest mission for us since that harebrained Sin Cruise.

Roger that.

Roger? You really are taking this military career seriously.

Hard not to. I haven't worked so hard since . . . forever.

Maybe I should come after all. I'd enjoy the spectacle of you working hard.

Very funny.

BTW, how are things going with that woman who was so suspicious of you?

Don't ask.

Uh-oh!

She's the biggest pain-in-the-ass woman I've ever met.

Could it be—?

No!

 he said, anticipating what Vikar was about to say.

Hey, it happened for me.

That's different. Mike made an exception for you because you were becoming almost . . . well, angelic.

I was not!

Trond could almost hear the indignation in Vikar's voice. One thing Vikings did not aspire to be was angelic. Leastways, they never had in the past.
  He thought about telling his brother that Nicole

thought he was gay, but decided not to. What he did not need was being made a laughingstock, thanks to the vangel gossip network, especially when he'd already made a laughingstock of himself with the *Michael* dance. Really, Vikings were worse than women when it came to passing on juicy tidbits. And Trond being a gay Viking would definitely be deemed juicy. He could just hear it now.

Trond the Gay Viking?

He always liked longboats better than swimming in tight channels.

Cruise any fjords lately, bro?

I always knew his arse was pretty, but . . .

After Trond promised to keep the VIK updated often, and Vikar told him he would make tentative plans for a fleet of vangels to deploy to Coronado on a moment's notice, they logged off. While the VIK and its cadre of vangels had lost a few special abilities when they stopped bouncing around in time, they still maintained many that would be helpful in situations like this, such as the ability to teletransport across wide areas. No delays for airplane travel or even cars. They didn't have wings yet of the type that could actually fly, except for Vikar, but they could move from one state to another in an instant. Even one country to another. And of course, they were vampires, with all the mystical powers that implied.

Karl had left the room when Trond had opened his computer. Now, mentally assimilating all that they would have to do, and how to do it in secret, Trond walked over and took a small packet of dried Fake-O out of a hidden compartment in his locker and added it to a bottled water. Downing the thickened "beverage" with a shiver of distaste, he carried the empty bottle with him to the bathing chamber, where he would rinse it out before discarding.

On the way back to the room through a mostly empty corridor, this being a Friday night, or rather early Saturday morning, he passed the kitchenette shared by the six rooms on this floor. Karl was in there. As he walked away, Trond heard the ping of the microwave.

He had to laugh then. Or cry. Poor Karl! Couldn't or wouldn't have sex while his wife was still alive. Oh well, men would do what men would do.

He could swear he heard Karl mutter, "Honey, I'm home."

The morning after comes to all of us . . .

Gay?

Nicole was still boggling at Trond's amazing revelation the next morning, even as she jogged for more than an hour along her neighborhood streets. She ran not because she had to—Lord knew, she got enough exercise in PT—but because she loved running. The freedom she felt when she ran was empowering. It cleared her head and made her feel in control of not just her body but her life. Not this morning, though, with her focus all scrambled up. All she could think about was, *Gay?*

On the one hand, her suspicious nature caused her to wonder if it was just a ploy the man had tossed her way to deflect her from investigating him. On the other hand, most men wouldn't in a million years put that label on themselves if it weren't true.

How could I have missed the signals?

Were there any signals?

What does it matter? It's not like I was going to hook up with him.

Was I?

On that disarming question, she showered with her favorite Jessica McClintock bath gel and forced herself to concentrate on other subjects, like her agenda for the rest of the weekend. Nicole was a list maker, and she liked to write things out, often on an hourly basis, everything down to household chores, errands, and even technical articles to be read. She bought so many Franklin Planners she ought to invest in the company.

After dressing casually in jeans and T-shirt, she sat down at the kitchen table to have a bowl of granola with fresh strawberries and milk, a glass of orange juice, and the weekly *Coronado Eagle* propped up against the cereal box when Donita walked in, wearing the same skinny jeans, stretch tube top, and boots as last night. Marie and Nicole had returned home alone last night.

Nicole arched her brows at Donita, who looked like she'd been ridden hard and put away wet . . . and not in a good way. She headed straight for the espresso machine, where she poured herself a small cup of the hundred-proof caffeine, then sat down at the table across from Nicole.

"For someone who presumably had her pipes cleaned a time or two or three, you sure look all clogged up," Nicole remarked, crunching on her cereal, which was incidentally very good. It was a special blend of granola mixed with nuts and dried fruit that she'd bought at a favorite natural foods store. She made a mental note to herself to put it on her grocery list for this afternoon.

Donita raised her head with obvious pain. "I passed out. After I puked on JAM's bedspread."

"Oookay."

"I'm a failure as a slut."

"Should I sympathize or congratulate you?" Really, the three of them donned slut outfits on occasion, but they weren't promiscuous.

"Both. Something strange is going on with JAM, by the way."

Something strange is going on with lots of folks. Sly and JAM, not to mention one hunkalicious guy who claims to be gay, even as he throws off sexual lures to women like a blinkin' fisherman. A fisher of women. "Strange how?"

"I can't explain it, but he's changed. For one thing, JAM would have had absolutely no problem last night nailing me, his best friend's girlfriend, or exgirlfriend. The JAM I thought I knew would have taken me home and tucked me in to preserve his friendship. Hell, Sly has changed, too. Do you know what Sly had the nerve to say to me last night? That if I kept shaking my goodies at every male in sight, I'd be having my ass fucked by a train in the parking lot."

Instead of weeping, she just seemed sad. And, yes, it was sad that such a good guy could turn out to be so bad. *Hah! Good guy/bad guy! When will I ever learn?*

"Maybe it's some bug going around," Donita mused.

"Men are the bugs, let's face it. I could lend you one of my favorite audio books: *Standing on Your Own Two Feet, Dammit!*"

"Or maybe we could make our own audio book. *Squash the Bugs, Dammit!*" Donita joked.

Well, at least Donita hadn't lost her sense of humor.

Nicole's cell phone rang just then.

Donita put both hands to her head as if the ringtone were an ear-piercing decibel when it was merely the theme from *Doctor Zhivago*. Looking at the message, Nicole immediately clicked over to the secure base line.

Donita's phone rang, too, hers a recent Katy Perry song, "California Girls." She switched over to the base line, as well.

Upstairs, they heard Marie's cell phone go off, too, the smile-inducing "Dum, dee, dee, dum! Dum, dee, dee dum . . ." intro to "Save a Horse, Ride a Cowboy."

They both exchanged glances as they peered at the messages from the command center. "Report for briefing. ASAP."

There was no code given, so this wouldn't be an immediate deployment. Still, the ASAP meant "mission imminent," usually.

Donita was chugging down coffee now, recognizing she had to get herself in shape pronto.

"I'm surprised that they would call you up after just returning from a mission," Nicole mentioned to Donita, even as she was gathering everything she would need in her backpack.

"Must be important. There've been rumblings about an Afghan compound with high-level Taliban in Davastan."

"Najid bin Osama!" they both concluded at the same time.

Could it be? They stared at each other with a shiver of excitement at the possibility. Neither of them had been involved in Geronimo. They'd love to be a part an important mission. Adrenaline ripped through her system. Not fear. That would come later, and it wasn't a bad thing, either. "Fear Is Your Friend" was a favorite SEAL motto.

Najid was the mysterious illegitimate son of Osama bin Laden, who had come out of the woodwork onto the world stage with a bang. Literally. Following an explosion in a U.S. shopping mall that resulted in hundreds of deaths and even more casualties, Najid disclaimed responsibility, but the world knew he was involved up to his lying mouth.

In many ways, Najid was even more dangerous than Bin Laden had ever been. Oh, Osama's death was a symbolic victory in light of 9/11. But Najid was a charismatic chameleon, a leader in every sense of the word, who charmed crowds whether he wore his thousand-dollar designer suits and spoke in fluent French-accented English or the traditional Arab kaftan and keffiyeh headdress as he stoked the anti-American fires of his fast-growing Muslim terrorist followers. It didn't hurt that he was suavely handsome.

"Take a quick shower, kiddo," Nicole directed Donita. "Five minutes max. I'll have the car ready."

"Bless you!" Donita took the stairs two at a time.

When the three of them drove off to the base a short time later, the town of Coronado was just waking up.

"I meant to ask you, Nic," Donita said from the backseat where she was nursing yet another espresso, "last I saw you last night you were dancing it up with Trond Sigurdsson. How did that go?"

Nicole rolled her eyes. "Don't ask."

Gay?

Seven

Mission Impossible . . . ?

The entire SEAL Team Five was assembled in the conference room of the command center, along with a half-dozen WEALS, and various other military personnel. The mood was serious.

Nicole quickly scanned the room as she sat in the back row with her WEALS mates. There were JAM, F.U., Sly, Cage, Geek, and several others who must have just come in off active duty . . . another indication that this mission must be important. The latter group included the Viking Torolf "Max" Magnusson, the Arab-Native American Omar ben Sulaiman, aka "Teach," Luke "Slick" Avenil, Kevin "K–4" Fortunato, Travis "Flash" Gordon, and Cody O'Brien.

Commander MacLean stood at the front of the room behind a podium on a raised dais. Geek sat below at a desk with a keyboard in front of him. Rumor was, Geek graduated college at sixteen, got his doctorate at eighteen, and had been in the Navy ever since then. Geek used his boyish charm to hide a wicked way with the ladies.

At a click of the keyboard that resounded around the silent room, the large screen behind the commander flashed an ominous message: "OPERATION OCTOPUS: Najid bin Osama."

The commander cleared his throat and pointed to the screen. "Gentlemen and ladies, we are about to embark on one of the most ambitious SEAL missions ever. Even bigger and more ambitious than Geronimo." He paused, then added, "Lieutenant Avenil will be leading this operation."

The SEAL best known as Slick stepped up onto the dais and stood next to the commander. Slick was old for a SEAL, mid to late thirties, she guessed. Very good-looking, with neck-length, black hair sprinkled with a tiny bit of gray. The rumor mill said he was divorced, badly, and still returned to court intermittently to counter his ex-wife's greedy alimony demands. In fact, she'd once overheard him telling a fellow SEAL, "You don't really know a woman until you've met her in court." Slick cleared his throat and told them without any preliminaries, "I just got back from Afghanistan with Max and Teach, and this is what we found."

An aerial photograph flashed onto the screen. Using a laser pointer, he showed them several strategic locations that would be of importance to them. "This is where we believe Najid's headquarters is located, his Afghan home, but that won't be our main target. Over here"—he pointed to what appeared to be another concrete complex of buildings a quarter or so mile away—"is Najid's harem, or the recent additions to it, anyway."

About twenty sets of male eyebrows rose with interest.

Men!

"But this isn't just any harem."

The next frame showed photos of several well-known girls and women . . . well-known in that they had disappeared or been presumed dead over the past few years. The daughter of a New York billionaire hedge fund owner who'd gained notoriety over contributions to a militant Israeli organization, a minor English princess whose stepfather had presided over the trial of terrorists, a Greek starlet who was married to a Jewish politician, the ten-member class of a private Christian girls' school in Switzerland who had presumably drowned on a boating field trip, and the Arab novelist Selah ad Beham, who'd written a blistering attack on Muslim treatment of women.

A communal gasp passed over the room. *Alive? They were all still alive. Oh my God!* Nicole studied the background of the photographs. The girls and women were lined up against a bare concrete wall, wearing Arab gowns, but they were not in purdah. No veils covered their faces, which were bleak and terrified. Some of them were marked with bruises. One even had an eye blackened to the point of being swollen shut.

"We have credible intel that Najid is planning a multipronged terrorist attack for September 11 of this year. Thus the code name Octopus. On that date, these females will be given to a troop of his most hardened soldiers to rape and brutalize. On camera. To be simultaneously televised to the entire world."

"Isn't that a huge risk? The outcry around the globe would be enormous," JAM pointed out. "Seems to me the bastard would lose half his supporters. It certainly isn't the Muslim way."

"Just the Muslim terrorist way," someone called out.

"Najid will deny any involvement, of course, and will probably be dining in Paris at one of those fancy restaurants that serve five-hundred-dollar mushrooms," Slick explained, "or have his mug on a timed security tape showing him filling the gas tank of his bulletproof Mercedes, which, last I heard, is worth a cool five hundred K."

Good Lord! The things people waste money on!

"I still don't get it. Despite his not being there personally, the world will know he masterminded the event." JAM was shaking his head with confusion.

"And he wants them to know that. If he could shout his involvement to the moon, he would." Slick pondered a moment, trying to come up with a better explanation. "Think of Hitler. He was proud of his death camps and his plan to annihilate the entire Jewish race, but he didn't personally give a press conference announcing his vile acts."

"I still say he's gambling big-time," JAM insisted.

"He is, but keep in mind," the commander interjected, "there are a helluva lot of people around the world who hate Americans, and there are bigots everywhere who still carry a Nazi mentality about Jews."

And wasn't that the sad truth?

"But that's not all," Slick went on. "There are multiple attacks being planned at the same time, around the world. We have three weeks to prepare 24/7 before we put boots on the ground in any of these various locations. I know that sometimes in the past, the Navy higher-ups have chosen a mushroom management approach. Planting you in a dark place, and then just letting the shit fall down on you."

"Could you be referring to that incident with the exploding camels in Kabul?" Sly shouted out.

Everyone laughed and Slick just grinned. "In any case, I'm not a higher-up but I guarantee that won't be the case this time. Believe me, this will not be a blind date," Slick told them. "I'll let K–4, Flash, and Cody tell you what they've discovered."

K–4, a darkly handsome Italian who'd joined SEALs more than five years ago after his wife died of cancer, said, "There are plans to simultaneously set off bombs in Arlington National Cemetery and Calvary, the spot in Jerusalem where Christ was crucified. Both of these are intended to be symbolic middle finger salutes more than attempts at mass human destruction. Consider those the second and third tentacles of the octopus."

Flash spoke then. "Cody and I just returned from Manhattan, where Najid spoke to a gathering of Muslim students . . . at a podium with bulletproof glass. Although the message was hidden in the sickeningly sweet talk he gave about Allah and Mohammed and world acceptance of his religion, he is, unbelievably, prodding them to riot on September 11 at—are you ready for this?—the World Trade Center memorial site."

A muttering of outrage rippled around the room.

Cody raised a hand for attention. "In addition, smaller incidents are planned for at least a dozen, possibly two dozen cities across the world. Everything from fires to riots to suicide bombings. The ultimate goal being chaos. Mass fear and hysteria."

JAM raised his hand. "Permission to speak, Commander, sir?"

The commander nodded.

"This seems bigger than any one SEAL team can

handle," JAM observed. "I mean, we SEALs tend to consider ourselves bulletproof, but even we aren't supermen."

"I doan know, JAM. I have a Mardi Gras cape that happens to be red," Cage drawled out in his lazy Southern accent.

"That is so gay," someone else said.

And Nicole cringed, glad that Trond wasn't here to hear that. Not that she was convinced he was gay. Still . . .

Everyone laughed, including the commander, who replied, "You're right, JAM. Everyone in this room is deemed mission essential, but we'll be working under the Joint Chiefs and the Central Special Forces Command in the Pentagon, the Agency, the Fibbies, all the special forces around the world, and that includes the U.S.'s own Delta Force, Rangers, and Night Stalkers, Israel's Mossad and Shayetet 13, and Britain's SAS and MI–6, to mention a few."

Slick interjected, "Here's the deal. Overall, this will be Octopus. Our squad going into Afghanistan will be OctoCat. Others will be OctoDog. OctoWolf. OctoBear. And so on."

"Well, dammit all, why can't we be big dogs or ferocious bears?" F.U. wanted to know. "They'll call us pussies."

"Uxley!" the commander reprimanded.

For once, F.U. had the grace to turn toward the women and mumble an apology.

"Besides, I prefer to think of us as tigers," the commander said. "In fact, I'll have our team's name changed to OctoTiger."

"Hoo-yah!" everyone yelled.

The commander rolled his eyes at the silliness of it all.

Someone in the crowd remarked, "Holy crap! With all those fingers in the pie, sounds like a snafu just waiting to happen." *Snafu* was the well-known acronym for "situation normal, all fucked up."

Slick shook his head. "Not if we can help it. We'll be following the KISS principle here as much as possible." *Keep it simple, stupid!* "Those of us here in this room, OctoTiger Squad, will be concentrating on the Afghan problem. Our primary goals will be divided along two lines. Keeping Najid in our cross-hairs, hopefully taking him down, now that we have the official go-ahead. And infiltrating the harem and rescuing those females before D-day. A snatch-and-grab operation."

"And all the ancillary events?"

"Other operatives will handle those . . . Wolf, Bear, Dog," Slick replied. "As for our entering the country covertly, I have no concerns about that, or about our ability to hide in plain sight. And, really, we have no choice. There's no time for force multiplication. We all know how to change our appearance so that we don't stand out, and we can use any friendlies who've helped us in the past."

It was true, Nicole thought. SEALs were masters of disguise. She'd been shocked on more than one occasion at how well they could alter their appearance to suit a mission.

"But there is one issue of concern to me," Slick continued. "Language. Omar is the only one of us who is really fluent in all the Arab dialects. There must be a frickin' fifty different variations. Oh, I know some of you have taken lessons, but you're only mildly proficient, with emphasis on mildly, and, yes, I'm looking at you, Cage. Arabs do not drawl. And they do not call an Arab woman *darlin'*."

Cage ducked his head sheepishly.

Slick continued, "Here's the solution. One of the Jaegers working here with us, Captain Trond Sigurdsson, is apparently a language genius. Omar assures me that he speaks the local lingo better than Omar does. Does anyone have a problem with me inviting him to join our team for this mission?"

Nicole was excited about the possibility of participating in such an important mission. It wasn't often that the teams let the WEALS join their operations as full-blown agents, instead of ancillary backup. That age-old military stigma against females in battle. Usually, they only allowed them into their elite ranks when there was a need for women on the scene, which was probably the case with the harem, or they had need for one of the WEALS' unique skills. She didn't care how she got in, she was excited to be included at all.

She suddenly had a sinking feeling in the pit of her stomach. She knew, *she just knew,* that somehow the jerk was going to be paired with her. Not that she should care since he was gay. Or allegedly gay. But her association with the mystery man would be wrong on so many levels, none of which was specific enough for her to raise an official protest.

"Since there are no objections, Max, you go out on the grinder and bring the grunt back here. In the meantime, let's talk about how our team will be divvied up." More charts were put up on the screen, this time with the various names grouped under certain categories.

And, yep, there she was. Harem Project: Nicole Tasso *and* Trond Sigurdsson. Oh, there were other people listed as well, like JAM, Omar, Slick, Sly, Kendra, Donita, and Marie, but she had a bad feeling about her and Trond being together on this project.

What I need is a guardian angel.

Where that idea came from, Nicole had no idea. Equally baffling was why the image of Trond Sigurdsson came immediately to mind.

Which was ridiculous, of course. If he ever sported wings, it would be as a bug, not an angel. Because he sure as hell bugged her.

It takes one to know one . . .

Trond Sigurdsson was royally pissed . . . or was that angelically pissed?

"Okay, I understand that I have a reputation for being a little bit lazy," he complained to Karl, who was huffing and puffing as much as he was as they twisted and turned to maneuver their way through the Weaver, one of many torture devices on the O-course, sometimes referred to as the oh-my-God! obstacle course. The trainees had to roll themselves over and under a series of metal poles arranged horizontally in an ascending, then descending pattern, without ever touching the ground.

Karl made a snorting sound and muttered something about "Little bit, my ass!" as he looked down at Trond from one of the higher rungs.

Trond ignored the snide remark and continued, "And I know the SEAL instructors are always spouting crap like 'The more you sweat in peacetime, the less you bleed in war,' but give me a freakin' break." He girded himself to roll his two hundred pounds over yet another level without breaking his neck, which would require him not just to repeat this evolution but the entire training program. When he got his breath, he continued, "That is no reason to test my energy and endurance to this extent."

Normally, they had to complete the entire course in two minutes, or try to, but this morning the rules were relaxed. They were almost done for the day. Hopefully.

"I suppose you blame Mike," Karl said, lying on the top pole for a brief moment before rolling over for the downward evolution.

"Of course. Yes, there is a legitimate vangel reason for me to be here, but I suspect my heavenly mentor is having a good laugh up above. Ouch, ouch, ouch." He felt as if he'd just pulled a hamstring.

"And lucky me that I get to suffer for your sins . . . as well as mine." Karl, who was done and bent over panting for breath, referred to his being assigned with Trond to Navy SEAL duty.

Trond felt a little guilty then for all his griping. Just a little. This *was* the most exercise he'd ever had in all his misbegotten life.

They were alternately freezing cold from the icy Pacific water, then hot from the blistering Pacific sun. And all the time, they were covered, head to toe, and inside every body orifice, with sand. They spit sand, they ate sand, and, some even claimed, they pissed sand. Add to that mix, bone-deep pain and exhaustion.

They'd started this particular day at dawn with a favorite SEAL torture known as Surf Appreciation. The Marquis de Sade, whom Trond had met one time with much displeasure, would be impressed at this assignment where several dozen trainees sat in water up to their shoulders, arms linked, as waves crashed over them. Then they were ordered to make "sugar cookies" . . . in other words, roll their wet bodies in the sand. And all that was preliminary to a short five-mile run in heavy boondockers along the beach. Followed by Volcanoes. Another idiotic rotation that called for a bunch of grown men to stand together in a tight cluster and toss sand in the air so that it would land on their sweat-sticky bodies.

All the time, the instructors were shouting out various inanities. Instructors always hollered, they never spoke in a normal tone of voice.

"The only easy day was yesterday!"

"There is no I in team!"

"You look like a gaggle of monkeys trying to fuck a hairy football!"

"Mind over matter, boys! We don't mind! You don't matter!"

"Haul ass! Bust ass! Get a move on it, assholes!"

"Work it out, maggots!"

"Embrace the suck!"

He had a few Old Norse sayings he would like to deliver to some of these instructors involving swords and dark places to sheathe them, but not wanting to do another bout of Gig Squad on a Saturday, decided to save the wisdom for later.

Now, it was almost noon—heaven be praised!— and their class was working out on the grinder, one last run through the O-course. They'd already finished the Skyscraper, the Slide for Life, the Wall, the Cargo Net, the Spider Wall, Parallel Bars, the Tower, and the Dirty Name.

"Stand easy, *boys*," called out the instructor, who was several years younger than Trond and would have had his tongue lopped off for such an insult back in Viking times. "That's it for today." He could have complimented them for a job well done, but no, pain was expected of them all, nothing to garner praise or commiseration. If he heard one more instructor say, "Pain is your friend," he might just hurl the contents of his belly, or hurt someone.

Just then, Trond noticed a man leaning against the fence watching him. His muscular body was covered with cargo shorts, a plain black T-shirt, white socks rolled over to the tops of his boondockers, and a brimmed San Diego Chargers cap over shoulder-length blond hair.

"I'm going to the chow hall," Karl remarked from his side. "You coming?"

"Later," Trond said, waving Karl on, still concentrating on the stranger who began to walk—no, swagger—toward him. An odd, mystical connection seemed to shimmer between them, the closer the man got. Two things became apparent to Trond then. The man was a SEAL, and he was a Viking. But something more, something not normal, in the same way that Trond was not normal. Or different.

"Who the fuck are you?" Trond inquired in Old Norse. And, yes, Vikings had known that ancient Anglo-Saxon expletive. The whole ancient world had, for that matter.

The man grinned and responded, in Old Norse, of course. "Better question. Who the fuck are you?"

The man was not a threat to him, Trond sensed immediately. He did not have a Lucie aura about him, either.

He grinned back at the man, extending a hand in greeting. "Trond Sigurdsson, but everyone here calls me Easy."

"Torolf Magnusson, but everyone here calls me Max." The man appeared to be a few years older than Trond's twenty-nine years. "Where you from, Easy?"

"The Norselands."

"Ah. Me too." Max eyed him suspiciously.

This has to be the first time I've mentioned the Norselands to anyone and not had them say, "Huh?" He eyed Max back just as suspiciously.

"This might sound like a dumb question, or might not," Max said. "What year were you born?"

"You wouldn't believe me if I told you."

"Actually, I would."

Uh-oh!

"I sense . . . I have a feeling . . . oh hell! I'm taking a gamble here by telling you this, but a number of the guys here already know . . ." Max hesitated, then revealed, "I was born in the year 984 and left the Norselands with my father and eight brothers and sisters in the year 1000 when I was sixteen years old, leaving a brother Ragnor and sister Madrene behind at Norstead."

"Norstead! I know where that is."

"Really? You'll have to tell me more. Later. Back to how my family got here. We arrived in America in the year 2003. Ragnor and Madrene followed us here later."

Trond's jaw dropped as he tried to assimilate all that Max had told him. There were so many questions. At one time, he would have said there was no such thing as time travel, but he'd learned the hard way that anything was possible. "Are you vangels?"

"Huh?"

That answers that question. "Are you human?"

"Uh, what else would we be?"

If you only knew! "You age like a human?"

"I *am* a human. Aren't you?"

Trond waved a hand dismissively. "You were picked up in one time period and landed in an-

other? You've been here eight years? And you're a
Navy SEAL?"

Max nodded, hesitantly.

"Why?"

"Why what?"

"Why would you willingly—I assume it is
willingly—undergo the torture to become a Navy
SEAL?"

Max grinned at his homing in on the most irrelevant of what he'd told him. "Seemed logical at the
time. Vikings, SEALs, same thing, really. We both
love the water, ships, fighting, drinking, sex . . ." He
let his words trail off and winked, as if they shared
a joke.

They did, except that the joke was on Trond.

Trond knew he'd have to answer Max's questions
soon or he'd have both him and Nicole riding his
ass. Nice thought, that, he mused with what was
probably hysterical irrelevance. *Oh crap! Is Max yet
another SEAL I must save? No, there's no sin scent. No
Lucie scent, either. Much more sniffing and people will
think I'm one of those drug-inhaling addicts. Like I need
another sin to add to my inventory!*

"You find me amusing?"

Trond shook his head. "No, it's our situation that
is amusing, and you will soon realize why."

"Cut to the chase, dude. The commander wants to
see you ASAP, and we're wasting time here. Are you
a time traveler, too?"

"Sort of. I was born in the year 821, and I died in
the year 850. Yes, *died*. Since then, for one thousand,
one hundred, and sixty-three years I have been
bouncing around through all the time periods, back
and forth, like a demented rabbit, on various missions."

"And you stay the same age?"

He nodded.

"Awesome!"

Trond wasn't sure how "awesome" it was to live on, and on, and on, or to have fangs, or to be forbidden some of life's greatest pleasures, like rampant sex. "I will be staying in present time from now on."

"And still staying the same age as the years go on?"

"Yes."

"Awesome!" Then he seemed to think of something. "Missions . . . you mentioned missions. For whom? Holy Thor! You haven't infiltrated the SEALs for some tango warlord, have you? If so, I'm gonna have to kill you, buddy."

Not gonna happen. In fact, can't happen. "My overlord is no tango."

"Are you working for Najid?"

"Who?"

"Najid bin Osama."

"No, I work for . . . uh, a guy named Mike." That's all he would say, for now.

Max narrowed his eyes at him. "But you are here on a mission, aren't you?"

Trond hesitated, then admitted, "I am."

"Fuck! Double fuck! I don't know what to do now. The CO wants you involved in an upcoming SEAL operation, but I can't in good conscience allow that until I know more about you and why you're here."

Trond put a hand on his arm. "Trust me. I suspect you and I are puppets whose strings are being pulled by the same master."

Max frowned. "Uncle Sam?"

Trond laughed. Looking up toward the sky, he said, "A higher authority than that."

"Good Lord!"

"Precisely."

Max was clearly unconvinced and confused. "Wait a minute. You asked me before if I was a vangel. What the hell's a vangel? Don't tell me, you're a bloody angel? Ha, ha, ha!"

You got the bloody part right. "Um."

"*What?* You can't be serious. A Viking angel?" Max hooted with mirth, slapping a hand on his thigh with delight at the idea.

"Better than that," Trond revealed. "A Viking vampire angel." Turning so that only Max could see, he flashed his fangs at him.

Max jerked back with surprise. If he weren't a Viking, he probably would have pissed his pants, the reaction vangels often got. As it was, all Max said was "Awesome!"

Eight

Some women have a taste for pigs . . .

Nicole shouldn't have been watching the doorway for Trond, but she was. Darn it! What was it about women and gay men? Women knew they couldn't change them, and yet there was this innate urge to try. Especially when they were so sinfully good-looking.

To her embarrassment, Marie had to nudge her a time or two to pay attention.

Finally, after forty-two minutes, not that she was keeping a precise count, Max returned to the command center with Trond, and the two of them looked like long-lost pals. Not gay pals—Max was married—just birds-of-a-feather, swaggering, SEAL-type buddies. Plus, they were both of Norse origin, she recalled. Who could figure out male bonding?

Trond must have been working out all morning. He was wet and sandy and badly bruised on one cheek and a forearm. Perspiration soaked his T-shirt and shorts. Despite all that, he looked healthy and downright virile.

He spotted her then, and their eyes connected. For only a second. But it was a powerful second. She felt as if he'd zapped her with some erotic shock, just by gazing at her. Then she noticed the odd expression on his face, and she realized that he was equally affected by this strange attraction between them.

Holy moly! Maybe I'm going to be the first woman in history to turn a gay guy?

No, no, no! I am not getting involved with him.

Why not?

I can't believe I'm arguing with myself.

You haven't had sex in a year, and that one time didn't really count. A year and a half would be more accurate. A one-night stand with a sailor suffering predeployment performance issues does not equal good sex.

I want a low-maintenance guy this time. Trond Sigurdsson would not be low-maintenance. He would demand too much. Expect to be catered to. Too much work.

Yeah, but the rewards!

"Tassy!" Marie hissed into her ear. "You're drooling."

Nicole felt her face flame. Luckily no one else noticed since the commander was addressing Trond. "Captain Sigurdsson, has Lieutenant Magnusson brought you up to speed on what we have planned?"

"Briefly, sir."

"Are you interested in joining our effort?"

As a visiting elite force member, not an actual SEAL, Trond did have a choice. "Definitely, sir. As you're no doubt aware, Pashto and Dari are the two primary languages spoken in Afghanistan. Mostly Dari. But the Turkish language is also prevalent, Uzbek and Turkmen, along with other languages, like Baluchi, Pashai, and Nuristani."

Okay, that's impressive. I have to give him credit for having a brain, darn it.

"In other words, we won't know till we get there what language or dialect is being spoken in the drop area," the commander concluded with an exhale of disgust.

"Correct," Trond said, "but if we look at a map of our insertion place, we can make an educated guess . . . subject to change, of course."

"And that's where your expertise would be invaluable," the commander commented.

Trond gave a nod of thanks at the compliment. "There's another thing, though." He paused and wiped the sweat off his brow with the back of a forearm. He and Max were still standing near the closed door. "My Jaeger comrade who came here with me, Karl Mortenssen, is just as adept at languages as I am, possibly better. I would respectfully suggest that you add him to this team, as well."

"We'll consider it," the commander said. "Is your participation conditional on our accepting Mortenssen?"

"No. I'm in, regardless, but it would be a lost opportunity for you . . . in my opinion, of course . . . not to utilize all the talent available. Sir," he added at the last.

"As I said, we'll consider it and let you know shortly. We'll catch you up later on what you've missed this morning after the lunch break, which we'll take at thirteen hundred. In the meantime, have a seat. Everyone," he said then to make sure the entire room was paying attention, "relax for a few moments while we set up the daily schedule for the next three weeks. Be prepared to work your asses off."

Max took his previous seat near the front next to Cage and JAM. For some reason, Nicole was not at all surprised when Trond, on the other hand, walked to the back of the room and sat down beside her. She heard Marie snicker on her other side.

While the commander and Slick were directing Geek on which slides to put up next, Nicole asked Trond in a whisper, "So, is Karl your lover?"

He didn't flinch at her question, which was rather disappointing. Had she been expecting him to tell her it was all a joke? "Nosy little bird, aren't you?" A slight grin twitched at his lips as he stared at her mouth.

Was her lipstick smeared? No, she hadn't had time to put makeup on. Maybe she had dried milk from her breakfast cereal. She licked her lips quickly to make sure.

His grin was full-blown now.

"Cut it out, birdbrain."

"Huh?"

"Stop looking at my lips," she said.

Blinking with surprise, he inhaled and exhaled with an odd hissing sound, and blinked several times more.

Crime-in-ey! Was there anything sexier than a guy with almost no hair and eyelashes like silky black fans? It made her wonder about other hair. Like, did he have a sweet Happy Trail veeing down to . . . oh my God! Her mind was out of control. She coughed to clear her throat and barely choked out, "Are you still in the closet?"

"What closet?" Seeing the glower on her face, he concluded, "Oh, you mean is my sexual activity a secret?"

She nodded.

"You could say that," he said, then muttered something that sounded like "More like nonexistent."

"Don't worry. I won't tell anyone." She put a hand on his thigh and squeezed in a gesture of reassurance.

"Oh no!" Almost immediately, the front of his shorts tented. He glanced around quickly to see if anyone had noticed, but everyone was busy with their own little conversations, and the commander and Slick were still speaking with Geek as he showed them something on his computer screen.

She jerked her hand back and tried not to look, but it was like watching a car wreck. You couldn't look away even when you knew you should. Tilting her head in question, she started to ask him to explain, but he beat her to it.

"It's a miracle!"

Nicole didn't believe in miracles, and the expression on her face must have told him so.

"Don't rub the lamp if you don't want the genie to come out."

"I did not rub your . . . *lamp.*"

"Well, if it's not a miracle, maybe some cocks are dumb and blind when it comes to male or female hands," he surmised, taking her notebook from the floor and setting it on his lap with a decided whack. He was teasing her.

Beware of men with teasing eyes.

"Dumb cock!" she concluded with a shake of her head.

"For sure!" he agreed.

"I think this is all some nefarious charade you're pulling on me."

"Nefarious?"

"You're a liar," she explained.

"I never lie."

"Is that a fact?"

"Practically a fact. Mostly a fact. Ninety-nine and seven-eighths percent a fact."

Despite herself, she laughed.

He turned fully in his seat and smiled, probably thinking her laugh was a signal that all was forgiven . . . or forgotten. Not a chance!

He smiled some more.

Beware of men with smiles.

It was one of those wicked, all-male smiles that women should take as a warning: *Hold on to your panties, baby. The seduction is coming.*

"I have an idea," he said, tapping his closed lips thoughtfully.

Beware of men with ideas.

"We should get together later and conduct some experiments."

That unsubtle suggestion was a bucket of cold water on her hot libido. *The lying son of a gun must think I'm stupid or something. First of all, he's purposefully carrying on this type of conversation in a crowded room, just so I'll be wary of how I react.*

He fluttered those erotic weapons at her some more, this time in a clearly deliberate attempt at exaggeration.

Beware of men with lashes longer than your own. "Experiments?" she asked, although by now her suspicions were on high alert.

"You know," he replied, waving a hand toward his notebook-covered crotch, "to see if it really is a miracle. Or——"

Beware of men who are players.

Hah! Two people can play games. Watch your six, sailer. I'm going to uncover your secrets. Just watch me. "Or?" she asked sweetly.

He just waggled his eyebrows at her, a trick she'd never managed to master herself, not even in front of a mirror.

Beware of men who can move certain body parts at will. With a bubble of laughter that had several people surrounding them turn to see what was going on, she said, "When pigs fly!"

"I'll take that as a yes," he replied.

Beware of men who surprise you. "You've seen pigs fly?"

"Sweetling, I've been called a pig more than once," he told her, and on that strange note, he stood and walked up to speak with Max, his erection no longer erect, she noted. He turned at the last moment, though, and winked at her.

All she could think was *Huh?* Immediately followed by *He is no more gay than I am. And I am feeling decidedly nongay at the moment.*

In her head, she could swear she heard angel voices sing, *Hallelujah!*

And she thought, *Hallelujah, my ass! You are dead meat, Easy. And it is going to be so . . . easy.*

Devils to the right of him, devils to the left of him, devils everywhere . . .

Chomping on a ham and Swiss sandwich he'd grabbed from the chow hall, Trond walked back to his room. He had a half hour to do twenty things before returning to the command center for the afternoon planning session, and all of them important. Top of the list, contact the VIK and get them out here ASAP, or at least some of them.

With his free hand, he punched in the programmed number on his cell phone for his brother Mordr and soon filled his brother in on what was happening. Trond and his six brothers were each guilty of one of the Seven Deadly Sins. While Trond's transgression had been sloth, Mordr's had been wrath. No wonder, him having been a berserker back in Viking times.

"This mission reeks of Jasper," he concluded, after outlining all his concerns, "especially that Najid asshole."

"I agree," Mordr said. "I've seen TV clips of his sudden appearance on the international scene. Reminds me of Rasputin. You know what I mean. You were there with me when we tried to save the Russian bastard, to no avail. The monk could present different personas to different people. Two-faced, he was. And diabolical."

"Diabolical? Funny you should say that. I watched a short video of one of Najid's speeches this morning. Is it possible the man might be a Lucie himself?" The hairs on the back of Trond's neck, what few were left after the last head shaving, stood out in alertness.

"Holy shit! This may be bigger than anything we've seen in years."

That's what Trond was afraid of. And only him and Karl here to fight what might be legions.

"Listen, I'm in Cuba at the moment. Don't ask. And, no, I won't bring you back any cigars. I'll be there in California tonight, hopefully with a few karls and a dozen other vangels."

Like ancient Viking society, the VIK was organized below The Seven into jarls, comparable to
earls; karls, high but not necessarily of noble standing; ceorls; apprentices; and thralls. Trond and
his brothers had been Viking jarls; now they were
Viking vampire jarls. Same thing, sort of.

Mordr continued, "I'll contact the others and see
who else is available."

"Maybe you should just come yourself or with
one or two others, for now. Until you get the lay of
the land," Trond suggested.

Mordr agreed and added, "Someone should probably contact Mike, too. Not that he won't already
know. But he likes to be kept in the loop. Remember
the time you failed to—"

"Yeah, yeah. Well, let someone else loop him. If
he comes here, he'll dig up more energy-sapping
things for me to do."

Mordr laughed. "Let's plan on getting together
later tonight, after midnight when the base is quiet."

Trond nodded, a habit he had trouble breaking
when on a phone. "You better bring a blood ceorl
with you. Karl's in bad shape, and I'm in need of
a feeding myself. It's been three months since I've
been able to take blood from a saved human."

By the time Trond clicked off his phone, he was
back at the BQ, where he ran into Karl coming out.
No doubt Karl had come back here over the lunch
break to sneak a cigarette, although his half day of
exercise was over and he could even leave the base.
That was, until Trond had volunteered him for this
operation, which the commander had approved a
short time ago.

He explained to Karl all that was happening.

It was true that Karl was fluent in the Arab languages. In truth, vangels could understand any language in any time period; they had these internal translators, he supposed. Writing the many languages was another thing altogether, something Trond had had centuries to master, while Karl had been a vangel only for a mere forty years.

Karl was as excited as he to go on active duty. If there was anything a Viking loved, even a lazy one like him, it was a good battle.

As they walked together back to the command center, Karl let him know that he was equally enthused about the arrival of a blood ceorl. "Man, I haven't wanted to say anything, but I am whipped. Any moment, I expect to look in the mirror and see that my skin has not only faded but it's gone transparent."

"I wouldn't have let that happen. You would have fed from me whether you liked it or not."

Karl's upper lip curled with distaste but he didn't argue. Smart guy!

"I should forewarn you," Trond said as he reached for one of the double doors leading into the command center, "Nicole will be on this mission."

"And I should worry about that . . . why?"

"She asked me if you were my lover."

Karl let rip a long chortle, but then he said, and he was serious, "I don't care if she . . . or anyone else . . . thinks I'm gay, but if you try to kiss me, I'm gonna punch you in your smirking mouth. I don't do male tongue."

They were both laughing, and he was squeezing Karl's shoulder in a comradely fashion when they entered the conference room, where the first person they saw was Nicole. Whose eyes were glued to his hand on Karl's shoulder.

Nine

Sweet temptation . . .

Trond appeared embarrassed and would have headed to one of the empty seats near the front of the room, Nicole could tell, but his "friend" Karl came directly toward her in the back row, where the most amazing thing happened. Karl looked at Marie, whom he'd apparently never met before, like she was a three-tiered birthday cake in an orphanage, and Marie looked at Karl as if he could blow out her candles anytime.

Nicole and Trond exchanged glances of surprise.

Karl sat down on Marie's other side, and Trond had no choice but to take his same chair as before, next to Nicole. He must not have had a chance to shower yet because he wore the same sweaty shirt and shorts from his morning workout, and, frankly, he smelled a mite ripe. Should have turned her off, but instead it gave him an odd appeal. Which would be an asset if she was going to launch a successful campaign to prove he wasn't gay and that there were indeed secrets behind his visit to Coronado.

He grinned wolfishly, as if sensing her attraction to him.

Stupid prick! "Looks like your boyfriend might be bi," she remarked, trying to put a defensive wall between them.

"About this boyfriend/gay business . . ."

Here it comes, here it comes. He's going to say he's not gay.

And, boy, would that would explain my inexplicable attraction to the man!

Of course, if he's straight, that would mean he's been playing me, for some reason, as I've suspected all along.

Bingo!

If he's not gay, we're back to the secret he's hiding. Maybe I should just go to Commander MacLean again with my concerns.

"Yeah? About the boyfriend business . . . ?" she prodded. She needed more time to think through her plan, but she would be a fool not to grab an opportunity when it fell in her lap.

"Never mind."

"What? You're just going to leave me hanging here? You should never start to say something, then change your mind." It drove women nuts. Men, on the other hand, could just let it go. One of the myriad differences between the two sexes. Okay, time to play him at his own game. She inhaled sharply for the courage to pull it off.

He arched his brows at her.

"Maybe . . . uh . . . since we'll be working together closely, you and I could . . . um . . . get together sometime . . . to, um, talk." Her face felt as if it was flaming. She was never that good at seduction. A devious seduction would be even harder to pull off.

"To, um, talk?" he repeated.

"Yes, I'm interested in the, um, Viking culture."
Oh Lord! I'm as subtle as an Abrams tank on a bike path.

"Culture?" He wasn't laughing. On the outside.
But inside she could tell he was amused.

"Here's my cell phone number," she said, writing
the number on her tablet, then tearing off that portion of the page. "Call me later, and maybe we can
meet somewhere."

"Do you do this often? Give strange men your
number?"

She should have been affronted, but she had
too many other things to be affronted about at the
moment. *"Are* you strange?"

"Very." He narrowed his eyes at her. "Are you
trying seduce me, Loo-ten-ant Tasso?"

Where's the nearest cliff where I can jump off? "No!
Of course not!" She paused, unable to even admit
she was hitting on him—a sure indication of how
well her plan would go. Or how poorly. "Are you
seducible? By a woman?"

"I don't know," he said with what she could swear
was exaggerated innocence. "I haven't had sex . . .
real sex . . . with a woman in years."

She wanted to ask what he considered real sex, but
was afraid of what he'd answer. "Is that the truth?"

"The God's honest truth." He made the sign of the
cross over his heart.

They had no chance to talk further because the
meeting was being called to order. She noticed,
though, that Trond slipped the paper into his shorts'
pocket, giving the pocket a pat, almost like a caress.

Folders were passed out to everyone in the room
then, and they were told to memorize every detail.
Before tomorrow! There had to be fifty single-spaced
pages of information about the mission.

"Here's your first order for this mission," Commander MacLean said. "Everyone in this room, all twenty-four of you, are confined to base for the next three weeks as of twenty-one hundred tonight. We're going to spend every waking moment on this project. That includes you married guys." None of the women were married. "You'll stay in a separate wing of the officers' quarters, the ladies on their own floor. Does anyone have a problem with this?"

There were lots of disgruntled faces, but no one spoke up. They all wanted to be part of what could be a historic event.

Trond leaned close to her and whispered in her ear, "Maybe we could have a sleepover. Bunkmates, that's what we'd be. I take dibs on the top bunk. I prefer being on top. How about you?"

She ignored his remarks. Truthfully, she'd asked for it by suggesting that they meet, and he clearly wasn't taking her "seduction" seriously.

The commander was still speaking. "Actually, I'll be heading to D.C. tomorrow, where I'll be your liaison with the Joint Chiefs. When you're not here or in a classroom learning every detail you can about this event, which I expect will be ever-changing as more intel comes in, or out on the grinder honing your physical stamina, you'll spend days on the shooting range or in kill houses being set up to simulate both Najid's home and the harem in the Davastan compound. We have diagrams of both buildings, right down to the type of doorknobs and locks, but, as you know, all the best planning can be a goat fuck in the real world.

"Then there will be one day at Fort Bliss training in their caves. Since part of Najid's Davastan compound involves a cave network, this could be essential. Also, there will be a day of jump practice at Fort Benning. Any questions?"

The next three hours were taken up with more logistics on the operation. A breakdown of the various jobs, such as securing the perimeter, breakout teams to breach doors and other barriers, snipers, lookouts, hostage rescue, medical care, and communications. If Nicole hadn't known before, she did now: SEALs were highly intelligent individuals. They had the skills of engineers, doctors, architects, and other professionals. If they didn't know how to do something, they learned how. Not such a bunch of testosterone-oozing apes! Or at least not all the time.

Nicole soon found out why the women were needed for this project. They were expected to infiltrate the harem and help facilitate the rescue from within.

How were they going to manage the infiltration?

Turned out a down-and-out, money-grubbing Arab goatherder had decided to sell his sisters and was going from tribe to tribe, where harems were still the norm. And guess who their brother was going to be?

Yep, Trond, aka Saleem ben Abdullah.

"At least you got the goat thing going for you," she told him when he grinned at her. "You smell like one." *Damn, damn, damn, I have to stop insulting the man. That is no way to get him to succumb to my charms, assuming I have any for him.*

He raised an elbow and sniffed his armpit. "Whew! You're right. Maybe I shouldn't shower for the next three weeks. To be more authentic."

"Or else we could roll you in goat dung when we get there."

"Cruel . . . you are a cruel woman." He was still grinning.

She was beginning to think she had the sex appeal of a prune, but she wasn't about to give up. No way!

The planning session ended at three, and everyone was given a break for the rest of the day so that those living off base would have an opportunity to tie up loose ends at home. Say good-byes where necessary. Put their wills in order . . . a standard ritual before any deployment.

Nicole stayed behind to talk with Slick about one of the elements that might be a problem for her— fast-roping from a helo. "I really haven't had enough practice with that," she confessed.

"I'll work with you on it," Slick promised. "No problem."

"Thanks for including me on this operation. I've been engaged in minor ops before, but this will be my first one of this magnitude. I'm looking forward to it."

"Well, you know how the military is about using women on the front, and we SEALs are probably worse than most. Political correctness isn't in our genes. Which reminds me. You might be hearing a little foul language." He smiled at her, sheepishly.

"Is that the best reason the SEALs or military can come up with for preventing women from serving on the front?"

"That and the fact that women haven't proven yet what they can do in the most dire situations."

No more than she'd expected. "Like I said, I welcome the opportunity."

After Nicole stuffed her paperwork in her backpack and slung it over her shoulder, she headed out toward the back exit and the parking lot, only to encounter Trond coming out the doorway of the training room, where he must have showered and changed clothes.

When opportunity knocks, winners have to be ready, she quoted one of her motivational tapes. At the same time, she groaned inwardly, *Am I really going to do this? Oh God!*

You're on your own, a voice in her head said.

Before she had a chance for second thoughts (or third or fourth), Nicole dropped her backpack to the floor.

She stared at him.

He stared at her.

Is he gay?

He doesn't look gay.

Hah! What does gay look like?

Yeah, but he doesn't act gay, either.

Her gaydar was silent as she wavered between *Is he?* or *Isn't he?*

"God help me!" she prayed, figuring she would need all the help she could get to pull this off.

"God's busy," Trond said with a laugh that sent a shiver down her spine. "He sent me."

That was it! Those teasing words sealed Trond's fate. At least, she hoped. Grabbing his hand, she pulled him into a utility closet. Ordinarily, she wouldn't have had the superior strength to make him do anything he didn't want to, but he was too shocked to react swiftly. Or maybe—in fact, more likely—he just wanted to see what crazy thing she would do next. In fact, he was becoming as suspicious of her as she was of him.

"What? Huh? Hey, what's going on?"

"Let just see how gay you are, bozo." Her words were gritted out as she dropped her grasp on him and locked the door behind them. At the sound of the click, Trond's eyes went wide, suspecting her intent.

There was a light on the ceiling that was becoming dimmer, one of those automatic turn-offs to conserve energy for when a door was shut. She could still see now, though.

Trond looked upward and said the oddest thing: "C'mon, Mike. Another friggin' test? I'm not a saint, y'know."

"I never thought you were a saint. Who's Mike?"

He just looked at her.

For the first time in her life, she understood what was meant by smoldering eyes. In fact, his blue eyes were so hot they appeared to be turning silver. And while he held a hand over his mouth at first, a seeming gesture of disbelief, she could swear his incisor teeth were longer than usual.

Hey, she was in disbelief, too.

That was the last logical thought to enter her head because in a motion so swift she surprised even herself, she shoved him back against the wall, raised herself up on her tiptoes, and grabbed his two ears to tug him downward.

"Gotcha!" she said against his mouth, and nipped his bottom lip.

"Nicole! Have you lost your mind?"

"Probably." She traced a fingertip along his jawline, and was inordinately pleased when he shivered. But wait. Maybe it was a shiver of distaste.

"I could sue you for sexual harassment."

Yep, distaste. Oh well, she was in it to win it. "Go for it, big boy."

"What do you hope to accomplish by . . . Holy crap . . . Did you just rub your breasts against me?"

It was dark in the closet by now, but she could feel his chest shaking against her breasts, which she had indeed rubbed back and forth across him. He was probably shaking with laughter. She didn't care. He wouldn't be laughing for long.

"This is so not a good idea." He spread his legs to give himself better support against her assault, but she used that advantage to press her hips against his belly.

He said some sharp words under his breath, probably Norwegian expletives.

"For a gay guy, you're awfully quick on the trigger," she remarked, undulating against his trigger.

She could hear him gasp. "See, that's the thing about triggers," he said, chuckling as he attempted to remove her arms from around his waist. "They're blind in the dark." He put his hands on her hips in an attempt to move her away.

She reached for his hands, but instead grabbed something else.

He didn't say anything, but the gurgling noise that came out of his mouth said it all.

"Oops!" Nicole didn't know a lot about homosexual men, but, whoo-boy, if he wasn't interested in women, she'd like to know how he'd be with a man.

She had her arms wrapped around his shoulders by now, and she proceeded to kiss him senseless. Or herself senseless. Or both of them senseless, for heaven's sake!

No soft butterfly kisses.

No sweet licks.

No soft murmurs against his mouth.

This was total, ravenous hunger unleashed.

She surprised herself.

And she sure as hell surprised Trond.

Ten

Sliding down the slippery slope of sin . . .

Trond was caught in a whirlwind of sexual ecstasy.

Every cell in his body was aroused and sensitive to the lightest touch—and, holy clouds!—Nicole was hot damn, sure-as-sin touching him! Everywhere. Even her breath against his neck was like a feather sweeping the veins of an overhardened cock. And, yes, a woman had indulged him with that fantasy one time. *I wonder if . . . no, no, no! No wondering!*

She pried his mouth open with her tongue and deep kissed him. He could swear she was tickling his tonsils.

And his tonsils liked it.

His knees, on the other hand, almost gave way.

In a desperate attempt to say something gay, the first time he came up for a breath, he told her in a falsetto voice, "I can taste your excitement. It's like honey with a hint of clove."

"I can taste your excitement, too," the saucy

wench countered, "like mint with a dollop of male pheromones." She was smiling against his lips. Smile kisses. "You are incredible," she said.

Wow! Gayness seems to have advantages.

"You have not experienced my incredible yet." He gave her a smile kiss in return, discovering something new in the sex arts: A little humor added spice to lust play.

Maybe a little bit of fooling around wouldn't hurt, the lackwit side of his brain decided.

It was dark.

Maybe she wouldn't notice how excited he was.

He could let her do all the work.

Maybe she'd think he wasn't straight enough to initiate anything.

Who was he kidding?

It felt too good to stop.

Not yet.

Just a little longer.

But then she thrust her tongue inside his mouth again, and he reflexively thrust his enthusiasm against her cleft. *Enthusiasm*, what a tame Viking word for the rock-hard erection he'd grown! And grown. And was still growing.

Did any man and woman ever fit together better than this? He doubted it. Their alignment, wet mouth to wet mouth, chest to breasts, cock to cleft, was pure perfection.

Something amazing and wonderful was happening here, unlike anything he'd ever experienced before. It was lust, of course, but more than that. He who had over the years faced demons and battle-honed warriors, even lions in the Roman Colosseum, found himself trembling. Surely, a sinner such as he did not merit pleasure of this magnitude.

Uh-oh! Is this yet another vangel test? he wondered, not for the first time. *A vangel sex test?*

Hah! Being a Mensa when it came to that kind of body sport, he would pass with flying colors.

Of course, that was not the outcome Mike would want from such a test. No, this was not a test. Trond preferred to think that what was happening between him and Nicole had come about naturally. Man to woman, even if he was not a hu-*man*.

Aaarrgh! I am supposed to be gay. What would a gay man do in this situation?

Not pant like a warhorse and tingle from his scalp to his toenails, that is for sure.

Her legs had somehow become wrapped around his waist, he noted, even in their dark space. *When had that happened?* And her hands were inside his shorts, cupping his bare behind. *When had that happened?*

Steeling himself with resolve, he reached up and pulled the cord on the light fixture. It would last for only a few moments. Time enough to say what he must. "This has to stop, Nicole. I know what you're trying to prove, but this has gone far enough. Whoa! What are you doing now? Oh no! Wait!" Then, after a telling pause, "God above!" He wasn't sure if his inadvertent exclamation was a prayer or an expletive.

She had crossed her arms and lifted her T-shirt up and over her head, taking her sports undergarment with it. She was bare from the waist up, with her legs still wrapped around his hips.

He put his hands on her bottom . . . just to hold her up, or so he told himself. He turned so that her back was to the wall, for more balance, or so he told himself. And then he proceeded to look. And look. What harm could there be in mere looking?

Her beauty stunned him. Her arms and shoulders carried the muscles of a military woman. Her skin was the color of winter wheat, sun-kissed to a golden hue. And her breasts . . . ah, her breasts were pure splendor. Full. The size of halved oranges, with pink tips that begged for his attention by blooming before his eyes into hard pebbles.

"Take off your shirt," she demanded in a sex-husky voice.

By the runes! She will be the death of me yet. "I can't," he said.

"Can't, or won't?" she accused. "I want to feel you, skin to skin, dammit."

Can a man faint from sex talk? "I cannot have sex with you, Nicole. Nothing personal. Believe me, if I could have sex with any woman, you would be my first choice." Of the moment anyway. "So, let's just call an end to this, and . . . aaarrgh!"

As the light went out, she shoved his T-shirt up far enough that she could brush his chest hairs back and forth across her breasts, bringing the nipples to even harder points.

Once he was able to speak above a whimper, he said, "All this you would do just to prove a point?"

He couldn't see her face, of course, but he just knew she was blushing. "To tell you the truth, it started out that way," she admitted, "but now . . ."

When she didn't continue, he prodded, "But now . . . ?"

"Now I just want you."

Her admission had to be a blow to her pride. He could respect that. He was a Viking. He knew about pride.

But, really, it was the worst thing she could have said! Or the best.

He was going to surrender, he knew that now, consequences be damned. But before he had a chance to say so, she arched her neck, causing her breasts to present themselves even more for his sex play, and her belly to press against him, then undulate in a rhythm he knew good and well.

Even though it was dark again inside the closet, he closed his eyes for a moment, fearing his eyeballs would be rolling back in their sockets. Then he took over the master role in this game as old as time. He needed no light to find his way.

He took her breasts into his mouth, licking and biting at the nipples, playing the tips like a fiddle string with his tongue. "You like that, do you, sweetling? Some women do not."

"How would you know, Mr. Gay Man?"

"I've heard. Anyhow, some women—"

"Shut up! Just do it!"

"Whatever you say." He laughed. A man had to appreciate a woman who knew what she wanted.

In many ways, sex in this total darkness was more enticing than in a lighted room. It heightened all the senses to a screaming pitch.

Her body was stiffening, her legs around his waist gripping him tighter, a sure sign that her body was racing toward a peaking. He began to pound her lower half in the game of near-sex he had perfected long ago. A dry run, some called it. Half-arsed satisfaction, he called it. But beggars couldn't be choosers, and right now he was at the begging stage.

His ballocks were hard and high. A violent shiver passed over him as he tried to forestall his own peaking. The urgent need to bite her neck prompted him to bite his own bottom lip in restraint. Another reason to be thankful for the darkness; she couldn't see his fangs that had a mind of their own at times like this, just like another body part.

Her long, unending stream of soft moans was his ultimate undoing. She showed her liking for each new thing he did to her by murmuring unintelligible words that he understood nonetheless, by sweet sighs that he shared, and then the type of breathy moan females make when they are ready for a man's penetration.

Penetration! The word zapped his dulled brain like a laser gun. No, no, no! He couldn't be doing this. "Wait," he said, or tried to say. "Wait, wait, wait!"

But it was too late.

"Nooot a chaaannnce!" she asserted. Her lower body was thrusting against him with short, hard strokes that hit him exactly where he wanted to be hit. And she bit his neck, probably to keep herself from screaming, but it resembled too much the way he would like her to feed on him. If she had fangs. Which she didn't. Not that he would want her to. Or would he? *Aaarrgh!*

Chest heaving, he surrendered then to the throes that whipped him into a frenzy of swirling, bone-melting ecstasy. She had already reached her peak, but he was by no means done with the tempting witch. He put his hands on her hips and held her just so, pelvis uptilted, and let loose with his own pounding rhythm, which caused her to begin another climb to orgasm.

He wanted to roar like a lion and charge like a bull. He wanted to penetrate her so deep and stretch her so far. He wanted to sink his teeth into her neck and drink her blood, just a taste. He wanted her to beg him to bring her to completion . . . again and again. He wanted so many things.

They came together then with his final thrust
that pinned her to the wall. To smother his own tri-
umphant yell or her cry of bliss, he kissed her deep,
very deep, and stayed buried in her mouth until his
racing heartbeat slowed to a mere gallop, and her
finger grips on the back of his neck lessened. Finally, he withdrew his tongue, paused, then leaned
in again and swept his lips across hers in a gesture
of thanks.

When he reached for the light cord this time, they
both blinked against the sudden glare, their eyes
having become attuned to the darkness.

Her honey-colored eyes were hazy with arousal.
A sex-flush pinkened her cheeks and neck. Even her
breasts were a beautiful shade of rose. Her lips were
wet and kiss-swollen.

His enthusiasm was rising again, just gazing at
her.

As he let her lower her feet to the floor, he had a
second peaking just from her body brushing against
him. If he were a cursing man, as he had once been,
now would be the time for him to say something in
Old Norse, like "God Almighty, what have you done
to me?" But instead he said in American English,
"What have you done to me?"

"Me?" she shrieked, obviously coming to her
senses, way too fast. Her undergarment and T-shirt
went back on as fast as her shaking hands could
manage. When he tried to help her, she slapped his
hands away. "What have you done to *me*, that is the
question here."

He wasn't going to argue with her. Even without
real sex, he was feeling mighty good.

His brother Cnut had a theory that every once
in a while a man needed to drain off some of his

man-sap to relieve the pressure, rather like pulling the bung on a barrel of fermenting beer. His cousin Olga, the most opinionated Norsewoman to ever walk the earth, on overhearing Cnut's remark one time, told him where she thought he ought to put his bung and it wasn't in a barrel.

The light was starting to fade and Nicole yanked on the cord, hard, before it could go dark again. "I do not do this kind of thing."

"And you think I do?"

That question seemed to give her pause, and he soon realized why. She shoved him in the chest with both hands. "You are so *not* gay!"

He had to think quickly, now that the fever of the moment was passing fast. "Do not be offended, dearling," he said with as much consideration as he could muster, which wasn't much, "I was thinking of Karl the whole time. It was the only way I could . . . you know . . . get it up."

She unlocked the door and stepped out into the hallway before turning to glare at him where he still stood propped against the wall. *Propped* being the key word. He was so sated he might melt down to the floor like a Popsicle in the hot sun.

"This is war," she declared then.

Having your hand slapped Navy SEAL style . . .

"Lieutenant Tasso! You have crossed the line."

Nicole was standing at attention before Commander MacLean's desk. Having gone to his office immediately following her encounter with Trond, she was beginning to think she might have acted prematurely. In fact, she *knew* that she had by the stern expression on the commander's face. She should have gathered more information before filing another complaint. "But I believe I have legitimate concerns about Sigurdsson . . . concerns that might affect the security of our operation, Commander, sir."

"Because you think the man is gay?" he scoffed.

"No. Because I think he's *not* gay, Commander, sir." She was still standing stiffly at attention.

The commander rolled his eyes. "Did it ever occur to you that the man used that as an excuse because he has no interest in you?"

"Sir!" Now she was indignant. The commander must think she'd been putting the moves on Trond. Well, she had, but with a purpose. Not because she had the hots for him. Well, not totally.

"Do you honestly believe that the Navy SEALs allow anyone onto our base without complete security clearance?"

"No, but—"

"Jaegers are as elite a group in Norway as SEALs are in the U.S. Do not for one minute think they're lax in their requirements."

"It's not that, Commander, sir. There is just some secret that I know he is hiding. He's a ghost. Honestly, I had an old police contact check him out, and he's not in any database. He doesn't exist."

"Good Lord! Every man here has secrets. Don't you?"

She was fighting a losing battle, Nicole realized.

The frustration on her face must have shown because the commander said, with less sternness, "I commend your motivation in wanting to ensure the security of our unit, but in this case, your concerns are misplaced. Now, let me tell you what *I'm* concerned about. Team unity. One of the things we emphasize from the very beginning in BUD/S as they do in WEALS training is the importance of teamwork. If you can't work together with every single person on the OctoTiger Squad, perhaps you need to step back."

"Oh no, sir! I assure you I'm a team player."

"Including Captain Sigurdsson?"

She gulped several times before agreeing, "Including Captain Sigurdsson, sir."

As she left the office, duly chastised, Nicole had to wonder, *Was I wrong? Are my instincts so rusty? Am I letting my hormones affect my judgment?*

One thing was clear, though. She would have to adjust her behavior toward he-who-was-driving-her-crazy.

Eleven

Angel flying too close to the ground,
or something . . .

If Nicole was already confused by Trond, she was stunned speechless the next morning when she finished her morning run and was walking toward the chow hall where she intended to have a big breakfast. She'd earned it.

As she approached the small, nondenominational chapel that served all Navy personnel, including the SEALs, she saw a small crowd outside, just standing about with the oddest expressions on their faces.

"What's going on?" she asked.

"Listen," one young sailor said.

The most glorious male voice was singing "Amazing Grace" inside the chapel. No, it was two male voices.

"Amazing Grace" was a wonderful hymn, and had been sung by some of the best singers in the world. Aretha Franklin's rendition on Oprah's last show had brought the audience to tears.

This was different.

She stood, transfixed, as did the others, when the choir moved from one song to another, including some in Latin, like "Sanctus, Sanctus, Sanctus," that Nicole remembered from her childhood in a neighborhood Greek Catholic church.

Finally, she couldn't resist and stepped through the open doors, even though she wasn't appropriately dressed for church. She shouldn't have been shocked at what she found, but she was. Trond stood in the front row with his friend Karl and they were singing their hearts out like . . . like angels. Jeesh! With voices like those, they could get music contracts, especially singing Christian music.

Just then, she noticed a man sitting at the opposite end of the last pew where she'd plopped down. He was staring intently at Trond and Karl, giving her an opportunity to study him.

Beautiful, that's the only word that fit. He wore a plain white T-shirt and denims with white athletic shoes. Nothing unusual there. And although he was tall and well-built, that was the norm here on the base. His face was sculpted out of pure, cream-tinted marble, or so it seemed. A strong nose. Full lips. Thick, dark eyelashes. His black hair hung smoothly to his shoulders. The sunshine filtering through the stained glass window cast a light that seemed to hover above his head like a halo.

Inexplicably, Nicole's heart was racing, and her hands trembled in her lap.

Then, as if sensing her perusal, the man's head turned, and he stared directly at her through eyes of an ethereal silvery blue color. Mesmerized, she couldn't have looked away if she tried.

The most incredible sense of peace came over her,

and in her head flashed vignettes of her entire life up to this point. And then it was as if an eraser wiped the slate clean of all the bad things in her past. All this happened in the blip of a moment.

The man nodded at her and smiled.

She blinked.

And between one blink and the next, he was gone.

Nicole found that tears welled in her eyes, but they weren't tears of pain or hurt. They were tears of joy.

That's how Trond found her when the service ended and he was exiting the church.

"Are you following me?" he accused. "More stalking? There aren't any closets here as far as I know."

Now, there was a mood killer if she ever heard one. Not that she'd been expecting sweet words after their bout of near-sex. Oh wait. Could it be that he was aware that she'd complained about him to the commander again? Still—

"No, I was out running when—"

"You were running? On a Sunday when you could have slept till noon, or lazed about doing nothing?" He sighed as if those were activities to be desired. Or nonactivities.

"Trond, Trond, Trond! You really do need some of my motivational books. *Peak Performance* comes to mind." The commander had warned her about pursuing Trond's "secrets," but that didn't mean she had to accept his lazy attitude.

His lips twitched with humor. "You really want to know how I perform when peaking? Methinks you already know that."

At first, she was confused. "Oh you! That's not what I meant." She felt her face heat with embarrassment. "How about this other tape, *Life Is Passing You By*? It's been a huge best-seller for years."

"Believe you me, I do not need a book to teach me that."

"Maybe you just need to be more organized." Okay, if she was going to be more cooperative with the guy, per the commander's edict, she could try being helpful. "I have some extra daily planners if you're interested. If you write down what you want or need to do for every hour of the day, you'd be surprised how much more productive you can be. I could show you how."

"You're serious, aren't you?" He shook his head with incredulity. "Do you write down times for visiting the latrine or doing laundry?"

Actually, sometimes she did.

"Amazing!" he said when she didn't respond, her nonresponse screaming, *Guilty as charged*, and he didn't mean it as a compliment. "Anyhow, if you weren't stalking . . . uh, following me, why are you here?"

She ignored his implication that she wasn't a churchgoing person, which she wasn't. Not anymore. But he had no way of knowing that.

"I was out running," she repeated, "when I heard the singing. Remarkable singing. So, I came in. You're very talented. Both of you." She nodded to Karl, who gave her a little salute as he approached and then walked on, following the rest of the congregation, leaving her and Trond alone.

Each of the men wore golf-type shirts with wing icons instead of little alligators or polo ponies on their left chests, tucked into neatly pleated khaki pants, with sockless loafers. Church clothes.

How could she reconcile the lackadaisical, seemingly lazy special forces guy who could kiss like sin on the hoof with a man who attended church and sang hymns? Well, her ex-husband used to attend Mass, too. For show. "Are you religious?" she blurted out.

"You could say that," he surprised her by saying. "Is that why you're misty-eyed? Because I sing so well? Or might be religious?" He smiled at her.

She hated when he smiled at her. Rather, she hated how his smiles made her feel. "If I'm misty-eyed, whatever the hell that is, it's because I just had the most remarkable experience."

"Oh?"

"I think I just met an angel."

Trond studied her for a moment, glanced over to the end of the pew where there was, incongruously, a small white feather, and said, "Uh-oh!"

Up close and way too personal . . .

Trond was taking a shower that evening, a cold shower, in the one of the private stalls in the bachelor officers' quarters . . . probably something set aside for visiting dignitaries wanting to brag that they'd jogged with the SEALs, ate with them, even slept in their barracks, in essence participated in the total SEAL experience. Hah! The real experience involved total lack of privacy and communal showers where everyone got to view each other's goodies. He'd like to see some white-haired politicians put their drooping gonads out on display.

When he raised his face toward the showerhead to rinse off the shampoo, Trond noticed a bare leg hanging over the top of the stall. A hairy leg. He jerked back, slipped on the soapy tiles, and fell on his ass, cracking his skull on the tiled wall.

When his vision began to clear, he saw that the man was climbing into the shower stall with him. First, he got an up close and personal view of a man's butt . . . a nice butt, if he did say so, not that he usually noticed that kind of thing on men. Good grief! Had word of his gayness spread already? Who else had that witch blabbed to?

The man, a tall man equal to Trond's height, was standing now, his long hair plastered to his head by the watery spray . . . the shower head having a wide spray span.

Trond wished he had his sword with him. As it was, he would have to use his hands, or maybe that washcloth could serve as a garrote.

But then the man turned.

"Oh my God!" Trond said, before he could bite his tongue.

Two things occurred to Trond then.

He was sharing a shower with St. Michael the Archangel.

He had seen St. Michael's bare ass.

Whoa! Hold the chariots! He was also seeing something else on the angelic being.

He scrunched his eyes shut so that he wouldn't go blind.

"What are you doing in here?" he asked as he reached for the shower doors and stepped out. A quick peek showed that St. Michael had stayed inside and seemed intrigued by the cool water spraying over him.

"I've never taken a shower before. I was curious."

Trond reached for a towel, thankful that he was the only one in the showering chamber at the moment. But then, he wasn't sure if anyone would be able to see the angel. He wasn't taking any chances, especially considering the fact that the archangel must have been in the chapel today, sitting near Nicole, and he'd obviously been visible to her.

"Why didn't you just open the door?"

"There's a door?"

Trond shook his head and quickly donned clean underwear, shorts, and a T-shirt. Then he slipped his feet into a pair of rubber thongs. The whole time he kept his back to the shower. "You better hurry up, or someone might come in," he warned.

"I'll just disappear if they do."

That answered that question.

"What is this substance in a bottle marked Axe?"

"It's liquid body wash. You can use it on your skin or to shampoo your hair."

"It smells heavenly."

Trond sat down on a bench and put his face in his hands, elbows braced on his widespread knees. Could his life get any more peculiar than this? "Why are you here?" *Sorry if that sounds rude, my angel friend, but you must admit this is not your usual modus operandi.*

Mike could read minds, and often did, but he must not be "reading" him this time because Trond could hear him whistling. *My brothers will never believe me when I tell them about this. They'll say I was* drukkinn *or that I made it up.*

"Ouch, ouch, ouch!" he heard come from inside the shower stall.

"What?" he asked. No way was he opening the door to see his heavenly mentor in the nude again.

"My eyes are burning."

"It's the soap. You must have gotten soap in your eyes."

"Soap? You did not tell me it was soap."

Trond rolled his eyes. "I thought angels knew everything."

"Only the important things."

"Just let the shower wash over your open eyes for a few seconds."

Before he could blink, faster than any human nanosecond, the archangel was sitting beside him on the bench, fully dressed except for shoes in jeans and a white T-shirt with the logo "Beam Me Up, Scotty," and reeking of Axe's Cool Mystic fragrance.

"You've been talking with Zebulan," Mike said right off.

So that was his reason for being here. "I have. Once."

"And you did not consider it important enough to notify us."

"I thought you saw everything."

"That does not excuse your keeping secrets."

"Hey, it wasn't a secret. Nothing happened. Besides, I notified my brothers of the presence of a high-level Lucipire in this area."

"I am more concerned with your impressions of Zebulan."

Trond hesitated to speak his mind, it was such an outlandish notion. "I wonder if . . . I don't think Zeb is all bad."

Instead of denying such a possibility, Mike nodded as if Trond had affirmed something he'd already known.

"Is there any possibility . . . I mean, has a demon ever turned?" Trond asked hesitantly.

"Turned what?"

Trond shrugged. "I don't know. Good."

"It has never happened in all the eons," Mike told him.

"What purpose would there be, after all?" Trond remarked.

"Have you learned nothing, Viking? Good is its own reward."

Trond was so sick of motivational sayings. From Nicole. From the SEAL instructors. And now from his heavenly mentor.

"Use him," Mike advised. "If Zebulan has a weak spot, bore in and take advantage."

"That doesn't sound very . . . um, Christian."

"Needs must for the greater good."

Blessed stars! Another proverb! "Can I promise him anything?"

"It is not for you to barter with the devil."

Okay, that put me in my place. Not that I haven't known exactly what my place is for oh, let's say, one thousand, one hundred, and sixty-three years.

"About the woman . . ." Mike started to say and then just stared at him. An archangel's stare was riveting. You couldn't look away. And with the stare, he saw everything.

"It was just a little playing."

Mike made a scoffing sound.

"When in Rome, do as the Romans do." Even Trond heard how pathetic an excuse his attempt at humor was.

And Mike wasn't laughing. "You've been in Rome, Viking, and did not like it. Fodder for the lions, you were, as I recall."

Trond shivered with distaste. If he never smelled lions' breath again, it would be too soon. He couldn't even go to a zoo, as Karl had once wanted him to, when a special panda bear exhibit had arrived from China. Too close to the lion cages.

"Temptation is a two-edged sword, Viking. You would do best to remember that."

Whatever that means!

"It means that while the pleasure can be great, the consequences can be greater."

Oh, so Mike is back to reading my mind? Just great! He could have given me warning.

"What would be the fun in that?" He almost smiled at Trond then.

Which almost caused Trond to topple off the bench with shock.

"In the vein of nothing ventured, nothing gained . . ." Trond scrambled to stand up with dignity, then flexed his fingers nervously. *Good grief! Now I'm quoting motivational sayings.* "I was wondering what exactly is the penance allotted for near-sex?" He wouldn't even bother to ask about full-blown, up-to-her-womb, screaming sex with a woman. The answer would no doubt scare him spitless, or was that sinless?

When he got no answer, Trond glanced sideways and saw that Mike was gone, leaving only a single white feather in his wake.

At the same time, Cage walked in, a towel wrapped around his middle, preparatory to taking his own shower. "Hey, Easy! Who you talking to in here?"

Trond twirled the feather between his thumb and forefinger and said, "Just myself."

Twelve

Angel to the rescue . . .

Nicole dreamed that night, and her dreams starred Guess Who?

Men got their satisfaction in wet dreams. Hers were hot and very unsatisfying. Thus, she was tired and cranky and no way ready for the voice mail she received from Commander MacLean after breakfast, just before heading to the command center for the first briefing of the day.

"Lieutenant Tasso: A woman named Cyndee Walsh is trying to reach you. Claims to be an old friend. Says it's important. Here's her number."

Oh my God! She hadn't talked with Cyndee for years, despite their having been next-door neighbors and best friends from grade school. In fact, Cyndee had been the only one who'd halfway believed her reports about Billy's abuse.

When Nicole had left Chicago, she'd cut off ties with everyone, fearing Billy would come after her. Later, when she'd become stronger and able to stand up to bullies like her ex-husband, she'd still kept her distance, not wanting anyone she contacted to suffer for association with her. As far as she knew, her dad was still on the force.

She sank down on a bench under a palm tree facing the beach. With heart thumping, she hesitated, then placed the call.

"Cyndee?"

"Nic, is that you?" She squealed, just as she had all through high school.

Nicole smiled, pleased that some things didn't change. "Holy cow! Cyndee Walsh! How are you?"

"I'm fine, but it's Cyndee Dillon now," she said. "Brad and I got married last year. *Finally.*"

Regret swept through Nicole in waves . . . regret that she hadn't even known that her onetime best friend had married. "I didn't know about the wedding, but, hey, it's about time. You two have been making googly eyes at each other since second grade."

"We still do."

"That's nice," Nicole said, and she meant it. "Remember the time in fourth grade when you socked him in the belly for sharing his baloney sandwich with Meg Kelly?"

"It wasn't baloney," Cyndee said with a laugh, "it was salami, and I've been reminding him of that ever since. Whenever he does something wrong, I bring it up again. He just doesn't understand how we women hold on to things."

And wasn't that the truth. Bad deeds had an eternal shelf life. Women might forgive the sins of their lovers, but they never forgot. "Oh, Cyndee, it's so good talking to you again. I've missed you."

She could hear the catch in Cyndee's voice when she said, "I would have invited you . . . heck, you were supposed to be my maid of honor, but I couldn't find a current address. Even your mother doesn't know."

If she'd told her mother, her mother would have told her father, and he in turn probably would have informed Billy. While seven years had gone by, Nicole couldn't be absolutely sure Billy wouldn't still seek retaliation. His fury at her leaving him—desertion, he'd considered it in his warped mind—had been monumental. It wasn't that she was afraid of him now. It was just that she'd put that part of her life behind her.

She wouldn't have gone back to Chicago for Cyndee's wedding, but she would have cherished the invitation. Cyndee had been maid of honor at Nicole's wedding to Billy. She should have been able to return the favor.

"As it is, I practically had to sign my life away with some commander named MacLean to get a message to you." Cyndee was still talking while Nicole's mind had wandered. "Where are you, Nic? I mean, I know you're in California, and you're in some kind of hotshot female SEAL program. There was that feature story in *USA Today* about all those women warriors."

Ah! That blasted newspaper article. When given permission to do the article, the reporter had promised not to use names or clear pictures of any of the women. Unfortunately, she and two other women had been front and center.

"Billy made fun of that story down at the station, by the way. Said it must be a troop of dykes."

"He would. The jerk!" It wouldn't have mattered what Nicole had done after she'd left him. He honestly believed she couldn't succeed at anything without him.

"You got that right. He considers himself the Irish stallion, but he's more like a horse's ass. You have no idea . . . well, I guess you do."

The fine hairs stood out on the back of Nicole's neck, as she wondered, despite herself, what else he'd done.

"Did you ever marry again?" Cyndee asked.

"Nope."

"Is there someone special in your life?"

For some reason, Trond's face popped into her head. He was special to her, all right. Special trouble. "Nope. No one."

"I bet there are lots of opportunities, though. I've seen some of those SEALs on TV, and they are pure hunks."

"Some are," she agreed. "Cyndee, you told Commander MacLean that it was important that you reach me."

She could actually hear Cyndee inhale deeply, as if for courage. "It's Billy."

Silence followed.

Maybe if she said nothing, she wouldn't have to know what the brute had done now.

Maybe it had nothing to do with her.

Maybe she was behaving in a cowardly fashion.

"What is it, Cyn? What about the bastard?"

"He's dating your sister."

At first, Nicole's brain couldn't comprehend what Cyndee had said. She'd even had to think, *What sister?* Then, "No! Teresa? No way! She's just a kid."

"She's eighteen, Nic, and she thinks he walks on water."

"Are you kidding me?" She was stunned, unable to grasp how this could have happened. Oh, she knew Billy could charm the skin off a snake if he wanted to. When she'd left him at age twenty-one, Teresa had been only eleven, but she had bawled endlessly and berated Nicole for being a bad girl for running around with other men. That was the story Billy had put forth for the breakup of their marriage.

If she had any regrets over her new life, or guilt, it was over Teresa. The other people she'd cut out of her life had been adults and mostly deserving of the cut, except for Cyndee. But Teresa had been a kid. She'd done nothing. And she was Nicole's sister. She tried to understand why she'd failed to contact Teresa the last few years, once she was firmly on her feet, and the only explanation she'd been able to come up with was that when she'd decided to have a new life, she'd somehow interpreted that to mean a *totally* new life. Now, she wondered if she'd been wrong.

"Does he love her?" Nicole asked suddenly.

"I don't know."

"Not that it matters. He claimed to be in love with me, and look what happened." Cyndee had been with Nicole the one time when she'd gone to a private clinic to set a broken arm and three cracked ribs.

"He acts more like a big brother around her, at least in public."

"He's ten years older than Teresa," Nicole said with a snort of disgust.

"That's not so much difference today," Cyndee said.

"Are you defending him?"

"Of course not. I called you, didn't I? Besides, Brad said that I had to at least make an attempt to let you know."

"Brad?" That was surprising news.

"He never disbelieved you, Nic, but he felt as if he was caught in the middle, being on the force with Billy and all."

Yeah, well, where had Brad been when she'd tried to file charges? She didn't say that, though. "What's different now?"

"He's seen things."

Nicole waited for Cyndee to elaborate but she didn't. Loyalty to her husband, no doubt. She couldn't blame her for that.

"I wiped my hands of the brute when I left him. He has nothing to do with me now." *But what about Teresa? She has something to do with me. Doesn't she? Damn, damn, damn, here comes the guilt train.* "Teresa is young. Maybe she'll get bored with an older guy, and—"

"They're getting married."

Nicole groaned. This was bad. Really bad. "Mom should be the one to put a stop to this. She knows what he did to me, and even if she did nothing to protect me, she would surely prevent it from happening to a second child."

"Your mother has stage three breast cancer. With the chemo and radiation, she doesn't have much energy for anything other than staying alive."

"Oh, Cyndee! No one told me."

"Can't you come home and talk to your sister?"

"Number one, Chicago has not been my home for a long time. Number two, I doubt Teresa would listen to me if she's under Billy's spell."

On the other hand, how can I not try? Oh jeez, I don't know. "What if he's doing this as revenge against me? It would be just like him to lay that kind of guilt trip on me."

"Or maybe he's trying to lure you back to Chicago

to hurt you in some way," Cyndee mused. "That's one reason I hesitated. Call me crazy, but women have been murdered by their ex-husbands for less."

Actually, that wasn't crazy at all. Oh, Nicole had absolute confidence in her ability to defend herself today. But bullies didn't play fair. They close-fisted defenseless women when they weren't looking. "When is the wedding?"

"Not till Christmas, but I heard she's already ordered her gown, and they reserved the Veterans' Hall for the reception."

The same Veterans' Hall where my reception was held? Taaaacky! Or sick?

Well, at least that gave her a few months to decide what to do, if anything. She could go into this mission with a clear head, no personal baggage hanging over her head. When she returned from Afghanistan, she would request a liberty of at least a week. Maybe. And go to Chicago to talk some sense into Teresa. Maybe.

"I'll see what I can do, Cyndee. And thanks so much for calling me. Let's keep in touch from now on."

"Absolutely. If you decide not to come, and I can understand why you wouldn't, maybe Brad and I could come to California sometime for a vacation. Of course we'd have to bring the baby with us."

"Cyndee! You have a baby?"

"Yep. Wanna know her name?"

"Of course. And give me your address so I can send a gift."

"It's Anna Nicole Dillon. We call her Nicky."

Nicole made a small whimpering sound. How many emotional surprises could she stand today? "Oh, Cyndee! I'm honored."

After they said their final good-byes, Nicole turned off her cell phone. No surprise that tears were welling in her eyes. That seemed to be the norm for her lately. For some reason, the image of the strange man in the chapel yesterday came to mind, and she was reminded that not everything in her past had been bad. There had been her good friend Cyndee, and now a baby . . . Nicole's namesake.

Before she had a chance to change her mind, she turned her cell phone on again and tapped in a number that hadn't changed for more than two decades.

After five rings, a weak female voice came on the line. "Hello."

At first, Nicole couldn't speak over the lump in her throat. "Mom?"

The only response was weeping and then loud sobs before her mother got herself under control. "Nicole?"

"Yeah, Mom, it's me."

"I prayed for this, my darling. I didn't want to die before hearing from you."

"I should have called, but I wasn't sure you wanted . . . well, you know what Dad said when I left."

"You're still our daughter. You're still my baby."

"I heard that you've been ill."

"I'm getting better. The chemo makes me weak, though."

"I wish I could be there for you."

"Your call is enough. I don't think your father is ready for . . . well, you know how he is."

So, nothing was different. Dad ruled. Mom submitted. Nicole was still not welcome. She'd shamed the family.

"I'm calling because I heard about Teresa and Billy. Oh, Mom, you can't really—"

"Who's that you're talking to? Why are you crying?" she heard a male voice demand in the background.

"It's a wrong number," her mother said and hung up.

Nicole listened to the dial tone for a moment. She was stunned to be cut off so abruptly, despite a family history that should have forewarned her. In the scheme of things, she was not a top priority. Not to her mother, who wanted peace at any cost. Not to her father, who demanded obedience, even at the cost to his daughter. And Teresa . . . who knew how her sister would feel after all these years?

What should she do? Just wipe her hands of the lot of them? Or go back to the town she'd vowed never to step foot in again to save her sister?

Well, she couldn't decide anything today. After she was back from this op, God willing, by mid-September at the latest, she would examine all the alternatives, perhaps make a few more phone calls, decide what to do, if anything. For now, she had to somehow shove it all to the back of her mind and focus on the mission at hand. Her job.

"Nicole, what's wrong?"

She glanced up to see the last person she wanted to talk to at the moment. Trond Sigurdsson.

"Nothing." She turned her head away from him.

"Nothing?" He sat down beside her, eyebrows raised in skepticism, and handed her a clean handkerchief that he pulled from the pocket of his cargo shorts. Like her, he would be going to the command center for the first meeting of the day in fifteen minutes.

She blew her nose loudly and swiped at her eyes. "I was just talking to my mother."

"And she made you cry?"

"I wasn't crying. I never cry." Hardly. Not till recently.

"Weep then?"

She glared at him.

"Get blurry eyeballed?"

She almost laughed.

"Tell me what happened, Nicole. I know that I annoy you on occasion." Seeing the expression on her face, he added, "All the time, then, but I can be a good listener. I've been told that talking about a problem helps, not that I know that personally." As an afterthought, he added, "Or so my gay lovers say." He took one of her hands in his and linked their fingers together.

She should have pulled away, but oddly, she did not, and just that clasp of skin on skin felt right somehow. That's probably why she spoke of something she never told anybody.

"I was married for three years. I left my abusive bastard of an ex-husband seven years ago. Now, he's about to marry my younger sister, and I don't know what to do."

"Abusive?" he said slowly, his brow furrowed with confusion. "Are you saying that you were physically harmed by this man?"

"Yep."

"You?" He was clearly shocked. "A strong woman such as yourself letting a man push you around?"

"I was different then."

"And your mother . . . you mentioned speaking with your mother. Where was she when this was happening? And how about your father? Did he not intervene?"

"No help from either quarter."

"And that's why you were so sad when talking with your mother? Nothing has changed?"

She nodded.

"Ah." He comprehended immediately why she was distressed. She never would have thought he had so much sensitivity in him. "In what way were you abused?"

"Beaten. Raped a few times. Lots of bruises and black eyes. Broken bones."

She felt him stiffen beside her. "In my time . . . I mean, back in Viking times, men were wont to wield a hard hand with women on occasion, but good men did not. There are bad seeds in every barrel."

"Bad apples," she corrected him.

"Apples, seeds, same thing. Shall I kill the nithing for you? *Nithing* is a Viking insult for a man who has no value, less than nothing."

She laughed, or tried to. "Would you?"

"Well, no, not unless he attacked me or some innocent, or he engaged in some demonic act, or if he was a terrorist, of course."

"He's demonic, all right."

His eyes lit up strangely with interest. "Really?"

"Believe me, that time when I sat in an emergency room with him holding my hand, hard, telling the physician that I'd lost my baby due to a fall down the stairs, I could swear he was a beast straight from hell."

"Nicole!" he said and pulled her into his arms, despite their being out in public where anyone could see.

She struggled to get free, but he just held on tighter. In fact, he lifted her onto his lap, pressed her face into the crook of his neck, and wrapped his arms around her. At the same time, he crooned softly what sounded like a hymn, something about the comfort of an angel's wings, while his big hands caressed her back from shoulder to waist, over and over. Oddly, she felt the same sense of peace as when that strange man had practically hypnotized her in the chapel yesterday.

Luckily, no one she knew passed by, and soon she had herself under control. Shifting herself off his lap, she stood and said, "I left my husband after that."

"And none too soon, I warrant." He stood, too.

"Now I have to decide, after this mission is over, whether to go back to Chicago and try to convince my sister not to make the same mistake I did."

He nodded. "But you fear a confrontation with your ex-husband?"

"That's about it."

"Not to fear. I will go with you."

Stunned speechless, she stared at him for a long moment, trying to figure him out. A lost cause, she'd already learned.

They both at the same time glanced at their watches and began to walk toward the command center. For a couple of seconds, they just walked in silence.

"Why would you make such an offer? You don't even like me," she asked finally.

"I plan on being your guardian angel." He waggled his eyebrows at her.

"Yeah, right. More like a fallen angel."

"Some of the best guardian angels fell at one time," he said. "Besides, I'm disliking you less since the near-sex episode."

"I want to apologize for practically attacking you." This was the least she could do in light of the commander's admonition.

Trond arched his brows at her. "So, you are now convinced that I am gay?"

"Not in a Coronado minute! But it's none of my business."

"Got smacked down by the commander, did you?" he guessed.

She felt her cheeks flush, but her shrug was the only reply she gave him.

He grinned at her, and, she couldn't fail to notice that he had a really nice, kind of lopsided grin. "I've been meaning to talk to you about that . . . um, near-sex event," he said.

Event? Nice way of describing a bone-melting orgasm. On my part, anyway. On his part, too, except he was fantasizing about someone else, if she believed him. "I'd rather forget about it, if you don't mind."

"Oh, let's not." He continued to grin. "I was thinking about giving you another chance to try again."

"Try again?" she gurgled.

"To turn me." He reached a long hand over and patted her bottom.

She slapped his hand away, but still she laughed. He was teasing her, of course. For now, the man had managed to turn her tears to smiles, which had probably been his intent. For that she could only be thankful.

That was before she glanced toward the command center and saw three men coming out, walking directly toward them. Rather, toward Trond, whose jaw had dropped and whose face had turned a decided shade of green.

The three men approaching them were tall, well-built, about thirty years old, give or take. In full military dress uniforms. She wasn't sure what country they were from, but they sported enough ribbons and medals to sink a ship.

"What the fuck!" Trond muttered under his breath, coming to a quick stop.

She stopped, too. "Who are they?"

"My lackwit brothers!"

"You have three brothers?"

"I have six brothers." He didn't sound too happy about that fact. Some people didn't like being members of large families. But *six*? Holy cow! She wasn't sure why that surprised her so much. Maybe because he'd never mentioned them. "Do you have sisters, too?"

"Not anymore."

She would have expressed her sympathy, except he didn't seem disturbed by the loss.

"They've been gone for many years," he said, sensing her disapproval. Then looking at his brothers again, he muttered, "I swear, I am going to kill someone. Several someones."

She glanced sharply at Trond, then at the men who by now had come to a stop a few feet away from them, then back to Trond. "Your brothers are admirals?"

"Huh?" For the first time, he seemed to notice the ranks exemplified by their uniforms and their impressive decorations. "Of all the half-brained things to—"

The three men saluted Trond, then grinned.

Trond saluted them, too. With his middle finger. And he wasn't grinning.

Thirteen

His brothers needed a keeper . . .

Could Trond's life get any more messed up than this? He didn't think so.

His three nitwit brothers were dressed up like big-ass Norse military men, parading out in public on the grounds of a seemingly secure special forces compound. Nicole was practically bouncing on her boondockers, anxious to have all her questions answered. And guess who would be expected to answer those questions once the three lackbrains took off for parts unknown?

"Nicole, these are my brothers. Mordr, Harek, and Ivak." He waved a hand at his three grinning brothers. "And this"—he took Nicole by the elbow and guided her forward—"is Nicole Tasso, a female SEAL, who happens to be my . . . um . . . friend."

Mordr stretched out a hand to her and shook it vigorously. "It is always good to meet one of Trond's . . . um, friends." He clearly thought that Nicole was more than a friend. She was. Sort of.

"I had no idea Trond had brothers," she remarked, still stunned by the spectacle before her.

Mordr, who didn't have a single funny bone in his somber body, made a tsking sound at Trond. "Trying to keep us a secret, are you, bro? And us being so close, too." He reached as if to pull Trond into a big bear hug, one that would nigh crush his ribs if previous experience was any indication. Of course Mordr had been trying to crush him at the time, really crush him, for some offense or other.

Trond ducked and hissed, "Do not dare."

Mordr chuckled. Another rarity. Mordr rarely engaged in mirth of any kind, being a serious kind of guy. Berserkness did that to a man. Sucked out the sense of humor, as well as most emotions, except rage.

Harek shook her hand then. "A female SEAL? Our sister-by-marriage Alex wrote a magazine story one time about female warriors. Trond, you should invite her home to Transylvania sometime. Alex might even forgive you for what you did at her wedding when you . . . well, never mind."

"Transylvania?" Nicole squeaked out to Trond. "You live in Romania? I thought you were from Norway."

Trond speared Harek with a glare. To Nicole, he said, "Transylvania, Pennsylvania. And it is not my home, precisely. More like the family homestead." Son of a troll! If she ever saw the rundown castle that was the VIK headquarters, she would run for the hills. Even he thought it was kind of spooky on a dark night, though Vikar was doing his best to renovate the monstrosity.

"There's a Transylvania in Pennsylvania? I had no idea."

He could tell she would have a million questions for him later. *Joy, joy!*

It was Ivak's turn to shake Nicole's hand now. And he did. In the most sensuous manner possible, involving his two hands sandwiching her one, with his thumb caressing her wrist. Ivak's sin had been lust, of course, and he looked at *every* woman as possible prey. Trond had once seen him put the make on Lucrezia Borgia, a move that had nigh cost him his head . . . a head that her politically ruthless family had demanded on a platter. Silver, of course.

Trond made a growling sound that seemed to surprise everyone, including himself. Nicole had to wonder at his sudden possessiveness.

"I thought you were in prison," Trond remarked, having to actually yank Ivak's hands away from Nicole's. He immediately regretted his revealing words, but it was too late to take them back now.

Nicole's eyes went as big as saucers at the mention of prison.

"I am in solitary for a week. They will not notice I'm missing," Ivak didn't skip a beat in declaring those outrageous words as he winked at Nicole.

Nicole appeared shell-shocked.

"Ivak is just teasing," he told her. "He is a prison . . . chaplain."

"Really?" Ivak, the halfwit, asked.

"Really?" Nicole parroted, clearly unable to see Ivak in the role as a minister. No one could, as evidenced by the snorts of his brothers.

She arched her brows at Trond then.

He ignored the silent questions that were piling up in her pretty eyes and advised, "Nic, why don't you go ahead to the meeting? I'll be there shortly."

She was about to resist, he could tell, when Mordr

said, "Not to worry, my brother. I already spoke to your commander and he has given you leave to speak with us for an hour." He smiled widely at Trond after making that announcement, which he had to know would be unwelcome to Trond. Interfering in another VIK's mission was not the way things were done in vangeldom.

"Didst know your commander is married to a Viking woman?" Harek added. "Small world, huh?"

Just how long were my brothers talking to Commander MacLean, and what did they inadvertently reveal?

Nicole left, reluctantly, and Trond led them into a small, empty office in the command center, where he immediately shoved Mordr in the chest. And Mordr shoved him back.

"Have you lost your overaged mind? You can't be out in public like this. Why didn't you just sail a longship up to the beach? You couldn't have created any more of a scene."

"We didn't think of that," Ivak said, as if he liked the idea.

"I thought you all were going to settle into a motel before contacting me," Trond griped.

"We settled, but they only had one room with two double beds. Try fitting two six-foot-four men in one bed," Mordr explained.

"Hah! As if anyone would share your bed after you ate those burritos with refried beans last night!" Harek commented, wrinkling his nose with distaste.

"None of us had to share a bed, truth to tell, since Ivak stayed up all night watching X-rated movies on the pay-TV," Mordr pointed out. "It will be too soon if I ever hear another woman fake-squealing 'Oh, oh, oh! You are sooo big, Lance! Can you stick it up my arse, too? Pretty please!' "

They all gaped at Mordr for a moment, and surprisingly, he blushed. "I could not help but overhear."

"Didst know you can put that candy called Pop Rocks up a woman's channel, then stick your cock in, and have little explosions go off all around your staff? Or sometimes, just fizzes." This from Ivak, the idiot.

Fizzes?

Now it was Ivak's turn to be gaped at.

"What? A Viking never stops learning about the sex arts."

Trond shook his head in dismay. He was living in bizarro-land, as Cage was wont to say.

"How did you like the one where the woman could suck her own nipples?" Ivak asked Mordr.

"I have no idea what you're talking about," Mordr said, but the heightened color in his cheeks told another story.

"Personally, I've always thought it would be great to lick my own dick," Ivak continued. "A dick is a—"

"We know what a dick is," the three of them said as one.

"You are unbelievable," Harek said to Ivak.

"I know," Ivak agreed, as if he'd been given a compliment.

"In any case, even if we didn't have to share beds, it was still crowded in that room," Mordr said, attempting to bring some order back into the midst of their chaos. "We were anxious to get out and about today."

"And I always wanted to know what it was like to wear a uniform," Ivak said.

Trond noticed then that they'd also gotten military haircuts. Since Vikings were a vain lot, that surprised him, but he supposed it was necessary to complete the admiral personas.

"I heard that women go apeshit over men in uniform," Ivak went on. "And, whoo-boy, do they ever! We practically had to beat them off with a battle-axe when we left the mall. Harek still had his battle-axe with him until the mall security guard took it away from him."

"Apeshit?" Trond said, homing in on the least alarming thing that Ivak had revealed. He did not want to know what they were doing at the mall or why Harek had been walking around with a medieval weapon.

"*Apeshit* is a word I learned in prison. It means—"

"I know what apeshit means," Trond interrupted with exasperation.

"Anyhow, why are you here on the base? I certainly hope you just vaporized here and didn't go through actual checkpoints. Jeesh! We're supposed to be a secret society. Not bleeping Viking vampire angel admirals."

"Bleeping? That is another good word," Ivak said. "Does it mean the same as fucking? Holy hummus! Prisoners do love the F word."

Trond and Mordr exchanged glances, then rolled their eyes simultaneously.

"Mike gave us permission to infiltrate the military base, just this once, to get the lay of the land, so to speak," Mordr told him. "From now on, we will work outside these fences, searching for Lucipires, whilst you work inside, on the mission, and on saving the two infected SEALs. How is that going, by the by?"

"Slowly. Karl and I intend to sit the two infected

SEALs down tonight and give it to them straight. By the way, where's the blood ceorl I asked you to bring?"

"Vikar is bringing Dagmar tonight. We had a minor emergency back at the castle that required all the blood ceorls."

Trond didn't need to know about the "minor emergency." They would tell him, if he needed to know. But what was this about Vikar? "Vikar is coming here, too? What? Are we planning a lackwit convention?"

Mordr shook his head. "Vikar won't be staying. He's setting us up in a suite at the Hotel del Coronado, then he'll return to the castle."

"The Del? From Motel 6 to five-star hotel?" Trond remarked. The Del, known for its red-roofed, castle-like appearance and the famous people who had stayed there over the years, was luxurious by anyone's standards.

"It's much closer to the base and convenient for you and Karl to come feed on Dagmar. Plus we would need an extra room for Dag anyhow."

He nodded. "How about you guys? Have you found anything since you arrived?"

"A faint scent, but just in the saloon parking lot that you mentioned. There is no large presence here . . . yet," Mordr replied. "Harek can tell you what he's found on the Internet."

Harek, their computer expert, comparable to the Navy SEAL nicknamed Geek, could do practically anything with computers. He was the one who'd first discovered plans for Jasper's Sin Cruise last year. Currently, to everyone's chagrin, Harek was helping Mike set up some kind of angel blog or website, which could prove interesting. A direct line from earth to God via the electronic superhighway. The twenty-first-century version of prayer.

"It's true, what your SEAL *hird* here has been told," Harek said. "Jasper is planning a huge international terrorist attack on September 11, and, yes, he is involved in some way with Najid bin Osama. It's not clear yet whether Najid is an actual Lucipire or a Lucie-in-the-making, a LIM, but I can guarantee you one thing. Najid is evil to the bone." Harek gave him additional details, some of which the commander didn't know about yet. Trond would have to be careful how he relayed that information, without disclosing his vangel ties.

"I can't have you guys hanging around the base, being visible. It will be hard enough to explain three frickin' admirals in my family to Nicole." As it was, the room they were in had a wide window over the grinder, and trainees could be seen walking by on the way to one evolution or another.

"We will be like ghosts," Ivak said. "Frankly, we just wanted to shake you up today." He waggled his eyebrows in a taunting manner.

The fool!

"The three of us will be in Afghanistan, behind the scenes, in case we are needed," Mordr said, in a way that brooked no argument, "just in case Jasper sends a large Lucie contingent there. Vikar, Sigurd, and Cnut will be working the other planned terrorist operations . . . the Twin Towers memorial site, and potential bomb sites. There are bound to be Lucies flocking in like flies."

Trond agreed. "We'll keep in touch then. I'll let you know later tonight what I learn in today's meetings. You can keep me up to date, as well. And, please, no more surprises!"

They were getting ready to leave when Ivak popped the question that had been like an elephant in the room, "So, is she the one?"

He knew who "she" was. He'd mentioned to his brothers a woman who was needling him to death here and they'd just met Nicole. Even so, he asked, "The one what?"

"Your life mate."

"Whoa! What leap of logic took you from nag to lover? Besides, vangels do not have life mates."

"Vikar does."

"He is the exception."

All three of his brothers were grinning at him, knowingly. Even Mordr, sometimes called Mordr the Dour.

"She is not my life mate."

And she thinks I'm a homosexual.

"She is a pain-in-the ass busybody who is suspicious of me and constantly nagging me to be more energetic."

And she thinks I'm a homosexual.

"She even wants me to listen to motivational tapes, for the love of a troll!"

And she thinks I'm a homosexual.

"If I were looking for an eternity mate, which I am not, she would be the last person I would pick."

He was blathering but could not seem to stop himself. And in the back of his mind, he still had her recent revelations about herself that he needed to assimilate. Nicole the brassy, strong woman, the victim of an abuser? An odd sensation squeezed at his heart when he thought of her being attacked by any man, let alone a man bonded by marriage to protect her. Not that he'd had any great experience with wedlock, and the Vikings he'd known never showed such softer emotions toward their wives. But these were different times, and he was different, apparently.

Aaarrgh! I have no time for this now.

Resuming his conversation with his brothers, he said, "Vikar might be willing to tie himself to one woman for eternity, but not me. No way!"

His lackwit brothers continued to grin at him.

"Just one question." Harek studied him in a way that made Trond squirm. "Have you near-sexed her yet?"

His silence was their answer, and the three of them were practically busting a gut laughing as they left the room. He heard Ivak remark to Mordr as they walked away, "He's a goner!"

And then she knew . . .

It was dusk and they were sitting on the ground outside the kill house, waiting for the strategists to reconfigure the walls and doors for the fifth exercise of the day using live ammo. This time a nighttime evolution.

Each of the evolutions was videotaped. Normally, they would go back to the command center in the evening and study all of their performances, but since it was so late already, that would have to happen first thing tomorrow morning. There was so much to do in preparation for a mission, even though SEALs and WEALs worked diligently to hone all their skills even when not under red alert.

Nicole was pumped up with adrenaline, practically hopping with excitement for this particular war game at the kill house, which was no game at all, but dead-serious preparation for the live op to come in Afghanistan. Even though Nicole and the women would be working from within the harem, without apparent weapons, they had to be prepared for all situations.

Trond, on the other hand, sat on the ground, back propped against the building, fast asleep.

She stood, staring down at him with exasperation. So much for trying to be friendly! All he did was annoy her by ignoring her efforts.

With a sigh, she took a long drink from her CamelBak, a backpack type hydration bladder of water with a tube leading over the shoulder. A soldier in the field had only to turn his head to the side to take a sip, no hands required. Then she tried again. "How can you fall asleep so quickly, in the middle of all this noise?" she asked.

Silence.

"So, three of your brothers are admirals in the Norwegian Navy, huh? None of them looks much older than thirty-two or thirty-three. That's awfully young for that rank, isn't it?"

Silence.

"And one of them a chaplain in a prison? Wow! I assume that would be a military prison. But an admiral chaplain? I've never heard of such a thing."

Silence, but then a little snore.

"I couldn't see much resemblance between the four of you, except for your height and body frames. Oh, and that odd little extension on the incisors of all of you. Not that it detracts from your smiles. You all have good teeth, but that little tiny protrusion of the incisors must be a family trait. I think it's kind of cute."

Still silence, but she thought she saw his lips twitch. Maybe not.

"Your brother Ivak is really hot. Is he married?"

Silence, but his teeth seemed to grind.

"Do your brothers know that you're gay? Have you declared yourself to your military? I know it's not technically necessary now that 'don't ask, don't tell' is outlawed. So, I guess not. Especially since you're presumably in the closet here."

Silence, with a little hint of a snort.

"What I told you about my ex-husband . . . all that personal stuff . . . please don't repeat it to anyone. It's embarrassing. I don't know why I told you. A weak moment, I guess."

More silence.

The whole packed-dirt area outside the kill house was filled with activity. Soldiers moving about. Some taking quick bites from MREs, like his friend Karl, who was looking decidedly pale. A few engaged in conversation. And, yes, a few of them rested, like Trond, though they didn't appear to be sleeping. Mostly, everyone was all jacked up, like her, waiting for the last evolution of what had been a long, information- and physical activity–packed day.

With Trond dead to the world, Nicole had a chance to study him a bit. His rifle was propped against the wall beside him, the safety on, she was quick to note. His K-Bar was secured in its sheath on his leg. He wore a drab green T-shirt tucked into camouflage pants, and heavy boondockers. Having dark hair meant he also had a dark beard that was emerging already, though he had surely shaved this morning.

His arms were at rest, his hands laced on his lap. The fingers were long and blunt-tipped. Sexy.

Now where did that thought come from?

Well, she knew, of course. It was the memory embedded in her brain of what those fingers could do to a half-clothed woman. Meaning her. Even when he hadn't really been attracted to her.

He had a nice, well-shaped face. A strong nose. Full, slightly parted lips. And beautiful eyelashes.

Suddenly, the suppressed imp in her rebelled and burrowed into her weary brain, causing her to blurt out, "I'm thinking about getting a Brazilian wax. Do men really like bare . . . you know?"

Flared nostrils, but still silence.

She'd never known a man to sleep so soundly. It probably went with his lazy personality.

She went for broke then and leaned forward to whisper, "Wanna have sex?"

His eyes shot open.

Apparently not such a whisper.

And apparently he'd been awake all along.

"Oops!" she said.

"Oops?" Trond stood in one lithe movement. "Still testing my sexual orientation, Nicole?"

She shook her head. "No, it just slipped out."

Trond arched his brows with disbelief and walked away.

A short time later, she got the answer to at least one of her questions. She came across Trond and Karl behind a storage shed. Trond was leaning back against the wall, and Karl was pressed up against him, his lips kissing Trond's neck. At least, that's how it looked to Nicole.

Trond's gaze connected with hers over Karl's shoulder.

This was no game to him.

He really was gay.

Fourteen

Was this *Candid Camera*? . . .

Enough was enough! Tonight was the night he and Karl would save a couple of sinners, or their souls be damned!

JAM had almost shot a round of ammunition into a dark, crowded room of his buddies this evening, and only Trond knew it wouldn't have been an accident. It had been late in the day, dusk, at the kill house and JAM had suddenly started shooting, randomly. Live ammo. Fortunately, Trond had sensed what was about to happen and tackled the man to the floor. Afterward, JAM had appeared stunned, unaware of what had just happened. Trond had explained away JAM's action to their superiors by saying JAM must have thought that was part of the exercise, to prevent a covert tango from taking out any of the team.

JAM had just stared at him afterward with a mixture of anger and confusion.

Kendra had broken off her short-lived engagement to Sly, for reasons unspoken. By the fear

Trond saw in her eyes when she glanced toward her former fiancé, Trond suspected he had assaulted her in some way.

Zeb or some of his Lucie cohorts must have been at these two SEALs again, possibly after Trond had left the Wet and Wild, before their lockdown on the base. The scent of lemons was so strong on the two of them that the sin taint was almost ensured. Usually the process was completed in one encounter, but the Lucie needed ten or more uninterrupted minutes to feed after stasis. One more fanging of JAM and Sly by a Lucie and they would be over-the-cliff evil sinners, ripe for the plucking to Jasper's version of Hell.

Trond and Karl had to complete this part of their mission tonight, or acknowledge failure in this particular battle of good against evil. He had no time to think about Nicole and the expression of shock, and maybe even hurt, on seeing Karl feed on him earlier tonight. It had been a necessity when he'd seen the state Karl had been in. No time to seek out the blood ceorl at the Del. No time for Fake-O, which would have been ineffective at that stage anyhow. It was all for the good that she would now be convinced that he was definitely not of the woman-loving persuasion.

So, why did it feel so wrong?

Why did he feel as if he'd crushed his best friend?

Shaking off these maudlin emotions, he waited outside the showering chamber for JAM. When the SEAL emerged, wearing only low-riding boxers and a towel wrapped around his neck, he stopped short, no doubt recognizing something different about Trond, who was in vangel mode.

"What's that blue cloudy stuff by your shoulders? Looks like wings."

Trond ignored JAM's observation. The wispy wings came out on occasion. He'd never seen them himself, but others had told them that the blurry images appeared when his emotions were high.

Nothing he could do about it. Instead, he insisted, "You must come with me."

"Where?"

"Just follow me."

"Without telling me where? Bullshit!"

"There are things you need to know."

"Is this a joke, Easy? Note, I am not laughing. Tell me what's up or get out of my face."

Trond shook his head. "These things must be said in private."

"What things?" JAM attempted to walk around Trond, but Trond blocked his way by spreading his ethereal wings, which JAM just walked through. "This is so not funny."

Trond sighed. Why couldn't these things go easy? "About your everlasting soul, my friend."

At first, JAM's jaw dropped, then his chest rumbled with laughter. "The only one who needs to be concerned about my soul, *my friend*, is me and the God I no longer believe exists."

"He exists, all right," Trond told him. "He sent me to save you." With those words, he flashed JAM his fangs and saw the SEAL's eyes fix on his mouth, then dart to the diaphanous blue wings at his back. "Jesus Christ!" JAM exclaimed, backing up from him with fright.

"Precisely." On that single word, Trond grabbed JAM by the upper arms and, despite their similar heights and weights, teletransported them both to a small lounge for maintenance workers in the BQ's basement. It contained only two straight-backed chairs, a torn leather sofa, a card table, and on the counter a portable TV and a microwave oven.

Karl, his fangs out but his color fairly good, thanks to his feeding on Trond hours ago, had been sitting on the sofa watching Sly squirm on the one chair, now joined by JAM on the other chair. Although neither SEAL was restrained, they could not stand up, for the moment. But their mouths could move, and they did.

"You fucking idiots! Who the hell *are* you?" Sly demanded to know.

"Are you tangos? Oh God, has Al-Qaeda infiltrated SEALs?" JAM added. He and Sly exchanged worried glances.

"We're not tangos. We're here to help you," Trond told them. To no avail, of course.

"Easy and Mortensen both have fangs," Sly remarked to JAM. "Like frickin' vampires."

"And wings," JAM remarked back to Sly. "Like frickin' angels."

Actually only Trond had the wings, but he and Karl did both have visible fangs now.

The SEALs turned back to him and Karl, eyebrows arched in question.

"We're vampire angels. Viking vampire angels, to be precise. Some calls us vangels," Trond told them.

"What the fuck? Am I sleeping? Is this a nightmare?" JAM wanted to know.

"Pfff! Can we both be having the same nightmare?" This from Sly.

"Let me explain," Trond said. "Are you willing to listen?"

Both men hesitated, then nodded.

"Thousands of years ago, Satan became impatient with the usual method for obtaining new souls for

Hell. That would be humans dying while in the state of sin. To speed up the process, he created demon vampires called Lucipires."

"Blah, blah, blah," Sly jeered.

Trond ignored the man's skepticism; he would be skeptical, too.

Karl picked up the ball for Trond by continuing the explanation. "When the Lucies . . . that's our nickname for Lucipires . . . sense a weak human being, one on the verge of sin, they sink their fangs into them, infecting them with a sin taint. Usually, the process is completed in one feeding, but sometimes they are interrupted, and must come back to complete the process. Then, when the human commits that contemplated mortal sin, or many others by then, the Lucies swoop in and drain them dry. Their human bodies dissolve, but their souls are taken to Lucipire hell, a place you do not ever want to visit."

"Some story!" Sly spat out at Karl. "What's up, Salt? You turnin' into some kind of Stephen King?" Salt was Karl's SEAL nickname, as in Morton salt.

"What has any of this crap to do with us?" JAM demanded, as well.

"You've both been infected," Trond replied. "Not once, but twice, I suspect. Maybe even three times. First time on San Clemente Island. Second time in the parking lot of the Wet and Wild on Friday night."

"Are we being punked or something? Is Ashton Kutcher gonna come jumping in here with a TV crew?" Sly laughed, but it was a fearful sound, unsure.

"Ashton Kutcher doesn't do that show anymore," JAM told Sly, even though it was obviously irrelevant to their situation.

"This is no joke," Karl said. "I was a Marine in 'Nam when I got saved."

Sly and JAM looked at Karl as if he were an alien.

Then Sly asked Trond, "And you, when did you get changed into whatever the hell you are now? In Viking times?"

Sly had not been serious, but Trond was when he said, "Actually, yes. In the year 850. My six brothers and I died and entered the realm of vangeldom."

"You've met God?" JAM asked, interested, despite himself.

Trond shook his head. "We work with a different heavenly being." He hesitated but then revealed, "St. Michael the Archangel."

JAM and Sly burst out laughing.

"Are you going to force us to become . . . whatever it is you are?" Sly wanted to know.

"Not at all. We're going to give you a choice. Good or evil." Time to cut to the chase, Trond decided. "Do you wish to continue on the course you are following now?"

"If this is about the incident today with my weapon going off, that was an accident," JAM proclaimed.

"Do you really believe that?" Trond asked, staring him in the eye and holding his gaze "Do you sense nothing different about yourself? A man who once contemplated the priesthood now talks about bombing an entire country, women and children be damned?"

JAM ducked his head, perhaps realizing at last that something had happened to him. "Lots of SEALs burn out after they get too good at killing."

"There's a difference in killing for a just cause but not enjoying it. When a man starts to enjoy killing, he has crossed a line." Trond knew that only too well. He and the other vangels had to restrain their killing instincts all the time. "And that goes for you as well, Sly. The powers above have noted your sinful slide as well, and not just in your lustful perversions."

Both men were released from their invisible bonds now. They could rise and leave the room, if they chose.

"What happens if we don't want to change? Maybe we like the way we are?" Sly's belligerence was telling.

"You'll die. Maybe not today or tomorrow or even next week. But soon," Trond replied. "And your destination will be horrific beyond human comprehension, but the greatest pain will come from the knowledge that you will never see your Heavenly Maker. I know, that sounds like a cliché, like something one of those Sunday morning evangelists would spout, but it is what it is. Still, you get to choose."

JAM suddenly dropped to his knees and made the sign of the cross. "Oh my God, I am heartily sorry, oh my God, I am heartily sorry," he kept murmuring over and over. Tears streamed down his face. "I want to change. I do."

Sly gave JAM a look of disgust. "What a crock! I don't give a rat's ass about God or being saved or leading the good life. I'm outta here."

"No one will believe you if you tell what you have seen and heard here tonight," Karl pointed out.

"Wanna bet, Salt?"

Karl just shrugged.

"One more thing . . ." Trond suddenly recalled an important fact. "Your brother Raymond who died in

the Twin Towers . . . he is in a better place now, and
he prays for your salvation."

Sly's hand was on the doorknob, already turning
it, but he stopped. "That was a low blow, asshole,
and total bullshit. Everyone here knows about my
brother Raymond." And then he was gone.

"In Sly's defense," JAM said, "I am more inclined
to accept your outrageous story because of my background in seminary and an innate belief in miracles, which I have apparently not yet lost completely.
Plus, I've been involved in some pretty way-out woo-
woo experiences with the other Vikings here. I refer
to the time travel, which I assume you are aware of
by now. I'm rambling, aren't I?" JAM sighed deeply.
"Okay, do your work, whatever it is."

"I must suck blood from your body," Trond said.

JAM cringed but didn't bolt from the room. In
fact, he was still on his knees.

Trond sank down to his knees in front of him.
"Ordinarily, my taking the sin taint from your body
by feeding on you would be enough, but you will
be weakened and might not be able to engage in the
strenuous SEAL exercises required of you tomorrow."

"So?" Jam asked hesitantly.

"After I feed on you, you will take blood from
Karl. Mine will be tainted by then."

"How will I take blood? I don't have fangs. Do
I?" JAM ran his tongue over his upper teeth and his
relief was obvious.

Hey, Vikings weren't too fond of the long incisors,
either. He understood JAM's revulsion perfectly.
"Are you ready?" Trond asked. When JAM nodded,
Trond made the sign of the cross, murmured a short
prayer, and put his hand to JAM's chin, tilting his

head to the side. With no further warning, he sank his fangs into the man's throat and drank greedily.

To a vangel, the blood of a sinner in the process of being saved was pure ambrosia. Sweet sustenance. He had to stop himself from taking too much. One time, in the early days, he had inadvertently drained a man to death. When he was done, he took a handkerchief from his pocket and wiped his mouth.

JAM looked like he might keel over with shock. Quickly, Trond went behind JAM to brace his shoulders, and Karl put his already lacerated wrist up to the man's mouth. At first, JAM balked, but then he, too, drank greedily from the open wound in Karl's wrist.

When they were done, all of them felt depleted, but in a good way. JAM was back to normal, the way he would have presumably been before his first Lucie fanging. JAM's blood in Trond's veins would sustain Trond for weeks. His skin color would improve. And he would not need to drink Fake-O as often. Karl would feed later from the blood ceorl, although he was not in as dire a need as he had been earlier when Trond had forced him to feed on him.

Which caused Trond to remember Nicole then, and the expression on her face when she'd seen Karl, seemingly in his embrace. What would she think of what had just transpired in this room? Could she, like his sister-by-marriage, Alex, ever accept him for the freak that he was?

Never! he answered his own question.

"Now what?" JAM asked, standing with effort, looking a little wobbly.

By now, Trond and Karl were standing, too. Karl handed JAM his own clean handkerchief, and JAM appeared stunned to see bloodstains when he wiped his mouth.

"Now, you go in peace and try to lead a good life," Trond advised.

"Am I going to be like a . . . I don't know . . . a saint?"

"Hardly," Trond said with a laugh. "We just stopped you from becoming demon fodder. That's a far cry from sainthood."

"Do I have to quit SEALs?" JAM inquired, clearly concerned that he might have to give up his long-time career. It was touching that he would apparently be willing to do so if it was deemed a necessity.

Trond shook his head. "Strong and good are not incompatible. A man can be a soldier for just causes, without sinning. The Bible is riddled with such men. Joshua, for one, comes to mind."

"I personally think there's a special place in Heaven for those brave warriors who fight to protect the innocent. They do the dirty work so the rest of the country can be safe and free, even the tongue-flapping hate mongers. I'd like to be at one of those cemeteries where lunatic fringes are picketing a dead soldier's funeral. I'd show them who earned them the right to rant and rave. I'd show them where they could put those pickets." Karl ducked his head with embarrassment at having spoken so passionately. Karl had been one of those brave ones, even if he'd been mired in evil at the end.

"You guys go on ahead. I need some time alone to . . . think," JAM told them. What he probably meant was pray.

Trond knew that JAM had many questions that he would be asking them over the next few days, but he was surprised by the comment he made now as Trond and Karl were about to leave. They were walking, not teletransporting this time.

"I wouldn't mind being what you guys are," JAM said.

"No!" he and Karl exclaimed at the same time.

At JAM's arched brow, Karl said, "Believe me, you would mind."

And Trond gave a two-word, succinct explanation: "Eternity sucks."

The only thing missing were the umbrella drinks...

"Bring me the girl."

Jasper's demand hit Zebulan while he was distracted, watching with morbid fascination as several of Jasper's hordlings turned the screws, literally, on one of the naked victims pinned to a butterfly-type display board down in the dungeon of Horror, Jasper's Arctic castle. They were sitting in soft chairs in Jasper's lounge, a revolving dais raised about ten feet above the stone floor. A sound system was blaring out that old Ricky Martin song "La Vida Loca." The demon master did like his material comforts.

While Zebulan nursed a cup of mead, Jasper sipped on a straw stuck in the neck of the shackled and gagged, kneeling Russian Spetsnaz that Zebulan had brought in this morning, along with a British SAS, both of whom had been already rotten to the core and very easy to turn. The Brit was in a killing jar in one of the anterooms, not yet accepting his fate.

All around them, down below, dead people who had been fanged by Lucipires were in various stages of torture, the ultimate goal being consent to join the ranks of the demon vampires. If they were smart, and they rarely were, they would agree from the start. But then the mungs, and hordlings, and imps would be deprived of their pleasures.

It's amazing how a demon like myself can become inured to the screams of tortured humans after all these years. At one time, I would have been cringing at the sounds of hundreds of cries for help, despite my black soul. And sympathy . . . hah! I lost the sympathy gene centuries ago.

He and Jasper were both in demon personas today. Red scaly skin, elongated fangs, burning eyes, and tails. Luckily, the chairs in Jasper's lounge were specially designed to accommodate their large tails. Once, these bodily changes would have been repugnant to Zebulan. He no longer cared.

But Jasper's demand finally registered with him. "What? What girl?" he asked, shaking his head to clear it.

"The one you said Trond was dancing with at that tavern."

"She's a woman. Not a girl. A female SEAL."

"Girl. Woman. Bitch. Harlot. Same difference."

"Why her? She isn't a candidate for Lucipire, not being evil or close to it. You can't turn her."

"Bait. If we have her, the VIK will follow. Plus I've kept a close eye on her. She has anger issues from her past. We might even be able to turn her."

"You're assuming that the VIK has affections for the woman."

"Doesn't he? I assumed . . ." Jasper waved a clawed hand dismissively. "The idiot is in one of those SEAL training programs, isn't he. Fidelity, loyalty, and all that crap. He'll want to protect the softer sex. But wait. This is even better. You said she was a female SEAL. Praise be to Satan! What a coup that will be for us! We can prolong her torture for years.

It will drive Michael insane to know that we hold her."

Zebulan shrugged. Taking the woman wouldn't require that much more effort since he hoped to "capture" Trond and the two SEALS, as well.

"What is happening with the two SEALs anyhow? I expected more of you, Zebulan. I thought we would have them here by now."

"I brought you two special forces soldiers," he said in his defense.

"You did, and I appreciate them," Jasper said, patting the Russian on the head. The eyes of the man darted right and left, frantic, but he was unable to move. "Would you care for a taste?"

Zebulan shook his head. "I got enough from both of them when I drank them dry."

"My reputation is on the line here, as well as yours, Zebulan. There are some who did not want you to head the project," Jasper pointed out. He was referring to Heinrich, of course. The Nazi hated Jews, and it could be said that Zebulan was of that persuasion, having been a Hebrew or Israelite.

Zebulan's face couldn't get any redder with frustration. How he'd like to tell Jasper what he thought of him and his reputation! "I fanged both SEALs twice now, but the second time was in a public parking lot, and I couldn't complete the sin taint. They are getting closer to their tipping point by now, I am sure, but the SEAL command has locked them onto the base."

Jasper nodded in understanding. There was some kind of barrier that prevented demons from entering the military base, probably something they'd inadvertently done with their security system. Jasper and his minions would figure it out, eventually. "I suspect the extra barriers are in place in preparation for the mission to Afghanistan," Jasper remarked.

"That would be my guess," Zebulan said. One of the sin-tainted SEALs, the black man, had revealed to him information about an upcoming mission to Afghanistan. Zebulan figured it had something to do with their new "friend" Najid. "It's almost impossible for us Lucipires to get into the restricted area without being detected now."

"Then you will take all four of them once they leave the country?"

"I will."

"Keep in mind that in this interim, while the two sin-tainted humans might be committing mortal sins that would merit Hell, the vangels also have an opportunity to save them."

"It's a gamble."

"I do not like gambles," Jasper hissed at him, the Russian's blood dripping down his chin. "The Sin Cruise was a gamble for which I paid dearly. Never again."

Zebulan hoped his "master" didn't blame him for that fiasco. He'd been in Somalia at the time, creating evil of another type. But he wasn't about to remind Jasper of that fact while Jasper was in his present foul mood.

"You will have two SEALs, the VIK, and the girl, that I promise," Zebulan said. *Or I will die trying,* he joked with himself. *If only I could die!* he quickly added, and this time he was not joking.

Instead of going back to the United States immediately, as he'd planned, Zebulan found himself teletransporting, almost against his will, to a country and place he avoided at all costs. Something strange had been happening to him of late, something that had never happened before, something that felt almost like regret. Deep, mind-rending, heart-aching regret.

At first, Zebulan kept his eyes pressed closed tightly. Even before he opened his eyes, he knew where he was. Masada, the ancient rock plateau at the eastern edge of the Judean Desert, overlooking the Dead Sea. It was a tourist attraction today, but in his mind's eye he saw it as the fortress it had been roughly two thousand years ago.

Where he'd lost his beloved wife, Sarah, and his eight-year-old twins, Mikah and Rachel.

It began as a whimper as Zebulan bent over at the waist, then fell to his knees. With his head thrown back, he howled like the beast of the night he had become.

When he was finally back under control and about to leave Israel, never to return again, he hoped, he sensed someone watching him. Could it be Jasper? If so, he would use his breakdown here today against him, to some Lucipire advantage. But no . . . Zebulan sniffed the air . . . not a whiff of Lucipire scent in the air.

Zebulan glanced downward then and saw the strangest thing . . . a luminous white feather. And not a bird to be seen for miles around.

Fifteen

Something was fishy in Denmark . . . uh,
Coronado . . .

Eat the fear, Tasso," Trond advised Nicole in the chow hall as they waited for the afternoon's evolution in Torture 101. He could see that she was only stirring the salad around on her plate as she practically shook with trepidation over what was coming up. "You eat the fear, sweetling, or the fear eats you."

"Bite me!" she snapped, not seeing the wisdom of his well-meant advice.

"I thought you'd appreciate a good motivational saying. Now you know how I feel when you are launching those word bombs at me all the time. Besides, I said, 'Eat the fear,' not 'Bite the fear.'"

"Could we just not talk? My stomach feels like a roller coaster."

"Drink this," he said, handing her a glass of iced water. When she balked, he said, "It will help. Take little sips."

This was the closest he'd been to her since she'd witnessed him in an embrace with his presumed lover two days ago. Now that he was out of danger from her suspicions, he should be relieved and keep his distance. Instead, he found himself watching her all the time, or seeking her out, as he had over this lunch break.

"Does everyone know I'm being such a scaredy cat?"

"Nicole! Why are you so hard on yourself?" Oh, he knew why after her revelations several days ago about her past. She was still trying to prove she was strong. If she stopped trying, her old weakness would rise to the surface. Which was ridiculous, of course, but she didn't know that. "Everyone is afraid of something. That's the purpose of torture, to put a person's fear at work against them."

Trond meant that literally. Today was torture day when the team members were being taught not how to torture, but how to withstand torture. And that didn't just mean pain and fear of death; it could be degradation, rape, or any other means of gaining classified information. Torture was a real possibility every military person faced when on a live op in enemy territory where they might be captured and subjected to interrogation techniques that defied international standards.

"You didn't seem to have much problem with the pain evolution," she remarked. "How could you stand to have it ratcheted up so far?"

He shrugged.

"What's your fear?"

Before he had a chance to curb his tongue, he said, "That I will always be like this. Forever and ever."

"Oh," she said with sympathy. "You mean, being gay."

"No! I do not mean being gay." Was that all she saw when she looked at him? Gay person? Probably. "I meant my life in general."

"Change your life then."

"I wish I could."

"I could help you," she said, reaching over and squeezing his hand.

He laughed at the hopelessness of this conversation and decided a change of subject was called for. "I wasn't too fond of the snake experience today. Is Donita all right?"

"She will be."

Everyone had a fear threshold. Donita's was reptiles, no matter the size, or whether they were poisonous or not.

"It didn't help when Sly put one of the buggers in her backpack after the exercise was over. What the hell is wrong with him anyway?"

If you only knew! Trond shook his head in dismay. Everyone had been appalled at the meanness of Sly's action when Donita's terror had been apparent to one and all. Only he and Karl—perhaps JAM now, too—knew the real cause for the sadistic turn in his personality. "It appears as if he's having a breakdown of some kind."

"Tell me about it. When he started spouting that stuff about you and Karl being demons and drinking blood down in the basement of the BQ, I thought the commander would go ballistic." She smiled shyly at him then. "At least I only accused you of being gay. I never said you were a vampire, although you do have those slightly longer incisors."

"You mentioned my teeth before." He smiled

back at her, then ran his tongue over his upper teeth. "I'm thinking about having them filed down a bit."

"Don't do that. Everyone can have perfect teeth today, thanks to aesthetic dentistry, but little imperfections like yours are cute."

"I am a Viking. If there is one thing Vikings do not aspire to being, it is imperfect. Or cute." He blinked at her with exaggerated hurt.

"Anyhow, Sly's accusation made him sound delusional, especially when JAM didn't back up his statements. My first inclination is to ask: What is Sly thinking? But honestly, I don't think he is thinking." She shook her head sadly.

"Well, at least he's someplace where he can conceivably get some help," he said. When Sly had gone nigh crazy, first with the snake episode, then the vampire charges, the commander had tried to talk some sense into him. When that failed, backup came in the form of security guards who escorted a cursing, flailing, threatening Sly to the psychiatric unit at the base hospital. He would be restrained and kept under twenty-four-hour watch for the next few days. At the very least, he would not be going on this mission. At the worst, he was jeopardizing his membership in the teams.

Trond's hope was that Sly would use that time to think about all he'd told him and ask for help when he and Karl returned from Afghanistan. There was little chance the Lucies would gain access to him in the secure hospital environment, and there was little chance of Sly having an opportunity to commit some grave sin there. When he was released, however, that would be a different story.

"Listen, Nicole," he said, turning on the bench to face her directly. Most of the other team members had already gone back to the grinder where the bus would transport them to the kill house, now transformed into torture house. Karl was off having a cigarette, and some of the others were taking bathroom breaks. He didn't have much time for what he had to say. "What is it about the next evolution that has you so terrified?"

"Waterboarding reminds me of a time when I was a kid and I almost drowned in the lake at summer camp. When you get right down to it, that's just what waterboarding simulates . . . the act of drowning. Over and over."

"But you know they'll pull you out in time."

"I know, but when I'm under the water, all logic disappears."

"You need to focus outside your body."

"Is that what you do?"

"Yes. Find some picture to put in your mind. A place. An event. Anything you can concentrate on, other than the waterboarding."

"For example?"

He thought for a moment and took both her hands in his. "Close your eyes. Picture yourself on some Caribbean island. The water is a clear blue. You can see all the way to the bottom where there are pretty shells and colorful fish. The waves are soft, lapping the shore."

"No sharks," she said with a smile, though her eyes were still closed.

He squeezed her hands. "No sharks. Picture the way you felt when we were in the closet, how you felt when I kissed you. Now you're floating on the water, and you're wearing . . . no, you're not wearing anything. This is a private island. No one can see you."

"You are so full of it. Don't think I don't know what you're trying to do. Take my mind off the upcoming evolution."

"Is it working?"

She hesitated. "Yes. Go on."

"The sun is so hot. It's beating down on your body, turning it a honey gold from your forehead to your toes, which are painted pink, by the way."

He saw a smile twitch at her lips. Who knew he could be such a storyteller? Maybe he should become a skald some day.

Or maybe not.

"So the sun is hot and my toenails are pink . . ." she prodded.

"Yes, but the water is cool under you to balance out the sun's rays. It's so peaceful. Nothing can intrude in your thoughts to mar this wonderful serenity. But wait, there is a large fish approaching under you. Not a shark. Don't be alarmed. It's—"

"Let me guess. A man?"

"Tsk, tsk, tsk! You've heard this story before," he accused her. "This man-fish is very large and very—"

"Naked?"

"Stop interrupting me."

"Sorry. Go on."

"At first the man-fish just floats on his back, underneath you, enjoying the view. Is there anything prettier than the small of a woman's back, the sensitive spots behind her knees, and of course her buttocks."

"Of course." Her voice was sarcastic but in a pleasant, companionable way. "Why is it that men always home in on a woman's butt?"

"Because it is a blatant sexual feature of the female anatomy. All those curves and indentations. Soft."

"If you say I have a squishy butt, I might just have to flip over and drown you, assuming you're the man-fish."

He laughed. "Nay, don't turn over. I . . . he has plans that involve you floating face upward."

"What are you . . . what is the fish doing now?"

"Just admiring the view. And blowing bubbles."

"Bubbles! I love bubbles. When I was a child—"

"No, these aren't children's bubbles. These are adult bubbles."

"Oh boy! That tickles. Are they supposed to be tickling me like this?"

"Definitely. Spread your legs a little bit, dearling. Feel the bubbles now?"

"Uh" was all she said. It was enough.

"The man-fish is standing now, looking down at your golden body."

"Standing?" Her voice was indignant. "I thought I was in deep water."

"No, it's only a few feet here. Waist-high on the man-fish," he said. "Keep on floating."

"What happens if I sink?"

"Doesn't matter. Did I not mention, you are a woman-fish?"

"Why didn't I think of that?"

"Because I am the one creating this fantasy. Besides, if you're a woman-fish, you will not panic when the water covers you, or even enters your mouth or nose. You will breathe evenly. Let it happen."

"Oh," she said, finally understanding what he was trying to show her about withstanding the waterboarding. "And if it becomes too much anyway?"

"Imagine the man-fish has decided to nibble and

suck on your sweet fruit. Your lips. Your nipples. And lower."

"Does he have fish lips?"

He laughed, pleased with how easily she entered the game. "No, they are manly lips, rather like mine."

"Good."

Good? What did she mean by that? Well, probably just that she didn't like fleshy fish lips on men. Hey, he wouldn't be too happy, either, if he was kissing a woman with fish lips.

"Aaaahhh!" She sighed. "I like that."

So do I. "In the end, if you feel as if you are drowning, pretend that the man-fins are wrapped around you, protecting you as you succumb to the pretend-drowning."

"What the fuck are you two birdbrains doing with your eyes closed?" a loud voice boomed behind them, jarring them both so they almost fell backward off their bench.

He and Nicole jumped to their feet, at attention, to see Commander MacLean glowering down at them. He wore his BDUs and must have just returned from D.C., where he'd been meeting with the Joint Chiefs. Was he planning to go to the kill house and witness their torture?

"We were practicing for my waterboarding test," Nicole said.

The commander's eyes went wide. "Call me crazy, but I don't know many soldiers who get turned on by waterboarding." He gave both of them meaningful full-body scans then, to prove his point. And, yes, they looked as if they'd been caught in the act. Sex-flushed faces and necks, hazy eyes, parted lips.

He and Nicole were both blushing as they followed the commander to the waiting bus.

Before they boarded, Nicole thanked Trond for his help, even if it had only distracted her from worrying so much. Then she added something that was both alarming to him and joyful. "I wish you weren't gay."

The only thing missing from this Halloween party was Freddy Krueger . . .

The Big Reveal took place a week later, and it was almost like a costume party. A dead-serious costume party. A dress rehearsal for what could be a life-or-death mission into Arab tangoland.

The OctoTiger project plans had been revised and revised to the point that Nicole, Donita, and Marie would be the only women going inside the harem, and Trond would be an unscrupulous trader in human flesh, not the brother to the three of them, which would have been ludicrous with Donita, anyhow, considering her ebony skin. The other women, to their chagrin, would be staying behind this time.

Their leader, Slick, kept emphasizing the importance of smaller numbers, and the ability to slip in and out of tight spaces. In the most successful battles, no shots were fired. Expectations hovered a lot lower this time.

Late arriving intel had revealed that Najid had a passion for blonde women; so that's what Nicole and Marie were, right down to their dyed pubic hair, which they hoped would not have to be exposed, but they were prepared for that eventuality if it happened. There was no changing Donita, but maybe her sharp contrast, dark to light, would provide an attraction of sorts.

The SEALs had an inside contact who'd made arrangements for Trond aka Saleem ben Abdullah to present the three women for consideration to be added to Najid's harem. Their charms had been highly touted beforehand, and the rest was up to Trond and the three of them to pass the inspection of the harem master, who in the old days would have been a eunuch. She rather doubted that even with a holy jihad, men today would be willing to sacrifice their manhood to procure or protect their leaders' women. In any case, Nicole wasn't sure she had the kind of physical assets that would please an evil man like Najid, but she was willing to try. Or pretend to try. She cringed to think what kind of mythical sexual talents Trond had hyped for the three women. She couldn't speak for Donita and Marie, but any skills she might have ever had were rusty from disuse by now.

Slick would be overseeing the entire OctoTiger operation in Davastan but would fill in wherever needed. No one could surpass JAM and Cage as sharpshooters. K–4, Cody, and Flash would secure the perimeter, meaning the wall that enclosed the home/headquarters, the harems, and other buildings. Geek would handle communications. Omar would go into the compound with the breachers, those experts at breaking down doors quickly and efficiently before anyone realized what was happening. F.U. would handle the caves. Karl and Max would be working the guards stationed outside the compound walls.

Then, too, there were all the operatives who

would man the Blackhawks going in for the insertion and the Chinooks coming out for the extraction, the assumption being they would have fourteen new "packages" to carry home. Most important might be the medics on the outgoing flight, in case they were needed either for the hostages or for any personnel wounded during the mission.

If all went well, once Nicole, Marie, and Donita were inside the harem and had the hostages in sight, the whole event should be over in less than an hour. Two, if there were glitches in the original plans. More than that meant snafu and a quick changeover to Plan B.

"Well, it's almost eighteen hundred. Are we good to go?" Nicole asked her two friends as they stood in front of the mirror in the ladies' room at the command center. Everyone involved in the mission was expected to report in a few minutes in full disguise.

They grinned at each other, although their smiles were not evident under the head-to-toe burqas they wore with only slits for the eye openings. Nicole and Marie's eyebrows had been dyed a lighter shade of brown to complement their new blonde identities. Donita's appearance remained pretty much the same, except that her hair was clipped short to the head; she looked like some Ethiopian princess of old. If Najid, or his harem master, didn't put aside his blonde preference for her beauty, he had to be blind.

As they exited the room, the three women pumped a fist in the air and gave a muffled cheer of "Game on!" Then they proceeded to walk down the hall with short, meek steps, heads bent downward in modesty. Their hands were folded neatly under their robes.

The first person they met at the doorway to the conference room was a short, mustached and bearded Arab with an embroidered skullcap, and a long white robe called a thobe that was traditionally worn by Arab men. It was F.U. He let out a hoot of laughter as he opened the door wide so they could enter.

The consensus within seemed to be: "Holy shit!" Especially when they took off the outer garments to show the revealing gowns they wore underneath.

"You can join my harem any day," someone yelled out, which was met with a communal "Hoo-yah!"

Sixteen

Where angels fear to tread, they send vangels . . .

On September 5, the night before they were to leave, Trond waited until everyone was asleep before teletransporting himself over to the Hotel del Coronado. Karl would keep a lookout for anyone straying into their room in the middle of the night.

"You are freakin' unbelievable," Trond said when he entered the luxurious suite.

No one even looked up.

A virtual buffet was set out on the dining table. Everything from crab claws to hot wings, enough to feed twenty hungry warriors just home from the wars. The only thing missing was a side of roast boar and a tun of mead, but wait, that looked like a side of roast beef. Ice buckets held dozens of different kinds of beer in cute little cans that any good Viking could consume in one swallow.

He assumed the mute blood ceorl Dagmar was behind the locked bedroom door to one side. She would be loath to witness that lackwit Ivak, wearing a T-shirt with the logo, "Do You Have Any Viking in You? Would You Like Some?," being lap-danced by a scantily clad woman—scantily, as in underwear: push-up half bra and thong—to the music of Lady Gaga blaring from a boom box. He hoped his brothers had at least had the good sense to offer Dagmar some food.

Through another open doorway he saw a circular bed on a raised dais. Lot of good it would do any of them! Ivak sure as sin wouldn't be doing anything with his lap dancer with his brothers here to rein him in, although they hadn't done much reining so far.

Harek, with his own ridiculous T-shirt proclaiming "I See Dead Pixels" was oblivious to Ivak's shenanigans, immersed as he was in something on his laptop that sat on an alcove desk. With eyes glued to the screen, he reached blindly for chips and beer on either side of the computer.

Mordr didn't wear any message T-shirt, but he was equally oblivious, and his usual dour self, as he watched a bloody World War II History Channel documentary on the widescreen TV. A multitasker as they all were, he was also oiling his specially designed Sauer pistol that shot bullets quenched symbolically in the blood of Christ. The bullets could dissolve Lucies into puddles of sulfurous slime if shot in exactly the right spots, and the VIK had had one thousand, one hundred, sixty-three years to practice their aim.

In this mix of luxury and dimwittedness, incongruously, a virtual arsenal of specially prepared weapons had been propped up against the doorway, ready to be used in the upcoming encounter.

In one swift swoop, Trond pulled the plugs on the boom box, computer, and television.

"What?" three stunned men said as one.

"Are you three demented? I could have been a Lucie coming in here and not one of you would have been the wiser."

"We sensor-wired the perimeter," Mordr said defensively.

"I got in without your noticing," Trond pointed out.

"Wired against Lucies and other nonvangels, lackwit," Mordr elaborated.

"And what would that be perched on Ivak's lap? An angel sent by Mike to soothe the savage beast?"

Mordr and Harek turned with surprise to see the woman still jiggling her arse on Ivak's thighs, as if the music was still playing. They all blinked for a moment, turning their heads this way and that, to observe the unique phenomenon—unique to them, leastways—of her making her buttocks quiver endlessly like vibrating Jell-O molds. *Could one learn to do that, or is it an inborn talent like wiggling one's nose, which I have never been able to master?* Trond wondered, then slapped himself upside the head, virtually.

"Where did she come from?" Mordr demanded of Ivak.

"She was with the serving staff who brought the food. I invited her to stay," Ivak revealed, not at all embarrassed or apologetic. "Don't mind them, sweetling," he told the stunned woman, who was probably only eighteen but made up to look years older.

"I thought I told you," Mordr said through gritted teeth, "No. Strippers."

"She's not a stripper. For shame, Mordr. She's a dance artiste. Someday she's going to be famous.

Maybe try out for *X Factor*. Aren't you, honey?" He glanced up at them. "Her name really is Honey, by the by. Isn't that amazing?"

Yeah, really amazing. She probably is a stripper, after all, with some stage name like Honey Pot, or Honey Cunt. No, that was too obvious. Honey Haven. Honey Showers. Yeah, that would be it. "You can lick my honey, Viking, if you'll just slip me a few coins."

"You're talking to yourself," Harek pointed out to him.

The woman had already gathered up her belongings, including the boom box, and was scurrying toward the door, clutching a handful of bills Ivak had given her in one hand. She smiled widely and gave them all a little wave as she left. It must have been hundred-dollar bills by the wattage of that smile.

"What in bloody hell is *Hex Factor*?" Mordr asked Ivak.

"It's a television show, and it's *X Factor*," Harek informed Mordr.

"You two have been watching too much television," Mordr decided. "They don't have anything like that on the History Channel."

"She has talent, all right. Quivering buttocks. That ought to go over great with the judges," Trond remarked.

"Actually, that's a popular dance move today," Harek replied. "Have you seen the latest music video from—"

"Aaarrgh!" Mordr said, standing and glaring at all three of them.

Why is he glaring at me? All I did was show up.

"You were supposed to be here hours ago," Mordr snarled.

"I couldn't get away till now. The guys were all amped up and wanting to talk about the mission. We're going to be wheels up by dawn, you know?"

Mordr nodded. "We'll be leaving at the same time, but while you'll have a stopover in Kabul, we'll be going directly to Davastan." He cleared the low coffee table and laid out some maps to show Trond and the others. "Here's the most up-to-date layout I sent Trond yesterday to slip into his commander's file. You're going to have a bitch of a time getting your female SEALs into that harem. There are four guards on the ground patrolling the harem building, two on the roof, and two more inside. Keep in mind that Najid has a harem of three wives, six concubines, who knows how many slaves, and all his children in one part of the harem. That's aside from the female hostages."

"Busy man!" Ivak remarked, not without a bit of envy. This past year of serving in prison had not been kind to Ivak's libido.

"We were there yesterday," Harek interjected, and opened a link on his laptop to show them another graphic. "This is a cave network about a mile from Najid's compound. It's overflowing with Lucies."

"Zebulan?" Trond guessed.

Mordr nodded. "He's there, although Haroun al Rashid is organizing the whole bloody operation."

"Numbers?"

"Hard to say for sure because they keep coming and going. I think Zeb and Haroun are the only haakai in the region, but there are lots of warrior mungs and hordlings, a few imps."

"And they are there in such numbers because . . . ?"

Mordr shrugged. "They hope to get a couple of

SEALs . . . JAM and Sly at the least . . . although they don't know you've saved JAM or that Sly will be absent. They desperately want some special forces guys, though. And you, of course, now that Zeb knows you're working with the SEALs. Aside from that, I expect they'll harvest all the evil tangos they can. They're not looking for innocent humans, like the hostages. They want humans who are evil to the bone, or leaning in that direction so that a little fanging will push them over the edge."

Trond nodded his understanding. "Do we know yet whether Najid is a Lucie or just on his way to becoming a Lucie?"

"Not a Lucie yet, but he's been fanged. And more than once," Harek said. "One of my men was close to him last week in Pakistan, and he said his scent was so strong he could have been a lemon meringue pie."

Interesting to know.

Trond studied the diagram carefully, knowing he would have to employ a double-pronged strategy on this mission. The SEAL one and the vangel one. Help to save the hostages. Kill as many Lucies as possible. Then, when he got back to Coronado, God willing, he would try once again to save Sly. After that, he didn't know what he would do, but oddly, Nicole's face came to mind. At first, he was alarmed, but then he thought, *Oh, that's right. I promised to go to Chicago with her where I intend to kick some husband-abuser ass. For a minute there, I thought my brain was actually considering a future with the woman. Ha, ha, ha!*

For the next two hours, they worked diligently, as a team, each contributing his own skills to the discussion. He and his brothers complemented each other in much the same way the SEAL team members did. They could set goals, establish priorities, assign duties, and follow through. Clean, mean, fighting machines.

And, yes, they were foolish at times, like Ivak with his lap dancer, but Trond could excuse that. In truth, he'd been the one most likely to screw up in the past. Still was, probably.

He stood and stretched his arms wide, yawning loudly. "It's two a.m., guys. I've gotta get back."

His brothers stood as well and joined hands. Bowing their heads, they prayed silently, a ritual they followed before every mission.

"Take care," he said, preparing to teletransport himself back to the BQ.

"By the by," Ivak said at the last minute. "I heard your 'friend' is now a blonde. Is it true what they say about blondes being more fun?" Ivak blinked guilelessly at him.

"I wish I knew."

The best-laid plans of mice and men . . . and vampire angels . . .

They were all in full military ruck as they sat on the bench seats of a low-riding, stealth-configured Blackhawk helo, even Trond and Karl, who were not official members of the U.S. armed forces.

Some would say that the lunar gods had blessed them with a moonless night, but Trond knew with a certainty that it was another God altogether guiding their fate. Even with the blessed darkness, the helo lights had been extinguished once they entered Davastan airways to avoid detection below. They could see one another, though, in that eerie, green-ish, pixelated filter of NVGs.

The rotors were relatively quiet, but the inser-tion into the hills of Afghanistan would have to be completed quickly nonetheless. They had prepared for this mission in any and every way they could, but there was always the element of surprise. Even in the seeming silence, a deeper silence reigned as awareness rippled through the aircraft of that Chi-nook that had been shot down by Taliban insurgents not so far from here, in which twenty-two SEALs had been among the thirty-eight fatalities.

They all wore bulletproof flak vests under their camouflage shirts and pants that made use of the numerous pockets and loops. Blow-out kits for field medical trauma, as well as kits for insertion and ex-traction, including money and various passports. Cammie paint and boonie hats. Little booklets that contained photographs of the tangos they hoped to apprehend, along with their significant others, such as Najid's wives and concubines, his sons, and close confidants. Every piece of the uniform served a purpose, whether a special sheath for K-Bar knives or thigh holsters, or slings for weapons. And Trond had to be impressed with the sharpshooters, or snipers, who carried a regular arsenal of differ-ent kinds of assault rifles, never being sure which would be needed for what terrain, whether air or land or sea, with their aim always being, "One shot, one kill." Some of the men also carried C–4 charges for blasting through metal doors, stun grenades for momentarily freezing an enemy, and even laser designators that could "paint" targets for airborne assaults.

Of course, they all carried backpacks with Arab

clothing that they would don on landing. The women couldn't fast-rope down from a hovering helo in a voluminous gown, nor some of the men who would wear long white robes, as well. On this op, those infiltrating the compound had receiving mics implanted in their right ears and sending mics implanted between the thumb and forefinger of their left hands. The women wore contact lenses with cameras in them, but they were fragile and might not hold up if they got themselves in a tight situation. Some of the SEALs, who would stay in uniform away from the fray, wore cameras on their helmets that televised everything back to the Pentagon, but more importantly to CentCom at its McGill Air Force Base headquarters, and to JSOC, the Joint Special Operations Command. The CIA and FBI would also be watching, and listening, he assumed. Lots of fingers in the antiterrorism pie, with good reason.

They'd landed at Bagram Airfield north of Kabul last night. Now, they were minutes away from Davastan, which was farther south.

"Are you afraid?" Trond asked, leaning close to Nicole's ear so he could be heard.

She nodded.

"That's good. Fear is good."

"*Now* you decide to appreciate motivational sayings?"

He just smiled and shrugged.

"Are *you* afraid?"

"More like excited. Death doesn't scare me so much anymore. Don't worry, though. I'll be watching your back," he assured her.

"Not always," she qualified. "Remember, once I'm inside, I'm on my own. With Donita and Marie, of course. But we'll be weaponless, for the most part, at least initially."

Trond shook his head. "You're not on your own. Ever. You might not see us, but we'll be there ready to jump in." He stared at her for a long moment, "I'll tell you this, though, if you were my woman, I would be scared shitless on your behalf. I would do everything in my power to keep you home under lock and key, safe and protected."

"That is so chauvinist," she said, but he could tell by the little smile she flashed at him that she was pleased. She must like the idea of being his woman. But, no, he was soon relieved of that opinion when she added, "If I were your woman, you couldn't be gay."

Gay, gay, gay! I am sick up to my fangs of the subject. "You have a point there." *Now can we drop the subject?*

Slick yelled out, "Everyone, stand ready. Two minutes."

Followed soon by "One minute."

"Thirty seconds."

Just then, the helo went into hover mode, the doors slid open on either side, and Slick waved his hand, motioning for everyone else to come forward. "Are we good to go?"

They all answered with a resounding "Hoo-yah!"

"God be with us all," JAM called out then, which caused a few eyebrows to rise, but no protests.

A rope was tossed out on either side and Slick yelled out, "Go, go, go!" as the sixteen bodies on board, minus the pilot and his assistant, quickly fast-roped or were lowered to the ground, Slick going down last. The goal was to have them all on the ground close together in an area no bigger than half a football field. Within seconds, the helo was gone, and they scurried to gather together and find the designated hiding place for their military gear, a small cave with an overhang, partially hidden by bushes. It was not yet daylight. So, for more than two hours all sixteen bodies crowded inside the space that reeked of old cook fires and dried animal dung. No one seemed to care, their focus on the mission to come.

By mid-morning it was time for Trond to get the three women inside the harem compound. They were in full purdah, while he wore a dirty *shalwar kameez*, the traditional tunic and drawstring, pajama-type pants whose legs were wider on top and narrower at the ankles. On his head was a red-and-white-checkered keffiyeh with a braided cord *igal* covering a shoulder-length black wig. His face sported a mustache and straggly beard.

"You look good with long hair," Marie told him.

"Ah, you should have seen me in my day. Hair like black silk. War braids laced with crystals on either side of my face." He pretended to preen.

"In my day?" Nicole mimicked. "Why do you sometimes talk like you're ancient?"

Because I am?

"You know what they call a beard, don't you?" Marie teased.

Actually, I do.

"Marie! I'm surprised by you," Nicole said.

I'm not. "A thigh tickler?" he guessed.

"Trond!" Nicole pretended shock.

"Would you like to know what a Viking man calls his mustache in the bed furs?" He winked at Nicole.

"No!" she exclaimed, and they all burst out in laughter.

"I must say, though, that I really like your head

cover. Stole someone's tablecloth, did you?" Donita teased.

He could tell they were all bantering with him because they were nervous. He understood that. And, frankly, he was nervous, too. Not for himself. But that window of time when the women would be on their own, unarmed, inside the women's quarters . . . well, anything could happen. And so he bantered back, "It's my own tablecloth. Notice the syrup here. I had waffles this morning." He waggled his eyebrows at the three women.

Nicole leaned up to whisper in his ear, "Bless you for making us smile."

He felt the whisper of her breath against the inner whorls of his ear, and felt blessed in a way she had not intended. He could see one benefit of the Arab attire, lots of hiding places for weapons and other . . . stuff.

Trond rode a donkey, and the three women walked docilely, eyes downcast, behind him for almost a mile until they approached the compound gate. The two guardsmen immediately raised rifles. Trond dismounted and began speaking rapid Arabic to them, with much gesticulating of hands, explaining that he'd been invited to bring these three women for their master's harem.

Much of the resistance was just for show. First came the traditional bribery known as baksheesh that had to be handled with finesse, even though it was an expected practice. Once Trond got through the arguments and the slipping of money into "greased palms," the guards looked the three women over and leered salaciously.

"I hope she has big boobs," the one guard said in a regional version of Pashtu. "Our boss, he likes the big boobies." The way he cupped his hands in front of his chest needed no translation for the women, who pretended embarrassment when they really felt like slapping the jerk up one side and down the other of his fool head.

"Do they speak Arabic?" the other guard asked. A little late for asking, if you asked Trond, which no one did, of course.

Trond shook his head. "Two of my sisters come from Sweden," Trond said with a wink, "and the other is from Somalia."

"Sisters!" The guards hooted with laughter, not just because of Donita's ebony skin, but because of the two blonde, clearly non-Arabic women, as well.

"And virgins . . . ah, if your 'sisters' are virgins, you will get a high price. The master does like a tight sheath for his sword. Ha, ha, ha!" The guard who was speaking made a rude gesture with a tightly closed fist and a forefinger.

By the tension emanating from the women, he decided a slap or five would be too mild. The women were thinking more in the vein of a steel-toed boot kick to the balls.

Trond tied the donkey to a post and patted the animal on the rump, which actually was a signal to his teammates through a mic under the tail that they were going in. There had been lots of jokes about what message would be transmitted if the donkey farted or performed some bodily function.

"Pigs!" Nicole muttered under her breath once they were allowed to go through the gates.

"Well, pigs they may be, but we have two more 'sties' to go through," Trond murmured to them.

"Oink, oink!" Marie said.

At least they still had their sense of humor.

Trond was surprisingly calm as he gazed around the compound, which was built up against a mountain riddled with caves, thus leaving the occupants a series of secret exits when under siege. Although Najid considered himself a prince of sorts, he clearly had not built a palace for himself in his Muslim fundamentalist homeland, where the kind of ostentation he favored abroad would be frowned on here. Still, it was large and could house hundreds of people, when necessary. At the moment, it was believed there were no more than seventy, including the women and children.

Najid was not in residence at the moment, and the OctoTiger team had mixed feelings about that. Rescuing the hostages might be easier without Najid here. On the other hand, it would be a major coup to accomplish both his demise *and* the rescue.

Most everywhere Trond looked there was concrete. Concrete walls . . . in fact, three concentric walls to reach the inner courtyards. Concrete buildings. Concrete cisterns. In the middle of all this concrete was a pounded dirt courtyard in the midst of which was an incongruous helipad. Concrete, of course.

Nothing fancy here, although Trond suspected things would be different inside. Najid did not strike him as the type to sacrifice his lavish lifestyle totally, even in his homeland.

There was something else Trond noticed. The scent of Lucipires, though faint, indicated they had been here, or were nearby. Plus, the strong scent of lemons. Lucies had been feeding here. In fact, he would bet his almost nonexistent wings they had been gorging on some of the evilest men in the world. When they were done draining a body, it dis-

appeared and went immediately to Hell, or Jasper's
version of Hell. Unless huge numbers of people had
disappeared so far, Najid's commanders would just
think the men had fled to the hills, or been killed
while engaged with some enemy.

The fur was going to fly soon, though, and Najid
would have to be aware of something happening in
his home compound.

The largest of the concrete buildings, Najid's
home and headquarters, was connected by open-
sided, roofed walkways to other buildings. The one
at the far end, of substantial size, must be the harem.
Thus far the diagrams they'd studied back at Coronado appeared to be accurate.

"Don't speak," Trond warned the women as they
approached the second gate that they needed to
get through if they wanted ultimately to enter the
harem sector. The first guards must have alerted the
guards here because they waved them through with
little interest as they watched some men rolling dice
on the ground nearby.

When they got to the next building, Trond
stepped inside the open doorway, waving for the
women to follow. He sensed instinctively that this
next hurdle would not be as easy as the first. Several men in Arab attire sat before computers at various desks, but this was not the usual office. Nope,
these guys had pistols sitting next to mouses, ammunition belts crisscrossed over their chests, flex
cuffs attached to belt loops, a machine gun propped
in one corner, and a wall-mounted TV playing an
unending stream of speeches showcasing Najid bin
Osama in Arab attire against an Afghan mountain
backdrop. Through a half-opened door at the back,
he saw bars. Presumably jail cells.

In any case, Trond would have to notify Harek about the computer systems here. Maybe he could do something to botch up the works, or use them to their advantage. Or maybe he should notify Geek of their existence. Yes, that would be the better way to go. Geek might be able to learn something about the Najid organization by studying the hard drives. Not that Trond knew how to remove a hard drive. Harek and Geek would know, though.

Bracing himself, Trond walked with confidence up to the first desk, where he handed the glowering man a packet of papers. Sitting on the desk next to his tapping fingertips, beside his Sauer, was an industrial-size bottle of Rolaids. Would seem some things about America weren't all that bad. A nameplate identified him as Rafi al-Hafiz, chief of security operations. There had to be an irony in rebel insurgents with the life span of a gnat going to the trouble of nameplates, but, wait, those were removable, sticky-backed gold letters, weren't they? Made sense. If anything in this volatile part of the world made sense.

"What you want?" Rafi barked out, causing his assistants to jump in their chairs.

"A thousand pardons, good sir." He did a salaam type greeting, bowing slightly and touching his chest, mouth, and forehead. "I am here to make a delivery." He glanced meaningfully to the three women.

"Pfff!" Rafi said with disgust after scanning the fake documents Trond had given him. "More women!" Motioning to one of his assistants, he ordered, "Frisk him." All this in Arabic, of course.

Trond had been expecting no less, and a routine sweep of his body by the guard who stood up from the second desk, Zafir bin Tahir, would reveal no weapons. Trond stood stiffly while Zafir ran his hands over and under all his various limbs and possible hiding places. They even made him take off his boots, but when they got a whiff of his specially malodored socks, they decided he'd taken off enough. The whole time Rafi and the other two guards in the room were sitting up with alertness, their hands close to their weapons.

Satisfied, Rafi turned to the women. "Now, the women. Burqas and shoes off!"

The women had been taught certain code words and body signals. Right now, Trond repeated the guard's order and blinked twice, a signal for them to begin weeping, as if mortified to be asked to remove their protective outer garments. It wasn't as if they were naked underneath, and hopefully would not have to be.

Rafi sneered with distaste at their tears and yelled, "Off! Now!"

With more softly spoken Arabic words to the women, only a few of which they would understand, the women removed their burqas and held their folded garments in front of them. The women kept their eyes lowered, which was a good thing. The eyes often revealed too much. Trond wasn't sure what would be more alarming if revealed, their fear or their rebellion.

They now wore full-length . . . to neck, wrist, and ankle . . . gowns of bright-colored silk, belted at the waist. Although they were modest by Western standards, they revealed plenty of the women's curves, and the hair, of course, which was considered a sexual temptation in some cultures. Nicole and Marie's blonde tresses hung down to their shoulder blades, while Donita's tight black curls glistened like a cap against her well-formed head.

"Strip them!" Rafi yelled, popping an antacid into his mouth.

"No!" Trond yelled right back and proceeded to argue, "You can't strip them. Only Najid or the harem master has the right to do that. They are an investment for me. If you shame them, they are worthless." He made a spitting gesture. "Less than camels. Less than my donkey outside. I will leave with my women if you insist. You can explain to Najid why the women were not delivered."

He motioned for the women to don their burqas again and turned toward the door.

The women had no sooner shaken out the outer garments than Rafi changed his mind. "Frisk them," he ordered Zafir, who smiled widely, displaying several rotten teeth.

The women stood stiffly—tears leaking from Marie's dark eyes, Nicole sobbing, and Donita staring straight ahead—while Zafir ran his fat hands over their bodies, sticking fingers in places they had no business being. The other two guards, still at their desks, watched avidly, wishing it was them. When Zafir was done, he winked at Nicole, who was probably restraining herself from doing him a favor by knocking out his bad teeth, and told Rafi, "They are clean."

Trond raised his chin with arrogance. "Did I not tell you they would be?"

Rafi shrugged, as if he were only doing his job, and stamped their paperwork, telling Trond how to get to the harem where the man in charge, Hamzah bin Hamzah, would want to examine the women further to determine if they would suit the master's taste. Meanwhile, the women had donned their burqas and shoes again. As they were leaving, he heard Rafi speaking into a phone, no doubt alerting Hamie of their upcoming arrival.

Trond exhaled as if he'd been holding a long breath and said, "Whew!" when they left the building and proceeded down another covered walkway to the far side of the compound. He told the women, "You did good."

"Hard to be bad when you're scared spitless," Nicole remarked.

"Fear is good," Trond said.

"Bite me," Nicole said.

He smiled. *If only!*

"Besides, you already quoted me that saying before. You need to expand your repertoire."

I have a repertoire? Please, God, don't let it be a repertoire of hokey skaldic sayings. Let it be something cool. Something sexy. Something . . .

How's this for a motivational saying? that infernal voice in his head intruded. *Hell is only one sin away.*

Trond decided the wisest course was *not* to compete with an archangel on anything. Even mind quotes.

So they were quiet as they walked now until Nicole remarked, "Why does it smell so strongly of lemons here?"

"You're right," Marie said, sniffing. "I don't see any lemon trees. Actually, I don't think lemon trees could grow in this climate."

"Maybe it's some kind of Arab air freshener," Marie offered.

"Too bad Trond couldn't put some in his socks," Nicole teased.

Trond had no time to react to the women's comments. For just a second, Trond thought he saw Zebulan sitting atop one of the walls, watching them. But when he did a double take, he saw just the sun shimmering off the barbed wire topping the concrete wall.

Seventeen

**When they pulled out the plastic gloves,
you knew you were in trouble . . .**

They'd come to the harem complex, and while they waited for the guard at the door to get another guard to escort them to the harem, Trond pulled Nicole aside. Marie and Donita were whispering to each other on his other side.

"Don't speak when you get inside."

"Take no chances."

"Be discreet in sending messages."

"Try not to show emotion . . . anger, pride, whatever, even with just your eyes."

Then he smiled at her. "Whatever you do, no motivational sayings to anyone, not even the harem women."

She smiled back at him. "Why are you looking so concerned? Did you hear or see something that alters our plans?"

He shook his head. "I just don't like the idea of you being in such a dangerous situation."

"Me personally, or all of us?"

"All of you, of course," he said, but she knew he meant her.

She tilted her head in question. "You confuse me."

"I confuse myself."

It appeared as if the guard was returning with their escort.

Quickly, Trond took her one hand out from the folds of her robe and pressed his lips to the palm, closing her fingers over the kiss. The whole time, his eyes held hers. Then he whispered, "Later."

She had no time to think about the import of that gesture, or of how a simple act could make her breath catch and her skin tingle, because they were inside now, and the heavy metal door clanged shut behind them.

And what a shock it was when they entered the women's quarters. Mosaic tiled floors. Plastered walls decorated with frescoes of ancient Arabia. Inner courtyards with bubbling fountains and huge green plants. A spa complete with whirlpools and massage tables.

She could only imagine how palatial Najid's living quarters must be at the other end of the compound if his women were treated so well. Materially, anyhow.

Of course, they only saw these things in passing as they were escorted to a room where they awaited the harem master, Hamzah bin Hamzah. A locked room. Oh, it was a comfortable room, with silky Persian carpets, low couches, and a coffee table soon laden with platters of fresh fruit, hummus, flat bread triangles, and iced glasses of pomegranate juice brought by a serving girl who avoided eye contact and said nothing, although Nicole sensed her curiosity. Before she left, the girl indicated they could take off their burqas, then showed them a rudimentary bathroom with basic toilet, bidet, and sink with a mirror above it.

Two hours passed slowly—they feared speaking in case the room was bugged—before Hamzah arrived to interview them. Accompanying him was a thirty-something woman whose gray-streaked hair hung in a neat braid down her back.

The heavyset, no-nonsense man of fifty-odd years carried a clipboard and a camera.

Nicole didn't want to think what that camera portended.

"Salaam," he said distractedly as he sank into a chair opposite the sofa where Nicole, Marie, and Donita were sitting. The woman eased herself down onto the chair next to him, waiting. Apparently, these kinds of "interviews" were nothing new for them.

Hamzah smoothed out the wrinkled fabric of his white thobe, placed the clipboard evenly on his knees that were pressed together, clicked a ballpoint pen, then asked them something in Arabic. When they stared dully back at him, he asked the same question in at least six other languages, including English, to which they schooled themselves not to react. The question he kept asking was: "What language do you speak?" Finally, he asked the question in French, and Marie jumped in with *"Oui!"* and told him that she and Nicole spoke passable French, but Donita spoke only Somali.

He nodded, taking notes. "Where are you from?"

"Nicole and I are elementary school teachers from Sweden. We were attending a conference in Paris when we were kidnapped. But not for ransom. No, these bad men sold us to slave traders." She began to weep.

Nicole joined in with the weeping and begged in French, "Can we go home now? I want to go home."

Hamzah waved a hand dismissively. "Your wants no longer matter. Allah will decide your fate now."

Or Najid, Nicole thought. *Like God, or Allah, would have any wish to be involved in human trafficking!*

"And this one?" Hamzah pointed his pen at Donita, who was staring ahead dully.

"She was taken in Somalia and sold to the same slave traders, that's all we know," Marie said. "Someone said she's some kind of African princess."

They all looked at Donita then, and she did resemble some regal black woman of importance, her back ramrod stiff.

"Hmpfh! That's what they all say," Hamzah remarked, writing on his clipboard.

The woman said something to him, to which he nodded. "Stand and take off your clothing," Hamzah ordered then.

"No, no, no!" Marie said on behalf of them all.

"Yes, yes, yes. It is necessary to see if you meet the master's requirements."

"Which are?" Nicole asked in her schoolgirl French.

"Beauty, of course. If we find you flawless, then we will take pictures and send them to Master Najid."

"Flawless?" Marie squeaked out.

"Pictures?" Nicole squeaked out, having no doubt he meant nude pictures.

"This is my daughter Layla. She is a nurse." He looked at the woman in the other chair with a smile of pride. "She studied in Germany."

Whoa! Why do we need a nurse?

Her unspoken question was answered immediately. "Layla will take blood samples to make sure you are AIDS free. And she will examine your bodies for viruses, like herpes, and yeast infections. Routine exams." He waved a hand airily.

Routine for him, maybe.

There was a short knock on the door and in came two guards wheeling a gynecological table. Layla was already pulling on a pair of plastic gloves.

The implications of that table caused Nicole and Marie and Donita to go into immediate, sphincter-tightening mode. The fact that the two guards stayed added a tightening of the fists as well.

They'd known this might happen. They'd prepared for the eventuality. And, thank God, in the bathroom a short time ago they'd removed the tampons that contained a C–4 mini explosive for taking down a metal door, a thin, razor-sharp switchblade that could slit a man's neck if necessary or substitute as a lock pick, and a stun gun . . . yeah, a real mini stun gun that could do the work of one of the big boys if aimed just right. They were taped in a hiding place under the sink.

The ordeal that followed was humiliating and even painful, but the three women bore it stoically and in the end were pronounced fit for an Arab dictator, barring any bad news from the lab. It didn't help that they'd been deemed nonvirgins. Even so, they would be taken to the spa shortly, where they could bathe, and then to a sleeping chamber.

But then Hamzah told them something as he was preparing to leave that changed everything.

"Master Najid will be arriving tonight. Late tonight, around three a.m. We should know by noon if he is interested in any, or all of you." He smiled then, as if he'd bestowed some gift on them.

Once the women were alone, they crowded themselves into the bathroom, turned on the water, flushed the toilet, and began to whisper urgently.

"We need to find the hostages ASAP," Marie said.

"We have to be out of here before Najid sees us," Donita added.

Nicole was the one who tapped the skin between her thumb and forefinger on her left hand three times, four times in a row, with pauses in between the sets. Then she spoke into her hand, "Tiger, Tiger, are you there?"

"Roger that," a voice said in their three ear mics.

"Cat here."

"Roger that."

"King Rat arriving oh three hundred."

A telling pause, then, "Have you located the kittens yet?" He referred to the hostages.

"Not yet. Going to try now."

"We're moving in. We have your six."

She sure hoped so.

When she ended the call, Marie said, "Well, ladies, shall we roll a few stumps and see what crawls out?"

"Hoo-yah!" Nicole and Donita replied at the same time, using the traditional Navy SEAL response pretty much meaning "Hell, yeah!"

Now it was time to see if they had what it took to be true-blue, female Navy SEALs.

He lost his ass . . .

Trond no sooner left the compound gates than he realized he had a problem. His donkey was gone. Not that he couldn't jog back to the bivouac site, or teletransport, but this particular donkey had been souped up. What he didn't want to do was chase the stubborn, braying animal all over the place, wasting time he didn't have to waste.

Thus, he was not in a good mood when he approached one of the guards, who was picking his teeth with the point of a stiletto. "Where's my frickin' jackass?"

"Your frickin' brother took it," the guard replied, repeating his expletive back at him.

"My brother?"

"Yeah."

Trond recalled then that his brothers were already here in Afghanistan. Of course they would want to connect with him.

"The one with a tail," the other guard explained. "Ha, ha, ha!"

Were these two drunk, or maybe suffering from sunstroke? It *had been* an especially bright day.

The first guard gave his friend a disbelieving glance. "He thinks your brother has a tail, but when I looked, there was no tail. Just the donkey's. Ha, ha, ha!"

Yep. Drunk. But then, the guard's observation sank in. *Zeb . . . it must be Zeb. Not my brothers.* "What direction did . . . um, my brother go?"

Both guards pointed west.

So Trond jogged along the dirt road, for once thankful for all those practice runs back at Coronado. To his surprise, when he turned a bend in the road, he did in fact run into his three brothers and about twenty other vangels camped behind some boulders about thirty or so yards off the road.

"Where's my damn donkey?" he asked Mordr right off.

"Huh?"

To Ivak, who was rucked out in so much military gear he could barely walk, he observed, "No tail?"

"Huh?" Ivak said, too.

"It's about time you got here," Harek said from his position where he sat on the ground, cross-legged, a mini computer resting on lap. "According to my data"—he pointed to the graph on his screen—"you should have been here a half hour ago. We've had a helluva time avoiding Najid's patrols."

Trond nodded to the various other vangels whose fangs were out, special weapons at the ready, anxious to do battle. They all sensed Lucies and their potential victims in the area. In great numbers, would be Trond's guess.

With only a few moments to spare, Trond updated his brothers on the OctoTiger project, and they told him what they'd been up to.

"I know I promised you backup, but we're going to leave you to the SEAL business, Trond. There is more than enough for us to handle with the Lucies," Mordr told him. "In fact, there are so many Lucies here, and victims who carry the sin taint, that I've called for more vangels. Saving these sinners is a tough job, they are so far gone, but we've managed to turn back a dozen of them." He pointed to a group of obviously confused Arab men and women huddled in the center of the clearing.

Trond noticed then the good color on his three brothers and some of the other vangels. They'd obviously fed on saved humans.

"As to the Lucies," Mordr continued, "the only haakai we've seen are Haroun al Rashid and Zebulan of Israel, but we haven't been able to get close yet."

Zeb was the one who'd taken his donkey then, Trond concluded.

"We have taken out a dozen mungs, though," Harek pointed out. "And at least twenty imps and hordlings."

"This is big, brother. *Big!*" Mordr said.

"So, your emphasis will be on the Lucies, and mine will be with the hostages," *and the safety of the three WEALS, Nicole in particular,* he summarized.

His brothers nodded.

Joining hands, they said a brief, silent prayer for heavenly support in their endeavors. Trond took off then, still searching for his donkey.

Finally, he caught up with Zeb sitting under a tree, munching on an apple. The donkey was munching on a dismal patch of grass. Zeb wore a baseball cap, jeans, white athletic shoes, and a pure white T-shirt with the logo "Devil May Care!" which usually meant carefree. Yep, that was Zeb. Happy-go-lucky demon, despite his all-American appearance.

Trond should just "kill" the demon. He knew he should. Instead, he asked, "Where's your tail?"

"Huh?"

"The guard said my brother took my donkey. The brother with a tail."

"Oops," Zeb said. "The tail comes and goes. Like our fangs. And your wings." Zeb glanced pointedly at his shoulders. His wingless shoulders.

"You stole my donkey," Trond accused.

"Oh, is that your ass? I thought it was a homeless ass. A sorry ass, at that."

Trond shook his head at the demon's warped attempt at humor and dropped down to the ground beside him, taking an apple from the basket on Zeb's lap. Both of their legs were extended to an almost identical length. They must be the same height.

"Are you sure we aren't related?" he asked of a sudden.

"Since when do Jews go a-Viking?"

He had a point there.

And wasn't that the oddest thing in this odd day in his odd life . . . an angel and demon, sharing an apple? Or maybe this was like the apple in the Garden of Eden offered by the satanic snake? Maybe he was going to turn bad after taking a few chomps.

He looked at the apple, looked at Zeb, then back at the apple, and shrugged. It was a really good apple. Plus, he'd already done the bad.

"What are you doing here, Zeb?"

"Harvesting sinners."

Trond arched his brows.

"There are a lot of sinners here, Trond. Mortal sinners. Some of these terrorists . . ." He pretended to shiver, with distaste or relish, it was hard to say. "Let's just say, they are irredeemable sinners."

"How many have you taken so far?"

"Personally?"

"Tsk, tsk, tsk! I'm not that picky. Overall, since you've been here for the past eight and a half days?"

Zeb's eyes widened at Trond's knowledge of the demon presence here in Davastan, down to the exact day they'd arrived.

"Seventeen souls," Zeb admitted, "but not to worry, you would not have been able to save any of them."

"And that's all you want . . . the already committed sinners?"

Zeb nodded, but his eyes did not meet Trond's.

They both ate another apple in silence.

Finally, Zeb broke the silence. "So, is she the one?"

The fine hairs stood out on the back of Trond's neck. "She who?" he asked. Then, "The one what?"

"The one you danced with."

"Are you still harping on that dance thing?"

"We demons do not harp. That is an angel thing."

"Pfff! What is it with you and the jokes today?"

"I get my jollies wherever I can."

"Jollies? Are you going over the edge, Zeb? Jollies?" he mocked.

"My friend, I went over that edge a long time ago."

"I am not your friend, Zeb. Nor am I fool enough to mistake your strange behavior as a sign of friendship."

"Methinks you are wrong. Methinks we could be comrades if you came over to our side. Let me fang you. I'd bet my tail your blood is more potent than aged Damascan wine."

Trond laughed. "Now you're a wine connoisseur?"

"Just because you Vikings prefer beer does not make it the superior drink. Actually, I had a small vineyard at one time. Very small, but it served the needs of my small family. It was in the hills beyond Jerusalem." He shook his head to clear it. "Suffice it to say, wine trumps beer any day."

Trond stared at Zeb, slack-jawed with amazement. He'd known Zeb a long time. This was the first time he'd ever shared any personal information.

"Back to your woman, have you bedded her yet?"

Whoa! What was it with Zeb's fixation on Nicole? "She's not my woman."

"I saw you kiss her palm today."

Uh-oh!

"Now, if you'd given her a tongue-down-the-throat kiss, I would call it lust. And a handshake or little air kiss, friendship."

"Air kiss?" he protested. "We Vikings do not do air kisses."

Zeb continued as if Trond had not spoken. "But kissing the palm . . . ah, you revealed yourself, vangel. Love is on the way."

"Idiot! A mere brush of lips over the palm leads you to think I've bedded her and am about to wed her?"

"Can vangels wed?" Zeb asked. He seemed to be jumping from one subject to another today. "Seems to me I heard that one of your brothers wed recently. Is that true?"

Trond stood and waited for Zeb to stand as well. Enough with this circling each other with irrelevant conversation. Were they going to face off now, a fight to the death . . . or something worse than death, if he lost?

No, Trond sensed that Zeb was here for some other reason.

"Jasper wants you, *and* the two SEALs."

No surprise there. "The one SEAL you fanged has been saved, and the other is not here."

"That is not good news. For me," Zebulan revealed.

So Jasper was leaning on Zeb. He wondered why. And what the repercussions might be if he failed. "As for me, no thanks. Tell Jasper I'd rather not visit at this time."

"You may have to reconsider if Jasper gets his other guest first."

Not the two SEALs. Who then? He waited.

"Your woman."

Trond's head felt as if it would explode with all the lurid images flickering through his stunned brain, images of what a master demon like Jasper would do to a woman like Nicole. Satan's disciple might not be able to turn Nicole into a demon since she was not in a state of sin or near-sin, but he could prolong her torture endlessly. For years. Until she finally died, which would be a blessing, or gave in, which would be hell on earth.

Trond's fangs came out and he hissed his outrage, prepared to launch himself at Zeb.

But the demon was gone.

Eighteen

Did G.I. Jane have to work this hard? . . .

The three women had been scrubbed, exfoliated, creamed, and massaged until they were cleaner and looser than wet noodles. Now it was time for action.

They'd gotten to "meet" the wives and concubines and what appeared to be servants or slaves, though "meet" a misnomer since none of the mostly Arabic women spoke English. There was a clear delineation of status here in the harem whereby the legitimate wives, assuming a wife could be legitimate when she joined four others, kept to one side of the small pool in the courtyard with a large spurting cupid fountain in the center. Apparently the wives' rooms were on the other side, too. Nicole, Marie, and Donita kept to the lower-class side, gladly. In fact, Marie had taken to singing under her breath that old Garth Brooks song, "I've Got Friends in Low Places."

Finally, they'd gotten a clue that the hostages were being kept in a locked, soundproof room down the corridor a distance when several servants were seen carrying trays of food and water. Not the succulent tidbits arrayed around the spa . . . fresh fruit, lamb kebabs, caviar, baklava, stuffed dates, and the like. Nope, the hostage trays seemed to contain flat breads, slabs of some kind of meat, several different cheeses, and plain water.

Nicole went into the bathroom first, and using the sense of touch and a wall mirror, was able to pull up the hairline filament tied to her molar, at the end of which, below her throat, was a slender plastic pod the size of a string bean. Inside was the liquid knockout drug she would put in all the drinks here in the spa. Also, she would hopefully be able to offer some drinks to the guards as well. Within fifteen minutes they would be fast asleep and stay that way for up to three hours, please God.

Nicole worked the room and outdoor area, on both sides of the fountain pool, by walking with Marie, seemingly chatting companionably in French, while they surreptitiously dropped the drug into the various fruit punch bowls. They had to make sure that all of them succumbed, lest others get suspicious; so, they made doubly sure that everyone had imbibed at the same time by offering to help the overworked servants place out fresh bowls of icy cold punch and icy bottled water with the caps undone.

While Nicole was doing a final check of the area, Donita and Marie went into the bathroom where they helped each other extract their own molar-anchored ampoules, both containing mini weapons.

Marie stayed behind, watching over the rooms, while Donita and Nicole hurried down the corridor as fast as they could in their long, revealing harem gowns and carrying a pitcher and two glasses.

Nicole even had a garnet glued into her belly button. She'd removed her belly button ring before the mission.

When they got near the metal door, they slowed and smiled seductively at the two guardsmen. In French, they offered the men a cold drink, on orders from the harem mistress, they said. Of course, the men didn't understand them, but they understood the gesture and drank greedily. Then they leaned against the wall and leered at them, especially at Donita, who was doing this eye-riveting thing with her breasts. Breathing in deeply, then out, then in, then out. Each time, her nipples and the surrounding areolas could be seen prominently pressing against the red sheer fabric of her bodice.

Soon, the men slumped to the floor, and it looked as if the gods of luck were with them. They wouldn't have to C–4 blast the door or spend time trying to pick the lock since there was a key ring on the one guard's belt. Plus they now had full-size weaponry— two rifles, a pistol, and several knives. Quickly, they opened the door, dragged the men inside, and shut the door firmly behind them, engaging the lock.

Then they turned.

Saints would weep at what they saw.

Lemonade, anyone . . . ?

"They're in!" Slick yelled to everyone in the cave, then muttered, "Son. Of. A. Bitch!" as he looked over Geek's shoulder at the video coming in from one of the WEALS' contact lens cameras.

The battery life on these mini cameras was less than five minutes, and even then they often malfunctioned. So the women would try one at a time. This first one was working. Too well. Even in the dark chamber where the hostages were being held, they could make out hazy images.

At the gruesome images, Trond's nuts shot to his tonsils over fear for Nicole, but then he breathed a sigh of relief when he saw Donita and Nicole moving about; it must be Marie's lens doing the filming. The three of them seemed to be unharmed. For now. Not so the hostages.

One of the hostages, older than the rest, which meant it had to be the author Selah ad Beham, was in bad shape. Lying on the floor on a threadbare blanket, she appeared unconscious, which would be a blessed relief considering her injuries. Even a rough eyeball analysis of her external injuries indicated severe beatings and possibly rape.

"Uh-oh! I count only thirteen packages, aside from Donita, Marie, and Nicole," Geek said.

An ominous silence followed as they replayed the visual scan of the room. "The Greek movie star is missing," Slick concluded, which was immediately confirmed by a hand mic transmission from Marie. "Athena Goldstein hasn't been seen since the first days of capture a year ago."

Morris Goldstein was a powerful politician. Heads were going to roll if his wife was dead. Not that heads weren't going to roll today, anyhow.

Marie continued, "Selah ad Beham is in critical condition. Both internal and external injuries. The skin on the bottoms of her feet is burned off."

He heard Nicole's voice mic interrupt then. "Several of the girls have been raped. We'll need rape kits. And Beth Hillman has had all her teeth knocked out, and is suffering severe gum infection." Beth was a young Manhattan beauty, a college coed, whose only crime had been that her father was a hedge fund owner who'd supposedly contributed financially to some Israeli militant group.

Trond understood now what Zebulan had meant about there being plenty of evil sinners for the Lucies to harvest here without going after the SEALs or the hostages . . . and him, of course.

"Medics," Slick said then. "We're going to need several medics on the incoming Chinooks. We have blow-out kits for cursory wounds, but these hostages are going to need lots more than we can provide. Geek, can you alert Kabul to have medics on the Chinooks when they come in for extraction? A physician would be even better. And ambulances should be waiting for our return. A lot of them."

"Roger that," Geek said, already transmitting the visuals and voice mail back to CentCom.

"Kitty, Kitty, are you there?"

"I'm here," Nicole said.

"And me," Donita and Marie both said into their own hand mics.

"Insertion into your chamber will be through a hidden cave entrance. Listen for a tapping on the wall. Five taps in a row."

"Roger," the three women said.

Slick then contacted all the men who were at various cave entrances to the compound. They weren't sure which entrance led to the place where the hostages were being held, and since there were foot-thick metal doors, explosives would have to be used.

They listened to the silence on the line as one after another of the SEALs reported no response to their tapping.

Finally, the women could be heard shouting, "We hear it. We hear it."

"It's F.U.'s location," Slick told the SEALs behind him. "Let's get this show on the road!"

Men immediately began to gather their gear, each heading toward the cave opening, each well aware of his job as part of the team, and knowing exactly where to go.

All their faces were rigid with fury.

Before they left, Trond heard Nicole exclaim, "What the hell is that? Shut the door, shut the door! Oh fuck! Do you see that . . . thing?"

"It's as big as a house and has a friggin' tail," Donita added.

"And scales. And fangs. Holy crap! It just attacked one of the guards. Wait, there are two of them."

"I smell lemons. An overpowering lemon scent," Nicole observed. "I think I'm gonna puke."

He heard a door slam shut.

The transmission then went dead.

When it came to road trips, he sure knew how to travel . . .

Nicole, Marie, and Donita worked quickly with the women to arrange them on the floor on the far side of the room, hands covering their ears, ankles crossed, and mouths wide open, as they'd been taught in WEALS training, to withstand the explosion to come. Otherwise, even with smaller C–4 explosives, they could sustain permanent damage to their eardrums.

In the case of Selah, the author, Nicole laid herself on top of her body as best she could. The poor woman probably wouldn't make it. Among the many injuries, Nicole suspected spleen damage.

And Nicole didn't even want to think about what she'd witnessed outside in the hallway a short time ago. Then, when she'd peeked through a short time later, all she'd seen was a pile of stinky slime. The lemon scent had disappeared.

Even though they'd been prepared for it, the first explosion caused them all to jerk with surprise, followed by the hostages screaming and crying. "Keep your positions," she yelled out over the chaos. "More to come!"

On the heels of her warning came another explosion, and a massive hole in the wall opened up. SEALs began swarming into the room. Immediately, Cage and K–4 came up to her with a stretcher and the three of them managed to get Selah on her way to safety with as little additional damage as possible. Other SEALs were carrying the girls in their arms, crooning sympathetic assurances to them. One of them had to be Cage, who said, "It's okay, darlin'. Uncle Sam sent us ta bring you home." Those hostages who could walk, or run, were already in the cave tunnels, rushing toward ultimate rescue.

She turned then and hit a brick wall . . . rather, Trond's chest.

"I swear, woman, I lost nine lives over you today." He yanked her into his arms and hugged her fiercely. When she started to say something, he gritted out, "Don't you dare mention my gayness. Not now. Don't. You. Dare."

"You're crushing me," she managed to get out, though she had to admit to liking the way Trond's arms felt around her. It just wasn't the right time. Nor would it ever be.

"Over here, Easy," Slick shouted, and Trond ran over to help maneuver the hallway door open so they could check out the rest of the harem for any women being held against their will. Not that they would be able to tell since they were still under the influence of the sleep drugs. Marie gave them a quick assessment of the individuals in the harem and held up the camera that held nude pictures of the three WEALS. With glee, she shot it with a rifle she'd picked up somewhere.

Just then, the sound of helicopter rotors could be heard overheard. It couldn't be the Chinooks so soon. Besides, the extraction point was at least a quarter mile away, and it would take the SEALs a half hour to get there with their "baggage." It must be Najid returning home.

Oh God! We've got to get out of here. All hell is going to break loose. Nicole turned, about to go after Trond and Slick to warn them, although they would have heard the helo, too, and she realized she was alone in the room. But not really.

There was a man near the cave opening, leaning casually against the wall, eating an apple. An apple! He was a good-looking man, wearing jeans and a T-shirt with the logo "Devil May Care!"

"Hello, Nicole," he said.

She frowned. "Who are you?"

"Zebulan, but you can call me Zeb."

Nicole pulled out the pistol from her belt, the pistol she'd taken from one of the guards in the corridor, one of the guards who had been attacked by . . . well, that wasn't important now. "Are you one of Najid's men?"

"Me? A Jew? Not even close."

"Are you with the SEALs? Or the other special forces?"

"Let's just say I'm a . . . um, friend . . . of Sigurdsson."

"Trond?"

He nodded.

For some reason, she had doubts. She couldn't quite explain why. And, besides, why were they just standing here when exit was of prime importance? Still, she found herself asking, "You're Trond's friend?"

"A friend of sorts, you could say."

"Are you, like, one of his lovers?"

At first, the man's eyes went wide. Then he slapped his thigh with wild laughter he couldn't hold in. "You think Trond is gay?"

"Don't you?"

The man . . . Zeb, he had called himself . . . just shook his head. "Trond is no more gay than I'm . . ." He seemed to hesitate for the right word. " . . . alive."

"What?" she gasped, especially when the man tossed the core of his apple to the ground and began to transform into the kind of beasts she'd seen outside in the corridor earlier. He grabbed her arm, then wrapped a scale-covered arm around her from behind, placing a knife blade at her throat, just as Trond burst into the room, pistol raised and pointed directly at Zeb. It was a strange-looking pistol, like a Sauer, but somehow different.

"Zeb, put the knife down," Trond said icily.

"You drop your weapon first."

"You don't want to do this, Zeb. I know you don't."

"You're right, but I have no choice. You know what Jasper wants."

"You have a choice. There's always a choice." Pounding footsteps could be heard coming down the corridor. Looking directly at Nicole, Trond said, "Slick has already left. It's just you and me here now. If we don't hurry, the Chinooks will leave without us." She noticed the oddest, scariest thing then. Fangs were elongating inside Trond's mouth.

Turning his attention to the man holding her, Trond said, "You can take me back to Jasper. Let Nicole go."

"No!" Nicole protested, sensing that if Trond left her now, she'd never see him again. He was sacrificing himself for her. Why that should matter so much was a puzzle.

"Too late!" the beast said as a key began turning in the corridor door. With his arm still wrapped around Nicole, the beast dropped the knife and grabbed hold of Trond's arm. With a whooshy noise and blinding mist, Nicole felt as if they were flying through the air. In what felt like hours, but must have been only seconds, she found herself in an empty cave with Trond and Zeb.

"What to do, what to do!" Zeb said.

"Was that Najid's men at the door back there, or Lucies?" Trond asked.

Nicole had no idea what Trond meant, but Zeb apparently did. "Both," Zeb replied.

Trond glared at Zeb, but then he cocked his head to the side, "You saved us, didn't you? You didn't bring us here to take us to Jasper."

"I'm still pondering my options." More confusing words, from Zeb this time.

On those strange words, Nicole felt the three of them swoosh up into the air, through the ceiling and roof. *Swoosh* was the only word she could think of to describe this in-one-place-one-instant-and-in-another-an-instant-later. For just a blip of a nanosecond they seemed to hover above the court-yard, where dozens of the tailed and fanged beasts swarmed over the helicopter and chased after flee-ing humans. At the same time, she saw fanged human-looking creatures with wispy blue wings at-tacking the beasts. Chaos reigned everywhere.

But then she seemed to go unconscious because next thing she knew the three of them were stand-ing on the deck of a cliff-side, bamboo-and-banana-leaf-roofed bungalow with a spectacular view of the turquoise blue waters.

Dazed, she looked around to see two fanged men—Trond and Zeb—high-fiving each other. She, on the other hand, felt like high-diving into the water to swim away from what had to be a mirage, or something worse. At the least, she would get great pleasure out of shoving the two dick-for-brains men—or whatever they were—over the cliff.

Instead, her stomach heaved, and she fought to find level ground so that the bile pushing its way into the back of her throat could be forestalled. Losing the battle, she bent over the railing and began to puke her guts out.

She hoped when she was done, this nightmare would be over.

Some hidey-holes are nicer than others . . .

Trond wasn't sure what to do first. Belt Zeb a good one for scaring the crap out of Nicole, or offer to help Nicole, who was still leaning over the rail-ing, retching. He chose the latter.

"Here," he said, pressing a handkerchief into her hand, his other hand holding her hair back off her face. "Can I do anything for you? A cool washcloth? An aspirin? Is there anything you want?" he asked, putting a hand on her shoulder.

She didn't raise her head, just tilted it to the side to give him a direct look of loathing before saying, "Yeah. Go fuck yourself, you lying, slime-sucking scumbag."

"Okaaay," he said, turning toward Zeb, who grinned at him.

"My wife told me the same thing in pretty much the same words in Old Hebrew when she was pregnant with our second child. Not the lying, slime-sucking scumbag words. The other ones."

"You had a wife. And children?" Why was he asking such irrelevant questions at a time like this? And why was Zeb sharing such irrelevant information at a time like this?

Zeb paused, seemingly surprised that he'd revealed so much. A cloud passed over his no-longer-grinning face. "Yes, I had a family. A long time ago." As if wiping an eraser across his expression, he rubbed both hands over his eyes and smiled, offering, "Wanna beer?"

"Thank you, God!" Trond replied, glad-handing the demon. A cold beer was just what he needed about now.

"Not God. It was me who hauled all those cases of brew up the mountainside. Will Blue Moon be okay, or would you prefer a pilsner?"

"Blue Moon would be perfect." He followed Zeb through the open glass doors into a large living room, complete with comfortable, buttery yellow leather sofas and recliners, a flat widescreen TV on one wall, and colorful, probably museum-quality oil paintings on the other walls . . . one of them a big-ass depiction of the open petals of a flower. It resembled the labia of a woman's vagina, if you asked Trond, which no one did.

Zeb walked into the kitchen that was separated from this main room by a wide, curved archway. It appeared to be all red granite and stainless-steel, top-of-the-line appliances. Corridors led in several directions, leading to bedrooms and bathrooms, he supposed. The place wasn't huge, but it was casually luxurious.

When Zeb returned, he handed Trond his bottle of beer and sank into the matching recliner beside Trond's. In the midst of these high-quality furnishings, Zeb had the foresight to provide the ultimate male comforts. They both drank deeply, then belched with appreciation. That was all right, Trond figured, since it was just the two men. He'd made a concerted effort centuries ago to curb his cruder, slothful habits, like belching and farting.

Trond placed his half-empty bottle in the special cup holder on the arm of the recliner, then stacked his hands under his head and leaned back, inclining the chair, with a sigh of comfort. "What is this place, Zeb?"

"My hidey-hole."

"Jasper doesn't know about it?"

"Not yet."

"I thought Jasper knew everything, or could find out everything."

"I suppose he can, but he never had reason to question my comings and goings. Not yet."

"You're going to be in deep shit over this, aren't you?"

Zeb shrugged. "Depends on what I do with you two."

Trond arched a brow.

"If I deliver the two of you to Horror, I'll be a hero. If I don't . . ." He shrugged again.

"Yes, I imagine it would be horror to be a captive of the lead Lucipire."

"It would be that, but I meant his home. Horror is the name of Jasper's castle. In your homeland, by the way. The Norselands. The far, far northern Norselands. Land of ice and . . . horror."

Trond shivered, despite his best intentions to appear unintimidated by Zeb's words. "Where are we, by the way?"

"Caribbean island, too small to have a name."

"Isn't your headquarters in Greece? In the honey-combed chambers of some volcanic ruins, as I recall."

"It is. Gloom is the name of my home there, deep in the ashy chambers under the old volcano. But this is where I go when I want to be alone . . . or not so gloomy."

"Why are you telling me this? Revealing Lucie secrets has to be a no-no, punishable by at least a flogging."

"Lots more than that," Zeb said ominously. "I figure either way it won't matter what I tell you now. If I deliver you, you'll know anyway. If I don't deliver you, telling tales out of school, so to speak, will be the least of my offenses."

"I won't go willingly," Trond told him.

"I never thought you would, but you'll go. I'm older than you, and stronger. Plus, I have a trump card." He glanced out onto the deck where Nicole was straightening and wiping her mouth on the sleeve of her gown.

"What do you want, Zeb? What will be the deciding factor?"

"I want you to kill me," he said.

Now, that stunned Trond. "You're already dead, lackwit."

"I don't mean *kill* kill in the usual sense. I mean, kill me with your special weapons so that when I dissolve I won't go back to being a Lucipire anymore. I am tired, *so tired*, of the endless killing and needless torture. Plucking out eyeballs loses its entertainment value after the first hundred times." Zeb's jesting tone was belied by his sad eyes.

"Yeah, but you'd still be a demon, wouldn't you. Just in a different place. You'd have to go to . . . oh! You would prefer to go to Hell? Do you have any idea how Lucifer would punish you? It would be beyond horrific."

"I know. Better that than this endless evil I'm engaged in now."

Trond knew how Zeb felt about the endlessness of their existence, but at least Trond's killings were for a greater good. "Ironically, because you've asked for this, I can't do it."

"Why the hell not?"

"If we'd been engaged in battle, I would have killed you . . . demolished your Lucipire essence . . . in a heartbeat. But because you ask me to kill you, it would be murder. Suicide by vangel just isn't—forgive my jest—kosher."

"That doesn't make any sense at all."

"Does any of this make any sense?"

They sipped at their beers before Zeb spoke again.

"I've always wondered, why did you . . . and your brothers . . . get a second-chance penance while so many of us sinners got condemned to this other sentence?"

"I don't know. Truly, I don't."

"Maybe my sins were so much greater."

Trond shook his head. "I don't think so. Ours were as bad as sin can get. Somehow, I think it was related to our being Vikings." He noticed Zeb's incredulous expression and said, "Go figure."

"I could be a Viking," Zeb decided, half joking.

At least Trond hoped he was joking because if this was a backward way of saying he'd like to join their ranks, Trond would have to disillusion him quickly. Through all the years only Vikings or those of Norse descent had been made vangels, and never had a demon been turned angel.

Sensing Trond's skepticism, Zeb sighed. "On second thought, I would make a piss-poor Viking. I'm not vain enough."

Trond would have reached over and punched him on the arm, but they were too far apart. Besides, Nicole was walking into the room, and she was not a happy camper, rather happy harem houri, considering she still wore the Arab gown that clung to her form but was raggedy along the edges, with one sleeve almost torn off. Her blonde hair was raggedy, too, and she had a bruise mark on her face from the melee that had occurred after the explosion. Her eyes were bloodshot, and her nose and mouth were red from her excessive vomiting.

Trond thought this brave woman was nigh glorious.

She paused in front of the two of them, glanced meaningfully at their recliners and the beers in their

hands, and concluded, "Dumb as dirt, both of you!"
Then she stomped off to open a door off the kitchen.
It was a broom closet, which gave Trond ideas. Sensual ideas. When he saw Nicole blush, he knew she shared the same *sensual* memories.

Slamming the door shut, she tried another door, but it led to a walk-in, climate-controlled wine closet.

"You have a wine collection?" Trond was both surprised and impressed. "Holy clouds! There must be a thousand dollars' worth of wine in there."

"More like twenty thousand."

Trond had to laugh. "A demon wine connoisseur?"

At Trond's amusement, Zeb shrugged. "I have so few opportunities for enjoyment these days."

Trond understood that.

As Nicole slammed yet another door, Trond got up and inquired as sweetly as he could, "What are you looking for, Nicole?"

"A bathroom with a shower. And some clean clothes."

Zeb got up, too, and pointed to the left. "Second door on the right is the bathroom. There's a Jacuzzi tub if you want to relax your muscles."

Nicole said something foul about relaxing that caused Zeb to grin.

"And there's clothing of mine you can pick through in my bedroom across the hallway. Don't think anything will fit you, but you could try the jogging pants or the spandex bike shorts."

"You bike?" Trond asked. He was the one grinning now. Somehow, the idea of a demon riding a bike just didn't fit. A demon bike-riding wine connoisseur. Who would have guessed?

"I tried biking, but my tail kept getting in the

way. Hey, I have to do something to keep in shape. We can't all be Navy SEALs."

Nicole was gaping at the two of them, as if they were lunatics. "What are you two?"

"I'm a vampire angel," Trond answered with a sigh of resignation. "A vangel."

"I'm a demon vampire," Zeb answered, not at all resigned. Just sad. "A Lucipire."

"You guys are weirding me out." Nicole shivered.

"Hey, I weird myself out sometimes," Trond said.

"Me too," Zeb said.

Nicole studied each of them. "I thought angels and demons were enemies."

"We are," Trond and Zeb replied at the same time.

She glanced at the beer bottles in their hands, the way they stood so close together, the his-and-his recliners, and shook her head with disbelief. "Beer-drinking buddies, more like. So, what happened to the fake fangs?"

She didn't believe a bit of their story, Trond realized. Why would she? It was too fantastical for anyone to believe. So he and Zeb did the only thing they could. They flashed their fangs at her.

Swaying on her feet, she held up a halting hand when Trond reached to help her. "Forget the beer and wine, I need a whiskey. Straight up. Make that a double."

On those words, she did in fact faint. He caught her just in time and carried her to the bathroom. If he was lucky, he might get a chance to take a bath with her in what turned out to be a very inviting blue-tiled Jacuzzi with a panoramic view of the tropical sea. *Holy hot wings! Where did that idea come from?*

Her eyes blinked open as he set her on her feet,

and she got her first look at herself in the one mirrored wall. Letting out a little yelp of shock, she glared at him, putting her hands to her head. "You could have told me my hair looked like a haystack that went through a wind tunnel."

"Huh?" He hadn't even noticed her hair, which, now that she mentioned it, was a little mussed up and tangly.

Then she put both hands on her hips and gave him what Cage was wont to call the stink eye, according to his Cajun mawmaw. "You are in such trouble, buster. Are you even a member of the Norwegian Jaegers?"

"Not exactly," he admitted.

From the open doorway he heard Zeb chuckle at his discomfort.

Then she narrowed her eyes at him. "More importantly, are you or are you not gay?"

Nineteen

The news was not good . . .

Two hours later, Nicole sat on the edge of the bed in a room at the far end of the hallway that she'd picked for her own. She would have to come out sometime and face the two bozos who kept knocking every five minutes to see if she was okay.

No, she was not okay.

Aside from being in bizzaro-land with the two woo-woo princes, she didn't know how she'd gotten here, or how she would get out. She'd tried going out one of the back doors and found there was some kind of invisible force field surrounding the property. Almost like one of those electrical fences they bought for dogs. Every time she tried to jump through, she got a shock and was jolted back inside the perimeter.

Then there was the mission, and her job as a WEALS back in Coronado.

Most of all, there was Trond. If he was not gay, he had a lot to answer for, and she already suspected why he'd told her that particular lie. His secret . . . if it could be believed . . . was out. The one he'd used gayness to cover. The black belt liar! He was dead, so to speak. A freakin' vampire angel. Putting that unbelievable story aside, if he was not gay, how was she going to be able to resist him?

Then, too, there was the issue of her sister and her ex-husband. Time was ticking for her to be able to help. If she could.

"Nicole, come out and eat," Zeb urged her. "I made seafood paella."

Nicole's stomach rumbled with hunger. She couldn't remember when she'd eaten last. Plus, the aromas wafting through the air were scrumptious. "A demon gourmet cook?" she said on a laugh. Why that would surprise her on top of all the other surprises boggled the mind.

"I watch a lot of Food Network in between . . ."

When he didn't finish, she finished for him, " . . . in between fanging people?"

"And other things." The tone of his voice bespoke some unpleasant things. In fact, *unpleasant* was probably too mild a word.

She heard footsteps and it was Trond who spoke now. "Stop being so childish and come out now before I break the damn door down."

"Oh, that's charming," Zeb said to Trond. "She'll never come out now."

The two of them whispered together and then Trond said, "Never mind. Zeb and I will just be watching CNN to see what they're saying about the mission."

She had to leave her room then, of course. When she entered the kitchen, she found the two nitwits sitting on stools at the counter serving themselves from platters of paella swimming with shrimp, scallops, and lobster, a green salad, and fresh-baked bread. Bottles of beer sat next to their plates. From this vantage point, they could see the TV screen in the living room—in fact, the big-ass man toy of a TV could probably be seen in Chicago—which was set to CNN, but a commercial was on at the moment.

Helping herself to the food, she sat down and said to Zeb, "Where did you get fresh lettuce out here?" She assumed the bread and everything else had been frozen.

"I have a little garden on the side. Salad greens, carrots, tomatoes, herbs, just a few things. And grapes, lots of grapes. I like to garden."

"A garden?" Trond choked on a sprig of lettuce and rolled his eyes.

"I could tell the tomatoes were fresh-picked. My grandmother always had the best plum tomatoes. We would eat them right off the vine with nothing but salt." She hadn't thought of her grandmother in ages, one of her early good memories she seemed to have buried along with Cyndee and so many other things under the weight of those harsh three years of marriage.

"I like tomatoes," Trond said.

She just ignored him.

Trond did not like being ignored. Not one bit. "Do you feel better since your bath?" he asked. Although he preferred her normal brown hair to this blonde, she looked fresh and healthy with a ponytail and no makeup, wearing Zeb's sweatpants rolled up to the calves, a short-sleeved T-shirt hanging down to her elbows and the bottom knotted at her waist. The toes of her bare feet curled around the side rungs of her stool.

He was wearing a pair of Zeb's jeans and a T-shirt, following his own shower, but he didn't look half as good as she did. And that wasn't vanity, either. It was a fact. Vikings were uncommonly handsome men.

When she didn't answer his question but instead conversed with Zeb about his recipe for paella, ignoring him, he found himself getting annoyed. "Why is it you talk with Zeb but not me?"

"Because I'm mad at you."

"What did I do?"

"You told me you were gay."

"Oh." Of all the things that had happened today, that seemed the most unimportant. Still, he had to say, "How do you know I'm not gay?"

She gave him a not-very-complimentary head-to-toe scan before disclosing, "Because Zeb told me you weren't."

He flashed Zeb a wait-till-I-get-you-alone, you'll-be-sorry glare.

"Busted!" Zeb hooted, but then he put both hands in the air. "She asked, and I couldn't lie."

"It wouldn't be the first time."

"Just out of curiosity, what lamebrain reason did you have for telling her you were gay to begin with?" Zeb wanted to know.

"Yeah," Nicole agreed. "Tell us what your lamebrain reason was, lamebrain."

He did not like Nicole and Zeb getting so chummy. "You kept bird-dogging me, Nicole, asking about my secret. How could I tell you that I was there as a Viking vampire angel on a mission to save some SEALs?"

"Huh? What SEALs?"

"Sly and JAM were fanged by your buddy here

and were on a fast track to joining the ranks of the Lucies."

Now it was Zeb who was subjected to Nicole's glare.

Zeb shrugged. "It's what I do. Fanging." Then he gave Trond a look of one-upmanship and disclosed, "Trond fangs, too."

Nicole's head swiveled back to him.

"Except I do it to save souls." *Mostly.* "Zeb does it to condemn them to a life of horror and sublime evil." He sliced Zeb with a so-there! look of triumph.

"Alas, Trond is right," Zeb said, fluttering his long eyelashes at Nicole. *Since when do I notice the length of a man's eyelashes. Maybe I am becoming gay. Aaarrgh!* "But all is not lost. I am hoping that Trond will be able to save me."

Whaaat? That was so low, bringing Nicole into their demon/angel arguments, that Trond couldn't even speak at first. But then he didn't have to because Nicole asked what he'd meant about Sly and JAM being his mission in Coronado.

He explained what he and Karl had done with Sly and JAM.

"I knew there was something different about those two, but I never suspected . . ." She cocked her head to the side, pondering. "Karl is one of you, too?"

Trond nodded. "He's a young vangel, though. He died in Vietnam."

"Good Lord!" Nicole was shaking her head, with disbelief or wonder, he wasn't sure which.

There were a series of staccato announcements on the TV:

"News Flash: Navy SEAL mission in Davastan rescues female hostages thought to be long dead."

"The biggest U.S. military coup since the killing of Osama bin Laden."

"Najid bin Osama missing and thought dead."

"Welcome, panel of experts, to discuss today's surprising news." The news anchor then introduced high-level military and news personnel.

Nicole, Trond, and Zeb, without speaking, picked up their plates and beverages and moved to the living room where they could better view the news report, using a low coffee table to spread out their food. For more than an hour, the network reported evolving news, had its various experts discuss the implications of the event and speculate on what the future portended in the war against terrorism. They showed graphic depictions of the Davastan geography and Najid's compound, before and after the mission.

It was a scene Nicole could barely accept . . . her sitting in a seemingly normal living room, eating dinner, watching TV, with an angel vampire and a demon vampire. It was a story to tell her grandchildren some day. If she lived that long.

First on the TV were the poignant pictures of the ten girls from the Swiss boarding school being reunited with their families at the airport in Kabul, preparatory to their return to the U.S. Some were on crutches. Two were in wheelchairs. One was on a gurney.

"Wait a minute," she said. "How long have we been here? There's no way those families could have been notified, flown across the world, and been taking their girls home in the hours since this afternoon."

"A day and a half," Zeb said blithely.

"What?" she screeched. All the strange happenings today were beginning to accumulate inside her.

Soon she would have a full-blown panic attack, not that she'd ever had one. She blew out a few times in a huffing fashion since she'd once seen someone do that on TV, except that person had been blowing into a paper bag. "How can that be?"

Zeb shrugged and took a huge bite of dessert—a strawberry cheesecake he'd defrosted for them that was, incidentally, delicious. "Demon time is different from human time."

That was another thing. What was this demon/angel/human nonsense? "Are you saying that you are . . . dead?" she asked Zeb.

"You could say that." He paused a moment, pinching his skin playfully. "Yep, I'm dead. How about you, Trond?"

Trond scowled at him. He was doing a lot of scowling today, though why he should scowl was beyond her. She was the one who had reason to scowl. Big-time.

"Yes, I am dead."

Her jaw dropped, and she just gaped at him.

She could tell he was uncomfortable with that disclosure. She had been contemplating a relationship with a dead guy. How pathetic did that make her? But then, she recalled the infamous utility closet incident and had to admit Trond sure knew how to kiss for a dead man. Probably lots of years of practice.

"What are you thinking?" Trond asked her.

"Nothing," she said, and avoided his gaze.

But Zeb just had to remark to Trond, "Her eyes got hazy for a moment, and her lips parted. I daresay her nipples are hard. Arousal would be my guess."

To give him credit, Trond reached over and swatted Zeb upside his fool head.

"What? I was making a simple observation."

"Some observations should be kept to yourself," Trond told him.

"Oh." Zeb turned to her then. "My apologies, m'lady."

Their attention turned back to the TV as the news-caster reported that author Selah ad Beham had just passed away of massive internal injuries, and there was a discussion of her various books and their poor reception in some parts of the Arab world. Various representatives of women's organization spoke with regret of her passing and her legacy that would go on beyond her death.

Nicole made a mental note to buy her books once she returned home.

If she returned home. *Oh God! I can't think about that now.*

The minor English princess, a cousin of Princes William and Harry about fifteen times removed, was already giving interviews; somehow, she would profit from the experience. But then, Nicole conceded, the woman deserved whatever she could bleed from the pain she'd suffered. They all did.

After that, the husband of the Greek starlet was interviewed. According to the surviving hostages, Athena had been killed during the first week of her captivity. One of the servants had let slip to Selah, who'd told the others, that Athena's torture had gone too far and led to her unplanned death. Planned or not, Morris Goldstein, Athena's husband, was dev-astated and furious. He swore he would get ven-geance, even if it took all his fortune.

The young New York coed refused to be televised until her dental work could be completed. She would regain her looks, the commentator assured the audience, though that had to be the least of Beth's worries, in Nicole's opinion. Her father, like Goldstein, swore revenge and said that if his contributions to a militant Israeli group had been what caused the punishment inflicted on his daughter, he would double, no, triple his contributions in the future.

Then there were the on-site reports. Pictures were shown of the compound that seemed oddly undamaged, except for the wall of the harem chamber that the SEALs had blown open. None of the harem women had been harmed, but there were very few men left in the compound. That included Najid, who was mysteriously absent, though observers claimed he had been exiting the helo when attacked by hordes of huge scaly beasts, with fangs and long tails. There were also reports of odd, fanged creatures with wispy blue wings who fought the scaly beasts. The only thing left were piles of sulfurous slime all around the area.

Al Jazeera featured representatives of Najid's now almost defunct organization claiming the U.S. military had engaged in chemical warfare of some type and demanding a UN investigation. As for the reports of prowling beasts, the experts put that in the category of bigfoot sightings, or possibly figments of near-death imaginations.

Nicole recalled the scene that she'd seemed to see when Zeb had mysteriously whooshed them out of the harem building. Had it been her imagination, too? Confused, she turned to the two men, "Are you beasts like those they're describing?"

"Not exactly," Trond said.

"Trond is being kind. I am a beast exactly as they are describing. He, on the other hand, is another kind of beast. A good beast." Zeb smiled at Trond.

"Thanks a bunch," Trond said. "And all this buttering up isn't going to change anything, my demon friend."

"Notice that he called me friend," Zeb whispered loudly to Nicole. "I think I'm making progress."

She gave Trond a look of disapproval, as if he ought to be helping Zeb.

Zeb just blinked those long lashes of his with exaggerated innocence.

"Let's back up the bus," Nicole said. "Exactly what are you two yahoos, and exactly what do you do?"

They both explained their histories, their astonishing—if they could be believed—histories. When they finished, Nicole had several questions for Trond. Well, actually, dozens, but two or three would suffice for now.

"Do you have wings?"

"No, not yet, except sometimes I'm told there are hazy blue shapes back there. I do have shoulder bumps for them to emerge sometime."

She blinked at him with incredulity. An angel? This seemingly lazy, no-motivation guy was an angel?

"His one brother has wings," Zeb inserted.

Trond cast Zeb another scowl.

"One of the admirals?" she asked.

"Admirals?" Zeb scoffed.

"Never mind," Trond said when she arched her brows yet again. "No, it's a different brother, but even Vikar's wings come and go."

"How old are you, Trond?"

His face flushed and he said, "I died in the year 850, that would be one thousand, one hundred, sixty-three years ago. Add on the twenty-nine years I'd already lived, and you could say I'm one thousand, six hundred, and ninety-two years old." When she frowned, he raised his chin in a so-sue-me! fashion.

"A mere youngster!" Zeb said. "I've been around more than two thousand years."

Is it possible I'm dead, and this is Hell? No, I don't feel dead. "Is this like some kind of massive joke?"

"I wish!" he and Zeb said as one.

She noticed something else about the TV report. Not one single Navy SEAL or other military personnel who had been involved in the mission was being shown, which was as it should be. Anonymity was essential to the Silent Warriors. But, oh, Nicole was so proud to be a part of this elite group.

Something occurred to her then, something she should have thought of long before this. "We should call the command center and let them know we're alive." She almost giggled then when she realized she was the only one alive in this group.

"No can do," Zeb said, licking the last of the cheesecake off his fork. "No cell phone reception here."

"You have TV satellites that work, but no sat phones?" She raised her eyebrows skeptically. Her eyebrows were going to go into whiplash soon with all this sudden lifting.

"You could try." He tossed her a phone that he pulled from the back pocket of his jeans.

No surprise that she didn't even get a welcome screen.

She looked at Trond then, who didn't bother to pretend surprise. With a clucking sound of disgust, she tapped the mic embedded between her thumb and forefinger three times, four times in a row, before speaking into her hand. She should have had a response in her ear buds. Nothing. Even after several tries. With disgust, she tossed the ear buds, as well as the specially designed contact lenses that had long passed their usefulness. "How about Internet?"

"I don't have a computer," Zeb said.

"Everybody has a computer," she contended.

"Not much use for social networking where I come from."

She was pretty sure that was a gurgle of mirth that came out of Trond's mouth, but when she glanced his way, he just stared back at her innocently. Yeah, right, as innocent as a fox in a henhouse.

"Can't you send mind messages or something to your brothers?" she asked Trond.

"Mind messages?" He laughed.

"Yeah. Telepathy or whatever you call it."

"Let me see." He closed his eyes and scrunched his nose. Then he opened his eyes. "Nope. No telepathy today."

"My force shield is very strong," Zeb explained.

She suspected they were both playing with her.

After the newscast and a quick cleanup of the kitchen, they were all tired and went to their separate bedrooms. Nicole had so many questions hammering her brain that she thought she'd never be able to sleep. Instead, she conked out within minutes and didn't wake until a brilliant sunrise woke her the next morning.

When she walked out to the kitchen, Trond was already up and fiddling with the luxurious coffeemaker with all its bells and whistles, trying to figure out how it worked. She slapped his hands away and made quick work of getting it to percolate. Only then did she ask, "Where's Zeb?"

His somber face told the story before he said, "Gone."

Fear rippled over her skin for some reason. "Gone? Gone where?"

He pointed to a note on the counter, written in bold masculine script:

Trond and Nicole:

I had to leave in the middle of the night. Jasper is calling. I won't return to Horror right away. Will go elsewhere to get him off your track. If I don't return within five days, the shield around the bungalow will disappear and you'll be free to leave. If I don't return within five days, pray for me.

                                        Zebulan

P.S. Take advantage of this time alone. You may never get another chance. Believe me. I know.

"Who exactly is this Jasper?" Nicole asked Trond.

"Zeb's boss. King of the Lucipires. One of the fallen angels kicked out of heaven with Lucifer. Evil to the core."

"What will happen to Zeb for having helped us?"

Trond kept his back to her and didn't speak.

"Trond, answer me. What will his punishment be?"

Trond turned then, and the expression on his face

scared her. He was being wracked by some internal pain. "Unspeakable."

She leaned on the counter for support. "Tell me."

"My brother Vikar was held by Jasper for a mere week. The things they did to him were so vile and agonizing I cannot speak of them. It took months for Vikar's physical body to recover, and we vangels have a tremendous capacity to heal almost instantaneously. Zebulan, on the other hand, will probably suffer much, much more and for many, many years until he breaks, as he will surely do, eventually."

Nicole walked over to Trond, shaking with shock. "You have to help him."

"I wish I could, but I can't." He shook his head sorrowfully.

"Don't you dare," she sobbed, pounding her fists against his chest. "Don't you dare say that you can't help. That man gave himself up for us. I don't understand half of this crap, but I do know, if there's a God, He is merciful." She hesitated before asking, "Have you met God?"

He shook his head. "No, we deal with someone else."

"Who?" she jeered, still finding it hard to believe his story.

"St. Michael the Archangel."

She almost laughed, until she saw how serious he was. "Ask him to help Zeb then."

He groaned. "Mike . . . that's what we call him . . . is, let's just say, unbendable."

"Everyone can bend," she insisted. "Can you bear to hear another motivational quote?"

He crossed his eyes with frustration, which she would have thought was cute under other circumstances.

"Friends are God's way of taking care of us. If Zeb's action doesn't exemplify the true meaning of friendship, I don't know what does."

"You don't understand," he said, holding her tight in his arms, despite her struggles to escape. "There is no reversing the penances handed down from on high."

She looked up at him with tear-filled eyes, surprised to see that his eyes were wet with tears, too. "You have to at least try."

He sighed and said, "I'll try."

Twenty

The lull before the storm . . .

Could a man die of horniness?

Better question. Could a dead man die *again* of horniness?

Ever since he'd read that P.S. on Zeb's note, and understood perfectly what he'd been suggesting, Trond hadn't been able to stop thinking about Nicole and what he'd like to do to her, or with her.

It was understandable, of course. Plant the idea of sex in a red-blooded man's brain, even a dead one, and it was all he could think about. Like an erotic splinter.

Even worse, every time Nicole came within twenty feet of him, his cock went on hair trigger alert. He swore the fool organ had jackknifed at least twenty times in the past three hours.

"What's wrong with you?" Nicole asked as she walked in off the deck and watched him rubbing an ice cube over his forehead. What he should have been doing was rubbing the ice cube someplace else, someplace that he was hiding behind the counter.

"Do you have to walk around half naked?" he grumbled.

"What?" She looked down at herself. The temperature was at least a hundred today and the humidity high; a storm was brewing. Thus she was bare-footed, wearing one of Zeb's tank tops tied below her breasts, with a pair of his spandex shorts cut off mid-thigh which were too big in the waist, so they sat low on her hips. Then she looked back up at him. "You're walking around shirtless. You're more half naked than I am. Honestly! I repeat, what's wrong with you?"

"I think Zeb must have sprayed the area with some kind of aphrodisiac before he left. I'm so turned on by you I can barely walk. How's that for honesty?"

Instead of being shocked, or offended, she said, "Is that what it is? I wondered why those bumps on your shoulders turned me on."

My shoulder bumps turn her on? Oh, that's what a man wants to hear. Not! Well, he could give her tit for tat. "Your toes turn me on."

She curled her toes, as if to hide them.

"I never had a toe fetish before, but I think I do now."

She gulped several times, and he could swear her nipples peaked beneath the thin fabric, though maybe that was wishful thinking.

"Have you contacted your, uh, mentor yet?" she asked suddenly, which was a hard-on buzzkill if he'd ever heard one.

"I've tried." In fact, after examining the entire property this morning and determining that the shield was indeed as strong as kryptonite, he'd actually knelt and prayed to Mike on Zeb's behalf. He'd gotten no response, but that wasn't surprising.

Mike rarely answered prayers instantaneously, if at all. And he solved problems in his own way and his own good time.

"Does that mean he won't help?"

"He who?"

"St. Michael, or God, or all the legions of angels, or whoever your boss is."

All of the above, sweetling. All of the above. "Prayers are always answered, just not always in the way we want or expect."

"Like that Garth Brooks song?"

"Huh?" What a country music singer had to do with God was beyond him. He shook his head to clear it. "We just have to keep praying, and wait."

"We? You said 'we.' You don't expect me to pray, too, do you?"

He shrugged. "It wouldn't hurt."

"I don't even remember how."

"No expertise needed. Just 'Hey, God! Long time no talk! I need a little help here.' Or something to that effect."

She looked at him as if he'd lost his mind.

He had. That, and a few other things, like his self-control. Next, his fangs would be coming out to scare the hell out of her.

"I will say one thing, though, Nicole. We're here because Mike wants us to be."

"Huh?"

"His powers are greater than Jasper's or anything Zeb might put in place. If Mike didn't want us to be here, we wouldn't be."

"I don't understand. Why would he do that?"

"Most of the things Mike makes us do rarely make sense. At first. In the end, sometimes his reasoning becomes clear. Sometimes not."

She pushed past him into the kitchen and made a pitcher of lemonade with ice and fruit slices floating on top. Filling two glasses, she handed one to him and said, "Come on. Let's go out on the deck and you can regale me with all your deep dark secrets."

His you-know-what shot out, like the back end of a bird dog on point, not just at her mention of his dark secrets, which were darkly sexual, but at the appearance of her rear end as she walked before him. Up, down, up down, up, down. God bless spandex! *Is that a blasphemy?* He hoped not.

The sky was still a clear blue, and even though there were distant, dark clouds and an electricity in the air portending the coming storm, it was a beautiful tropical setting anyone would appreciate. The lush plants about the property with their fragrant flowers only added to the allure.

Sitting in side-by-side teak loungers, which Trond had deliberately placed under the porch overhang for shade, he told her stories about St. Michael the Archangel. First of all, how they called him Mike with irreverence, just to annoy the hoity-toity archangel. How Mike always called them Viking, with equal irreverence. Usually it was, "Can't you do anything right, Viking?" or "Did you really think near-sex didn't count as a sin, Viking?"

Then he told her how Mike had talked Harek into setting up an archangel website, still a work in progress, so that the celestial beings could get in tune with the twenty-first century. When some of the VIK had resisted, Mike had replied, "God doesn't care if his followers come to him via a palm-waving crowd on a Jerusalem roadway, or via some palatial cathedral, or via the Internet superhighway. Just so they come."

Nicole was wiping tears of laughter from her eyes when he told her about some of the jobs he'd had over the years, including his days as a gladiator fighting lions in the Colosseum. "You do not want to get up close and personal with lion breath," he assured her.

Her eyes went wide with interest when he told her about the run-down, long-abandoned castle in Transylvania, Pennsylvania, built a hundred years ago by an eccentric lumber baron, that his brother Vikar had been sent to renovate, and was still renovating, and would be renovating for centuries to come. She giggled when he described the antics of the strange town that used vampirism as a tourist attraction. And he told her about the extended family of vangels, aside from his six brothers, hundreds of them, who inhabited the castle from time to time, including Lizzie Borden, their cook, and a witch who was always threatening to put a curse on the male vangels' favorite body parts when they misbehaved, and even the young teenage vampire angel Armod, who fashioned himself a reincarnated Michael Jackson. "You do not want to see a vangel moonwalk," Trond assured her.

When he took a break in his long-winded blathering, she smiled at him. "You really are one of those . . . things. Aren't you?"

"If you mean a vangel, for my sins, yes, I am."

Then, she homed in on the least important thing he had said, or maybe not so unimportant, "What is near-sex?"

"I'll tell you later," he choked out. He didn't think Zeb's thong—yes, he was wearing a new pair of Zeb's thongs—could stand the strain. It was the only new underwear he could find in the drawers. It was either that or go commando, as many of the Navy SEALs did. He hoped his brothers never found out; he would never live it down.

"No, seriously, sex is sex, right?"

He rolled his eyes. "Let's just say when you belong to a society that proclaims sex outside of marriage as a mortal sin, a man must be inventive. I have the distinction of being the master of near-sex."

She smiled.

He loved when she smiled at him. She did it so rarely.

She tapped her forefinger on her closed lips as she pondered his words of nonwisdom.

He loved her lips, closed or otherwise. But the subject they were discussing was a dangerous one for him. A temptation.

"I imagine chastity itself would be a sort of punishment," she continued. "For some people, anyhow."

"Oh, it is. Believe you me, it is."

"So, sex with penetration is a big sin, but near-sex isn't?"

He almost swallowed the lemon in his glass at her explicit word and the image it brought forth. *Oh damn! Can I really engage in such graphic talk without giving her a demonstration? Down, boy, down!* He wasn't about to look at his lap. He didn't have to. "No, I didn't say that near-sex is permitted. I'm just hoping the penance is not so great. Of course, I told my brother Vikar about near-sex, and his experiments landed him in a marriage for life."

"Vangels can marry?"

"No. Vikar is the exception. Besides, there are too many complications." Like the VIK staying the same age and his wife aging and eventually dying. Like vangels being unable to have children. Like centuries with the same partner, if they could both live the same life span, would be a penance in itself.

"And you can get off with near-sex?"

I should go take a cold shower. No, I can't stand. Please, don't let me disgrace myself like an untried, overeager boyling with his first tup. Think about something else. Stinky gammelost. Cold Norse winters. Fish guts. When he was under control, he said in as calm a voice as possible, "Yes."

Luckily she changed the subject. "Your family sounds wonderful . . . eerily weird, but wonderful. And the castle, I would love to see it sometime."

"Maybe you can," he offered before he had a chance to check himself, "*when* we get out of here."

"I like your confidence."

"Now, you tell me about yourself," he said, "but hold that thought. I'll be right back." He went inside to Zeb's fully-stocked fridge and came back with a plate of assorted cheeses, olives, a peeled and sectioned orange, several clumps of succulent red and green grapes, and crackers, placing it on a small table between them with little cocktail napkins that said a lot about Zeb. He also refilled their glasses of lemonade.

"This is nice," she said. "If it weren't for my worry over Zeb, and our failure to report back to headquarters, and my sister, I could almost relax and enjoy this brief respite. I can't remember the last time I took a vacation."

He wasn't surprised. "I noticed you're not jumping up and down with constant—"

"—peppiness?" she finished for him, repeating back his criticism of her in the past.

"Now tell me about your life. It can't all have been bad."

"It wasn't." She told him about her childhood when her paternal grandparents, immigrants from Greece, had been alive and lived down the street from them. Their Old World values had been implanted in her early and deeply and were what eventually had her joining the WEALS.

"Were you always so . . . peppy?" he teased.

"I was, actually, and I confess, I was even a high school cheerleader. I lost it for those few years with Billy."

Trond teased her about her energetic attitude, but deep down he had to admit that inside his slothful, nonenergetic self was not peace and calm, but dead chaos. If a person didn't care, he didn't get hurt. Could it be that apathy was a defense mechanism? Could it be that subconsciously, all those years ago, that's what he'd been doing? Seemed rather preposterous to him, but an interesting idea to ponder on a long, lonely night, which this was not.

" . . . but I won't apologize for my personality. Uh-uh!" Nicole had continued talking while his mind had wandered. "It's too easy to be a pessimist and depressed. Even if I have to force myself to be bubbly with all my motivational tapes and stuff, I'd rather that than the opposite."

He put up his hands in mock surrender. "Hey, your personality is growing on me."

"Is it?" she asked, suddenly serious.

He reached over and linked one hand with hers. Their gazes held. "Yeah, it is."

They both felt the erotic shock between their clasped hands.

"Do you think it's some demon dust Zeb sprinkled around?" she asked huskily, puzzled by this strong attraction between them. "Oh, I admit, it was there before, but not so powerful, or compelling."

"I hope this is Zeb's doing," he said, because if it wasn't that, it was something more. Something bigger that he couldn't begin to contemplate or handle.

Sweet surrender! . . .

Nicole was strung tighter than a sexual Slinky, and she didn't know how much longer she could hold the coils of her control together.

As they ate leftover paella and reheated bread for dinner, she watched Trond eat, fascinated by his lips.

When he steepled his fingers and pinioned her with his take-no-mercy eyes, she whispered, "Mercy!"

When he walked outside to check the shutters in preparation for the hurricane that was expected to sweep the Caribbean, according to the TV, which had just gone on the blink due to the storm, his wide shoulders, slim waist, and hard butt drew her eyes. In fact, the backs of his knees, of all things, attracted particular notice. And, yes, she was developing a toe thing, too.

He had pulled on a T-shirt with the message: "Heaven: The Best Gated Community Ever" on the front, and on the back, "Hell: The Worst Gated Community Ever." You had to appreciate a man with a sense of humor, even it had been borrowed from Zeb.

He brushed past her to get a screwdriver from the

kitchen utility drawer, and she barely stifled a groan at the sexual zing. How could she have such a powerful reaction to someone who was *dead*?

When he looked at her with his intense blue eyes, turning strangely, hue by hue, to a silvery grayish blue, she knew he shared her growing arousal.

She was even turned on by the slight presence of his fangs, a sign of the testosterone raging inside his body.

The question was: What would they do about it?

The answer came that evening when the lights went out, the candles were lit, and they drank not one, or two, but three glasses of Zeb's fine red wine. The house shook, the shutters rattled, lightning struck, and it was nothing compared to the storm brewing between them.

She headed toward the closed glass doors to stare at the stormy sea, and he came up behind her.

"I surrender," he said, rubbing himself against her behind, his hands braced on the glass on either side of her head.

"Me too," she groaned. "Won't you get in trouble for this?"

"Oh yeah. You play, you pay." He nibbled at her neck, exposed by her hair being piled atop her head with a rubber band. "You have no idea how much I want to bite you."

"Maybe later."

His body jerked reflexively against her. Then he did in fact nip at the sweet curve where her throat and shoulder met. "Tease!"

"I haven't begun to tease you yet," she promised, and tried to turn within the bracket of his arms.

"Not yet." He winked at her. "I have plans."

"Oh boy."

"I'm a man. Not a boy," he growled. "That you will discover before this night is over."

"Promises, promises," she taunted him playfully.

Outside the bungalow, it was black, except for the occasional lightning, but there was enough glow from the many candles they'd lit that they could see their images in the dark glass.

Because of the storm that battered the cottage, because of the danger that hovered around them outside this temporary safe harbor, the world seemed to narrow to just this room and the two of them. All her senses were on high alert. The sound of thunder and crashing waves. The scent of Trond's skin, soapy clean and all male. The feel of his warm breath on her neck and his body pressing against her back. His male essence cloaked her in an erotic fog, as dark and enticingly dangerous as the mists outside.

How can he be dead?

"Let's play a game," he suggested as he lifted her shirt over her head, leaving her bare from the waist up, her breasts pressed against the cool glass being whipped by the rain. "Do you like games, Nicole?"

"Like Monopoly?"

He laughed and put the flats of both hands inside the waistline of her cut-off biker shorts, shoving them down to the floor, where she kicked them aside. "No, dearling, nothing like Monopoly. More like tennis where the ball, so to speak, is in your court, then my court, then yours, and so on. Or a roller coaster, with all its ups and downs. No, the best comparison would be a play we are putting on, with many, many acts."

"Would there be a grand finale?"

"Definitely." He put his hands back on the glass, in fact his entire forearms on either side of her head.

She sensed, rather than saw, his smile behind her.

"But each act would have its own satisfying conclusion, if you get my meaning."

"And the rules of this game?"

"We take turns being the director. And one thing, and only one thing, can take place during each act until the last one. Kissing. Touching. Looking. Talking. We will be creative. I'll go first. My act will be called Statues. What do you think?"

She turned in the circle of his arms, stood on her tiptoes, and looped her arms around his neck so her breasts were even with his chest. The pleasure was so intense that the blood drained from her head, and she had to hold on to his shoulders for support. "How come you get to go first?" she finally managed to squeak out.

"Because I'm bigger, and I thought of it, and . . . because I say so." His hands cupped her buttocks, tugging her closer into the cradle of his hips. "That. Feels. So. Good." He seemed to be having trouble getting the words out, and he let her slip back to her feet.

Even that slipping was an erotic experience. "Okay, Mr. Director," she agreed, her words a little wobbly, too. "So, first act, Statues. I assume you've put on this particular game . . . uh, play before."

Now he was swaying from side to side, brushing his chest hairs over her already hardened nipples. "You don't play fair," she complained, halfheartedly. His grin told her loud and clear that he knew very well what he was doing to her raging libido. "If you're not careful, the finale is going to come . . . *come* being the key word . . . before there's ever a first act."

He let her put a little space between then, but

only so he could give her a full-body survey, one that caused the corded vein in his neck to pulse. She would bet her boxed set of *Mind over Matter* tapes that another part of his body was pulsing, too. She'd deliberately not allowed herself to look "down there" yet, wanting to prolong the anticipation.

"No, sweetling," he finally answered her question, "I have never played this game before. Near-sex has many variations. This is one I was saving for someone special."

She was pleased by that admission, but this was a game, and she couldn't let him win so early with a mere compliment or two. So, she slanted her eyes up at him and boasted, "You have no idea how good I am at games. I was the tennis champ in high school, and I adore roller coasters."

The edge of his lips quirked into that lopsided grin she found so boyishly endearing, but there was nothing of the boy in the feral predatory gleam in his now fully silver eyes. "Game on, sweetling."

Twenty-one

**He was no gambler,
but tonight he was a winner . . .**

Sometimes life deals you dream cards, and Trond was looking at a royal flush.

He stepped back to get a better look at Nicole's naked body as she leaned back against the dark window. He wished he had about two dozen more candles, and a floodlight or two, to get the full effect. Still, he could see enough that his knees felt weak, and his heart started thumping against his rib cage.

Nicole Tasso in full military ruck was attractive. Nicole Tasso in the nude was sex personified. Especially when she struck a pose with her arms raised above her head after releasing the rubber band on her hair and gave him a little Mona Lisa smile. Shy she was not! Which he considered another dream card in this game they were playing.

She hadn't been lying. She was a good game player. Really good.

"Do you think I'm a slut?" she asked suddenly.

Whaaat? Oh, she must mean a wanton. Modern women were so strange about their inhibitions. "Not yet. Hopefully soon."

"Don't you think we should level the playing field?" she asked in a smoky voice . . . a voice made husky by her arousal, he hoped.

"Oh?"

"Drop the shorts, cowboy."

He smiled. *Forget inhibitions. My Nicole apparently has none. Did I just say . . . think . . . "my Nicole"? Yikes! But, really, you have to love a woman who knows her mind.* And being a cooperative kind of guy, he did as she'd ordered. But slowly, as he shrugged out of his shorts and undergarment at the same time. Hey, he was a game player, too. With a lot more years under his belt, and below, too.

Her quick intake of air through parted lips told him loud and clear that she liked what she saw when she gave him tit for tat in the full-body survey business. Which was just the reaction a virile man wanted in a situation like this. Ergolf the Arrogant once had a bawdy maid laugh when he dropped his braies. A cockstand leveler, if there ever was one.

"Are all vangels so . . ." she waved a hand at his rampant erection " . . . endowed?"

"No, only me."

She arched her brows.

"Well, Vikings are known to be uncommonly endowed." He thought for a moment. He was pretty sure women wanted a man with something substantial in his package, but maybe she was different. "Don't you like . . . endowed?" He felt himself wilt a little at that prospect.

"I love endowed."

Wilting forestalled.

He led her to the middle of the room, closer to the candles, and arranged her body in the way he wanted. "Remember, the main rule in Statues is that you can't move, no matter what I do." During her momentary silence while she pondered the implications of his rule, he used his foot to spread her bare feet slightly apart. Then, he raised her arms so that her fingers combed through her hair, raising the swaths up and off her neck. Her position caused her breasts to jut out, as if begging for his attention, which they would get, eventually.

He moved behind her, needing to get his arousal under control without her noticing his dilemma.

"So, do you always go freestyle?" The question was casual, but her tone was pure arousal. She must be trying to get herself under control, too.

He couldn't allow that. With just his fingertips touching her, he feathered matching lines on each side of her body, from neck to shoulder to elbow to wrist. As expected, goose bumps followed in their wake.

But she didn't move. Good girl! Instead, she asked in the calmest of voices, "You never answered my question about your lack of underwear." She was good, really good if she could ask such a nonsexual question in the midst of this sexual heat that was enveloping them.

She must not have noticed that thong. Good! "I usually wear boxer briefs, but not always. Sometimes I wear the hokey boxers my brothers pick up in their travels, like the 'Kiss My Wings' one with wings right over, well, you can guess where, or the 'Trust Me, I'm an Angel' one, or the 'My Halo Is Bigger Than Your Halo' with a little strategically placed gold ring. But, today, the only new under-wear I could find of Zeb's was a package of thongs." He grimaced with distaste.

The whole time he was blathering, he was ad-miring her backside. Really, a woman's form, even her backside, was like a work of art. He could un-derstand how the finest sculptors loved doing the human body. Her shoulders were muscled from all the physical activity of WEALS, but not so much to make her masculine. Her waist was narrow and ta-pered over pretty hips enclosing the luscious globes of her buttocks. In fact, he went down on one knee for a second and licked first one, then the other of the tempting palettes. He would save the crease for later.

She yelped, "Trond!" and almost shot forward but he stood quickly and held her in place by the waist, then made sure she resumed her former pose. "Tsk, tsk, tsk, Nicole, have you forgotten the rules already. No moving."

She said something under breath that sounded like, "Just wait until act two."

Continuing his study of her body, he noted how he especially liked the twin indents at the small of her back, and the dimples at the backs of her knees. He didn't dare touch her yet, except for those impul-sive butt licks, for fear he wouldn't be able to stop. And he had much to do before he reached that point. He realized belatedly that Nicole was laughing.

"What?"

"You mentioned thongs. Zeb bought those thongs to use as slings to hold up his cantaloupes that have been rotting on the ground in his garden."

"Whaaat? That's the most ridiculous thing I've ever heard." He felt a little bit foolish, but how was he to have known that? "Is that a demon gardening thing?"

"No. A Hint from Heloise, or Eloise, or whatever, that he was going to try. Those household hint mavens are always suggesting you improvise with things around the house, like old pantyhose or worn-out thongs. Unfortunately, Zeb had neither around. So he bought some for his garden. An experiment."

"I can't believe I'm discussing gardens when I have the most beautiful woman in the world standing before me in all her naked glory."

"I can't believe you are, either," and defying his order not to move, she turned. "I want to see what you're doing."

Zeb allowed himself to feast then. A visual feast.

Her breasts were round, like the perfect halves of large navel oranges. Their creamy skin only acted as a backdrop to pink areolas, also perfect circles, with rose-hued nipples in their center, engorged with her want of him. Then he looked downward. "I wondered if you would be blonde there," he remarked huskily. He also wondered if her nether curls would be damp with what Vikings called woman dew in the old days. He would find out soon enough. "Blonde is nice, but I prefer your natural color. How long will it take to grow out?"

"As soon as I can get a bottle of hair dye, I'll be mousy brown again." She seemed rather shy at his examining her there and squirmed a little.

"Light brown, with honey highlights," he corrected, patting the soft curls. That's the only touch he could allow himself now, lest he begin delving for . . . honey. "Your brown hair has highlights of pure gold."

"You really are good at gaming."

"I forgot this was a game," he told her in a raw voice of utter candor. "I want to make love with you. Every way I know how. I want to create new ways of loving. With you. I want . . ." He let his words trail off because that was the throbbing element in his body at the moment. *Want.* He *wanted.* So many things. And they all revolved around this woman.

"Then do it," she whispered in an equally raw voice.

He lifted her with arms around her waist and walked her to one of the recliners, kicking it with his toes into an almost level position. Then he tossed her down and crawled up and over her. Shifting this way and that till he got their body parts aligned, especially his unwieldy erection, he then leaned on his elbows over her and smiled.

She smiled back.

"Do you like lip kisses, Nicole?" he asked, pressing his lips lightly against hers. "Or would you prefer that I move right to your breasts?" He raised himself on one elbow so that he could palm a breast, rubbing in a circular fashion. "Or shall we go directly to the main course?" Back to being braced on both elbows, he thrust his cock against her female parts several times in succession.

"All of the above," she whispered, her hands already framing his face and pulling him down to her. Against his mouth, she inquired impishly, "Are we still playing Statues?"

"Movable Statues," he decided, nipping at her bottom lip, which was curved into a smile.

He kissed her then. For a long time. With his fingers tunneled in her hair, gripping her head. Usually, he spent only a moment on a woman's body above her neck, but he found himself relishing all the different aspects of her mouth. He molded her lips into changing patterns until he got the perfect fit. He forced her mouth open with his thrusting tongue. He settled into slow, drugging kisses, then took her mouth with a savage intensity.

And she kissed him back. With equal fervor. Not at all repulsed by his fangs. In fact, she seemed to enjoy licking at them in fascination. Her tongue seared his when she dared to enter his mouth. Then she sucked his tongue deep into her own mouth.

Between kisses, he whispered things to her, naughty things he wanted to do to her later.

Between kisses, Nicole, bless her wanton heart, whispered things back at him, naughty things she would do to him later.

They were both panting for breath when he raised his head. Staring down at her, he saw her honey eyes were dilated and dark with arousal. Her sweet mouth was swollen from his kisses.

He moved down her body then, placing his face over her breasts. At first he just lapped the outer edges, moving closer and closer to her areolas and then her pebbled nipples. When he flicked his tongue over one of them, she let loose with a long moan. Her limbs went stiff. And the joining of her thighs spasmed against him.

She was coming to orgasm from this little bit of sex play? By the runes! This was going to be a night to remember.

"I am so embarrassed," she said, turning her face to the side. "It's just that it's been so long, and my breasts are sensitive, and—"

"Shh, dearling, your pleasure is a compliment to me." He proceeded to minister to her breasts in earnest then. And for a long time. He kissed the taut nipples and tantalized the buds with the tip of his tongue before plucking on them gently with his teeth. Each time he sucked on them, deeply, he could tell there was an answered draw in her woman's channel because she raised her hips in counterpoint and moaned her unceasing pleasure.

Trond had read a woman's magazine of Alex's one time, not that it was his usual practice. Most of them just made mock of men. In any case, this magazine article said a woman's mammary glands caused men's neurological systems to shut down. That was probably true. He did love looking and touching a woman's breasts, and most especially he was enjoying Nicole's.

He kissed his way over her muscle-honed abdomen, tonguing her belly button that was sans its gold ring today, jewelry not permitted in active military ops, but he remembered how it twinkled there that night in the tavern. Her belly was slightly concave with a tattoo on her right hip, which he traced with his fingertips and then the tip of his tongue. It was a letter V.

Raising his head slightly, he arched his brows at her. "The letter V?"

"For victory. I got it after I left Billy. And it symbolizes some of the other hurdles I've overcome as well."

"I like it," he said.

He skipped over the part of her body he most wanted to feast on, and instead used his fingers to touch and his mouth to kiss down one thigh and knee and calf and ankle and foot and toes, then up the other leg till he was at sex central. He knelt on the floor, took her by the rump, and yanked her forward, then used his shoulders to separate her thighs wide, placing her feet on the edge of the chair. In fact, he pulled the table between the two chairs closer. It had two candles on it. Reaching behind him to the coffee table, he picked up the two candles there, too, so that he had more light to see that hidden part of the female anatomy that was so fascinating to men.

"I don't know, Trond," she protested, trying to draw her knees together.

He wouldn't let her. "I want to see."

"I'm too open." She was leaning up on her elbows, looking down at him.

He shook his head. "Not open enough." He paused then. "I will stop if you want me to, but . . . let me, please."

She nodded hesitantly.

For a second, he just looked at her there, the golden curls glistening with her arousal. He knew without checking that his cock would have a bead of semen on it, as well . . . man dew. The anticipation of touching and tasting her there was wonderfully unbearable.

With trembling fingers, he parted her folds and could have cheered at the slickness that beckoned him. With just one fingertip, he traced a line from just above her clitoris, that knot of nerves where a woman's joy was centered, down the side almost to her bottom, then back up the other side. While she watched him, he put the fingertip in his mouth and sucked. "Sweet." Returning to that swollen bud, he touched it lightly, then flicked it from side to side.

She arched her back up off the recliner, keening, "Too much, too damn much!"

"Never enough," he murmured back.

At the same time he put his mouth to the bud and began to suckle her there, he stuck a middle finger inside her woman's channel. Immediately, her inner muscles began to convulse around his finger and she thrust her hips against the intrusion. Out of her parted lips, she kept moaning, "Oh, oh, oh, oh!"

Finally, when her body slumped, he'd had more than he could handle. Lifting her limp body up higher on the recliner, he laid himself over her again, and with his cock nestled in her folds, he began to pump himself to a raging climax. In the end, his head and shoulders reared back and he shot his semen against her folds. It wasn't the kind of sex he would like to have with her, but it was still good.

When he was able to move, and it took a while, he kissed her lightly on the lips and said, "Stay here. I'll be right back." Her eyes were still closed, and she didn't respond, but there was a smile on her lips.

He went into the bathroom and cleaned himself off, then came back with a warm soapy cloth to do the same for Nicole, who was sitting up now, staring at him as if in a daze. Thank goodness the chair was leather and easily wiped off.

She stood and stretched, then said, "If that was near-sex, I'd like to know what not-so-near sex is."

"You liked it?"

"Wasn't that obvious? So, are we still playing games? Is the play still on?"

"If you want," he replied hesitantly.

"Definitely. Act one is over. Time for the lady director to start the second act. Against the wall, my friend, I'm going to show you how we female soldiers torture our prisoners."

Trond wasn't sure he liked the idea of that. Oh, who was he kidding? Anything she did to him would be a pleasure. If she breathed on him, he would probably come again.

"You are not to move, unless I tell you to," she said. "You could say this is Statues Redux."

He braced himself facing the wall between the living room and the kitchen with his arms folded over his head, his forehead pressing against the plaster.

She traced the palms of her hands over his shoulders and upper arms, then seemed to be fascinated by the bumps on his shoulder blades. She touched them, she kissed them, she pressed her fingertips against them as if she expected something would pop out. "And you will have wings here someday?"

"Possibly."

"Do you like that idea?"

"Not particularly. Not any more than I like the fangs. They are a fact of my existence."

She kissed her way down his back and seemed to like the small of his back the way he liked the small of hers.

"I really, really like your butt," she said with a laugh.

He laughed, too. It was funny the way modern women fixated on the buttocks, their own and men's, as well. He couldn't recall any women in Viking times ever commenting on that part of his body. Now, his cock, that was a different matter.

"Marie and I were talking about it one day. Marie called it prime."

"You and Marie were discussing my ass?" Now, that surprised him.

"I like the backs of your knees, too," she said. "They have dimples."

"I do not have dimples. Anywhere," he insisted.

"Turn around, big boy," she ordered then. "Let's see what you've got."

Plenty. That's what he had. Again. Already.

"A Blue Steeler," she said with admiration, running her fingertips briefly over the blue veins of his thick shaft that reared out from the thatch of black hair at his groin. In invitation.

Instead of taking him up on the unspoken invitation—he had visions of her leaping up with her legs wrapped around his waist, undulating him to another orgasm—she examined his nipples with her fingertips, then her teeth and mouth, suckling him. He liked it, but it was not where he wanted her mouth at the moment, not that he would expect *that* of her.

But, of course, she did just the opposite of what he'd expected. She sank to her knees, gripped his buttocks with the fingertips of both hands, then spread her lips over the flaring head of his cock.

His mind went blank, and he almost came. "Easy, now, Nicole. You don't have to do this."

"Yes, I do," she said, looking up and holding his gaze as she took him inch by inch inside her mouth. Her eyes were large and liquid with her own excitement. Her cheeks hollowed as she drew on him.

That she would do this for him touched a spot deep inside him, one he'd sheltered and kept hidden for ages. The intensity of feeling for her that spread through him like wildfire almost scared him into pushing her away from him. But he didn't, of course. What man would?

He tunneled his fingers in her hair then and guided her, his heavy-lidded eyes following her every move. For the next five minutes, or was it five seconds, she brought him to the epitome of male ecstasy.

When it was over, he sank to the floor with her, succumbing to the sensory overload. With her just cradled at his side, their backs to the wall, he kissed the top of her head. "Thank you," he said.

"My pleasure." She cuddled closer.

For several minutes, they just sat, listening to the winds batter the bungalow that had apparently been built to withstand such storms. Who knew when the electricity would come back? Who cared?

Finally, she drew away from him and smiled. "So, what's the score so far in our game?"

He didn't hesitate for one moment before saying, "You win. Hands down, sweetling. You win."

Twenty-two

Act four . . . or was it five? . . . and oops! . . .

Nicole was in love with Trond.

Unbelievable as it was, unacceptable as it was, she had to admit she'd fallen, head over boondockers, for the big galoot. And it was unbelievable that it had happened so quickly and with a man she had taken such a dislike to, initially. And it was unacceptable because the guy was a freakin' vampire angel, for heaven's sake!

Not that she would tell him about her love.

He would probably laugh at her.

It was now roughly two a.m. He'd made love to her on the recliner. She'd made love to him against the wall. They'd made love to each other standing in the dark shower. And none of it with penetration. Amazing!

By feel she'd made her way to the kitchen to get a drink of water while Trond was trying to batten down one of the shutters that kept banging in the wind. He came up behind her, soaking wet from the rain, and hugged her from behind.

"You're wet and cold," she protested.

"Warm me up then," he said, then complained, "You got dressed,"

"Just with a T-shirt."

He inserted a hand under the hem to check and smacked her rump lightly for good measure.

"Let's go," he said then, grinning at her. "We haven't had near-sex in at least, oh, fifteen minutes."

She grinned back at him, already becoming accustomed to his fangs that he apparently couldn't control when in a state of "feverish arousal," his words. Seemed to her, his "feverish arousal" was lasting a long time, which she chose to view as a compliment. "Poor boy! Fifteen whole minutes!"

They both picked up candles to carry to his bedroom. When they got there, he flipped the coverlet off, totally. Then, eyeing the sheets and her, he said, "I have an idea."

She had to laugh at that. "Honey, you have way too many ideas."

"Are you tired? Do you want to sleep?" The hurt, puppy dog expression on his face was almost comical, especially with the fangs.

"No, Trond, I'm not tired."

Immediately, his expression went joyful. He picked her up by the waist—a habit of his—and tossed her up and onto the bed, facedown. He crawled up over her, not like a puppy, but like a cat, a big scary cat. In fact, he growled in her ear and whispered, "The things I am going to do to you, lady!"

"Should I be scared?" She turned her face to the side on the pillow and nipped at his chin.

"Very, very scared."

For the next hour, and, yes, it was at least that

long, they tortured each other with bone-melting caresses and multiple orgasms, for both of them.

He forced her to all fours and made love to her doggie-style, without actual intercourse. The way he tortured her front while engaged in that particular bout had her screaming an unending orgasm at the end.

They rolled over and over, taking turns on top as they set each other aflame, fueling the fires of desire over and over. It was too much and not enough.

This time when she forced him to his back, perspiration beaded her forehead. Her blood raced alarmingly as she rode the back side of his penis that lay pressed against his belly by the weight of her body. Suddenly, accidentally, she had pressed against the tip of him and he was inside her, halfway.

"Oops!" she said.

His body went stiff, and he shut his eyes, clenching his teeth.

"I'm sorry." She started to lift herself off him.

He slapped his hands on her butt to hold her in place. "Do. Not. Move."

To her humiliation, her inner muscles began to clench and unclench him. She was having a blasted orgasm with him only partially penetrating her.

He groaned. A long groan.

"Am I hurting you? We can stop now. No harm, no foul."

He started to laugh then, and she felt it right down to his erection that seemed to be shaking inside her. "Stop now and I might have to kill you," he said.

On those words, he flipped her over and slammed into her body, full-tilt boogie all the way to heaven, or at least her womb. Glancing downward, she saw his dark pubic hairs blend with her blonde ones in an oddly touching way, like they were meant to be together, those hairs.

Trond was a big man. When she said he filled her, she meant he *filled* her.

"Hold on tight, sweetling. I haven't done this in two hundred years and I have a fierce need."

He wasn't kidding. So energetic were his thrusts that he actually lifted her off the bed, moving her across the mattress until she hit the headboard. The wet sounds of their mutual slickness was carnal music they created together.

He told her what it was like to be inside her, like a tight glove of warm syrup.

She told him what it was like to have him inside her, like silk on hot marble.

With chest heaving, his hips rolled wildly, and he continued to ride her hard. He couldn't seem to stop himself. She didn't want him to stop.

She caressed his shoulders. She soothed him with warm whispers of encouragement. "It's okay. Don't worry. I can take it."

In the heated pitch of excitement, he whispered against her ear, "You are more than I ever expected or wanted, more than any woman I have ever had. You are . . . everything."

She wasn't sure what that meant, but she was pleased nonetheless.

The hurricane was hitting full-force outside if the whistle of the wind was any indication, but it was nothing compared to the storm in the bedroom. Trond became the wild creature he was beneath the civilized soldier. His eyes were shards of pure silver now. His fangs were extended. His nostrils flared.

She wasn't scared of him, though.

Even while he started the short, pounding thrusts

into her body, and she felt herself literally melting around him, her female ejaculation wetting his balls, she gently fingered the edges of his damp, military-short hair and caressed the rigid cords of his neck. Then she held on for life to his wing bumps.

Trond threw his head back and roared his male triumph as he began the crescendo to his climax. Something pulled deeply inside Nicole, and her inner body welcomed his finish with a nonending series of hard spasms that tried to keep him inside her, and thus increased the delicious friction.

They came together and he fell upon her, holding her tightly, as if he never wanted to let her go.

She didn't mind his weight. In fact, she relished it. And, although she didn't say the words aloud, as she ran her palms across his back, caressing, she thought them.

I will love you forever.

The end was fast approaching . . .

Four days later, Trond had made love more times and more ways, some of them rather amazing, so that it was a wonder his cock wasn't worn down to a nub. Instead, it seemed to be growing with each use, so much so it was almost embarrassing. Well, not really.

They'd changed and washed bed linens so often it was a wonder the threads weren't worn out. And wasn't it amazing how many Egyptian cotton sets Zeb had, all with fifteen-hundred thread counts from high-end department stores?

He had no idea when Zeb had started the "clock" on his five-day shield, but it could be as early as

tomorrow when he and Nicole left this bungalow.
He had mixed feelings about that. He wanted to go
back and complete his missions, and yet this inter-
lude with Nicole had been a time he would never
forget, especially since he would be paying for it for
God or St. Michael only knew how long. Even so, he
wasn't ready for this time with her to end.

There were some problems that niggled at him,
though.

One, every time he looked at Nicole, and not just
when she was naked and doing something wonderful to him, he got this odd ache in his chest. Like
heartburn, but not. He was afraid to think what it
might mean.

Second, he was worried about Zeb. Very. Worried.

Third, his feeding off JAM when he'd saved him
should have lasted him for at least a month, but he
had been outside in an extremely hot and bright sun
too many hours each day here, including days of
clearing up the storm debris. Without Fake-O or a
blood ceorl as a backup, his skin was growing paler.
He hadn't lost energy yet, but he would. Feeding
would have to be a top priority on his return.

Four, Mike had been uncommonly absent. It had
to be deliberate.

In the meantime, he was trying to stay away from
Nicole. He could literally smell her blood, and it was
driving him nigh crazy with the urge to feed on her.

He was watching a sports channel on the TV, sitting on the low sofa (the recliner posed too many
memories), his long legs propped on the coffee
table. He wore a shirt with his shorts today because
Nicole had told him repeatedly how his chest made
her horny, and she had a habit of touching his wing
bumps every time she passed by. She came into the

room, carrying a basket loaded with tomatoes, lettuce, carrots, onions, green and red peppers, grapes, cantaloupes, and oranges from an overladen tree outside. In fact, grapes were boiling on the stove right now to be made into jelly.

"Nicole! There isn't any way we can eat all that stuff before leaving here."

"Well, I can't leave it out there to rot. I'll put it in the fridge for when Zeb returns."

He saw the tears in her eyes, and he didn't know why, and was afraid to ask, if it was because Zeb might not ever return or because they would be leaving.

"Do you want to play cards?" she asked.

"No!" he replied too sharply, then chuckled. "The last time, I lost my . . . Well, never mind."

She grinned impishly at him. "*Interview with the Vampire* is on one of the cable channels at three o'clock."

"Pfff! Tom Cruise is the sorriest vampire I've ever seen."

She was chopping up some of the vegetables she'd just brought in and washed in the sink. Probably making yet another salad for their lunch. He was going to turn into a rabbit pretty soon. He needed to go out and hunt a boar . . . or something. Of a sudden, he recalled the one winter when he was a boy and food was so scarce that even grass, let alone a salad, would have been welcome. Anything that walked ended up in the kitchen cauldron.

"Why are you smiling?" she asked.

"Did you ever eat boiled wolf?"

"Huh?" she said, then added, "Have I told you how much I like your lopsided smile?"

Only a dozen times. "I do not smile lopsided."

Leastways no one had ever told him that before. "Nicole! What are you doing now?"

"Taking off my shirt."

"Why?" he choked out, trying not to look at her bare breasts, which was impossible. *Is she going to cook bare-breasted? That could be dangerous, but then she's not cooking over a hot stove. She's making a loathsome cold salad. Aaarrgh! My brain is melting.*

"Because it's hot, and because I want to get an all-over tan before we leave." On those ominous words, she set the bowl of salad greens aside, walked out of the kitchen, shrugged out of her shorts, then pranced right in front of him toward the deck and a waiting chaise longue. At the open doorway, she paused and looked at him over her shoulder, "Want to join me?"

He shook his head. He could not speak over his long fangs. He put a hand to his mouth to make sure his tongue wasn't lolling or that he wasn't drooling.

Over the next hour, Trond did everything he could to avoid looking at Nicole's nude body glistening in the sun, including two cold showers. Finally, he did what any good vangel did. He dropped to his knees in the bedroom and prayed.

"Dear Lord, please help me to resist this woman because the worst possible thing has happened. I love her."

Bite me! ...

Nicole was hurt and puzzled by Trond's behavior, and she'd had enough.

For four days they'd screwed each other like bunnies in every room, on every surface, even outdoors.

And now he avoided her like the plague. In fact, he'd gone to bed early, in a different bedroom.

Well, enough was enough.

She tried the door handle, and it was locked. That hurt. But it wasn't about to stop her.

"Trond, let me in. We have to talk."

Silence.

"I mean it. Let me in, or . . . or I'll do something drastic."

Silence.

"I'll cut off all my hair."

He laughed. Apparently, that wasn't drastic enough.

"I'll set the door on fire."

A snort of disbelief.

She tried to think of the most drastic thing she could say.

"I'll get back with my ex-husband Billy to save my sister."

The door flew open. "That wasn't the least bit funny."

Oddly, he was sitting on the side of the bed, his face in his hands. How had the door opened? She shook her head to clear it. Really, it didn't matter. What mattered was the state Trond was in.

"What is it, sweetheart?" she asked, coming up to put a hand on his shoulder.

"Don't touch me," he said, jumping up and putting some distance between them.

Which gave her an opportunity to study his appearance. He looked like hell. His eyes were not just silver, but a glowing silver. His fangs were elongated. Perspiration covered his body, and his face was flushed, the flush being more apparent because of the paleness of his skin.

"You're sick."

"No, Nicole. I'm not sick. I just need to feed."

Suddenly, everything became clear to her, based on things he'd told her about vangels over the last few days. And an idea came to her . . . a scary, distasteful idea. "Trond, does your brother Vikar feed on his wife?"

"Yes, but—"

"Is she a vangel, too?"

"No, but—"

"Then you can feed on me." *Oh Lord! Did I just say that? Did I just offer myself up as Dracula bait? No! Trond is the man I love. If he is a Bram Stoker creation, then he's a good Dracula. Maybe Dracula had a nonevil brother.*

"No! Absolutely not!"

"Would you hurt me?"

"Of course not."

"Then do it." *I don't like needles. How am I going to bear teeth piercing my skin? Don't start shaking, Nicole. Do. Not. Shake.* "Besides, you're hurting me now by shutting me out. You have to know that I love you, Trond. Oh, don't get that sick look on your face. I'm not asking anything from you, and I know we have no future. But there it is. I love you, get over it. And I want to help you."

Trond just stared at Nicole, his heart aching in that odd way it did of late. He could have wept at the pleasure of the love she claimed to have for him, and he could have wept at the pain of knowing he was unworthy and therefore unable to accept what she offered so freely.

But he needed his strength in order to get them back to Afghanistan and do all that he must in the next day or two. "I accept your generous offer, Nicole." He held out a hand to her.

Instead of taking his hand, she rushed at him and clung to his shoulders, burying her face in his neck where he felt the wetness of her tears. "You brute! You louse! Shutting me out like this!"

"Shh," he said. "Shh." That's all he could say.

"How do we do this?" his brave girl asked, even as her bottom lip quivered with fear.

He laughed and framed her face with his hands, kissing her softly. "Not so fast. If we make love, it will be easier for you."

"It won't hurt?"

"Just the first time. A little."

She laughed now, too, and swiped at her eyes. "Sounds like all the guys when they're trying to talk a girl into giving it up the first time."

"I am not like 'all the guys.'" He pretended affront.

"I know," she said.

Trond drew her to the bed and proceeded to make sweet love to her. He paid homage to every part of her body with caresses, kisses, and whispered words of admiration. He started gently, stoking her fires, needing her molten and ravenous for fulfillment before he would take her blood.

"Did I ever show you the famous Viking S-spot?" he asked silkily at one point, wanting to lighten the somberness of their lovemaking.

"You're making that up," she told him with a laugh.

"Am not," he said and showed her exactly where it was. With his tongue.

That brought her close to her first climax, but he wouldn't let her go over the top. He had to have her mindless.

But she was not happy. She pushed herself up

and over him, sitting on his belly. With excessive sweetness, she inquired, "Have I ever shown you the Cowgirl Twirl?"

She hadn't, but she did, and it took every bit of restraint to lift her off before they both exploded into a mutual orgasm.

"You're driving me crazy," she moaned.

"I need to." He used all the expertise he'd gained over eleven hundred years then to bring her to a keening, arms-flailing, hips-bucking arousal.

He played with her breasts until she grabbed his head and forced him down hard against her, wanting more and harder suckling. Instead, he eased himself away and teased her with light, feathery touches until she reached the point that his breath on her wet nipples brought her close to peaking. Even the hair on his legs rubbing against her legs was enhancing her excitement.

Once again, he stopped. And this time just stopping wasn't enough to dampen down his excitement or hers, so he tried a different tactic. Lying on his back with his arms folded under his neck, he asked, "What's your favorite food?"

She looked at him with disbelief, then down at his amazingly huge cock and said, "Sausage."

He barely stifled a grin. "Your favorite color?"

"Flesh."

"You're not taking my questions seriously. Your favorite song?"

" 'Sex Machine.' "

"Nicole! Your favorite book?"

"*Men Are from Mars, Women Are from Venus.*"

"I give up," he said then, and rolled over on his side, staring down at her.

She resembled a furious tiger kitten as she glared

up at him through bruised lips. Her eyes were misty with arousal. Her nostrils flared with either anger or arousal. Probably both. Her hair was bed-mussed, or rather sex-mussed. In other words, she was nigh irresistible.

"I want you so much, Nicole," he murmured against her mouth.

"Not half as much as I want you, Viking," she murmured back.

He kissed her ravenously then, and at the same time used his fingers to delve into her soaking folds. Putting first one, then two, then three fingers inside her, he stretched her inner muscles, then began pumping her. Her liquid pleasure coated his fingers. He felt a wetness on her face, as well. Salty tears seeped down to their joined lips. When he raised his head to look down at her, she said only one word, "Please?"

His knees trembled and there was roaring in his ears when he finally, finally, finally mounted her. As tortuous as it had been for Nicole to forestall her orgasm, it had been twice . . . nay, thrice . . . as hard for him. And even now, he had to fight against the coils of tension in his body that yearned to let go, especially when her inner channel clutched at him on each backstroke.

Her head was tossing from side to side, her eyes closed, as Trond thrust himself hard inside her, his pubic bone hitting her clitoris. He leaned down then and clamped his teeth against her neck. He heard her gasp of shock, then her sigh.

His strokes into her climaxing folds were short and hard then as he drank greedily from her. So sweet. Her blood was so sweet and nourishing to him. Lifeblood. Forcing himself to stop, finally, when they'd both climaxed together, he licked the bite marks on her neck and lay atop her, his cock now quiescent inside her.

"Thank you," he murmured against her neck.

At first there was no response, but then she slapped him on the shoulder.

"What?" He raised his head.

"You didn't tell me I would enjoy it so much."

If Trond hadn't fallen in love with her before, he would now. Throwing his head back, he laughed joyously. In this moment there were no jagged splinters of his horrid life. This woman, and this woman alone, had shown him what life could be without all the dark shadows.

Before he could bite his foolish tongue, he kissed her lips and said, "You are mine." *Forever.*

Twenty-three

He never actually promised her forever . . .

The following morning, they were back in the Davastan cave where the SEALs and WEALS had hidden before the hostage mission, and it had all happened so easily. She'd dressed in the same tattered Arab robe, and Trond put on the smelly socks and Arab garb he'd worn when "selling" her and Marie and Donita for Najid's harem. One minute they stood in the garden, Trond holding tight to her hand, and then they teletransported, or whatever it was vangels did. Whoosh, in an instant, they were on the other side of the world.

Thanks to materials that had been stashed at the back of the cave, they'd been able to contact Cent-Com and a helo was being sent for them within the hour. She and Trond had rehearsed over and over the story they would tell the commander on their return. They'd been captured by some of the terrorists at the end of the mission and kept in one of Najid's hidden caves farther away from Davastan. The ragtag band hadn't been sure what to do with them these past five days, and they kept arguing over whether to torture information from them, kill them as examples of U.S. military intrusion in Afghanistan, or ask for ransom. The tangos had been waiting for word from Najid's successor who was supposed to arrive from Pakistan when she and Trond had managed to escape, and it had taken them two days to find their way back to the cave hideout near the compound. At least, that was the story they were telling.

"I hear the helo," Trond said, helping her to her feet. Instead of walking out immediately, though, he pulled her into an embrace, a tight embrace, as if he didn't want to let her go.

"Hey, we have plenty of time for that when we get back," she said, kissing him lightly on the chin. They both picked up backpacks containing small items left in the cave.

"They'll be putting a harness down for us," Trond said. "They don't want us rappelling up without gloves."

She nodded.

The helo was already hovering nearby when they walked the short distance to the extraction site.

"Listen to me, Nicole," he said against her ear at the last minute. It was hard to hear over the chopper's noise. "I'm not going back."

"What? Wait."

"No, listen to me, heartling." He held her by the forearms. "I must go after Zeb. There will be an explosion any minute now in the cave. You will tell the authorities that I went back to get something, and I must be presumed dead."

"Nooooo!" she wailed. "I want to stay with you. We'll help Zeb together."

He shook his head. The sadness on his face was heartrending, for both of them.

Just then, two things happened at once, a harness was dropped for her about a hundred yards away, and the cave exploded. Into the flying mist, Trond was already beginning to disappear. She couldn't hear him, but she saw him mouth the words, "I. Love. You."

Where there's a will, there's a way . . .

Nicole had been back in Coronado for four days, and following ten different debriefings, her life should have been back to normal, or as normal as it would ever be after the experiences she'd had. Sometimes she wondered if half of it had ever really occurred.

But, no, if she denied those horrid beasts devouring humans in Najid's courtyard, or the concept of teletransportation, or men with fangs, then she would have to deny her love for Trond, a Viking vampire angel.

Aside from yet another debriefing—and she'd been questioned and questioned, then questioned again about what had happened to her and Trond in Davastan—all special forces operators when they returned from a mission involving deadly force were required to meet with the base psychologist. To make sure their heads were still screwed on right. Killing changed people, and the military wanted to make sure they handled their roles in taking out tangos without going bonkers. Some did.

The Octopus mission was deemed a success. Well, not a total success since two of the hostages had died, and Trond was gone and presumed dead, but overall there had been none of the planned explosions, thanks to careful special ops planning, and most of Najid's followers had been destroyed or scattered to far parts. Oh, there had been efforts to pull the stragglers together in Osama's name by another of his illegitimate sons, but the effort petered out. That did not mean it was the end of terrorism, by any means, but hopefully one more step had been taken, making the world a little safer and freer.

She was worried sick about Trond, of course. And Zeb. If only she'd realized that Trond would give himself up to that evil Jasper to save Zeb—and that is what she was convinced had happened now that she'd had time to think about it—she would have tried to do something to stop him. What, she wasn't sure. She presumed it was the angel thing to do. The right thing to do. That didn't make it any easier to handle the images in her head of what horrific torture he might be undergoing at the moment.

As soon as the commander released her from questioning the first day back, she'd gone seeking Karl to see if he could help her find Trond, or contact St. Michael the Archangel—she'd felt foolish even saying such a thing—to see if he could help. But Karl was gone, too, supposedly back to his Jaegers unit in Norway, but she knew better.

Interesting, though, that before he'd left, Karl had been meeting daily with Sly over in the mental wing of the base hospital, and apparently Sly had recovered his mental faculties. Karl must have saved him.

And here was the icing on the cake. Sly and Donita had reunited and gone off to be married in Las Vegas, where they still were, honeymooning.

Torolf "Max" Magnusson had taken her aside

yesterday and questioned her about Trond. "I really regret not having gotten to know him better. My father will be especially sorrowful at not having made a connection with a fellow Viking."

Nicole had been given another week off from her WEALS duties, only reporting for her daily psychiatric session with Dr. Feingold and light PT. Marie had gone home to Louisiana for a short break. So, she was home alone at one a.m. when the doorbell rang.

At first, her heart raced, thinking it might be Trond, but, no, he wouldn't bother with any doorbell or a door, for that matter. Her visitor was equally surprising, though.

A girl stood on her doorstep, wearing skinny jeans, a cropped T-shirt, and too much makeup. A small suitcase sat at her feet on the stoop.

"Nic?" the girl said.

She tilted her head to the side. "Teresa?"

The girl, whom she could see now was not a girl but a young woman of about eighteen, nodded and started to sob.

Nicole gathered her baby sister into her arms and led her inside. "What's wrong, honey?" As if she couldn't guess.

After much blubbering and a half box of tissues, and words like "the ass," "Daddy said," "college," "a slap," and then an amazing, "Mom told me to come to you," the gist of it was, she didn't want to marry Billy, the ass, who'd told her she couldn't continue her college classes when they married. She'd been planning to go to nursing school. When she'd protested, he'd slapped her, and their dad had told her she must have deserved it because she was getting mouthy at home, too. "But Billy told me he was sorry right away," she'd quickly amended.

The same old Billy!

"And Dad said Billy would probably change his mind about college after we were married."

Yeah, right!

"So, what do you want to do?" They were in the kitchen now eating store-bought cookies, hers washed down by a cup of herbal tea and Teresa's by a cold Pepsi.

"I don't want to get married right away. And . . . and I don't think I want to marry Billy at all."

"Okay. What *do* you want to do?"

"Nursing school, but not in Chicago. I was accepted at three schools. One of them is in Florida. That's where I want to go."

Good idea. Get away from them all. "Will Dad pay for your school?"

"Grandma put some money in trust for my education. She put money aside for you, too."

Well, that was news to Nicole. "When do classes start?"

"Next week."

"Are you sure about this?"

"Yes. Can I stay with you for a few days?"

"Of course, sweetie."

"I admire you so much, Nic."

"You do?" The compliment pleased her inordinately.

"But I missed you. And you never came home." She started crying again.

They both did.

And over the next two days, while Nicole handled the phone calls to her father—not pleasant!—and the two of them went shopping for school clothes appropriate for a warmer climate, and Teresa went googly-eyed over all the hot men in uniform, they got to know each other again. Billy made a half-hearted attempt to change Teresa's mind, but her little sister was braver by phone, and convinced him it was over between them. He blamed Nicole, of course. By the time Nicole put her sister on a plane, they had bonded as if the past seven years of separation had never existed.

Oh, there had been some arguments. Mostly over little things, but Nicole came to a long-overdue realization as she drove home, one that would probably require her to make an effort to reconcile with her mother, despite her father. Her sudden epiphany was ridiculously simple: Family is so important.

Which suddenly caused a spark of memory to light in Nicole's lately dulled brain. Trond had family. There was a family home.

With a little yelp of glee, she pounded on her steering wheel, causing other drivers at the red light to stare at her as if she'd gone crazy. Maybe she had.

Phone calls to the commander cemented her one-week liberty. She spent the rest of the day packing and making travel arrangements. She played some of her motivational tapes, which she'd been ignoring since her return, having forgotten the importance of optimism.

She needed to find out what had happened to Trond. As horrific as that news might be—she was imagining the worst types of torture anyhow—she needed to know. And maybe, just maybe, there might be a way for her to help him.

She was going to Transylvania. Transylvania, Pennsylvania.

Home, Sweet Castle . . .

After Trond had left Nicole in Davastan, he went immediately to bloody damn cold northern Norway searching for Jasper's Arctic castle. But there was an invisible shield around the perimeter that he couldn't breach.

So, while he stood shivering in his head-to-toe furs, contemplating his next move, he glanced sideways. Then did a double take.

There stood Mike leaning against a stark, leafless tree, wearing nothing but a white, belted gown. He wasn't shivering at all.

"Going somewhere, Viking?" Mike asked coolly.

He nodded. "I have to save Zeb."

"Oh, really?" Sarcasm from an archangel was not a pleasant thing.

"Zeb gave himself up for me and Nicole," he explained, which was silly of him to point out, really. Mike undoubtedly knew that already. He knew everything, it seemed.

"And how, pray tell, did you plan to do that, Viking?"

"Um."

"Perchance, were you going to offer yourself up in his place?"

Trond gulped. Despite his best attempts at bravery, he feared what would befall him once he entered Jasper's domain. "Yes."

"And did you ask my permission to do so?" When Trond didn't answer, Mike added, "Ah, you must have forgotten."

"Mike, I beg of you," he said, "Zeb is not all bad. He deserves . . . something."

"The arrogance of a Viking!" Mike shook his head

from side to side with seeming dismay. "When will you learn? That is not a decision for you to make."

And before Trond could blink the snow off his eyelashes or wipe the frozen snot hanging from his nose, he found himself flat on his ass in the back garden of the Transylvania castle with Mike hovering over him, wings widespread. Sternly, the archangel admonished him, "Do not dare move from here, Viking, or you will suffer the consequences." By past experience, Trond knew what "consequences" meant, and it wasn't a light slap on the hand. But then, Mike added, "And no contact with humans outside the castle." He meant Nicole.

Trond made his way into the castle kitchen, where their cook, Lizzie Borden, was grumbling over an enormous pot she was stirring on the stove, something about, "Pasta, pasta, pasta! What do they think I am? A bloody Eye-tal-yan?" Her fangs hung over her lips as she glanced up at him and she didn't even bother to say hello.

He found his brother Vikar on the floor of the main parlor playing with the two little toddlers, Gunnar and Gunnora, that he and Alex had adopted or inherited or something. The sight was amazing. A six-foot-four Viking warrior letting little gremlins crawl all over him.

"Welcome home," Vikar said, as if it was not unusual for him to show up suddenly. Well, actually, it hadn't been unusual in the past.

Trond mumbled something about this not being his home, not that he had any other home, and he didn't want a home. Nicole immediately came to mind. He pushed that impossible thought away.

"Have you met our prisoner yet?" Vikar asked.

"Huh?"

"Mike delivered a prisoner to us." Vikar was tickling one of the twins' bellies while the other was doing jumping jacks on his buttocks.

"He did? When?"

"Yesterday." Vikar looked up at him then, grinning, a clue that Trond was not going to like whoever this prisoner was.

"Where is this prisoner?"

"In the dungeon."

"You have a dungeon?"

"Well, no. Remember, we converted the dungeon into a weight room. We have the prisoner locked in the tower."

"Alex's tower?" When Alex had first come to visit the castle as a reporter, Vikar had kept her locked in a tower bedchamber. Later it became their love nest. Somehow he couldn't see these two lovebirds, wed only a few months, turning their special room into a jail cell.

"No, the other tower."

"The one with all the bats?"

"That would be the one." Vikar was grinning again.

Trond took the steps two at a time, all two thousand of them—or what seemed like two thousand—before he got to the second of four towers. He tried the knob, and it wasn't even locked. Some dungeon/ jail!

Inside, eating a bowl of Lizzie's pasta, was none other than . . . Zeb.

The demon didn't seem at all surprised to see him as he casually dabbed at his mouth with a cloth napkin. Some prisoner! Where were the chains and torture implements?

"You idiot! I went to the Norselands to give

myself up to Jasper in exchange for your freedom while you sat here basking in luxury."

Zeb gave the stone walls and cobwebbed corners a disbelieving survey. Then he bowed his head at Trond. "You were going to sacrifice yourself for me. I was going to do the same for you. Tit for tat. It appears as if we both failed in our noble attempts. I wonder why."

They both exclaimed at the same time, "Michael!"

Trond couldn't help himself then. He pulled the man up into an embrace and hugged him. In a manly fashion, of course.

He soon learned that the shield around Jasper's castle had been Mike's, not Jasper's, and when Zeb had attempted to return to Horror—that was the appropriate name of Jasper's domicile—Mike had jerked him back, just as he had Trond. And dragged Zeb by the ear—it would have been the tail, if his tail had been out, according to Zeb—back to the vangels' headquarters in Transylvania.

Michael's admonition in placing him here had been similar to Trond's as well: "Do not dare move from here, demon, or you will suffer the consequences."

So now, a week later, Trond was stomping about, missing Nicole, complaining, complaining, complaining.

Although there were dozens of vangels working about the place, Vikar was his only brother in residence. The others were out on various missions. Vikar told him to go talk with Zeb, that he was personally sick of sharing in Trond's misery.

Trond found Zeb on his knees working in Alex's flower garden out back. "Some prisoner you are!" he observed.

"I guess you could call this work release," Zeb replied. For some reason, Vikar and Alex and the other vangels sensed the same thing about Zeb that Trond did. There was goodness in the demon, enough so that they did not fear his presence in their home, even around the two toddlers. It was puzzling, really. And scary. Because if there could be goodness left in an ancient demon, there could be evil left in an ancient vangel.

He plunked down on a bench and sighed.

"I think this place needs a grape arbor," Zeb said right off. "I used to be a vintner, you know. The climate's not perfect for vines, but some varieties would do well here. Maybe along that sunny wall there. We could even press a wine, or two. It's not that hard."

Trond hated to break the news to Zeb, but he probably wouldn't be here long enough to see any vines take root, let alone stomp any grapes. He wouldn't tell him that, though.

"I have a philosophy," Zeb said. "The man who has garden dirt under his fingernails is planting seeds of grace in Heaven."

"Bet that philosophy went over great in Jasperland."

Instead of being offended, Zeb just smiled and tossed what smelled like cow shit onto the roots of some roses. At least he hadn't thrown it at Trond, as he deserved.

Trond braced his chin over one fist with his elbow resting on his knee and contemplated his fate, whatever it might be.

"I don't understand why you're so miserable," Zeb said. "It's wonderful here."

Trond glanced around at the crumbling castle

that had scaffolding up on four sides, as it had for months for workmen to repoint the stonework and reglaze the windows. The slate roof was apparently intact, but not much else. There were seventy-five rooms, give or take, in this gray monstrosity. It would take Vikar forever to get it in shape. But then he had forever, or close to it.

"You have family. You have a roof over your head, such as it is, and a warm bed to sleep in. You have good work. You have peace and . . . and hope."

Now Trond felt guilty for being so mean-spirited. Still he had to say what was on his mind. "But I don't have Nicole."

"Ah!" Zeb said. "Would you like to hear my philosophy about bad men who love good women?"

"No!"

"Then help me plant some winter onions. There's nothing like gardening to soothe the soul."

Trond said something foul as he stood abruptly. Zeb was laughing as he stomped off to complain to someone else, someone more sympathetic. Maybe the twins. Better yet, maybe he should have a beer, or five.

Twenty-four

Not your run-of-the-mill castle! . . .

After several connecting flights, Nicole finally ended up at Harrisburg International Airport, where she rented a car with a GPS set to Transylvania, Pennsylvania. In one hour, she would be at Trond's home.

What awaited her there?

At the very least, she hoped for news. Would they know what happened to Trond once he entered Jasper's version of Hell? Would Jasper have even released Zeb in trade for Trond? After all, Jasper was a devil. He didn't have to obey rules of ethics, like promises, or deals.

One after another, little things surprised Nicole as she approached the small town.

First of all, Trond had failed to mention that he lived in Amish country. Rolling hills and neat farmsteads charmed the eye, along with quaint Amish buggies on the highways and side roads. Life certainly moved at a different pace here.

Her first clue that she was entering Land of the

Weird—surprise number two—was when she saw the words on the local Catholic church's outdoor bulletin board: "Vampires Welcome." Driving through the main street, she saw stores and restaurants and bars, all catering to the touristy allure of vampires, with names like Good Bites, or the Dark Side, or Drac's Hideout. Even Suckies. Everywhere she looked she saw people wearing capes and fake fangs. A dentist advertised a teeth filing service. Yeech! A banner near the town hall announced a Fall Festival featuring a costume ball, a blood-drinking contest, aka Kool-Aid, a stake-throwing event, and a marathon of vampire movies, everything from Bela Lugosi to *Twilight*.

The gas station attendant who gave her directions to the castle warned her, "They won't let you past the gates up there."

She'd see about that!

As she approached the castle up a winding, narrow dirt road, she was astonished. Trond hadn't been kidding. A huge, *huge*, rundown castle rose up against the mountainside. Even from a distance, she could see scaffolding and workmen's trucks and vans, but from here it appeared as if only a tiny dent had been made in the renovations. Who would have built such a massive edifice in the middle of nowhere?

When she neared an iron gate, a guard stood there, holding up a halting hand. He pointed to the "No Trespassing" sign and motioned for her to turn around and leave.

No way!

She got out of her vehicle and approached. Before she'd met Trond she might have been frightened by a six-foot-five, blond Viking with pale, almost albino-ish skin, faded blue eyes, and real, not fake fangs, but now she was only mildly frightened. "Hi! I'm Nicole Tasso. Here to see the Sigurdssons."

"Aren't you all?" the Prince of Snideness responded, arms folded over his chest.

"I met Trond Sigurdsson in California recently and he told me to drop by any time."

"Is that so?" He twirled his fingertip for her to go back to her car.

"I'm not leaving." She folded her arms over her chest, mirroring him.

She thought she saw a smile twitch at his red lips, but it was hard to tell with the fangs. In fact, he made a hissing sound at her to scare her away.

"Oh please!" she said. "I've been hissed at by better than you. In fact, you need to work on your hiss."

"What's wrong with my hiss?" he asked before he could catch himself. "Never mind. Listen, lady, I don't care where you've come from. You are not on the list of expected visitors, and therefore you are not coming in. Don't make me get physical with you."

Just then a black SUV drove up with a woman driving. She blew the horn and waved at the guard.

"Are you going to move, or do I have to toss you over my shoulder and carry you back to your car? That's the boss's wife and I need to let her through. You're blocking the way."

"That's Alexandra?" she asked, and before the guard could grab her arm, Nicole ran back to the SUV. Speaking as fast as she could, she said through the open window. "Hi, I'm Nicole Tasso. A . . . a, um, friend of Trond's. The guard won't let me pass."

The woman tilted her head to the side. "Nicole? The female SEAL?"

She nodded.

"Thank God!" Alex exclaimed.

Nicole had no idea what that meant, but it had to be good. Unfortunately, she was the only one who heard it.

The guard had a hold of Nicole's arm now and was trying to drag her away.

"Let her go, Svein," Alex called out. "This is the woman Trond has been driving us crazy over."

Svein looked more closely at her, and not in a complimentary way. "I can see why she would drive someone crazy. She says I have a bad hiss," Svein grumbled.

"Maybe we can finally get some peace here. Hop in," she told Nicole. And to Svein she said, "Move her car and bring it around back, please. I can't wait to see Trond's face."

Nicole got a better look at the woman driving now that she was inside the vehicle. A strawberry blonde with green eyes . . . probably Irish, she was tall, about five-eight or -nine, wearing a white silk blouse tucked into black jeans with sandals. While Nicole glanced at the overladen backseat, Alex told her, "I've been grocery shopping."

For an army?

Just then, the implications of what Alex had said on first meeting her sank in. "Trond is here?" Nicole asked as they drove through the gates, to the front, then around the side of the castle.

"Yep. He's been here for ten miserable days."

"He's here? He's safe? And he didn't even call me?"

"Uh-oh!" Alex murmured, then, "I think he's out back planting onions with Zeb. Or maybe it's grape vines. He's sort of between missions. So is my husband, and they're both antsy."

"Zeb is here and safe, too?"

Alex nodded, no longer sure she should be revealing so much to a stranger.

"I'm going to kill the man. And I don't even care if Trond is already dead."

Alex laughed and reached over to squeeze her hand. "Welcome to the club, honey."

First they entered a huge kitchen with commercial-grade appliances and freezers. An older woman was hacking away at several whole, raw chickens with a cleaver. "Chicken cacciatore *with pasta*," she said with snarl of disgust, thus exposing her fangs. "Honestly, Mrs. S., I'm making pork and sauerkraut tomorrow, and everyone better eat it, too."

The fragrant pot of tomato sauce already simmering on the range must hold at least twenty quarts. As she cut the chicken into portions, she tossed them into an equally huge frying pan already sizzling with green peppers, onions, and garlic.

Alex smiled and said, "Nicole, this is Lizzie Borden, our cook."

Nicole looked at the woman dressed in a Victorian-era, long, lace-trimmed black dress with an equally long white apron. Her gray hair was gathered in a bun at her neck. Nicole looked again at the cleaver that could be construed to be an axe, she supposed, and connected the name with the implement. *Surely not*, she thought, but Alex grinned and gave her an inconspicuous nod. Nicole recalled then that Trond had told her about Lizzie one night while they were at Zeb's hideaway.

"And Miss Borden, this is Trond's friend Nicole."

"Do you like pork and sauerkraut?" Miss Borden asked her curtly.

"Uh, yeah." *Sometimes.*

"The vangels in residence have taken a liking to pasta lately," Alex explained, "and Miss Borden is getting tired of making the same kind of food every day."

"Just because it looks like blood don't mean it is blood," the old lady complained.

"Do you have any idea where Trond is?" Alex asked Miss Borden.

"He and Zeb are babysitting your little ones."

"Where's Vikar?"

"He had some important business with . . ." Miss Borden rolled her eyes upward.

Nicole wasn't sure if she referred to God, or St. Michael, or just that he was upstairs. It wasn't her place to ask.

Just then, Nicole noticed a young man, about sixteen, sitting at the other end of the kitchen on a high stool before a counter, with a small DVD player in front of him while he crunched away at a bowl of cereal. His black hair was slicked back off his face, and he wore a red jacket and white-sock-exposing black pants, just like . . . Oh, this must be the Michael Jackson aficionado that Trond had mentioned. He had fangs, too, and was oblivious to them even being in the room as he watched the DVD player playing . . . what else? A Michael Jackson video.

As Alex led Nicole in a search for Trond, she couldn't help but be impressed by the interior of the castle that was indeed in the process of renovations, but the bones of this edifice were unique and potentially beautiful. Deep-grained woods. Marble veined in various colors. Murals-in-progress on some walls. Massive chandeliers. And the architectural details were probably of historic importance, especially the highly carved staircase in the front hallway.

Fanged men, and some women, were busy at work everywhere they passed, everything from scrubbing floors to computer work. Finally, they came to what might once have been a formal second parlor but was now a "family room" with widescreen TVs—three of them—toys, deep comfortable sofas, and lamps with soft lighting. On the carpeted floor, Zeb lay on his back with a little boy dressed in denim coveralls bouncing on his chest. In a far corner, Trond sat in a rocking chair reading a book to a little girl—*The Three Little Pigs*, by the sound of it. On one of the TV screens, a sports channel was showing highlights from a recent NFL football game. On another of the screens, it was *The Lion King*.

"And he huffed and he puffed and he blew the house down," Trond said in a deep, gravelly wolf voice when he glanced up and saw Nicole standing, frozen, in the doorway. She wasn't sure if the sudden heightened color in his cheeks was from shock or embarrassment at being caught in such a cozy situation.

Zeb sat up, also surprised, but there was pleasure on his face at seeing her again. "Hey, Nic!" he said amiably.

But she had no time to think about Zeb now. It was the other jerk in the room that consumed her attention. While Nicole had wept buckets over Trond, unable to sleep at night, worrying about the torture he was undergoing, he'd been home all along. Eating frickin' pasta. Planting frickin' onions. And playing with children.

And he'd never bothered to contact her, never considered her feelings, was apparently okay with a permanent separation. And she, pathetic, love-struck woman that she was, had chased after him. "You slime-sucking, two-bit jerk!" she gritted out.

She had to get out of here. Right away.

Swiveling on her heel, she began to run back the way she'd come. If she could make it to her car, she would escape with at least a little of her pride intact.

"Nicole! Wait! I can explain," Trond yelled behind her.

The time for explanations had long passed, in Nicole's opinion. When would she ever learn not to trust men? Trond had told her that he loved her that last day. Well, not really *told her*. He'd mouthed the words as he'd disappeared.

That kind of love she could do without.

Not the reunion he'd been hoping for . . .

Nicole was here!

She'd come looking for him.

All his misery of the past week and more melted away, and he smiled. He'd been stunned with surprise, but it had been a good kind of surprise. Setting little Nora on her wobbly toddler feet, he'd stood and started to smile with happiness. But wait. Was that look of loathing on her face directed at him?

Oh yeah, he'd immediately answered himself when she'd tossed those expletives at him and rushed away. Time for some damage control.

Alex and Zeb were laughing at him, which caused Nora, short for Gunnora, and her twin, Gunnar, to laugh, too, thinking Trond had done something to amuse them. He called after Nicole but she ignored his pleas to stop, and being a WEALS, she could run really fast.

He caught up with her just as she was about to climb into her rental car. Her eyes were misted with tears, but he suspected they were tears of anger more than sorrow, at this point.

"C'mon, Nic, give me a chance to explain." He grabbed her arm and slammed the car door. Pinning her against the frame, he said, "I missed you, dearling."

"Fuck you!" she snarled.

"Maybe later."

She was not amused by his response and tried to squirm out of his grasp. When that didn't work, she tried kneeing his groin.

A part of his body that had been especially happy to see her just barely escaped injury.

"Let me go, Trond. My coming here was a mistake."

"No. It was not a mistake." When she continued to fight him, he picked her up and slung her over his shoulder fireman-style. Alex, Vikar, and about three dozen vangels were out on the back verandah or at the back windows on all four floors watching him make a fool of himself. He didn't care.

Walking swiftly to the garden gazebo, he sat her down on a cushioned wicker chair and planted his braced hands on either side of her. Only inches separated their faces when he asked her, "Why are you so upset?"

At first she balked and turned her face away from him. When he refused to let her go, she sliced him with a glare and said, "You're safe, and you never bothered to tell me."

"I couldn't."

That response surprised her. "Why?"

"Mike stopped me right outside Jasper's place in northern Norway and wouldn't let me go in."

"Why?"

"I don't know. He hasn't come to talk to me yet. I suspect . . . *I know* . . . I'm in big trouble, but Mike doles out his punishments when and how he chooses."

"That doesn't excuse your not contacting me and telling me you were safe. Even if you don't love me, it would have been common courtesy—"

"Don't love you? Where would you get that idea?"

She stared at him as if he was a thickheaded lack-wit.

"Oh. I guess you thought my silence meant—"

"That's exactly what I thought."

"I'm as much a prisoner here at the moment as Zeb is."

"That's another thing. Both of you are jerks for making me care about you, then leaving me in the dark. And, frankly, this place resembles no prison I've ever seen."

"Mike ordered me to stay here and make no contact with anyone outside the castle until he decides my fate."

That seemed to soften her a little bit. "Well, now that I know you're okay, I'll go back to Coronado."

He laughed. "Not a chance!"

"You can't make me stay."

His arched brows told her loud and clear without words, *Wanna bet?*

"Why do you want me to stay?"

"Do you honestly need to ask me that? Because I love you."

Any response from her was stalled when Vikar yelled out to him, "Mike is coming. He'll be here within the hour."

"That's my brother Vikar." Trond looked at Nicole then, putting a hand to her face in gentle entreaty. "Will you stay, at least until after Mike leaves?"

"St. Michael the Archangel is coming here?" Her eyes were huge with a mixture of wonder and disbelief.

He nodded.

Coming closer, Vikar nodded a greeting at Nicole. "One more thing. Mike wants to talk to her, as well."

"Me?" Nicole squeaked out, putting a hand to her heart in dismay. "How did he know I was here?"

He and Vikar both gave her a look that pretty much said the archangel knew everything.

"What could the archangel possibly want with me?" she asked Trond as Vikar walked back to the castle.

Trond didn't have a clue. "He probably wants to know your intentions toward me," he teased, but then he wondered, *Could that possibly be true?*

Do-overs sometimes *are* possible, it seems . . .

St. Michael the Archangel arrived with a flourish of widespread wings. Sometimes it was necessary to establish his authority with a show of angelic strength.

These vangels! Even after all these years, they behaved like little children. Rules needed to be spelled out to them. Over and over. They thought the world revolved around them and forgot they were here by the sufferance of a higher authority. They needed to be punished.

Forget the vangels! He had someone else to deal with first.

"You!" He pointed a finger at Zebulan and motioned the demon vampire toward the library.

It was a fabulous room, even by angelic standards, with a rich burgundy and cream Oriental carpet, floor-to-ceiling bookshelves, a highly carved fireplace mantel with Rookwood tile surrounds, a stained glass screen, and a massive walnut partner's desk at one end, in front of which were arranged beautiful armed chairs with leather seats.

Zeb was impressed, too. He could imagine peaceful winter nights sitting in an upholstered chair with a footstool beside a roaring fire, reading a book, maybe even the Bible, perhaps sipping at a glass of fine wine. Or was that his vision of what Heaven must be like?

Sitting down behind the desk, Michael adjusted his wings over the chair back and glanced at a folder he'd brought with him. Zebulan stood nervously at attention before the desk.

"Tsk, tsk, tsk!" Michael clucked as he read.

Zebulan flushed, but he remained ramrod stiff.

"You have sinned mightily," the archangel pronounced, slapping the folder shut.

"I have."

"There are vangels . . . one in particular . . . who have interceded on your behalf."

Zebulan started to speak, then stopped himself. "I did not ask him to." Not precisely, anyhow.

"Are you sorry for your sins?"

"Desperately," he answered without hesitation.

"What would you have me do?"

"End it. I do not want to be a Lucipire anymore. Send me to Hell if you must, but I can no longer bear to perpetuate evil. I hate myself."

Michael nodded his understanding. "You were willing to give yourself up for Trond and his woman. I cannot discount that. However, I cannot excuse your sins."

Zeb felt tears well in his eyes. He had been a

Hebrew, but he'd betrayed his people by serving the Roman armies, all in hopes of saving his vineyards and his family, of course. Beautiful Sarah and the adorable twins, Mikah and Rachel. Little had he known that his family had fled to Masada for refuge while he'd been gone, and the siege in which he'd participated had led to their deaths, as well.

"It is not that sin I refer to, Zebulan. 'Tis the centuries of sin you have done on Jasper's behalf."

Zebulan bowed his head in contrition. His shoulders slumped, realizing there was going to be no easy forgiveness here.

"God has noticed the speck of goodness left on your black soul, Zebulan, and He is offering you another chance. If you will go back into Jasper's world and work undercover as an agent of mine for fifty years, your sentence as a Lucipire will end."

"And then?" The demon cocked his head to the side.

"And then you would become a vangel."

"But I have no Viking blood. I thought only those of Norse descent could become vampire angels."

"You will be the first non-Viking to join their ranks."

Zebulan smiled then. "I can imagine how happy that will make The Seven."

"It is not for them to be happy or unhappy about my decisions."

"There's a problem, though. I've been gone too long, and I haven't followed Jasper's orders to bring him Trond and Nicole. He won't accept me back into his wicked fold."

Michael shrugged. "I will give you three dozen evil humans . . . sinfully unredeemable souls . . . for you to present to Jasper in reparation. You will tell him that you were unable to fulfill his demands, but that you gathered these humans together in the meantime. Jasper will not be happy but he will accept your 'gift.' "

"Only fifty years . . . a mere half century?" Zebulan asked, time meaning something different in the demon/angel world.

Michael nodded and smiled at him.

As Zebulan dropped to his knees, Michael walked around the desk and placed his hand on the man's head. "God be with you!"

Angels wept at that moment.

Twenty-five

The road to happiness is long and winding . . .

Zeb smiled at Trond and Nicole when he left the office.

"Do you have to go back to Jasper?" Trond whispered to Zeb.

Zeb nodded, but he said nothing more. And, oddly, he was still smiling as he sauntered down the hall toward the kitchen. He'd probably been given orders to keep his fanged mouth shut. At least for now.

Trond would have liked to question the Lucipire more . . . assuming that's what Zeb still was, disheartening as that prospect was, but it was his turn to enter the office for his showdown with Mike.

He squeezed Nicole's hand. They'd had no chance to talk yet, but they would later. He hoped. He noticed that she didn't return his squeeze.

Mike had his desk chair tipped back precariously. The edges of his wings, tucked in behind him, swept the floor. His long, denim-clad legs were propped on the desk. His pure white T-shirt bore the logo: "Faith Makes Things Possible, Not Easy."

Should Trond be scared by that message?

The archangel didn't look up when Trond first came in. Instead, he studied a folder.

Those damn folders again! Vangels had come to hate them when called into a meeting with their mentor. Trond couldn't wait until Harek got Mike to convert everything to computers. If Mike had been staring at a computer screen when Trond walked in, he might just as well have been playing Solitaire, or IM-ing with God or one of the other archangels. Not deciding on his fate, based on a few missteps documented in a folder.

When Mike set the folder down, his gaze pierced Trond. "With all the years you've been a vangel, when will you learn?" Mike asked him.

Talk about trick questions! If I answer wrong, I might be volunteering information he doesn't have. "Are you talking about my trying to save Zeb?"

"Of course. What else would I be referring to, Viking?"

"It seemed like the right thing to do. The only thing to do. If Zeb was willing to offer himself for me, shouldn't I have been willing to do the same for him?"

"Your motives were pure. Your execution was not. What gives you the right to make such a decision? When you were given a second chance and became a vangel, you offered yourself up to God. You belong to God. How dare you offer yourself to Jasper?"

Trond hadn't thought about it in quite that way. *I am in bigger trouble than I thought.*

"I'm not going to add more years to your penance for that offense, but I am going to give you a mission that you might consider a penance of sorts."

Uh-oh!

"You will get U.S. citizenship papers, after which you will apply to become an official Navy SEAL. For years to come, you will be assigned to that post where you will save those SEALs who teeter on the edge of sin. Jasper has not given up on his mission to turn some special forces men into Lucipires."

This would indeed be a penance because Mike knew full well how much he hated extreme exercise, and he would probably have to start from the beginning in SEAL training with all that involved, including Hell Week. Ironic, really, since he'd volunteered to go to Hell.

But he could foresee many problems with this mission, not just his hate for hard work or hell in any format. "How can I take on a contemporary job? My comrades in SEALs would grow older, while I remained the same age."

Mike thought for a minute. "Ten years, then."

Trond wouldn't even bother to ask about all the complications of security clearances and Jaeger history, the red tape of joining an elite military group, even explaining his absence for several weeks. Mike would handle all that. He knew *people*.

"I'll be like a red light blinking target for Jasper."

"That you will, but you will have Zebulan to work with you, from the other side."

Ah! He was beginning to understand. "Zeb is going to be a good demon?"

"There is no such thing. He will pretend to be a demon."

Trond tilted his head in confusion. "What is he then? Surely not . . . a vangel?"

Mike waved a hand dismissively. "Zeb's status is his concern; you need only to work with him."

He wondered how long Zeb's sentence . . . uh, penance . . . would be. Surely not as short as ten years.

"What about Karl?" Trond suddenly realized that he hadn't seen or heard from Karl since he'd been back.

"Karl's human wife died. He is grieving. Later, I will decide his future missions. Probably not SEALs."

Now they came to the real complication of Trond's returning to Coronado and a military career. Nicole. How was he going to withstand the temptation of being around her and not acting on his baser inclinations? How was he going to stand loving her and not being with her? Was that to be the punishment in his new mission?

As if reading his mind, Mike asked, "Was she worth risking your immortal soul?" He was referring to the sex, of course.

"Yes, it was worth whatever punishment you will levy." Trond doubted that meant his immortal soul. That would be too harsh a punishment. "Honestly it didn't . . . doesn't . . . feel wrong."

"I wonder why."

"Because I love her?"

"Aha! The Viking has a brain, after all."

Mike's snideness on occasion was something Trond and his brothers had learned to abide, but that didn't mean they liked it.

"What are you going to do about this love of yours?"

"Nothing."

Mike raised his angelic eyebrows.

"I have nothing to offer her."

"Material wealth is easy to come by."

Trond shook his head. "I am a shell. I am not worthy of her."

Mike laughed. "Dost know nothing, Viking? Men are rarely worthy of the good women in their lives."

Trond had no clue where they were going with this conversation.

"There will be no more premarital sex. Not even that ludicrous near-sex that is fooling no one. You will either mate with this woman for your eternal life, or stay away from her. Totally."

A choice. He was being offered a choice. He assumed it would be under the same conditions as Vikar had with Alex, something they'd all thought was a one-time exception. Married forever. Fidelity required. She would live only as long as he would. No children. "But . . . but . . . but I'm not sure she would have me."

"You'll never know unless you ask." Picking up a cell phone on the desk, Mike pressed a few numbers, then spoke into it. "Vikar, send the woman in."

"You," Mike said, pointing to Trond, "sit down before you fall down."

Trond sank into one of the two chairs in front of the desk and watched as Nicole walked hesitantly into the room and sat in the chair next to him. She seemed frightened to look at Mike, who was studying her through steepled fingers. She avoided looking at Trond, too. Not a promising sign.

"Miss Tasso," Mike finally said.

She looked up and gasped.

Trond could understand that. Mike was a formidable sight, even in modern clothing. His features were just too perfect. And ethereal. Plus, there were those wings. And the sun shining through a stained glass window gave the appearance of a halo.

With what was probably hysterical irrelevance, Trond noted that he probably hadn't earned his wings on this last mission. Probably wouldn't ever. No big loss there.

"What are your feelings toward this sorry excuse for a vangel? A Viking, no less!"

The question surprised her, but then she smiled. A slight smile, but a smile nonetheless. "He lies. He has the sensitivity of a rock. He's arrogant. He—"

"That comes from being a Viking," Mike interrupted. "The whole lot of them are full of themselves." He waved a hand for her to continue. He was obviously enjoying her criticism of Trond.

"He's lazy. Refuses to listen to motivational tapes."

"I love motivational tapes!" Mike said. "Have you ever heard Roger Atwood speak on 'Listening to a Higher Power'?"

Trond looked at the archangel as if he'd lost his mind.

Nicole's smile was getting wider. "You should order Trond to listen to motivational tapes," she told Mike.

"Wait a minute here," Trond protested. That really would be punishment.

"Be quiet, Viking. I am talking to your woman."

He wasn't the only one who caught Mike's reference to "your woman."

Nicole didn't correct Mike, but her face flushed with color. "I'll tell you what really bothers me about this man. The lout!" she resumed, talking to Mike. "Can you believe a man would tell a woman he loves her . . . well, not in actual words, but mouthing the words? And then just disappear—poof!—into thin air and never contact her again, letting her think he was being tortured in some devil's lair."

"Tsk, tsk, tsk!" Mike said. "I had no idea."

"Oh, that is so unfair," Trond complained to Mike. "You had every idea. Besides, you wouldn't let me contact her."

"Did I say that?" Mike tapped his head as if he didn't recall. "In any case, Miss Tasso, the lout has something to ask you."

"I do?" Trond asked. Then, "Yes, I do."

He got down on one knee before her chair and took one of her hands in his. "Will you marry me, Nicole?" Before she had a chance to answer, he quickly added, "It would be for life . . . the length of my life, which can be eternally boring after a while. And we would never have children, ever. And while I could be in Coronado for the next ten years, I would have to move on to other assignments then, and you would have to decide whether to stay there in WEALS or move with me."

"That's your idea of a proposal?" she asked with affront, tugging her hand out of his grasp.

"Pitiful, isn't he?" Mike remarked, a hint of mirth in his voice.

"The only upside to that lamebrained offer that I can see," Nicole remarked, "is that I could torture him for life with my peppiness and motivational tapes."

"Is that a yes or a no?" Trond snarled.

"It's a 'Hell, no!' You are an idiot." There were tears in her eyes that he couldn't understand.

"What am I missing here?" Trond asked.

"The most important thing," Nicole and Mike said at the same time.

"Ah!" He stood, dragged her up and into his arms, kissed her hard on the mouth, and then said, "I love you desperately. More than my life. I think an eternity with you would not be enough. I don't care if you play motivational tapes or nag me to stop being a slugabed or make me jog even when I don't have to. As long as we can be together." He kissed her deeply. Then pulled away. "Will you marry me, Nicole Tasso?"

"Yes!"

They were kissing again, oblivious to their surroundings when they heard a discreet clearing of the throat. Mike stood, his wings outspread and touching both opposing walls. He blessed them with a sign of the cross in the air and just before disappearing, wagged a forefinger at them. "No more sex before marriage."

Trond looked at Nicole and said, "Can we get married tonight?"

Turns out they couldn't, but that was another story.

Epilogue

Vikings, Vikings, everywhere,
and not a longship in sight . . .

The wedding of Trond Sigurdsson and Nicole Tasso took place one month later. To everyone's surprise, the ceremony was held at Blue Dragon Vineyard in Sonoma, California, home of Magnus Ericsson, Max's father and the father-in-law of Commander MacLean.

Trond and Nicole wanted to wed sooner and in the Transylvania castle, but they wouldn't have been able to invite any outside guests. Too many young vangels unable to control their fangs. Plus, the location of the VIK headquarters had to remain as secure as possible.

The SEAL command was not happy about their decision to marry, just as they had disapproved of Sly and Donita tying the knot and others in the past. It was the Navy contention that if they wanted their men to have wives, they would have assigned them ones of their choice. But facing a possible resignation by Nicole from WEALS and Trond's possible change-of-mind regarding the new BUD/S class, they acquiesced.

When Max heard about the wedding that Trond and Nicole were going to hold in the base chapel—just a small affair—Max insisted they hold a grander event at Blue Dragon Vineyard where he'd been married himself to another Viking, Hilda Berdottir. "Vikings need to stick together," Max had said.

So, here they stood on their wedding day on a gorgeous estate.

Unique speckled-bark oak trees lined the drive up to the massive Victorian mansion with its wrap-around porch. The low stone walls on either side of the road were dotted every ten feet or so with enormous, dragon-design terra-cotta planters spilling over with baby's breath and crimson roses, especially filled for this wedding. Wildflowers in every color of the rainbow appeared especially bright today on the lawns, as if knowing it was a special day for them to shine. Beside a spring-fed pond framed with willow trees, tents had been erected for today's reception. Behind the house were several hundred acres of plump grapes awaiting next week's fall harvest. A white carpet led from the side of the house to the arched, rose-twined trellis with its makeshift altar where the ceremony would be held.

It would be a Christian ritual, but the couple did bow to the Blue Dragon patriarch's wishes in one regard. Trond and Nicole would wear Viking wedding attire passed down in their family.

Nicole wore a long-sleeved, collarless chemise of gauzy white linen . . . ankle-length in front and pleated and slightly longer in back. Metallic gold, green, and white embroidery portraying intertwined roses edged the red bands about the wrists and circular neckline. A crimson silk overgown, open-sided like typical Norse aprons, had matching bands of embroidery in reverse colors along the edges. Rosebud shoulder brooches held the gown in place.

Trond had balked but eventually donned a black, long-sleeved, cashmere wool tunic that hung to mid-thigh over slim trousers. At the waist was a wide leather belt with a solid gold buckle. A white, silk-lined mantle of the same fabric, embroidered with roses matching the bridal attire, completed the outfit. The roses were what had Trond balking. "Men do not wear roses!"

Magnus, a massive, barrel-chested Viking, still impressive even in his fifties, overheard Trond and smacked him upside the head. "I wore roses. My brother wore roses. My sons wore roses. You'll wear roses and be happy about it."

Trond wore roses.

What had started out to be a small affair was now a huge wedding reception. Nicole had declined to have her father at her wedding, choosing Commander MacLean to "give her away." His wife, Madrene, a gorgeous Amazon of a Norsewoman, had been very helpful to Nicole in planning the quick ceremony. Almost like a mother, although she wasn't really that old.

Nicole's sister, Teresa, was her maid of honor, with Marie, Donita, and Alex as her attendants. Trond had all six of his brothers as his best men when they'd all argued for that honor. Of course, their SEAL buddies were there: JAM, Sly, Cage, Geek, Slick, F.U., and a few others. And all of Magnus's children, all twelve of them, from teenagers to thirty-somethings, along with their extended families; Magnus prided himself on being a very virile Viking.

When Nicole walked along the white carpet and saw Trond for the first time under the arch, she missed a step, so impressed was she at her vampire angel in Viking wedding attire. But then, Trond gasped himself on seeing his beautiful bride.

A local priest was to perform the ceremony, but at the last minute Michael stepped forth in regal church vestments. Afterward, everyone wanted to know who that remarkable clergyman had been, but he seemed to have disappeared.

When they were pronounced man and wife, and turned to face the crowd for the first time as a married couple, Trond whispered in Nicole's ear, "Look over there, under the willow tree."

There stood a handsome man in a black suit, pristine white shirt, and a red and black striped tie. It was Zeb. He gave them a little wave, then faded away into the now milling crowd.

Between the service and the setup of the reception tables, Trond led Nicole into a little sewing room off the kitchen where he flipped up her gown and "swived her silly"—his words—up against the wall. "These thirty days of celibacy seemed longer than centuries of celibacy," he told her afterward.

Between the dinner and the cake cutting, Nicole told Trond she wanted to show him something in the wine-pressing building. Once inside, she shoved him onto a table and had her way with him. "Celibacy sucks for women, too," she'd told a laughing Trond afterward.

When it was time for dancing—a band was about to play on the portable dance floor that had been set up—they did the traditional bride and groom dance. No father-daughter dance for her, but she didn't mind. In the glow of Trond's family and all their friends, she had enough.

Just then, the band struck a particular note, and Trond turned on her. "Nicole! You didn't!"

"Me?" she asked, putting her hand over her chest with exaggerated innocence as "Chain of Fools," began.

Trond and his brothers looked at each other with disgust—Mordr was particularly disgusted—as they walked out onto the dance floor with resignation, and formed a line. While the band belted out "Chains, chains, chains," and the rest of the guests joined in, the seven brothers did the *Michael* dance. And they were good. Really good. For a long time afterward, people said it was the best entertainment they'd ever witnessed at Blue Dragon, and that was saying a lot. Vikings knew how to have a good time. There was even a video of it up on YouTube for a day before someone yanked it off. Probably Harek.

When Trond sat down next to a smirking Nicole, he pinched her behind and said, "I have a surprise for you."

"Uh-oh! Is this payback?"

"No, this is a gift from Zeb. I found it in my jacket pocket."

He handed her plane tickets and a set of directions. Her eyes were wide with wonder and a slight mist of tears. "His hideaway? For our honeymoon?" They both bemoaned the fact that the demon had been unable to participate in their celebration. They both also feared for Zeb, back in that horrible den of evil, but this was a time for happiness. They would worry about Zeb later.

That night, when they were on a plane with Nicole's head resting on Trond's shoulder—no teletransporting this time—she inquired sweetly, "I was wondering, honey, if you would teach me that *Michael* dance later."

He paused and then laughed, "Only if we're both naked."

Glossary

Al Jazeera—Arabic news network.

Al-Qaeda—Military Islamic organization formed by Osama bin Laden; a terrorist network.

A-Viking—A Norse practice of sailing away to other countries for the purpose of looting, settlement, or mere adventure; could be for a period of several months or for years at a time.

Baksheesh—Bribery.

BDUs—Battle dress uniforms.

Berserker—An ancient Norse warrior who fought in a frenzied rage during battle.

Bivouac—A military encampment with tents and improvised shelter.

Boondockers—Heavy boots.

Boonie hats—Wide-brimmed hats with loops for hanging vegetation for camouflage.

BQ—Acronym for bachelors' quarters.

Braies—Slim pants worn by men.

British MI–6—British secret intelligence service.

BUD/S—Basic Underwater Demolition SEALs.

Burqa—Enveloping outer garment worn by women in some Islamic countries.

Catacombs—Ancient human-made subterranean passageways for religious practices or burial.

CentCom—Central Command.

Ceorl (or churl)—Free peasant, person of the lowest classes.

Cher—Male endearment, comparable to friend.

Collateral damage—Unintended or incidental damage to the intended outcome.

Cossack—Russian military warriors during czarist times.

Delta Force—Elite tactical combat group, affiliated with Army but including other service branches, as well.

Drukkinn (various spellings)—Drunk, in Old Norse.

Eunuch—Castrated male.

Extraction Point—Place where military forces are extracted from enemy territory.

Fibbies—FBI.

Fjord—A narrow arm of the sea, often between high cliffs.

Force multiplication—A factor that dramatically increases the effectiveness of a group, including the training of friendlies within an enemy nation to multiply the size of the fighting forces.

Friendlies—Those within an enemy nation who are friendly to the attackers, e.g., rebels within Afghanistan.

Gammelost—A pungent Norse cheese with a greenish-brown crust.

Gig Squad—A punishment inflicted during BUD/S whereby a SEAL trainee is forced after a long day of training to do many vigorous exercises outside the officers' quarters.

Grinder—Asphalt training ground in the middle of the SEAL compound in Coronado.

Gunna—Long-sleeved, ankle-length gown for women, often worn under a tunic or surcoat, or under a long, open-sided apron.

Haakai—High-level demon.

High-and-tight—Military haircut.

Hird—A permanent troop that a chieftain or nobleman might have.

Hordling—Lower-level demon.

Houri—Beautiful woman, often associated with a harem.

Igal—Rope or band used to hold the head scarf in place.

IM—Instant messaging.

Imps—Lower-level demons, foot soldiers, so to speak.

Insertion Point—Place where soldiers insert themselves into enemy territory.

Jaegers (or jagers)—Jaegerkorpst, Scandinavian special forces.

Jarhead—Nickname for U.S. Marine due to high-and-tight haircut.

Jarl—High-ranking Norseman similar to an English earl or wealthy landowner, could also be a chieftain or minor king.

Jihad—Religious duty, or holy war.

Kaftan—Silk or cotton, ankle-length and wrist-length garment, buttoned down the front, belted with a sash.

Karl—High-level Norse nobleman, below a jarl or earl.

K-Bar—Type of knife favored by SEALs.

Keep—House, usually the manor house or main building for housing the owners of the estate.

Keffiyeh—Traditional Arab headdress fashioned from a square of cloth.

Longship—Narrow, open water-going vessel with

oars and square sails, perfected by Viking ship-builders, noted for their speed and ability to ride in both shallow waters and deep oceans.

Lucifer/Satan—The fallen angel Lucifer became known as the demon Satan.

Lucipires/Lucies—Demon vampires.

Manchet bread—Flat loaves of unleavened bread, usually baked in circles with a hole in the center so they could be stored on an upright pole, like a broom handle.

Mead—Fermented honey and water.

Mossad—National intelligence agency of Israel.

MRE—Meals ready to eat, what used to be called K-rations.

Mungs—Type of demon, below the haakai in status, often very large and oozing slime or mung.

Muslim—A religion based on the Koran with the belief that the word of God was revealed through the prophet Mohammed.

Nithing—A Norse insult meaning that a person was less than nothing.

Norman Vincent Peale—Famous for his book *The Power of Positive Thinking*.

NVG—Night vision goggles.

O-course—Grueling obstacle course on the training compound, also known as the oh-my-God! course.

Odin—King of all the Viking gods.

PEZ—Type of candy available from unusual, mechanical pocket dispensers.

PT—Physical training.

Purdah—Practice in certain countries of screening women from men or strangers with all-enveloping clothes.

Roger—As in "Roger that!" meaning "I understand," or "I hear you."

Runic—Ancient alphabet used by the Vikings and other early Germanic tribes.

Salaam—Arab greeting meaning "Peace!"

SAS—British special forces.

SEAL—Sea, Air, and Land.

Seraphim—High-ranking angel.

Shalwar kameez **(or** *gamez* **or** *kamiz***)**—*Shalwar* is the long shirt of tunic, thigh or knee-length, worn over the *kameez* which are pajama-style pants with drawstring waists, usually wider on the top and narrow at the ankles. Women would complete this outfit with a loose scarf over the top.

Shayetet 13—Elite naval commando unit of the Israeli Navy.

Skald—Poet or storyteller.

Spetsnaz—Umbrella term of any special forces in Russia.

Stasis—State of inactivity, rather like being frozen in place.

Taliban—Islamic military and political organization that rules large parts of Afghanistan.

Tangos—Bad guys, terrorists.

Teletransport—Transfer of matter from one point to another without traversing physical space.

Thobe—Long white robe.

Thor—God of war.

Thrall—Slave.

Tun—Roughly 252 gallons.

Valhalla—Hall of the slain, Odin's magnificent hall in Asgard.

Vangels—Viking vampire angels.

VIK—The seven brothers who head the vangels.

WEALS—Acronym for Women on Earth, Air, Land, and Sea.

Wheels up—Mission under way, plane in the air.

Zydeco—Type of Cajun music.

Keep reading for
a sneak peek at

KISS
OF
TEMPTATION

The next book in
the Deadly Angels series,
coming soon
from Sandra Hill
and
Avon Books

Prologue

The Norselands, A.D. 850, where men . . .
and life . . . were always hard . . .

Ivak Sigurdsson was an excessively lustsome man.

Ne'er would he deny that fact, nor bow his head in embarrassment. In truth, he'd well earned his far-renowned wordfame for virility. On his back. On his front. Standing. Sitting. On the bow and in the bowels of a longship. Behind the Saxon king's throne. Deep in a cave. High in a tree. Under a bush. On a bed. In a cow byre. Once even with . . . Well, never mind, that had been when he was very young and on a dare and another story entirely.

He liked women. Everything about them. Not just the sex bits. He liked their scent, the feel of their silky skin, the allure of their secrets, the sound of their sighs and moans, the taste of them. And women liked him, too. He wanted them all.

You could say lust was a sixth sense for Ivak. He was a Viking, after all.

He'd been twelve years old when, swaggering with overconfidence, he'd tried his dubious charms on his father's eighth concubine, who'd laughed herself into a weeping fit afore showing him exactly which hole he should aim for. Now, twenty years and at least two hundred bedmates later—he'd stopped counting after that incident in Hedeby— there was naught he did not know about sex. Men came to him for advice all the time. Women, too.

The cold Norse winds blew outside his keep now, but he and his comrades-in-arms were warm inside as they sat before one of the five hearth fires that ran through the center of his great hall at Thorstead. Their body heat was aided by the mead they were imbibing and the satiety that comes from having tupped more than the ale barrel, and it not yet eventide.

When bored and having no wars to fight, or any other time for that matter, taking an enthusiastic maid to the bed furs was always a worthwhile pastime. Leastways, it was for Ivak. You'd think his jaded appetites would have waned by now. Instead, he found himself wanting more and more. And the things he tried these days pushed even his sensibilities for decency . . . but not enough to stop him.

And, of course, when bored and having no wars to fight, men did what men did throughout time. Drank.

In fact, Esbe, the widow of one of his swordsmen, walked amongst them now, refilling their horns from a pottery pitcher. When she got to him, she smiled, a small, secretive smile that Ivak understood perfectly. Women told him that he had an aura about him . . . a presence, so to speak. By leaning against a wall just so, or just staring at them through half-slitted eyes, or, gods forbid, winking at them, he sent a silent message. Here was a man who knew things.

He smiled back at Esbe, who shared his bed furs on occasion, and watched appreciatively, along with every one of his men, as she walked away from them, hips swaying from side to side.

Another thing men did when bored and having no wars to fight, and especially when drinking, was talk about women.

"Tell me true, Ivak," demanded Haakon the Horse, a name he'd been given because of a face so long he could lick the bottom of a bucket and still see over the rim, not because of other bodily attributes. Haakon was a master at swordplay if ever there was one, a soldier you'd want at your back in battle, but an irksome oaf when *drukkinn*, and he was halfway there already. "There must have been times when your lance failed to rise to the occasion. It happens to the best of men betimes."

Ivak exchanged a quick glance with his best friend, Serk the Silent, who sat beside him on the bench. Serk, a man of few words, did not need to speak for Ivak to know that he was thinking: *Here it comes!*

Ivak tapped his chin with a forefinger, as if actually giving the query consideration. He could feel Serk shaking with silent laughter. "Nay, it never has, though there have been times I've had to take a vow of celibacy to give it a rest." He cupped himself for emphasis.

"For how long?" scoffed Ingolf, his chief archer. A grin twitched at Ingolf's hugely mustached upper lip, knowing when Ivak was about to pull a jest.

"Oh, a good long time. Two days at most," Ivak admitted.

Everyone, except Haakon, found amusement in his jest, including Kugge, the young squire he'd been training of late. Gazing at Ivak in wonder, Kugge blurted out, "Did it hurt?"

"The celibacy or the excess?" Ivak asked, trying to keep a straight face.

A blush crept over Kugge's still unwhiskered face as he sensed having made a fool of himself.

Ivak patted Kugge on the shoulder.

Haakon glared at him, his question not gaining the results he'd wanted . . . a fight. Ivak returned Haakon's glare, his with a silent warning that Haakon thankfully heeded. Haakon stood, tossing his horn to the rushes, and stomped off, hopefully to sleep himself sober.

Ingolf took a long draught from his horn of ale, cleared his throat, and proclaimed with a chuckle, "To my mind, a man's cock is like a brass urn."

"Oh, good gods!" Ivak muttered.

"How true!" Serk encouraged Ingolf and nudged Ivak with an elbow to share in his mirth.

"Now, hear me out," Ingolf said, stroking his mustache. "Everyone knows that brass needs polishing from time to time, and—"

"Mine is especially shiny these days since I got me a second wife," one of the men contributed.

Ingolf scowled at the interruption and continued, "Of course, a one-handed rub will do to ease the throb, but best it is if the polishing is done in the moist folds of a female sheath's choke hold."

"I don't understand," Kugge said to Ivak.

"It's a mystery," Ivak replied with dry humor.

Ingolf, who fashioned himself a master story-teller, was on a roll now. 'Twas best to let him finish. "The thing about brass is that too much rubbing and it loses its luster. Even grows pits." Ingolf pretended to shiver.

"Pits? Like a peach?" Kugge whispered.

"Nay. Like warts," Ivak told the boy. "You do not want warts down there, believe you me."

"Even worse," Ingolf told Kugge, "tainted oil in the sheath can spoil all it touches. Remember that dockside whore in Jorvik." The latter Ingolf addressed to the other men. "Now that was a woman with teeth *down there*."

"She had a lot more than teeth," Serk remarked, "as many men soon learned."

"The difference, my friend, is that some cocks are solid gold." Ivak motioned a hand downward.

The other men rolled their eyes and guffawed uproariously.

"Mine is solid silver," Bjorn No-Teeth said, his lips twitching as he attempted to hide his gummy smile. "I'm thinking about having it . . . etched. Ha, ha, ha!"

Others offered their own self-assessments:

"Mine is ivory, smooth and sleek, and big as an elephant's tusk betimes. Not that I have e'er seen an elephant."

"Mine is a rock. A rock cock."

"Mine is iron, like a lance. A loooong lance."

"Holy Thor! Do not make me laugh anymore lest I piss my braies."

Someone belched.

Someone else farted.

More bragging.

Ivak sighed with contentment. It was the way of men when they were alone with time to spare.

Their merriment was interrupted by the arrival of Ivak's steward announcing Vadim, the slave trader from the Rus lands, who had come from Birka before circling back home. He would probably be the last one to make it through the fjords before they were frozen solid for winter.

Ivak and Serk left the others behind as they went out to the courtyard and beyond that to an outbuilding that usually housed fur pelts. It was empty now, the goods sent to market, and cold as a troll's arse in a blizzard. He waved to a servant, who quickly brought him and Serk fur-lined cloaks.

Vadim was a frequent visitor at Thorstead. As often as he dealt in human flesh, Vadim also traded in fine wines, spices, silks, and in Ivak's case, the occasional sexual oddity . . . dried camel testicles, feathers, marble phalluses, and such.

Serk joined the steward, who was examining some of the wares on display in open sacks while Ivak, at Vadim's urging, walked to the far end of the shed.

"Come, come, see what delights I have for you, Lord Sigurdsson."

Ivak was no lord, and he recognized the obsequiousness of the title dripping from the Russian's lips, but it wasn't worth the bother of correcting him. "So, show me the delights."

Three men were roped together against one wall. Nothing delightful here. An elderly man that Vadim identified as a farmer from the Balkans. With the rocky landscape at Thorstead, Ivak had no need of a farmer and certainly not a graybeard. Next was a boyling with no apparent skills; Ivak passed on him, as well. The third was a young man that Ivak did want—a blacksmith's apprentice. He and Vadim agreed on a price, although Ivak did not like the angry exchange of words in an undertone between this last man and Vadim that the trader dismissed as of no importance.

Next came the best part. The delight part. The women. Ivak always enjoyed checking over new female slaves. Serk, who had finished examining the household wares, joined him.

The five women were not restrained, but they were shivering with cold, or mayhap a bit of fear, not knowing that Ivak would be a fair master. They shivered even more when Vadim motioned for them to disrobe. While Ivak pitied them this temporary chill, he was not about to buy a piece of property without full disclosure. Once he'd purchased a prettily clothed slave in Jorvik only to find she had oozing pustules covering her back, from her neck to her thighs.

"I see several you would like," Serk whispered at his side.

Ivak agreed, a certain part of his body already rising in anticipation.

The first was clearly pregnant, normally a condition that would preclude his purchase—there were enough bratlings running about the estate, including some of his own—but he had a comrade-in-arms who had a particular taste for sex with breeding women, so he motioned for her to join the young blacksmith at the other end. With an appreciative nod of thanks at her good fortune, she quickly pulled on her robe and drew a threadbare blanket over her shoulders.

"This one is a Saxon, a little long in the tooth, but an excellent cook," Vadim said.

"I already have a cook," Ivak demurred.

"Ah, but does she make oat cakes light as a feather and mead fit fer the gods?" the heavy woman of middle years, whose sagging breasts reached almost to her waist, asked in Saxon English. The Norse and Saxon languages were similar and could be understood by either. She'd obviously gotten the meaning of his remark.

Ivak liked a person with gumption, male or female, and he grinned, ordering her to join the other two. Besides, a Viking could never have enough good mead.

All the thrall bodies were malodorous from lack of bathing . . . for months, no doubt . . . but this next one—an attractive woman of thirty or so years— had a particular odor that Ivak associated with diseased whores. He gave Vadim a disapproving scowl and moved to the fourth woman.

"This one is a virgin," Vadim said. "Pure as new snow. And a skilled weaver."

Ivak arched a brow with skepticism as he circled the shivering female who had seen at least twenty winters. He doubted very much that a female slave could remain intact for that many years. Still, she would be a welcome diversion. New meat for jaded palates. Not to mention, he had lost a weaver this past summer to the childbirth fever. He nodded his acceptance to Vadim.

And then there was the fifth woman . . . a girl, really. No more than sixteen. Red hair, above and below. Ah, he did love a redheaded woman. Fiery, they were when their fires were ignited, as he knew well how to do. He could not wait to lay his head over her crimson fluff and . . .

He smiled at her.

She did not smile back. Instead, tears streamed down her face.

He ran his knuckles over one pink, cold-peaked nipple, then the other.

She actually sobbed now, and stepped back as if in revulsion.

The tears didn't bother him all that much, but the resistance did. Thralldom was not easy for some to accept, but she would settle into her role soon. They usually did. They had no choice. Not that he would engage in rape. Persuasion was his forte.

But wait. She was staring with seeming horror at something over his shoulder.

Ivak heard the growl before he turned and saw the smithy tugging to be free from the restraints being held by both Vadim and his assistant. At the same time, the young man was protesting something vociferously in what sounded to Ivak like the Irish tongue.

"What is amiss?" Ivak demanded of Vadim.

"He's her husband, but you are not to worry—"

Ivak put up a halting hand. "I do not want any more married servants. Too much trouble." He started to walk away.

"You could take one of them," Vadim offered.

Ivak paused. The woman's skin *was* deliciously creamy and her nether fleece *was* tempting. "I'll take her. You keep him."

The husband didn't understand Ivak's words as he spoke, but Vadim must have explained once Ivak and Serk left the building and headed back to the keep because his roar of outrage would be understood in any language.

"Is that wise, Ivak?" Serk asked. "Separating a man and his mate?"

"It happens all the time, my friend, and do you doubt my wisdom in choosing good bedsport over good metalwork?"

Serk laughed, but at the same time shook his head

at Ivak with dismay. In some ways Serk had gone soft of late, ever since he'd wed Asta, the daughter of a Danish jarl. Six months, and Serk was still besotted with the witch. Little did he know that Asta was spreading her thighs hither and yon. Ivak knew that for a fact because he'd been one of those to whom she'd offered her dubious charms. He would have told his friend, but he figured Serk would grow bored soon enough, and then it would not matter. As long as she did not try to pass off some other man's baby as his own. When Ivak had mentioned that possibility to Asta, she'd informed him that she was joyfully barren. That was another thing of which Serk was uninformed.

And women claimed men were the ones lacking in morals!

That night he swived the Irish maid, and she was sweet, especially after having been bathed. It was not an entirely satisfying tup, though. The girl was too willing. He kept seeing her husband's face as he was dragged away. No doubt his distaste would fade eventually, but tonight he had no patience for it, and he sent her away after just one bout of bedsport. In the end, she begged him to be permitted to stay, but he wanted no more of her for now.

He drank way too much mead then, which only increased his foul mood. That was the only excuse he could find for his seeing Asta slinking along one of the hallways and motioning him with a forefinger to come to her bedchamber. Another round-heeled woman with the morals of a feral cat. He knew for a fact that Serk was serving guard duty all night.

Mayhap he should tup Serk's wife and then

explain to him in the nicest possible way on the morrow what a poor choice he had made in picking this particular maid for his mate. Ivak would be doing his friend a favor, he rationalized with ale-head madness.

Asta was riding him like a bloody stallion a short time later, and while his cock was interested, he found himself oddly regretting his impulsive invitation. Bored, he glanced toward the door that was opening, and there stood Serk, staring at them with horror. This was not the way he'd wanted his friend to discover his wife's lack of faithfulness.

"Ivak? My friend?" Serk choked out.

"I can explain. It's not what you think." Well, it was, but there was a reason for his madness. Wasn't there?

At the stricken expression on Serk's face, Ivak shoved Asta off him, ignoring her squeal of ill humor, and jumped off the bed. By the time he was dressed, his good friend was gone. And Asta was more concerned about having her bed play interrupted than the fact that her husband had witnessed her adultery. To Ivak's amazement, she actually thought they would resume the swiving.

Ivak searched for more than an hour, to no avail. It was already well after midnight and most folks, except for his housecarls, were abed. His apology and explanation to Serk would have to wait until morning. He had no doubt that Serk would forgive him, once he understood that Asta was just a woman, and a faithless one at that. Oh, Ivak did not doubt that Serk would be angry, and Ivak might even allow him a punch or two, but eventually their friendship would be intact.

Still, he could not sleep with all that had happened, and he decided to walk out to the stables to check on a prize mare that should foal any day now. What Ivak found, though, was so shocking he could scarce breathe. In fact, he fell to his knees and moaned. "Oh, nay! Please, gods, let it not be so!"

Hanging from one of the rafters was Serk.

His friend had hanged himself.

What have I done? What have I done? She was not worth it, my friend. Truly, she was not. Oh, what have I done?

Ivak lowered the body to the floor and did not need to put a fingertip to Serk's neck to know that he had already passed to Valhalla. With tears burning his eyes, he stood, about to call for the stablemaster in an adjoining shed to help him release Serk's noose, when he heard a noise behind him. Turning, he saw the young Irish blacksmith, husband of the red-haired maid he'd bedded, running toward him with a raised pitchfork. Vadim and his crew were supposed to depart at first light. The man must have escaped his restraints.

Before Ivak had a chance to raise an alarm or fight for himself, the man pierced his chest with the long tines of the pitchfork. Unfortunately, he used the special implement with metal tines that Ivak had purchased this past summer on a whim, not satisfied with the usual wooden pitchforks for his fine stable. So forceful had the man's surge toward him been that he pinned Ivak into the wall.

"You devil!" the man yelled, tears streaming down his face. "You bloody damn devil! May you rot in hell!"

He was given a choice: Hell or something like Hell . . .

"Tsk, tsk, tsk!"

Ivak heard the voice through his pain-hazed brain. *I thought I was dead. I must be dead.* Opening his heavy lids, he glanced downward, beyond the sharp tines that still pinned him to the wall, to see his life-blood pooling at his feet. *Definitely dead.* Raising his head, he saw that Serk still lay in the rushes where he'd lowered him. And the blacksmith was gone. Apparently, neither he nor Serk had been discovered yet. Well, it would be too late for either of them now.

"Tsk, tsk, tsk!" he heard again, and this time realized that the voice came from his right side. "It is never too late, Viking."

If Ivak hadn't been dead, and if he hadn't been immobilized by a pitchfork through his heart, he would have fallen over with shock. Standing there, big as he pleased—and he was big, all right—was an angel. A big, black-haired man with widespread, snow-white wings and piercing blue eyes.

Ivak knew what angels were since he practiced both the ancient Norse religion and the Christian one, an expedience many Norsemen adopted. Apparently, he would not be off to Valhalla today with its myriad of golden shields and virgin Valkyries. "Am I going to Heaven?" he asked the frowning angel.

The angel made a snorting sound of disbelief at his question. "Hardly!"

"Hell, then?" he inquired tentatively.

"Nay, but thou may wish it so."

Enough of this nonsense. Dead was dead. "Who are you?" Ivak demanded. "And how about pulling out this pitchfork?"

"Michael," the angel said, then eyeing the pitchfork, added, "Thou art certain I should do that?"

Before Ivak had a chance to reconsider, the angel . . . Michael . . . yanked it out, causing excruciating pain to envelop him as he fell to the rush-covered floor, face first. If he were not in such screaming pain, he would have been impressed at the strength of the angel to have removed, all in one smooth pull, the tines that had not only skewered his body but had been imbedded in the wooden wall behind him, as well. Like one of his muscle-honed warriors who hefted heavy broadswords with ease, this angel was.

He realized in that instant whose presence he was in. Staggering to his feet, he panted out, "Would that be Michael the Archangel? The warrior angel?"

The angel nodded his head in acknowledgment.

"Am I dead?"

"As a door hinge."

"Is this what happens when everyone dies? An angel shows up? You show up?"

"No."

"I'm someone special? I get special attention?"

"Thee could say that."

Ivak didn't like the sound of that. "Stop speaking in riddles. And enough with the *thee*s and *thou*s!"

The angel shrugged. "You are in no position to issue orders, Viking."

He sighed deeply and tried for patience, which had to be strange. A dead person trying to be patient. "What happens now?"

"That depends on you."

More riddles!

"You are a grave sinner, Ivak Sigurdsson. Not just you. Your six brothers are equally guilty. Each of you has committed one of the Seven Deadly Sins in a most grievous fashion."

"My brothers? Are they dead, too?"

"Some are. The others soon will be."

Ivak was confused. "Which horrible sin is it that I have committed?"

"Lust."

"Lust is a sin?" He laughed.

The angel continued to glare at him. No sense of humor at all.

Ivak laughed again.

But not for long.

The angel raised his hand and pointed a finger at him, causing him to be slammed against the wall and pinned there, but this time there was no pitchfork involved. Just some invisible bonds. "Sinner, repent," Michael demanded in a steely voice, "lest I send you straight to Lucifer to become one of his minions. You will like his pitchfork even less than the mortal one that impaled you."

"I repent, I repent," Ivak said, though he still didn't see how lust could be such a big sin.

"You do not see how lust can be sinful?" Michael could obviously read his mind. The angel gaped at him for a moment before exclaiming, "Vikings! Lackwits, one and all!" With those words, the angel waved a hand in front of Ivak's face, creating a cloudy screen in which he began to see his life unfolding before him, rather the lust events in his life.

It didn't take Ivak long to realize that not all the girls and women had been as eager to spread their thighs for him as he'd always thought, but most of them had. What surprised him was the number of husbands or betrothed who'd suffered at his hands—rather his cock—for his having defiled their loved ones. Serk hadn't been the only one. And babes! Who knew he'd bred so many out-of-wedlock children . . . and how many of them lived in poverty! He would have cared for any of his whelps brought to his keep, but these were in far countries.

And then there was this past night's events . . . the thrall he'd taken to his bed furs knowing she was wed. Worst of all, his betrayal of his best friend.

He shook his head with dismay as shame overcame him. Raising his eyes to the angel, he asked, "What can I do to make amends?"

Michael smiled, and it was not a nice smile. "I thought you would never ask, Viking. From this day forth, you will be a vangel. A Viking vampire angel. One of God's warriors in the fight against Satan's vampire demons, Lucipires by name."

Ivak had no idea what Michael had just said. What was a vampire?

But then, it didn't matter because his pain-ridden body became even more pain-ridden. Every bone in his body seemed to be breaking and reforming, even his jaw and teeth, after which he hurtled through the air, outside his keep, far up into the sky. Then he lost consciousness.

When he awakened, he found himself in another keep of sorts. But it was made of stone, not wood, as Thorstead was. And the weather here was almost unbearably warm, not the frigid cold of the Norselands.

The sign over the entryway read: "Angola Prison."